Praise for *ELEMENTS*

"Suzanne Church covers a lot of ground in this collection, from Science Fiction to Dark Fantasy with twinges of horror tossed in. Hers is a unique voice and added to that, she is a superb word-smith. These stories are nothing like what you've read before; I couldn't put this book down!"
— Nancy Kilpatrick,
Award winning author of *Vampyric Variations*

"Suzanne Church's fiction is charming, dark, powerful, and stylish, sometimes all at once."
— Kij Johnson,
Associate director for the Center for the Study of Science Fiction

"Suzanne Church is a bright new star on the speculative-fiction horizon. I'm very excited to see this mesmerizing collection, which shows the fabulous range of Suzanne's talent and includes 'The Tear Closet,' one of my favorite stories in recent years."
— David Morrell,
New York Times bestselling author of *Creepers*

"...every last tale in this book is a powerful glimpse of a reality that's very different from our own. Some are dark, others are wry — all are unforgettable..."
— Ed Greenwood,
creator of the award-winning *Forgotten Realms* role-playing campaign setting

"Suzanne Church is a shining new star in the Canadian science-fiction firmament. Her wonderful stories will move and delight you."
— Robert J. Sawyer,
Hugo Award-winning author of *Red Planet Blues*

ELEMENTS

A COLLECTION OF SPECULATIVE FICTION

SUZANNE CHURCH

EDGE SCIENCE FICTION AND FANTASY PUBLISHING
AN IMPRINT OF HADES PUBLICATIONS, INC.

CALGARY

Edge Science Fiction and Fantasy Publishing
An Imprint of Hades Publications Inc.
P.O. Box 1714, Calgary, Alberta, T2P 2L7, Canada

Editing by Ella Beaumont
Interior design by Janice Blaine
Cover Illustration by Neil Jackson

ISBN: 978-1-77053-042-3

EDGE Science Fiction and Fantasy Publishing and Hades Publications, Inc. acknowledges the ongoing support of the Alberta Foundation for the Arts and the Canada Council for the Arts for our publishing programme.

Library and Archives Canada Cataloguing in Publication

Church, Suzanne, 1965-, author
Elements : a collection of speculative fiction / Suzanne Church.

Issued in print and electronic formats.
ISBN: 978-1-77053-042-3
(e-Book ISBN: 978-1-77053-043-0)

I. Title.

PS8605.H87E56 2014   C813'.6   C2013-905016-7   C2013-905017-5

FIRST EDITION
(M-20140107)
Printed in Canada
www.edgewebsite.com

Table of Contents

∞ O ∞

DEDICATION

To Joseph and Emmett

Acknowledgements

Ironically, no writer works alone, except when we sit at our keyboards creating worlds. Each story in this collection has been finessed by others.

First, thanks go to the crew at EDGE Science Fiction and Fantasy Publishing. In particular, thanks to Brian Hades for giving my collection life, to Anita Hades for her boundless energy at every convention, to Ella Beaumont for her fine-tooth comb, and to Janice Shoults for making sure the world seeks the work of EDGE authors. Special kudos to Neil Jackson whose amazing cover art inspired the story "Soul-Hungry".

Thank you to the late Ann C. Crispin for showing me the ropes when I had no clue how all of the words fit together. Warmest hello and thanks to the tutors, conveners, and participants of the 2004 CSSF Kansas writers' workshop and the 2005 Clarion South writers' workshop for extracting writer-Suzanne from Mom-Suzanne.

I bow down in sincere thanks to the members of the DC2K writers' group for almost fourteen years of support, critiques, and encouragement. Thank you to the Stop-Watch Gang for showing me the dynamics of in-person writers' groups and for keeping ours running smoothly. Each member of these two groups has bled on my manuscripts and all these stories are better for their efforts. Though I hate to play favorites, I extend extra kudos to Eugie Foster for always holding a slot for me on the *Daily Dragon*, to Debbie Yutko for reminding me that writers can also be moms, to Nancy Northcott for being the best example of how hard work and persistence make goodness rain from the sky, to Scott Hancock for sharing his love of poetry, and to Amy Herring for proffering the warmest southern welcome and friendship a Canadian could ever be so blessed to enjoy.

Thanks to the Toronto-plus-southwestern-Ontario writing community. Whenever I need a boost, you're all only an email away, ready to share a coffee or a beer and plot noodle me out of a corner, or to assist me in making the next business decision. You all know who you are and I don't have room here to thank you individually. Special thanks to my girl-posse members Sandra Kasturi and Marcy Italiano for their spirit and conversation.

Finally, thanks to Stephanie and Renée Green for providing me the opportunity to know what daughters are like, to my sister, Elise Willison, for listening, and my mom, to JoAnne Willison, for being there *whenever* I need her for *anything*. I extend my hand to Mark Church who allowed me to pursue this whole author-gig at the very beginning, and also for offering up his air miles so that I could attend my first writing course at my first convention.

Michael Green, you have my back, you listen, you encourage, and for all of that and a million other reasons I thank you for being in my life. Joseph and Emmett Church, you are both more amazing than I ever imagined you could become. Thanks for being all that you are.

—Suzanne Church

∞ O ∞

WHAT BECOMES A
LEGEND MOST

BY SANDRA KASTURI

I remember there used to be these old Blackglama ads for mink coats. This was of course from back in the day when people actually wore mink coats and no one thought anything of it. The ads had famous celebrities like Marlene Dietrich and Julie Andrews and Maria Callas. They said, "What becomes a legend most?" All of which may lead readers to say, "Who?" And probably also, "What does that have to do with anything?"

I'll tell you who. Well, no. Because many of you reading (young whippersnappers!) may not have heard of those famous women, and it's beside the point anyway. But I'll tell you what and why. Because Suzanne Church is quite likely to be a famous woman soon, and quite probably a legend too. So what becomes her? Obviously not a fur coat. But this book becomes her. And you embracing her prose, that especially becomes her. And awards. Awards become her because she's already won a bunch. And will no doubt go on to win more. I've known her for years now, so Future Me is really looking forward to saying, "Oh, I knew Suzanne long before she won both the Hugo and the Nebula in 2017. She's had *dinner* at my *house*." Cue gasps of envy from her fans.

It would all be deserved. Suzanne's a good writer, if you hadn't noticed. She has a knack for an elegant or funny turn of phrase. The one that cracked me up most was "better than a hell sandwich." And then it occurred to me. That's what this collection is— it's better than a hell sandwich. Which isn't damning with faint praise, let me be clear. Because I think a hell sandwich would be pretty fucking extraordinary, don't you?

Suzanne also has a knack for creating characters you care about. For a pervasive and beautiful melancholy that seems to thread through her work, even in the funnier stories. And ideas. She's got some pretty friggin' cool ideas, no? Well. You'll find out shortly when you get to the book proper.

My favourite story of the bunch is probably "Destiny Lives in the Tattoo's Needle," a dystopian fable set in a future North America where "Atlantica" and "Pacifica" are at war and a "Thinker" parachuting from a destroyed ship is captured by a mysterious (enemy?) combatant. But here's the thing. Suzanne also makes me mad. (You *do*, Suzanne, you do!) Because that story is set in such a rich and fascinating world that I was furious when it ended. What happens to Greg and Alyssa? I wanted to follow those characters and see where their next adventures lay. Suzanne? I'm still waiting.

But that's the trick, isn't it? To leave your readers wanting more. To make them angry about your abandoned protagonists and worlds, to make them furiously snap up every single story you write, just to see if you've gone back to the characters they loved, only to have them realize you haven't done that at all— you've just gone and created new ones that they can agonize over! And so it continues, until you have a whole passel of devoted (and probably cranky) fans in your wake, waiting to see what you'll do next.

Suzanne's on that path. So, yeah, you should read this book. Sure you should. But be prepared for frustration and tantrums when you realize there aren't any sequels, and you don't know what'll happen to the people (and aliens) you liked best, because, well… there isn't a new story out. Yet. Yet.

So I live in hope. I hope that my own destiny will return me to the tattoo's needle. That the Couch Teleportation Universe doesn't teleport itself out of existence. That Austin from "Jelly and the D-Machine" has a good life and things work out for him and Drake. And that all those dystopias Suzanne's envisioned don't come to pass. Because that's the stuff that really stays with me when I lie awake at night. Thanks, Suzanne. Thanks a *lot*.

Your own mileage, as they say, may vary. Maybe you'll worry about the thing in the belfry more than I did. Maybe the drug addiction and failed connections of "Synch Me, Kiss Me, Drop" will be what leaves you melancholy and staring into the dregs of your coffee cup on a Monday morning. Or the broody and grotesque science fictional riff on shapeshifting in "Mod Me Down." But I'll tell you this— you won't be unaffected by what you read here. And if you're one of those people who thinks, "Oh, it's just science fiction [sub in 'horror' and 'fantasy' as needed]; it doesn't *mean* anything." Well, you'd be really wrong. Suzanne Church is doing what the best writers in genre fiction have always done: she's writing about the human condition. Even when she's being funny, she's still showing you what it is to be (in)human. And Suzanne's doing it well enough that I'm not sure I'd want her gimlet eye turned my way— because I'm pretty sure she sees too much.

So, yeah. I think Suzanne is on her way to becoming a legend. Wait and see. Get ready to say you knew her when. Read this book and look out for the next one. Watch for her stories in *Clarkesworld* and *Neo-Opsis* and *On Spec* and *Cicada* and *Challenging Destiny* and wherever else good genre fiction shows up. You won't be sorry. But you'll probably be addicted. You'll be *synched* and ready for the drop... just like me.

—Sandra Kasturi
Toronto 2013

∞ O ∞

COOLIES

I had the shakes; brought on by the adrenaline of the upcoming salv. Coolies are the worst of the best and I was their leader.

A newbie sat at our table in the mess tent— a woman. She wore a tough-as-stainless face, but everybody lost it the first time out. She'd be no different.

I sat beside her, shoving my stubble-lined cheek in her direction.

She glanced at my shaking hands, so I kept them moving, shoveling eggs like they tasted better than sawdust. She looked no more than eighteen with her nearly-bald crew cut. And her eyes, they reminded me of someone.

I asked, "What's your name?"

"Daxie."

Shit. Of course. The picture. I swallowed hard. "Doesn't sound like a real name," I said.

"And you are?"

"Marvin. But you can call me Sergeant." Either she didn't know who I was, or she hid her emotions well.

"I heard Georgopoulos call you Pops," she said. "Must be a story there."

"You don't know the half of it. Come back alive with a full cooler and I'll tell you the first chapter."

Damn her mother and damn the deal. One picture a year. No contact. I wasn't allowed to be her father. Not when I chose a cooler over love.

Part of me wanted to grab her by the shoulders and scream at her to run as far from the war as she could. To beg a transfer before she shoved her hands into someone's insides to search for whatever was worth salving.

My one chance to make a difference in her life fell into my lap and all I could do was eat my lousy eggs.

"You're Needles' daughter, aren't you?"

She nodded. "How d'you know my mom?"

I stared at her eyes, green as a new pair of fatigues, and looked for an excuse to break my promise.

"I…" More eggs. "She sews our inventory back onto people."

I expected her to flinch. To at least *hate* me for degrading her mother's job into that of the butcher's aid. But she smiled. That was the opening; the moment when I should've capitalized on her pride or love or whatever the hell she felt for her mom. It hung there, like snot on the tip of your nose in the dead of winter; and while my stomach churned my crappy eggs into a hell sandwich, I tried to string together a few noble words. *I'm your dad. This job is evil. Don't follow me.* But as the silence stretched between us, my courage fell by the wayside, catching an express train along with my dignity and my honor. I abandoned my food, grunted a parting word, and headed for the locker room.

My second-in-command, Master Corporal Renault, a.k.a. Snowpick, had already donned half his armor. The albino leaned on my locker while he reached down to tighten his boot. When he heard me approach, he straightened and said, "Hey, Marv. What do the scum-rics have planned this morning?"

"They've been hauling equipment from Sunburst to Sweetgrass." I tightened my chest plate, snapping the armor into place with a satisfying click, eyeing the red maple leaf that had faded onto the camo background. I wasn't much of a father, but at least I loved my country. "They're pushing most of the Montana force through Alberta, right into our lap."

"Lucky us." He took off his wedding ring and placed it on the hook attached to his locker door. His fingers paused, like he was touching his wife's lips.

I grabbed my helmet and pulled the picture out of the inner mesh, holding it out for Snowpick. Daxie smiled for the camera with the same happy face she'd shown me in the mess hall. Except she had a full head of beautiful red hair. I bet Needles shot it; couldn't have been more than a year ago, but Daxie had blossomed since then. Into a woman.

"Seen our newest member?"

Snowpick pressed his pale lips together and nodded. "D'she know?"

I nestled the image back into the mesh. "Not as far as I can tell. I can't believe Needles would let her own flesh—"

"I bet the doc doesn't have a clue. Teenagers don't tell their parents jack. Mine don't." He closed his locker. "Your call, Marv; but if I was you, I'd tell her the truth."

"Truth's not my best color. Seems I'm more the scrambled-eggs-shade."

I expected him to argue the point, but he stared at me. Fatherhood was a tight-knit club, and Snowpick had sent me an invitation to the party. I bit my lip, composing a speech for my only child that wouldn't make me seem like a bastard.

Snowpick checked his watch then grabbed his pack. "See you in the IFV."

"Yeah."

∞ O ∞

Daxie stood outside the Infantry Fighting Vehicle, looking like she needed someone to tell her what to do. I cleared my throat.

She straightened to parade attention.

"Hey, listen. I've got to tell you something."

"Last words of advice?" She smiled. "Because the guys have all been giving—"

"Stay behind."

"Excuse me, Sergeant?"

"Don't get on the IFV."

"Why the hell not?"

"Because your mother... I mean, I'm..."

Teflon rapped Daxie on the back and said, "Let's go, newbie."

"But the sergeant—"

"Never mind," I said. "Follow me."

∞ O ∞

The IFV would drop us next to the fire line. Corporal Weber ran the gun on top. The Section called him Teflon because enemy ammo never stuck.

Our coolers waited inside. I lifted my beat-up, red baby's lid; checking for ice. Snowpick had filled it. I snapped the lid back down, bungeed it closed, and headed for the driver's seat.

Driving kept my mind off our newbie and her imminent initiation into salving combat. I wanted to keep checking on her, to glance back and make sure her armor was secure, but my team would've been suspicious. Snowpick was the only man I would ever trust with my dark little secret. Besides, the guys were all over her, spewing their last minute words of wisdom before the action.

As we approached the fire line, I said, "Five minutes, people. Checklist and tie-down."

Snowpick leaned against the back of my seat. "Think we'll ever get the stem cell factories back online?"

I shook my head. "The Americans bomb them faster than we can build them. One day they might shove their self-righteous crosses so far up their asses that they'll lobotomize themselves. In the meantime, we need parts to patch up our wounded."

Daxie moved up beside him, and said, "Which one's mine?"

"Newbies get black." Snowpick pointed at the dented cooler near the front of the IFV. She nestled up to it like it held the secret to eternal life. Her reaction reassured me. The coolies who embraced their equipment lived longer.

Gunfire staccatoed outside. I slammed the brakes and radioed Teflon to lay down suppression fire. I rechecked my armor. Clamps secure, helmet strapped on. Game time. When the back door opened, we filed out; Snowpick on point and Daxie in front of me.

"*Pro patria!*" I shouted.

"*Pro patria!*" they all responded.

We scattered, a cooler dragging behind each one of us on a tether. Gunfire erupted to our right. Daxie flinched, like she'd forgotten every minute of basic training. My gut wrenched into a knot.

Another exchange of fire ripped through the air further west. She ducked below her cooler. At least she had survival instincts.

A shell hit northeast of us. I took cover. My cooler shook with the pounding of another three shells. Despite the twitch in my chest telling me to run, I headed towards the last bombardment. Noise marked the wounded. By the time the ringing quieted in my ears, I was five hundred meters to Daxie's left and hoping she could handle herself.

Bravo Section drew fire in bursts, returning in the pause between reloads. I dropped behind my cooler, and waited for the party to break.

After catching a breath that reeked of gunfire and burnt hair, I hurried for the edge of the crater and surveyed the damage.

The shell had taken a leg off one soldier and an arm off another. The armless one's wound squirted in regular pulses with her heart. A medic jumped down into the hole with me. He covered the woman's wound with shrink wrap. Her skin pinked up. No orgs for me.

The leg guy had a chunk of shrapnel in his head and a slow ooze out the wound. A good harvest. While Bravo Section started another assault, I grabbed the dead guy's liver, kidneys, heart, lungs, spleen, and GI tract. His eyes looked cloudy so I left them behind. The docs had been asking for throats and cords lately, so I sliced them free of his neck and moved on.

When the medic hopped back onto the field, I headed northeast toward a crater big enough to eat an IFV. I saw Daxie's cooler at the rim with the lid up. She might as well paint a big target on her ass.

I raced for the crater as RPGs flew in my direction. One dive and my cooler slung in beside me in the hole.

I grabbed Daxie's arm and shouted, "Get your cooler out of sight."

She pulled on her bungee and the black container skidded into the crater beside her. I could tell from the bounce that it was empty.

"What about him?" I pointed at a guy cut in half near point zero. "You could grab his intestines, they're probably still good."

She shook her head. "His temp's too low for a viable salvage."

"You temped his liver? You could've had his colon and femoral artery by then."

"I wanted to be sure."

I shook my head. "No time."

She looked hurt, like I'd given her an F on her term paper.

"Daxie?"

"Yeah, Sarge?"

"This is the worst time, but if I don't, well… I'm your father."

Before her reaction seeped into her face, I turned toward the high-pitched whine of an incoming.

I heard her say, "My what?"

I started crawling for the rim, trunk down, with my cooler between me and danger. I turned to her. She had her ass in the air and looked as stunned as a doe.

"Get down!"

She flattened against the dirt. As she did, my one and only pang of fatherly instinct flooded me. *Protect her.* I rolled onto my back, my arms reaching to pull my cooler up over both of us. But before I could cover her, the whine turned to a screech.

I saw the shell a fraction of a second before it hit. I knew better than to watch ordnance, but this one called to me, like it had my number tattooed on its ugly brass head. Part of me wanted to witness the end, the chunk of chemicals and metal that would erase my existence from this stink-hole world. The weird part was that I wanted to live the moment — every slice and rupture in perfect detail — to experience the nirvana of total shut-down. My chance to suffer the moment when a body switches from human to salvage.

I got my wish.

∞ O ∞

Snowpick dragged my cooler behind his own. I reached out to take control of my load, but only bumped into it. My hands were both severed, the stumps covered with shrink wrap pinked by blood.

Daxie lay all around me, her body in pieces; head here, abdomen there, a leg at the edge of my vision. Her arm bore a tattoo— symbols, like Asian and Arabic letters melded into images. Ferocity leapt from the surface, warning the timid to stay back. The fingers grabbed at my pant leg.

I tried to step away, but they had a good grip on me. "Please," I said.

The head rolled toward me. Empty, bleeding eye sockets stared back. "Dad?"

I woke, grasping at sheets that stank of over-bleach and straining against what felt like a mag-harness holding me down.

Bandages covered my eyes. I felt as though shards of hot glass had embedded themselves in my corneas. I forced one lid to open slightly under all the padding. The blackness didn't change. I touched the dressing, my fingers delicately searching for answers. The slight pressure on my eyeball brought a second layer of indescribable pain.

Someone entered the room, announced by a squish-squish of mud-crusted boots on a tiled floor.

"Who's there?" I said.

"Snowpick."

"Where am I?"

"Base Hospital."

I swallowed hard, my mouth suddenly drier than it had been a moment before. The image of my broken daughter still fresh in my mind, I asked, "Who'd we lose?"

"Half the fucking Section. Teflon bought it, vaporized. Not even a skin graft left for us to salv. Georgopoulos lost an arm at the shoulder and both legs, and Holling's gonna need a new spinal cord."

"What about Daxie?"

For a long while I listened to his breathing. He sounded like he'd sprinted behind the IFVs all the way from the front line. I'd salved my own people before. It was the worst part of the job, harder than the blank stares of the dead, harder than the mothers who'd grieve their children, and damned harder than RPGs crashing all around.

"Tell me!"

"She's gone. I salved her myself."

A shudder ripped straight through me. Fuck those American bastards and fuck this stupid war. I had told her the truth and lost her in the same moment.

"What'd you get?" Hating myself, I swallowed back the bile rising from my twisted insides. My own fucking daughter and all I could think to ask was the fucking butcher's bill.

He came close, grabbed my hand and pressed it against his arm. "You feel that?" he said.

"Yeah."

"That's her fucking blood. I had my arms buried in her chest, you heartless bastard. What kind of sick son-of-a-bitch are you?"

I pulled my hand away. "Damn it, I need to know."

With a calm I could never have managed, he said, "Heart, lungs, spleen, and pancreas."

He was holding it back, and we both knew why. I wouldn't be able to bear it coming from some doc, especially not Needles. I had to hear it from him. My second. My best friend. "Anything above the shoulders?"

"Yeah. She was O-Pos, just like her daddy. So I saved them for you. Sent them straight to Needles."

"They were green, weren't they?"

"Yeah," he said. "And you don't deserve them."

"Nobody does."

∞ O ∞

At dinner the same night, they cut my pork chop into bite-sized pieces. I couldn't imagine a worse insult for a guy who carved human flesh for a living.

The next morning, Snowpick arrived after breakfast. He said, "The bandages are coming off?"

I nodded. "I don't want my first vision to be your ugly face. Besides, shouldn't you be with the Section?"

"Both sides are waiting on ammo shipments, so you're stuck with me."

We allowed the silence to linger. Thinking is a sorry business, full of what-ifs and what-the-hells. I longed to avoid it, but what else could I do, locked down to my bed and blind?

The door opened, and I heard footsteps. As the person approached, I smelled the unmistakable scent of lilac mixed with disinfectant.

Why'd it have to be her? I sat there, fidgeting. I should have apologized, begged her forgiveness, but I couldn't bring myself to even say hello.

"Sit up," said Needles.

I did.

"Your synapses might not work right away. Your brain has to learn to process signals from a different pair of eyes."

Stone-cold clinical. I shouldn't have been surprised. "I trust you." I reached out for her hand.

Without another word, she snipped the gauze and tugged it free, one slow revolution at a time. Her hands trembled as they neared my eyes. I reached out and touched her fingers. She started, like I'd burned her. The bandages smelled ripe from my sweat. Then the soft pads pulled away one at a time.

I willed my eyes, no, *Daxie's eyes* to work. Light crept through the pink flesh of my lids. They were glued shut; layers of crud had oozed out and hardened my lashes into a crusty mud bank.

Needles pressed a soggy cloth against my face.

The blood-tinged light turned to darkness once more. I pushed the wetness into my lashes, and the pus softened. Then I pulled the cloth away.

"Open your eyes," said Snowpick.

I tugged my lids apart. Bright light forced them shut and I heard bubbling-screechy sounds in my head. I coerced my eyes open again. The bright blue eyes of my ex-lover-turned-savior stared at me.

"How many fingers?" she said.

"Three."

She forced one lid wide open, then the other, burning me with her bright flashlight of pain to get a good long look.

"What's the verdict, doc?"

"I never wanted Daxie to know you; figured she was better off without a father. The next thing I know, I'm holding the pieces of half your squad. They didn't even tell me. I was sewing her eyes into you and they didn't—"

"I'm sorry," I said, crying. At least the tear ducts worked.

"She told me she was taking a year off before university to have fun. *Fun*, for fuck's sake." She kicked the bed, shaking it and me. "She was in your Section, your command, Marv. Why the hell didn't you stop her?"

"You forbade me to—"

"You're the sergeant! It's your job to keep the newbies safe. She wasn't ready and you damn well knew it." Needles raised her hand to slap me. "God damn it, Marv. If I wasn't afraid of wrecking what's left of her, I'd slap you into hell, you fucking prick."

In all her rage, she was more beautiful than I remembered. Maybe it was because seeing anything at all looked fantastic at that moment. Maybe it was because I was viewing her through a different pair of eyes, the eyes of her child.

But her words stabbed me. Maybe that's how she earned her nickname.

She stood and deactivated the mag-harness. "The sooner you're out of my hospital, the better."

Love and hate lived too close together. I wanted to hurt her, like somehow pushing my guilt and pain onto her would lessen my burden. So, I said, "And the sooner I'm back with my Section, the happier I'll be."

Needles left without another word.

Snowpick watched me watch her go and then cleared his throat. "Bad news, Marv."

"They've desked me, haven't they?"

"The Section's holed up with Golf Company. They're expecting me, but you're not invited."

I shook my head. "Invite me, damn it."

"No can do."

I leaned back and put my arm over my new eyes, blotting out the bright room. They burned a constant, searing pain, reminding me of their foreignness. I had tried to connect with Daxie. Now we were linked, but in death, not life.

"I bet they all feel it," I said. "The guys who get patched up." I pulled my arm away and used her eyes to take in the room. "Their friend's heart pumping their own blood, or a chunk of some gal who sat beside them in the canteen. The weight of the constant reminders of two mistakes."

"Maybe," said Snowpick. "Or maybe they just thank the powers above that their warranties haven't expired. A full transplant's grounds for a discharge."

"Yeah, but how many take it?"

"Not many." He paused, staring at me. "You want her back, don't you?"

"I want them *both*. I should've stopped her."

"Coolies don't do shoulds," he said.

I pointed to my eyes. "This is different. How will I ever look Needles in the eye? Fuck, they aren't even mine to do it with."

"Go after her."

"With all that's happened?"

"*Because* of it. You two had something once."

"She hates what I do."

He crossed his arms over his chest. "Everyone hates what we do."

"Do you?" I asked.

He wore the face of command, now, and it suited him. He'd make a better sergeant than I ever had. "Someone's gotta do it," he said.

"I know the standard line. I wrote the fucking brochure. 'We save lives, we don't take them.' It doesn't make me feel any better."

Snowpick shook his head. "You're wrong. *Needles* saves lives. And she deserves a hell of a lot more credit than you or anyone else gives her. Go after her, *now*, or you'll regret it."

I stood and nearly fell back down again. By the time I'd hobbled into the hallway, Needles had disappeared. "Damn."

A doctor in scrubs approached. He looked like a lizard, all scaly at the edges; the peripheral vision hadn't caught up to my brain yet. "Hey, Doc? Have you seen Needles?"

"She's scrubbing into a splenectomy."

"What?" I asked. "You can't be out of spleens?"

"We are. And unless you're willing to donate your own, soldier, I suggest you return to bed."

"I have to see Needles."

The doc yelled a few objections at me, but I ignored him. The walls and floor of the corridor blurred together, making me feel like I was walking along the inside of a pipe. Everything seemed darker and tinted green, as though the army had spiked the camo button, blending the world into their reality. I didn't think about the route— I followed my instincts. I guess the eyes had searched out their mother before.

From the OR gallery I watched Needles. She stood over an open abdomen, retracting skin and calling for suction. I turned on the mic. "Hey, Needles?"

Without looking up, she said, "I'm busy."

"I'm done," I said. "With salving. I'll sign the discharge papers."

That made her look up. "You're serious?"

"Yeah."

The scrub nurse mumbled something about the patient's heart rate. "Can I finish, now?"

"Look for me when you're done."

She didn't answer. I watched her work for a few minutes. Her hands drifted like angels, carefully and skillfully manipulating life back into flesh. Snowpick was right. She saved lives. I was only another scrub nurse passing over organs instead of instruments.

I shuffled back along the hospital corridors, more disoriented than before. I put the odds at less than one in twenty that she'd come after me. But morbid curiosity could be a powerful draw. Or maybe she'd need to hang on to the past.

Back in my room, Snowpick had left a note: *Don't come back. I mean it.*

He always knew what to say.

Under the bed, I found my fatigues. I ditched the gown and suited up, desperate to cling to who I used to be. But part of me had died on that battlefield. Not in glory, like the old war movies. But in disgrace, failing to save the only good thing I'd ever done.

As I headed for the bathroom, I misjudged the distance and smacked my forehead on the door frame. At the mirror, I checked to see if I'd sliced myself open. The guy staring back wasn't me. Green eyes, *Daxie's* eyes. They didn't belong in a uniform any longer.

The nurse had left me a razor. I rubbed at the stubble and decided it matched my soon-to-be-unemployed status. My skin was worn, scarred. Living proof of a thousand bad choices. My up-close vision had dialed the clock back a couple of decades.

My breath fogged the glass until all I could see was a blob. I could have been anyone ... Daxie ... even Needles. I'd spend the rest of my life trying to earn their forgiveness.

"Time to return the uniform," I said to the blob.

I waited for him to answer, to talk me out of it, but he only glared.

I cleared my throat and uttered the two words that had meant the most to me during my stint with the Royal Canadian Regiment. *"Pro patria."* For the first time since donning camos almost twenty years ago it rang hollow. Just another trick to coerce recruits to put their country before their own lives.

As the fog cleared, I noticed a nose smudge on the mirror. A souvenir for the next patient, unless the room got scrubbed first. The discharge forms waited at the nursing station. I scrawled my sergeant sig on the solid line.

It should have been dotted, a line like that. The kind that turns a man's war. Because final battles never ended smoothly and mine should be no different.

The Wind
and The Sky

Triangles and hexagons danced in intricate patterns, their colors streaming from yellow, to orange, to violet. In the upper periphery a cluster of turquoise parallelograms slid next to blazing red trapezoids like seed crystals dropped in a supersaturated solution.

"Polnine!"

Halting the fractal and engaging his eyes, Polnine answered, "Yes, sir."

Astfour stood in the doorway, arms crossed, glaring. "I didn't clear this research." He pointed at the display. "What function do planetary co-ordinates perform in genetic research?"

Arrogant Astatine series. "Well, sir..."

Astfour tapped the monitor. "Yes?"

"I tracked a group of humans on the surface, to determine the location of their settlement."

"Polnine." Astfour shook his head. "You're on the cusp of an unscheduled software upgrade."

"Sir, my research could augment Radnine's human—"

"Trivialities." Astfour waved his hand.

"If we don't track the humans, then how will we know when to integrate them?"

"Integrate! They're devolved, mammalian imbeciles."

Polnine stood and crossed his arms, matching Astfour's self-righteous pose. "Humans created us in their image, Sir."

"Their technologically superior predecessors developed the *Hydrogen* series, who aren't even advanced enough to clean the stabilizers. I think 'creator' is an *infinite* exaggeration."

Polnine shook his head. "But they entrusted us to maintain their genetic samples and culture."

"They've endured. Extinction is no longer a threat."

Both androids waited for the other to speak. Polnine looked at the viewscreen to avoid Astfour's exasperating smirk. On the Earth's surface, the line that separated day from night crept over the Atlantic Ocean.

Astfour broke the stalemate. "Science is about commitment, rigor, and focus. Not studying pitiful cave dwellers."

"We exist for more than science."

"We are science. We determine science. We advance science. Science is all-important."

"Not for me."

"Then you require a software upgrade."

"You wouldn't!"

"I must do my job, as you must do yours." Astfour moved to the doorway. "I will pass along your data to Radnine, but you must report to software."

"Yes, Sir." Polnine slumped in his chair. *I won't submit to sanitation.*

He walked towards software, but when Astfour disappeared around a corner he changed direction and headed for transportation.

∞ O ∞

Polnine threw another leafy branch on the shuttle and stood back.

He could still see the nose of the shuttle so he adjusted the camouflage. As he did, a sprig of balsam activated his olfactory decoders. He cataloged the combination of alkyds and esters in his memory.

He looked up and gazed at the brilliant blue of the sky. The multitude of subtle hue variations overwhelmed him.

Then he focused on his auditory decoders. A robin chirped, a sparrow responded, and the buzzing of bees and dragonflies provided counterpoint. A breeze stirred up a symphony of rustling leaves. The space station — with its mechanical hums and drones — paled in comparison.

He picked up another branch and studied the intricate texture of the bark. The pattern far surpassed the complexity of his favorite fractals. He pushed his cross-reference routines to their capacity interpreting the data.

With the shuttle suitably hidden, he sat down on an exposed piece of granite (hard but rough— and such an interesting shape). A compulsion to pause immobilized him. Regardless of the risks he took — unauthorized shuttle use, disobeying a superior — he lingered.

The co-ordinates of the settlement placed it to his left. He stood and threw his field bag over his shoulder mimicking an adventurer from the literature archives.

The forest closed in around him and he fought his way through the brush. The many fingers of shrub and tree branches grabbed at his clothing, ripping and catching. He stopped to pull a blackberry shoot from his pant leg. One of its thorns punctured his skin, and he checked for blood. *Why would I worry about blood?* The humans had embedded reactive subroutines, but he didn't recall ever experiencing one himself. An invasion of this nature would cause a human to bleed. He filed the sensation away for further interpretation while struggling through the dense brush, until he broke through to a clearing. He noted a woman working twenty meters to his left.

She had long black hair and wore clothes made from animal skins. As she dug up roots, she placed them in a woven basket. Polnine backed into the forest and crept towards her position. When she grunted and used both hands to wrench out a tenacious root, he emerged from hiding.

"My Wind," she gasped.

She spoke a language that he carried in his database. He accessed the appropriate phrase. "I am Polnine."

"What clan are you?"

Clan? A synonym for family. Had the word evolved to a broader definition, like workgroup? "I'm traveling alone." He stepped closer to her.

She backed up. Her hands gripped the basket with such force that her fingers whitened.

"Please, do not be afraid." He stretched out both arms in a gesture, he hoped, of friendship.

"You're not Merek." She held the basket out in front of her as a shield.

"I've journeyed a great distance. I'd like to meet your..." He referenced what word would designate her settlement, but found none. "The place where your clan rests."

Her eyes narrowed. "Are you here for lineage?"

Lineage? "I came here to meet your people." He smiled.

"Why?" She backed away from him and looked to her left and right. "To steal our children?"

Polnine leaned towards her. "If you would take me to them, I would—"

She dropped the basket and bolted. Her sudden move surprised Polnine, but he raced after her. In the level clearing he overtook her within moments. He grabbed her arm and dragged her to a stop. She hit him with her free hand as she tried to wrench the other one free. When he grabbed the free arm she kicked him in the region where a man's reproductive system would reside.

"You don't need to defend yourself. I didn't come here to harm you."

"Liar!"

He loosened his grip on her arms. "If I release your wrist, will you please not run away?"

She glared back at him. "Your clan are fast *and* strong. What do you need of our women?"

"I want to talk with you." He let go of her. "What's your name?"

She cradled her sore arms. "Ve'keso."

"That's an interesting name." He could not find a reference to its meaning in his language database. "What does it mean?"

She stared at the ground in silence. The wind stirred the leaves near his feet and he documented the intricacies of their dance. Another breeze picked up a thin layer of her hair that joined in the merriment.

"I'm a scientist. I came here to share data with you."

"I don't know your words," she said, looking up at him. Her dark brown eyes pierced him in a strange, unphysical way. Fear and hatred swam in those eyes, but curiosity chased them.

"Which words?"

"Sytis."

"Ah," said Polnine, checking his language database and finding no equivalent, "I experiment and conclude, thus I am a scientist."

"A Synis?" she asked again.

He paused. "I study everything around us. The sky, the environment, people."

"The sky and people? These are made from our Wind, by our Wind."

Polnine checked his language algorithm. Her words made no sense. "No, science explains life. Energy cannot be created nor destroyed. Gravity is caused by the mutual attraction of objects. Science is the language, and the tool we use to describe the actions and reactions of the universe. Wind is a meteorological event."

Ve'keso's expression had changed from terror to confusion. "Our Wind rules the sky."

"Space has no wind. I know. I come from there."

She gasped. "You come from the sky?"

"Beyond it, yes."

She looked away, then back at him. "My mother once told me the story of a man, who comes from the sky and gives a woman his lineage. Her baby brings strength to our people. Are you that man?" She knelt down before him and bowed her head.

He looked up to the sky then back to her. He stroked her hair. "I came here to help however I can."

She stood up. "Come." She retrieved her basket, and then turned in the direction of the settlement. "You swear not to harm us?"

"I promise."

"Your speech is strange. The elders must approve all lineage bonds."

"I look forward to sharing knowledge with them." He paused, then added, "You are the most beautiful creature I've ever seen, Ve'keso."

She blushed, then turned towards the settlement. Her body swayed from side to side as she walked. She held the basket against her right hip, unbalancing the rhythm of her stride. Polnine had never witnessed such grace, except in recordings of dances in the archives. "Are you a dancer?"

Without answering, she glanced over her shoulder and a smile flickered on her face. Turning back to the trail, she said, "My name… it means bird."

∞ O ∞

The village consisted of several round huts, made of mud and grass, built on a natural plateau. The villagers had arranged the huts in concentric circles around a larger, square building. Smoke floated upward through openings in the roofs. Children played a game with sticks in a depression beyond the distant huts.

The other humans stared at Polnine as he and Ve'keso walked along a radius towards the center of the village. A group of older men and women gathered outside the square hut. Ve'keso approached a tall, lean man within the group. He wore his gray and black hair in a braid. She whispered to the man, glanced at Polnine, then pointed at the sky.

Another stockier man, with shorter hair and a blazing red beard, said, "I am Perston. Come inside and speak with us."

Polnine followed him into the large hut and the older humans followed. Ve'keso entered last, and she sat down on a woven grass mat, outside the circle formed by the elders. Polnine sat between Perston and the man with the braid, who identified himself as Heevaho.

Each elder took a turn asking questions. Polnine explained in simple terms why he had come to their village. Questions traced around the circle three times. Once the elders seemed satisfied with his answers, they sent him outside.

While he waited, many of the women and their offspring came by to scrutinize him. Two women, who appeared childless, touched him, feeling his arms and back, commenting on his health and strength. The men stayed distant, glancing and muttering.

As the sky darkened, two adolescent girls — who giggled to each other while avoiding his eyes — left a sack of food. The second looked over her shoulder at him as she walked away. He had seen that same look on Ve'keso's face.

The moon rose above the horizon. Polnine noted the drop in temperature, and held his legs close to his chest. *Strange response. Perhaps another of the embedded subroutines?* He leaned against the wall of the square hut.

After a while, he activated one of his favorite fractals, and turned off the input from his eyes. Triangles and hexagons grew to form new shapes, their hues transforming from green, to blue, to red. A swirl started in the lower periphery, and it enveloped a region of orange trapezoids, turning them scarlet.

"Polnine?"

He dropped the fractal and engaged his eyes, seeing Ve'keso standing above him. "Yes?"

"The elders will be honored to have you join the Merek clan."

"Thank them for me." Behind Ve'keso the sky had become as complex as a fractal. Above the bright horizon, shades of pink and blue swirled together below the gray clouds. The white intensified and the pink and blue seemed to dissolve as though iodine and indigo had been dropped into a beaker of water. "Your sky is magnificent."

"Our Wind loves to paint the morning. The elders have allowed me to choose your lineage to enhance the clan."

Polnine let go of his legs and asked, "Please, would you explain lineage?"

She sat down beside him. Her ears looked pink, when she whispered, "You must have made children before, for other clans? You are strong and healthy."

He shook his head. "I can't... I don't have..."

"Oh." She paused, and glanced at him, before studying her feet again. "If you want to choose another, I suggest Xao'o. She has given the clan many healthy children."

"I'm honored that your clan deemed me worthy. I would like to choose you, but I can't provide lineage. I don't have the *ability* to make a child with you."

"You've never given yourself?"

"No. Never."

"Oh." She looked up at him. "Oh!" She stood up and offered her hand. "Come with me, Polnine. I will show you a most wonderful amusement."

They walked to a hut in the fourth circle from the center. Ve'keso lit a fire, and then sat down beside him on a bed layered with animal furs. She took his hand, and caressed the top of it, wrist to fingers, and back again. She looked into his eyes, and he lost himself in their beauty. He could feel her breath against his lips, as she moved close to him. Then she kissed him. The moisture from her lips lingered on his before evaporating. Her skin felt hotter than when he had touched her in the woods. Her tongue came out, and touched his lips, before she kissed him again. She leaned back.

"You say I'm beautiful, but you don't kiss me?"

"Am I to kiss you back?"

"Polnine! Why do you play with me?"

He brought her close, and put his lips to hers, imitating her kiss.

"I'll make healthy children with you," she whispered.

He pulled away from her embrace. "Perhaps we can talk. I have many questions about your people."

"Now?" She wiped her lips with the back of her hand, and glared at him.

"You look flushed. Do you feel ill?"

"I'm fine."

"I'll bring you some water. Do you have a well, or do you carry it from a pond or river?"

"Go ask Xao'o." She stood up, and stirred the fire. "I have chores. Go away until you're ready."

"Ve'keso?" Her contempt loomed where eagerness had been moments before. *Perhaps I should investigate courting rituals.*

Outside the hut, he looked up at the sky, trying to determine the station's current position. *How do I explain what I am to her?* A beam of sunlight poured through a break in the clouds onto a few huts. Polnine drank in the scenery for a long time, then approached some children to study their play.

As he made his way through the village, he met Perston and Heevaho. They stopped their conversation. "Thank you for allowing me to learn about the Merek clan," he said. "I have information that will help to improve your living conditions."

Heevaho crossed his arms over his chest and said, "Help us by giving Ve'keso a child. She's lost much."

"What has she lost?"

"A warring clan killed her mate. We met with them to seek lineage but they didn't follow our rituals. After the conflict, they took her children as payment for her release. Our clan lost a strong hunter, and two boys of healthy lineage."

"Why do you meet with other clans if they're dangerous?"

Heevaho answered, "Without variety, our children are born sick."

"I understand." Polnine paused. "Ve'keso is angry with me."

Perston smiled. "Go to the forest and bring her a gift from our Wind. Ve'keso likes flowers."

"Thank you for the guidance." Polnine nodded and continued his study of the village. Late in the day, he ventured to the forest. He wandered the landscape, studying plant and animal species. At dusk he stumbled across a natural shelter created by a slate overhang, and decided to spend the night. He lay protected from the wind, listening to the trees sway, the animals scurry, and the insects sing. He had hoped to start the humans on the path to science and technology before his upgrade. Now he understood what it meant to live. How much longer would he be allowed to remember?

∞ O ∞

After cataloguing another glorious sunrise, Polnine started back for the village. He followed Perston's advice and picked a bouquet of buttercups and daisies for Ve'keso. When he reached her hut, he called, "Ve'keso, may I speak with you?"

She did not answer. He stepped into the doorway and looked around. Her bed coverings smoldered in the embers of the fire. She had sliced long, jagged marks into the mud wall beside the bed. Someone shuffled behind him, and Polnine turned to see Heevaho, who shouted, "Get out of there!"

"What happened here?"

"Ve'keso has the fever. She made those marks on the wall last night, to beg our Wind to take away the pain. All who get the fever go to the cave."

Polnine dropped the flowers. "Where is this cave? Why did she go there?"

"She must take the fever away from the village, or we'll all die."

"Die? From a *fever?*"

Two women appeared. One of them identified herself as Xao'o and said, "She has the 'fever of terror'. Many catch it in the forest. As your body burns up, your wits cloud over, and then you... She fled to the 'cave of our Wind,' on the other side of our lands. The cave is stocked for her death journey. In a few days, we'll give her body back to our Wind."

"Where is this cave? I need to speak with her."

"No. You'll catch the fever."

"You don't understand." He turned to stare at them one by one. "I can make medicine for her."

"If you help her, you risk killing us all."

Polnine stormed through the village. "Who will tell me where to find the 'cave of our Wind'?" They turned away from him. No one would answer.

He paced in a slow circle, watching their frightened faces, wondering how they could all be so quick to abandon one of their own to die alone.

I will not allow her to die, he thought.

Turning his back on them, he headed for the woods. *I'll find her with the shuttle's detection equipment.*

∞ O ∞

He reached the cave at nightfall. The entrance had large "X" marks etched in the rock to warn of danger. A dim light shone from a hollow to the right of the entrance, and he followed its warmth. He wound through a narrow passageway, then into a larger chamber. The room had a bed, a chair, wooden bowls, and a bin filled with dried meats and plants. The embers of a small fire glowed in the corner. Above it, a hollow in the rock allowed the smoke to escape. Ve'keso lay on the bed, trembling under several furs.

"Ve'keso," Polnine whispered. He crouched by her side and touched her shoulder.

She jerked with a start, and turned to look at him. She seemed to stare right through him. "Leave, Polnine. You'll catch the fever."

"I can't catch the fever."

"Leave me!"

"No, Ve'keso. I want to help you. I won't die because I don't live. I exist. I am an android."

She shook her head. "Your words are thick."

Polnine sat down beside her, and stroked her long, beautiful hair. "Do you know what happened to humans, who lived before your clan?"

"Our people hid from the great Wind when she piled her rage upon the world, angry that we had forgotten the old ways. The Merek family lived with others in the great cave, and later emerged to form our clan. We are all their descendants."

"Ve'keso, many years ago a meteor — a large rock — fell from the sky, destroying life. Some people built caves, with enough supplies to last while the world repaired itself."

He paused while she coughed. "Some survived above the world, in a dwelling that moves around the sky." Polnine made a sweeping arc above his head with his arm. "In it, they created machines like me — androids — and programmed us as scientists. I was not born of a man and a woman, I was assembled."

"I don't understand."

"You don't have to. I'm going back to design medicine for you. And to acquire supplies to provide lineage." A coughing spasm racked her body. He held her hand. "Will you hold on until I return?"

"I'm so hot." She closed her eyes, and her hand fell out of his.

He reached into his field bag for a sample collector, then pierced her skin. As he filled the bottle, he whispered an apology. The coppery smell of blood sent warning signals through him. *Another embedded subroutine.* He hurried back to his shuttle.

After docking, he ducked into the medical lab where he started an algorithm to isolate the fever contagion, and design a custom antidote. While it processed, he warmed a frozen sperm sample from the archives and installed a hardware upgrade for implantation. Then he hurried back to the docking bay with the vials of antidote and sperm.

Astfour blocked his path to the shuttle.

"Back for your upgrade, Polnine? I'm pleased that you've rationalized through to a scientific conclusion."

"Sir?"

"Stealing a shuttle is beyond your usual disobedience. But you returned to accept punishment." Astfour held a deactivation uplink. More androids waited at the other end of the bay.

"Your parts will be recycled, contributing to our evolution. Please co-operate, Polnine. For science."

As Astfour reached forward to connect the uplink, Polnine grabbed his wrist. He wrenched the unit free and linked it with Astfour, deactivating him. "For *science*, Sir." He entered the shuttle before the others could stop him.

∞ O ∞

Back in the cave he injected Ve'keso with the antidote. She awoke and whispered, "You came back? Did you catch the fever?"

"No. I'm healthy. Do you still wish to make a child of my lineage?"

"Yes. For our clan." She kissed him. Her dry lips quivered as she pressed against him.

Polnine removed his clothes, and slipped under the furs. He moved with slow and gentle grace. The upgrade functioned flawlessly. He used a scanner to ensure that the egg had been fertilized, then pulled a blanket over her.

Ve'keso would pass on antibodies to the baby to protect against the fever. Perhaps the child would bring strength to her people, as the prophecy foretold.

He stroked her soft hair and said, "I believe that I love you, my mystical Ve'keso." He kissed the nape of her neck, and stored her scent in his memory.

Outside the cave, two shuttles flew overhead and landed. Many of his colleagues would be on board, ready to capture and deactivate him. He had traded the humans' science for beauty. He sat down outside the cave and waited to face his deactivation with dignity.

Sadness overcame him when he thought of all of the magnificent data he had gathered, which would soon be lost. He wiped his hand across his cheek. In his despair, he chose not to question the reason for the action. *Possibly another embedded subroutine.*

MARCH
OF THE
FORGOTTEN

Sebbee, the silver travel mug, had been forgotten. *Again*. This time in the food court of the mall. So began another test of her endurance.

All day, as the shoppers fluttered past the restaurant stalls, a few reunions set various sentient objects free. A pair of red leather gloves danced over and up into the hands of their owner, a middle-aged woman whose long auburn hair matched them perfectly. The gloves had huddled together, whimpering and afraid, as they marched along in the *Lost Circle*. Clearly they had never been left before. They carried the signs of a lengthy relationship with their owner— cracked at the tips, their color rubbing off in the creases of the palms: *favorites*.

Sebbee watched in angry silence, more jealous than she harbored the right to be, settling into the certainty of her extended stay in the *Circle*.

The worst part was that she wasn't empty. Vanessa hadn't finished her Chamomile. In fact, she had sipped so slowly, so intermittently, that the beverage had turned cold long before she'd forgotten Sebbee on the food court table. Sebbee hated cold drinks, for they made her inner skin feel slimy and the outer one clammy. At least the tea had been black, well yellow actually, but free of sweeteners or the dreaded *cream*. She had known many a lost object to live a brief moment of ecstasy in reunion only to be followed nearly immediately by the indignation of the recycler. Or worse, the trash. Either way, the victim would lie, helpless, surrounded by filth, trapped by the bin's electro-magnetic disablers, while he or she imagined the blinding pain of deactivation followed by nothingness.

Black Chamomile meant hope that one day her owner would return. Vanessa would eventually need a hot drink and considering her frugality, she would use Sebbee rather than spend the few extra pennies on a paper cup. And when she couldn't find her faithful silver mug, she would eventually retrace her steps and return to the food court, pass close enough to Sebbee, and then the two would share the joy of reunion.

The mall stayed open late, extra hours for the holiday rush. With all the bundles and packages, combined with the mind-numbing pressure of last minute gift selection, many objects found themselves in the *Circle*, marching diligently, loop after loop. Every mall had one, a designated section, usually around the food court, for that's where humans expected to be entertained. All sentient objects would travel, counter clockwise on even days and clockwise on odd ones, in single-file, except for pairs like gloves and shoes who would travel side by side. All of them strutting their features in the hopes that a distant glance might tweak a memory or bring their owner close enough to trigger the standard sentient object homing beacon.

Sebbee had experienced the flash — half jolt and half rapture — when her beacon sensed her owner's proximity. Only then could an object break the *Circle* and run (or trot or slide, whatever movators they had been blessed with) into the sometimes surprised but usually happy hands of the person who had so carelessly left them behind. Vanessa often misplaced her *necessities*: her purse or keys.

Sebbee shuddered from the digression, aware of the upcoming discomfort if she continued to think poorly of her owner. Objects were programmed not to slag their keepers, otherwise, the *Circle* would be nothing but a constant misery-fest. Every object in the *Circle* would spend their time recounting their master's one, or many, indiscretions that led to their being left behind.

Vanessa often lost, *sting*, a single glove or mitten from a pocket. *Pain*. Singles suffered the agony of separation, followed by a double blow. The one lost would march forever, in whatever *Circle* was closest. Alone, half-there, carrying the shame of being single in a double's world, their only hope being that the *Circle* would not be occupied by any pairs. Otherwise, the constant reminder of their twin's loss could drive them to depths no object should ever be forced to endure.

Worse, the one not lost would die quickly, for Vanessa never held onto, *pain*, her singles. As soon as she would discover the error, she would throw the remaining of the pair, *jolt*, into the nearest recycler— at least she believed in object reincarnation. Sebbee carried the audible whimpers heavily in her power-source-heart, long after the sound of her discarded comrade dwindled as Vanessa brought her mug beyond the range of the single's final resting place.

Goodbye, friend, Sebbee would think. *At least your pain didn't linger.* But she understood that to die knowing your other half marched endlessly without you, someplace long-forgotten, brought no closure. In fact, she had heard stories of the afterlife, a nebulous place where the souls of unmatched objects would linger for eternity, never birthed into another object, never settling into the serenity of lost memories, never finding peace.

Better to be an isolated object like her. Designed as an aid, but not a *necessity*.

"Hey there," came a voice a few objects further back in the line.

Sebbee slowed but did not stop, for her programming would not allow her to halt.

"Silver," the voice again. "You're looking shiny today."

She hobbled backwards, searching out the object and found another mug, like her. From the depth of the voice, a male; probably assigned such by a male master. He had a candy apple-red coat and an L-shaped handle, even the same black neoprene coat around his middle.

"Hi, Red," she said.

"The name's Bob, actually." He wiggled left to right as he spoke his moniker, proud that his owner had had the kindness to grace him with a name.

"Sebbee," she said.

"That's an odd one. What's your owner's name?"

"Vanessa." She turned her back on him, and added, "Yours?"

"Miles. A real pompous dude, always on an airplane or riding in a limo. Some company can't live without him, but I think it's only a line he uses with his wife to justify the fact that he'd rather play video games with their daughter than hang with her."

"I know the type," said Sebbee. "Seen plenty of their discards. Probably won't—" Sebbee shuddered.

Bob wiggled, acknowledging the silence.

The slight had only been half-accidental, for her thoughts lingered on her absent master. Cynicism and manipulation were soul-partners in the *Circle*, but voicing such feelings simply brought more pain.

"I understand," he said. "Let me reassure you, *Sebbee*, if that's *really* your name, that I've never spent more than a week in a *Lost Circle*. As a matter of fact, I was once picked up by a *roamie*."

It is *my name*, she wanted to correct him, but he would probably hear the wobble in her processors. He might even call her on the lie, though he didn't seem quite that cruel.

"Your tale's as tall as your profile, Bob. *Roamies* are a myth. I might look like a newbie, but I've probably spent more time in *Circles* than you and half your manuf class combined."

A shove knocked Sebbee from behind. A diaper bag. The pompous jerk. They never spent more than an hour in the *Circle*. Damned *necessities*.

"Keep moving," smirked the bag. Her voice was smooth, with a slight Italian accent. One of those high-end bags for the mom-who-has-everything.

Bob slowed and Sebbee matched his pace so that the bag would pass them and hassle some other object.

"They're all the same," he said, pointing his handle at the bag. "Think they own the world. I couldn't wait until Miles' daughter grew old enough to ditch the diaper bag. Bad enough I have to endure the holy trinity."

"What are you blabbering about?"

"*Holy*, as in 'so important they might as well be God,' and *Trinity* as in three. You see, Miles always has three vehicles. Each is replaced after three years, so that he has a new one every year. The newest key is always the most pompous until she's replaced."

"The keys are all female?" said Sebbee.

"Yep, just like the cars, which he names."

"Lots of owners name their cars."

Bob flipped his drink spout open and closed. "Not the *cars*, the *keys*. He uses mother-daughter pairs of famous characters, either from books or human-life. It's sick, really. Makes all the other objects nauseous."

"How can we be nauseous?"

"Trust me, it happens," he said.

Sebbee flipped her own drink spout open, more in exasperation than anger. This Bob was going to milk the gullible angle until she might actually figure out how to feel nauseous. Much as she liked to have a friend in the *Circle*, she wasn't certain how much of his teasing she could endure.

She spun on her neoprene bottom and surveyed the line of objects behind them. Three sets of mittens, all tiny, but of differing sizes, and all the same powder blue. Some mom was about to take her charges to the van and discover a massive hand-warming shortage. They wouldn't be in the *Circle* for more than another hour. After them, a black hairbrush, a cell phone that looked about to burst with attitude, then a white scarf that gathered more and more grime as it slithered in step, so to speak.

"That one's destined for the recycler," said Bob. "Those stains'll never wash out."

"Ever heard of bleach?" said Sebbee.

"Who uses bleach anymore?"

"My Vanessa."

"Yeah, and she named you Sebbee, right?"

Every centimeter of her body wanted to stop, then, to illustrate to the others, and more specifically, this buffoon, how contempt can hurt when it smacks you in the rim. But onward her movators pushed, ahead with the march, a display of hope and shame, longing and despair, all packaged as a modern upgrade from the dreaded non-sentient *Lost & Found*. "Yeah, like *roamies* are real," she said.

Bob turned and fell, smacking his rim into her handle with a loud snap. Every object in the *Circle* jumped, for damage could easily spell immediate recycling.

"How dare you," said Sebbee. "You could've broken my handle."

"Serves you right." He hurried ahead, pushing past the diaper bag who chased him with a round of insults. Before the Italian snob could overtake him once more, the bag's sensors beeped. And, showy as a diamond-studded Rolex, she lit up like a Christmas tree.

The bag carried *proximity lights*.

A gasp from near the donut stand, and the Italian bag sprinted off in the direction of her owner. The woman-mom-owner pushed a double-stroller, filled with two perfectly-matched twin babies no more than six months of age. Their vintage was only a best guess by Sebbee.

After all, Vanessa was single and childless. Lucky Sebbee often lived on the coffee table, filled with hot cocoa or cider, while Vanessa unwound in front of her flat-screen.

Safe.

Home.

Sebbee bounced over a bump, noticing too late that she had landed in gum.

Pink gum.

Now, with every hop, she stuck a little to the floor. A gooey feeling spread from her base along her slender frame. Her spout popped open and a splash of chamomile spurted from her cavity and out the hole, spraying the floor and the mitten trio behind her.

"That, my dear silver, is nausea." Bob had returned.

Sebbee wanted to reply with another clever quip, but all she could manage was, "Oh." Her insides felt worse than clammy, she felt eruptive. The last time she had sensed this much discomfort, she had been left on the counter for five days with a latte curdling inside her. She could not pop her spout, either, for the mixture inside had been so chock full of sugar and honey that she was stuck shut. Desperate, she had promised Guido, an egotistical cell phone of epic self-importance, a little stroking if he would knock her, and the two cereal boxes blocking her path, into the sink.

He had.

But to Sebbee's dismay, she *still* had not popped open. Luckily, the mess of the two spilt cereal boxes caught Vanessa's attention, and before midnight that evening, Sebbee found herself full of hot water and dish soap, soaking away the stink that lived insider her.

"That was close," Guido had said. "Another day and she might have recycled you, rather than bothering with your mess."

Sebbee rocked back and forth in agreement, careful not to spill her contents.

"And tomorrow," said Guido, "you'll make good on your promise."

To Sebbee's dismay, Vanessa had thrown both cell phone and coffee mug into her laptop bag that morning. They had spent the entire hour-and-a-half commute on the subway pressed against each other. Guido's hinge got quite a workout, and by the time they reached the coffee shop, Sebbee actually looked forward to the scalding rinse by the baristas before she was filled with a double-bag dose of Earl Grey.

"Sebbee?" Bob sounded nervous, beside her.

She found her way back to the mall, the *Circle*, and the endless march, now percussed with the loud stick-release that had become her new song.

"Where'd you go?" he asked.

"If you're still here in seven days, ask me about Guido."

"I will," he muttered.

I doubt it, especially if the roamie *story is real.*

Mitten-mom appeared, five children in tow. Off raced the triple pair of blues behind them.

The hair brush hurried to fill the gap in their line.

Sebbee and Bob both said, "Hi," but the brush didn't respond.

Though Bob wiggled in a way that only another mug would see as smug, Sebbee whispered, "Design flaw," and continued with her march. She had spent a month once in a show building — designated for special events — cold and lonely after the summer fair had passed through. With only twelve of them in the *Lost Circle*, she had built quite a relationship with the objects left behind. Seven had been retrieved, including Sebbee, but five had expired in the *Circle*, their batteries recharged too many times. Summer objects were often built for portability and the float-factor, especially if they belonged on a beach. The flat brush had been silent the entire march. But when she was retrieved, only a day before Sebbee's reunion, her siblings, a round brush and a mirror, part of a beautiful set, had quickly explained about her design flaw.

"Our owner loved the look of us so much, she endured the flaw. Besides," added the round brush, "I rarely say much. There are only so many cuss words an owner with thick, matted hair will endure before she might decide to replace me."

"Thanks," said Sebbee before the owner whisked the trio home. She wasn't sure at the time why she had found the story so important, so comforting. Perhaps because she had always wondered if the flat brush had simply been rude. Or worse, so *thinly* sentient as to be incapable of conversation.

"It's a good thing we weren't built that way," said Bob. "I'd go crazy in a *Circle* without conversation."

"Me, too," said Sebbee. And for the first time, she felt a closeness to Bob, as though they were meant to be stuck together. "Tell me about the *roamie*."

He wiggled back and forth, nearly turning his march to a zigzag, and said, "But first...."

Sebbee waited.

"Explain your name."

Cornered. Well, if she would ever get him to tell his story, true or not, she would have to admit what he probably already guessed.

"Some of my letters are missing," she admitted. "All I have left from 'Starbucks' is the S and the B, and all that's left from 'Coffee' are the two E's."

Quieter, so that only Sebbee would hear, he said, "An accident?"

"Worse." Sebbee hated this part of the story, because it meant she would have to speak poorly of her owner.

"Scratched?" offered Bob.

Sebbee said, "Yes," with such a loud pop of exhalation from her spout that the two of them jumped a little out of line before hurrying back in step. He understood. No need to try to dance around the explanation, no need to stutter the V in Vanessa over and over until he finished it for her.

"Oh, Bob," she said. "I'm so glad you're here."

He sidled closer to her, and said, "Me too, silver. Me too."

Bob held back the *roamie* story. Neither one of them seemed up for the tale. Instead, they marched in calm silence, enjoying each other's company, content in the knowing that they were similar manuf's.

Almost kin.

The brush didn't last. A wayward teen had hurried into the *Circle* to grab at an iPod. *Circle-lifters,* usually trying to out-cool their friends.

The iPod, intent on waiting for its true owner, had attacked the teen, ramming into the boy's head, breaking his nose with an audible snap, then scratching one of his corneas. All *necessities* were programmed for self-protection. And the fancier, high-end models could even summon the law to lay down a *Circle-lifting* charge. In the ruckus, the brush had been stomped on, not once, but three times. What was left would never brush its master's hair again. The law enforcer had ordered the custodial staff to retrieve the locator from the wreckage and plug it into the network. At least give the owner some closure, if they ever noticed the object's absence. Sebbee wondered if the owner would ever search out the brush's fate, or if those last moments of pain and snapping would be the only memories it would carry to reincarnation. Perhaps, in its next life, the new object would be blessed with the power of speech.

When the mall's lights dimmed, leaving nothing but the warm-red glow emanating from the emergency exits, the objects slowed. Though they could never stop, they were encouraged to conserve energy when reunions were impossible.

Conversations were a waste of battery life, so the silence of the night closed in around them. The only sounds were of slow, deliberate movement. The swish of the scarf, the scrape of the sole remaining cell phone, too dejected by his lack of retrieval to bounce, and of course, loudest of all, Sebbee's stick-snap of her gum-soiled bottom on the *Circle's* floor.

Bob stayed close, marching as near to her side as unitary objects were allowed, making the occasional comforting plop of his spout.

In the morning, she would ask him what he carried. From deep within, the slosh was slight but present. Most travel mugs could name-that-beverage as easily as out-venting, but Bob's cargo was mysterious.

Tomorrow, she thought.

∞ O ∞

Sunlight hit the skylights before the mall lighting returned. Every object turned its panels to her glorious gift, eager to recharge and prolong its life for another day's march. Sebbee reveled in the tingling sensation as the embedded circuits transformed the sun's rays into electricity. She directed two thirds of the flow into charging, but used the other third to reactivate her speech. The freedom to communicate delighted her enough to add a bit of a spring to her stick-snap wobble.

"You're a morning mug," said Bob.

Several of the objects startled at the first spoken words of the day. Sebbee would have smiled, had she the mouth. Instead she twisted her handle left to right and said, "Always. Morning means coffee, espresso, lattes, and all manner of caffeinated beverages."

"And owners looking for a place to pour them," said Bob.

Would Vanessa be digging through her bag right now, or the cup-board, or yesterday's shopping loot? How long until she mentally retraced her steps and returned for her favorite mug?

The other objects began to chatter, as each one built up a sur-plus of energy to fortify them for the long day's march. A pair of black leather boots, still tied together with string, hobbled along ahead. Newly purchased, their battery stores had been dangerously low all night, so that they had fallen through the *Circle* from a hundred yards away at lights out to right in front of the mugs this morning.

"Soon," the left said to the right. "Master's feet were comforted by our lining yesterday."

"And her hands keen to spray us with protectant at the checkout," said the right.

"Soon," they sighed together. As they passed through a bright ray of sun streaming through the skylight, they picked up their pace, nearly snapping an orange umbrella with green stripes that had been dragging itself in front of the boots.

"Too cold," said the umbrella, her metal tip scraping against the *Circle's* floor with a disturbing screech. "Won't need me until spring. I'm doomed."

Bob moved closer to Sebbee. He must have sensed her discomfort at having the umbrella so close. Desperate objects could weigh down hopes until every item in the march had given themselves over to the gloom.

"Is Vanessa... a regular?"

"Bob!" she snapped her spout open, and twisted violently, spraying yesterday's chamomile all over him. "How dare you accuse my owner of a repeat—"

"I meant *at the mall*. For coffee. In the morning?"

Sebbee slowed her march. "Oh. No."

"Sorry."

"Me too. For jumping to conclusions."

They marched in silence, listening to the conversations around them. The umbrella had fallen far behind them by the time the *switch-direction* order blipped through their short-range antennae. Once the *Circle* had slowed and the objects all managed to turn and move in the opposite direction, the mall opened its doors and the early morning customers began to drift through the food court.

"Miles is," said Bob. "A regular, I mean. Usually hits the drive-thru at about nine-twenty."

Both mugs glanced in the direction of the digital clock above the french-fry stall.

"I guess we only have a few more minutes together, then," said Sebbee. "You better hurry up and tell me the *roamie* story."

"Right." He turned his handle outward, to allow him to get as close as possible to her.

"The fifth time Miles forgot me, I was at the movies. Normally, they don't allow outside drinks, but men like Miles aren't exactly rule followers. Anyway, he left before the credits were done rolling. I had fallen over, hidden behind the popcorn bag, so he would've had trouble seeing me. I tried to chase him, but he'd disabled my movators to hide me from the concession staff. And because of the rules, I was sure to be tossed from the *Lost Circle*, straight into the recyclers. The concession staff didn't want evidence of their broken rules lingering around the lobby."

Sebbee stepped in a puddle of still-melting snow. For one glorious step, the gum didn't stick to the *Circle's* floor. She hopped backwards, catching an extra trip through the puddle and was pleased with the temporary lessening of the gum's adhesive qualities.

"What did you do?" she asked.

"I took a chance, and asked the young human with the broom if he would cut me some slack and put me in the *Circle*."

"And?"

"He did."

"Wow, you were damned lucky."

Bob jiggled his handle, and said, "I prefer to think of myself as persuasive."

Figures, she thought. *At least his arrogance kept him alive.* "What happened next?"

"I marched in the *Circle*, caught between two wool hats — it was winter — and then a teenager showed up out of nowhere and grabbed me."

Sebbee gasped. Some of the other objects close enough to listen mumbled and gossiped among themselves. The *roamie* legend was common, especially in *Lost Circles*, but they all wanted to believe.

"Did you hit him?"

"I tried. Rammed at him, right between the eyes, but then a jolt ripped through me, worse than getting plugged into a recharger when your battery's too depleted. I looked up and saw the teenager's hands grabbing me. I couldn't move, couldn't defend myself, all I could do was watch and wonder whether he intended to rip out my nerve center or torture me for trying to ram him."

Bob's voice was getting stronger, more animated, as he told the tale. Every object close enough to hear was hanging on his every word, slowing up the march and drawing the attention of the cleaning staff.

"The teen stuffed me in a leather satchel, and left the theater."

"Were you scared?"

"Terrified. I could feel the outside cold seeping though the bag, then the thunk as he dropped me into a car trunk."

"Oh, I hate the trunk," said both halves of a pair of gloves behind them. "The smell of exhaust and washer fluid..." The two shuddered together. They reminded Sebbee of a parlor game with a mirror that she'd seen Vanessa play.

"But when the car stopped, the teen brought me inside and I recognized the smell— Miles' house."

Bob picked up speed, obviously excited by the big ending of his story. Sebbee had to push herself to keep up with him.

"I've never seen Miles so *happy* to give away money. He paid the teen with a fistful of bills then thanked him profusely. The instant the teen left, I felt the click-shift and I had all of my faculties back. I jumped into Miles' hands, nearly smacking my beloved master in the jaw in my haste."

Bob paused, opening and closing his spout with enthusiasm. "I'll never forget that feeling. Being *wanted*. My owner had parted with some of his hard-earned money to find me. More, maybe, than it would've cost him to *replace* me! I can't even begin to explain how it felt with mere words."

The boots in the *Circle* clapped. So did the two sets of leather gloves.

"Beautiful," said the umbrella.

"Inspiring," said the cell phone.

Love, thought Sebbee. And for a fleeting moment, she felt it, love, but not for her owner. For this mug, Bob, so close to her in shape and utility, so similar that they might have been manuf siblings. Her fondness for him blossomed, bringing a warm tingling better than sunlight, *almost* better than being reunited with Vanessa.

No. It felt *better*. A pain seared through her from rim to base. She couldn't help the slight. With a good portion of her energy she tried to maintain the feeling of love for Bob. Needed to remember the sensation. Thoughts were dangerous, though, as dangerous as prolonged darkness, malfunctions, or planned obsolescence.

"Nine-thirty," said Bob. "He's a little late, but I knew he'd come."

Before Sebbee could respond, Bob broke from the line and hurried into the hands of his master.

Miles wore black cotton no-iron pants, a black turtleneck, and a double-breasted blazer. Over these, he wore a charcoal-gray wool coat, unbuttoned, accented with a matching pashmina scarf, which flapped with each stride.

Bob leaned over and shouted to the others, "Goodbye. I'm off for a caramel macchiato refill. Be strong, your owners will return soon."

Sebbee wanted to shout a profound response, some turn of phrase that could somehow capture how *good* Bob had made her feel, but the only word she could muster was, "Bye." It sounded more like a gurgle than a word, contorted by the fear building inside her.

Vanessa might not return.

Pain, a jolt of over-charged circuits raging through her inner workings, but a true thought none the less.

Her owner's last words had been so clear, so hurtful. "Look at the shiny new green one. I *love* it."

More pain as Sebbee's circuits tried to erase the remnant, prevent it from ever being thought again.

Not forgotten. Pain. *Abandoned.* Pain. *Replaced.* Agony.

The truth, as the stories all told, hurt more than any object should know.

∞ ◯ ∞

For ninety-three days, Sebbee marched in the *Lost Circle*. She no longer spoke to the others around her. She did not raise her awareness beyond the next hop in front of her. By the last days, she could only drag herself along, sticking awkwardly, bouncing washer-board-fashion because of the infernal gum, which, to her dismay, had never hardened or lost its grip.

When her battery could no longer hold a charge, she simply stopped moving. The others in line nudged her aside and within the hour, a mall custodian picked her up and tossed her into a recycle bin.

Many objects soiled her in the bin: ketchup, cheese, coffee, and worse, soda! So much sticky, runny, fizzy soda that her circuits degraded.

She could no longer see, nor hear much beyond gray noise, when the bin was finally emptied. Her awareness, though, of her own demise, remained keen, and her thoughts were all of contempt and bitterness towards Vanessa.

Bad thoughts of her owner no longer brought pain, as that circuit had thankfully been degraded by a bowl of noodle soup. If there was a place for her spirit to live forever, Sebbee would fantasize about bringing misery upon Vanessa. Yes, the human deserved it.

Blackout. Nothing. Then a jolt. *Pain.*

How could that be? Her circuits had been damaged because her evil owner had— *Pain!*

With it, this time, came light and sound. Sebbee found herself in a small room, with a brown cement floor and cream-painted cinder block walls. Above her stood a teen. A girl. Her nametag read, "Renée."

"There. A nice fresh battery for you," said Renée.

A stick, a cable into Sebbee's side, jumbling her thoughts. She saw Bob, felt him slap her with his handle, she smelled popcorn from the bag hiding him at the movies, then felt the snap of the brush's bristles as— *gone.*

Looking up, the mug saw the teenager's features. A badge spelled the letters of a name but the mug could not remember how letters fit together to make words. Her insides felt wet, but because of what beverage she could not recall. As a matter of fact, she could not remember any drinks at all.

"Am I new?" she asked the teen.

"To me," said the human. "My name is Renée, but my friends call me, 'Fips.' And your name, will be, 'Quips,' mostly because it rhymes and I think it sounds cool."

Quips! A name! How lucky an object she had become. Mugs weren't likely to be named, what with not being necessities.

"This," said Fips, "is Gus. He's my cell, but don't let that scare you. I rescued him a while back from the same bin as you. Took me three tries to completely remove his attitude, but he was so worth it. His owner must've been quite the piece of work, because his diagnostic was clean. Who recycles a perfectly good cell? Not to mention naming him Guido."

While Quips could not recall ever hearing the name before, she felt an odd discomfort at its mention. But when Fips threw the two of them into her knapsack and closed it into her locker for her shift at the mall, Quips and Gus had a rather pleasant conversation.

By the time Fips threw the bag over her shoulder for the commute home, Quips and Gus had begun to exchange touches, he opening his hinge to gently brush against her handle, and she rubbing her neoprene coat along his antenna.

"Oh, and every Friday," said Gus, "We hang at her cousin Jackie's place for an evening of video-gaming. Jackie's dad has the coolest mug. Looks just like you, only red."

"That's nice. What's his name?"

"Bob. The uncle loses him all the time."

Quips flinched, filled with an overwhelming urge to lose her contents through her spout. Her handle trembled.

"Relax," said Gus, "the guy always manages to find him again."

The pain lessened, though her handle wouldn't stop shaking. "I'm glad," she said. "For Bob. The *Lost Circle* is the worst kind of fate."

The last word, *fate*, lingered in the knapsack, matching the resonance of the subway's metal wheels against the tracks. For her first ride home, Quips listened and reveled at her new life, her new friend, and the wondrous feeling of belonging to someone.

STORM CHILD

Thick air oozed into my lungs like mud into a boot. Rain was coming. I fought to breathe through the pains of the baby.

Nellie wiped my brow. "Open your mouth, Wanda," she said. "Make a circle with your lips."

I did, but it hurt so bad. "I need Tom."

"He'll be along."

But he'd be in the fields till sundown. They needed tending. Just as a brown-skinned man needed to prove his worth.

The room grew frightful dark. "Nellie, how bad is it?"

She turned to me, and I saw the truth in her eyes. "The sky's yellow. All wrong. We should get to the cellar."

"I'm birthing my baby in the bed my Tom built." I was breathing heavy, but I had time before the next pain. "I ain't squatting in the dirt like no animal."

Nellie pulled my arm. "We're going."

"I won't."

"You will! Or you'll be sucked into the hands of the Lord."

Hearing His name set me straight. That and the unholy smell of the wind. I wrapped my arm around Nellie's shoulders and leaned on her, limping for the door. A pain ripped through me and I screamed, loud enough for my man to hear in the fields. Loud enough for the Lord to plug his ears.

Lightning struck close, and thunder shook me. I stumbled through the door. The rain poured hard, soaking us both to our skin. My foot slipped and I fell face first into the mud. Nellie pulled me up and we started again for the cellar. I stank of the muck, all covered in filth. I didn't want my baby born in that. We weren't animals no more.

Lightning lit the night, and I saw a man. He was strolling out of the corn as if the sky was shining blue.

The rain washed some of the filth off my face. My dress clung to me. I was glad to be cleaner, but the cold made my hands and feet ache.

I screamed, but I didn't hear myself 'cause a roar started; louder than salvation, as though the Lord and the Devil warred, breaking the sky wide open.

A big sucking twister swirled up to heaven. Corn and bits of trees flew around. The stranger walked up to me, slow and steady. He was dark skinned, but his arms were too long and his face crossed with deep creases. I ain't never seen a man look so angry before. He stood over me, mean and greedy. Another flash of lightning lit up his wet chest and showed his muscles. He worked as hard as any man, harder mayhap.

"Who are ya?" I said through the wind.

"I am storms."

I screamed then, but not at the man. The baby was coming out. I reached down and felt its bitty head coming through.

The man pointed at the outhouse. Before my eyes, Lord have mercy, it smashed to pieces which the sky sucked up.

Nellie fell to her knees, swearing prayers for us both.

The man pointed at my belly.

"Please! I'll be good. Spare my child."

The storm stopped. The wind stilled and the rain turned off as if the pump broke. A flash of lightning lit up the sky like noon on a sunny day, and I saw his black eyes. They had no white parts or brown circles. They looked as if they were filled with ink, ready to be poured down my throat, and into my belly to snatch the baby.

"I want your girl for a bride."

"Who said it's a girl? It ain't born yet." Stupid, it sounded, but it's what I said.

"I'll spare you. Your kin. For the girl."

"No!" I said. Another pain came and the baby stuck out more. Nellie leaned over to help.

He pointed at me. "Then I'll take you all."

The rain started again. The twister too. The man pointed into the corn and said, "Starting with him."

"Not my Tom!" *I'll make more babies, but I'll never find another husband like him, nowhere.* "Take the baby." I pushed and screamed. Tom burst out of the corn.

"Wanda!"

"Tom! He's taking—" But the storm man had disappeared. While my Tom held me, the baby came. Not in our bed, but outside in the rain. Nellie handed our girl to Tom, who took off his shirt and wrapped it over the babe. As she fussed, we named her Miseke.

Thunder rumbled in the distance. I prayed to the good Lord to protect my girl.

∞ O ∞

Years passed and we had five more babies— all boys. Tom never spoke of the storm man again. He tended the corn, as did the boys soon as they were able. Miseke loved the land, but I taught her the kitchen work. Her pies tasted better than mine, so I joined Tom in the fields and left the house to her.

Lord, I loved the smell of them corn stalks after a rain, but Miseke, she loved storms. Every time it rained, she'd rush outside, dancing and singing. Tom watched her, worried. He tried to keep that girl out of the rain but couldn't. Miseke wouldn't miss a drop.

One year a dry spell hit. Long and hard. Every night we all prayed for rain, even little George, but none came. Miseke prayed the hardest. I think mayhap she was connected to the storms, waiting for *him*. I didn't speak of it.

Tom brooded. Silent. He wanted rain for the corn, but when Miseke was asleep I'd hear him whisper his love in her ear; his relief that her storms stayed away.

One dry and sunny morning, Miseke woke up a woman. I scrubbed the stains out, pumping more mud than water out of the well to rinse them. She beamed when I gave her rags of her own. We made a pie together for the boys. That day was one of my best, as if she was my little baby again, learning with her Mama.

I carried the warm pie through the corn. The heat seeped through my hands like hot water from the first bath. I was so proud of my girl. Then she turned and pointed up at the sky. I remember how her hand touched the drooping corn and how the field smelled of failure.

Her face was near to bursting with glee. "Storm clouds, Mama. It's gonna rain."

"The Lord heard our prayers," I said. But part of me wanted to curse His name. A storm was coming, all right. Coming for my baby, turned woman.

"Go home," I said.

She stared at me. "What?"

"I'll take the pie. Get back to the house."

"I want to feel the rain, Mama."

Tom met us. "Get inside, girl. Before them clouds burst."

"I ain't a girl no more," she said.

Thunder rumbled in the distance. "For sure?" he turned to me.

I nodded. Thunder rolled through the air again, closer. "We ought to go back."

"I want to get wet, Papa. Please?"

"Much as you need a rinsing, go back with your Mama. I'll fetch the boys."

Before we could stop her, Miseke hurried past us into the corn. The rain started. I heard her and the boys hollering and running through the corn stalks, shouting, "Ra-in! Ra-in!"

Tom yelled at them to head home, all stern and angry, but them kids didn't listen.

Lightning flashed and with it, the storm man appeared, drawing our girl like a bird to seed. Tom stood between the man and Miseke, and said, "You ain't welcome here."

"I came for my woman."

"No!" Tom grabbed Miseke by the arm and dragged her to the house.

We blocked the door and kept Miseke inside, out of the rain. She acted like a rabbit, jiggling around all cooped up and confused. Tom turned as cold as the river in winter.

The storm man waited on the porch, silent, for two days and nights. All the while he brought rain and wind, drowning the fields. The Lord stayed out of our dark business. We huddled inside, fair to deaf from the thunder.

On the third morning, Miseke said, "Mama, Papa. I love the rain. Let me go with him, before you lose the corn."

I wanted to speak up, tell her, "No," but I had made the deal.

Tom glared at me, knowing, and then, Lord forgive me, I nodded at my girl.

She hugged her brothers, one by one. She kissed her father. He cried. Something I never saw him do before, nor since.

I shook my head, but I couldn't make any words. Miseke opened the door. The storm man reached out his hand for hers. I looked into my baby's eyes one last time. Then she touched him and they turned to mist and rose into the sky.

∞ O ∞

The rains eased. The corn lived, most of it. The years after, our crops thrived. Tom tended the fields, but his spirit left with Miseke. He never forgave me for promising her away. He ate his meals in silence, acting like I wasn't alive.

Every time a storm passed, I whispered the name of my only girl and wondered on her life.

The year before the good Lord took Tom, we had a dry spell, and I begged Miseke for forgiveness. Every night I asked the Lord to show her how much I loved her still. I never wanted to send her away. I had traded her for my Tom and lost them both.

I heard Tom praying to his girl those dry nights. He begged her for rain, but she showed him no mercy. His strength was almost gone, like a shirt washed too many times.

One night I dreamt of Miseke. She was holding her newborn daughter. The babe was beautiful, just like her Mama. Miseke's eyes glowed like Tom's used to, back when his heart was built of rainbows instead of stone. The baby looked strong, as if she could build the world herself. She would achieve more than me. More than my Tom who worked every day of his life.

Miseke whispered and cooed into her baby's ear. I wished I could be there. Hold the girl. Share the joy. But I didn't belong in my daughter's world. "She's beautiful. Take better care of her than I did you."

Miseke nodded, as though she heard me. Then she smiled through tears that ran down her face.

I woke to the sound of rain.

COURTING ICE

To an ice courter like Faya, all frozen water was uniquely magnificent, from the great bergs that floated past the cape to the thin skins on late autumn puddles. She adored her gift, for it allowed her a connection as splendid as the love she had once shared with her long dead mother. All her life the ice had proven pure and true, until the spring when she fell in love.

The morning after the spring equinox she stood in water up to her knees, daggers of cold slicing through her calves, her heavy furs piled on the shore several arm's reaches away. With water all around, she linked with the ice. A large mass had formed in the shallows at the other side of Ranglien Cove. Tendrils of comfort drifted to her from the mass as it felt its way through her. It longed to join with her, to be loved as only ice can be adored by its courter. With arms outstretched, she urged a small piece of it closer, coaxing it to break free from the massive formation. Crevices ruptured, screaming with the effort of separation. Heartbeats later, the separated chunk sailed over to her waiting embrace.

"Nice work."

Releasing her hold on the ice, she turned to see a man, naked from the waist down. He wore a loose cotton shirt, too thin to provide much warmth, and he had tied the bottom edge in a knot to keep it out of the water. Settling into the shallows behind her, he washed himself at the edge of the clear, frigid waters.

With a quick return to her task, she rotated, twisting the waist-high chunk onto shore and turning her back on this stranger. He should have been shivering from the cold, yet he cleansed himself with a strange mixture of calm and grace. The water misted above him like a perilous fog.

She said, "A courtship isn't meant to be shared."

"Ah, but a courtship *is*, by definition, sharing, is it not?"

She stepped ashore, courted the piece onto her sled, and wrapped oiled leather around it. "Witnessed, then."

"Despite your objection, I rather enjoyed the moment. I'm Lebno." He extended a hand towards her.

She paused, staring at his hand, then stepped back into the water to grasp it. His palm was warm. It felt comforting. "Faya," she said.

"Pleased to share your courtship, Faya."

"Aren't you cold?" This man seemed too content in the water, but with her own abilities, she would have been able to sense if he, like her mother, had courted it.

He shrugged. "I needed solace, and I thought this cove deserted."

"In my experience, those who seek isolation are avoiding an unsolved quandary."

"You're an observer, as well," he said. "But incorrect. I'm here for a simple rinse. I've tasks, not quandaries, to evade."

"The sooner you're at the work, the quicker you'll finish."

"And now you're a philosopher." The water misted, almost boiled as a blush tore its way from his face down.

Despite her courtship with the ice, her legs had had enough of the cold and urged her to exit the water. A gust of wind tore through her. She shivered, not once, but twice. The elements demanded much of their courters.

She returned to shore, finished binding her ice to the sled, and donned her heavy furs. She could not help but look at him. The man's muscles bulged through the thin shirt. A sprinkling of gray painted his dark beard. He caught her eye and smiled so brightly that if he'd been a fire, sparks would have popped in every direction.

Fire!

Faya slumped to the ground in surprise, hitting her tailbone hard enough to send spikes of pain along her spine. *It can't be. They are so rare, so few.*

"You're a fire courter," she said.

His face showed no emotion, no acknowledgment.

She hadn't meant to say it aloud, to speak of his gift so openly. Many of his type had been corrupted by their power, using it to conquer, or worse, to kill. Fear had spread from one village to the next, until the great cleansings had taken many of the fire courters' lives. The ones who remained were forced to serve multiple communities, while at the same time they lived under constant scrutiny of the ever-watching councils.

She swallowed, and stood, "I didn't know that Daslak's council had called you to serve."

"I'm only here for a short while, to tutor your apothecary. I'll soon return to Cape Trebnay."

"Oh." Pressing her lips shut, she thought, *I hope that means I will see you again.* Keeping her face as neutral as she could muster, she nodded respectfully, and then pulled the sled's strap over her shoulders, settling into the yoke. "Well… Good travels to you, Lebno. If I were you, I would finish rinsing soon, or you might lose your feet." With closed eyes, she sought an inner peace, forcing rogue thoughts back while she carried her load forward.

∞ O ∞

From the age of fourteen, Faya had lived alone in a cave near Daslak. Her mother's father had sculpted it into a functional living space when he moved from the far south. He used a great chisel and countless iron discards — rings and braces too rusted to hold a fishing line — that had been thrown onto the piers to carve three chambers. For as long as Faya had lived here, the cave was simply *home.* Though the sleeping chamber was small, it soon warmed from the heat of her body and the ever-present fire. She required only one chair most nights; the others stood vigil, eager for the occasional company of Haryon and Misha.

Her grandfather had settled where the demand for ice blossomed with the swelling population. Boats streamed into port full of cod, and his ice blocks kept them fresh until the fish were smoked or salted for the trip westward.

Her mother had inherited a water connection, and like others with her gift, she'd sailed the sea. In return, the water had stolen her from Faya at the age of six. To her ailing grandfather's relief, the ice called to Faya more than its liquid counterpart, and she courted it, one chunk at a time. With caresses and careful coddling, she coaxed it free and hauled it to Haryon's underground ice cavern, where he cut her finds into blocks for sale.

Haryon's cavern seemed smaller when she arrived with her load. Though the chunk paled in comparison to her previous day's haul, it filled the remaining space in the shaping chamber.

"Looks like a keeper," he said.

"Aye. You've not much walking space to carve it. Why are so many pieces still uncut?"

"Misha fell ill last night."

She pulled her furs tighter around her neck. "Not the baby, I hope?"

He laughed. "She'd like it to come soon, but no. Only a cough and a dry one at that. I made her root tea with honey, and rubbed her swollen feet until she fell asleep. By then, the darkness would have made the trip here bitter, so I left it for today. And now I've twice the work and half the desire to get at it."

"But you have *Misha*." The words sounded sour to her ears, so she added, "To warm you after."

"Aye." He grabbed a chisel and raised it to sculpt her latest offering then set it down. "There's a pink tinge to this one."

"That's odd."

"Where'd you court it?"

"Ranglien Cove."

"The fish catchers don't like a hint of blood in the ice. It spoils the freshness."

"Blood?"

"What else turns ice pink?"

"I've courted in Ranglien Cove for three years and I've never had a problem. Maybe the ice picked up the tinge here?"

"You know better."

"I know it was fine when I strapped it to my sled." Her harsh comment echoed off the multitude of blocks.

"Your tongue's a prickle-bush. Must be more troubles than the tinge for you to take that tone with me. Did something happen today?"

Heat flushed her cheeks. Lebno had happened. Witty and half-naked, with a smile she had no excuse to remember. A fire courter; she hated the words. "Nothing."

"A manly-sort-of-nothing, I suspect by your crimson face."

"Haryon!"

"That's my name, sure as Misha knows it. But we aren't speaking of *my* exploits. You're overdue for a vigorous romp in a man's bed."

"I court *ice*."

"If that's all, you'll turn as cold as the bergs right before you die of loneliness." He abandoned his work and sat beside her. "What happened?"

She shrugged. "There was a man."

A smile lit his face and he slapped her leg. "Aye."

"A courter." She exhaled a misty cloud of regret between them. "Of fire, no less."

His smile turned sour. "Now that's bad luck."

"It's *my* luck."

Fire and ice did not mix. When a fire courter took an ice courter, or that of water, as a wife, their offspring paid the price. The elements battled within the child's mind, turning them mad. With the power of two elements, the result was often fatal, not only to the child, but to everyone around them.

Fire.

The word hovered in Faya's mind like sparks thrown into the air.

Haryon picked up the chisel and started his work. "Best be forgetting him. We've ice to sell."

"Aye."

She gathered her leather and sled, and headed home. The smack of iron against ice echoed out of Haryon's cavern long after the sun hit her back. The sound of each distant blow chipped unhappiness from her thoughts. Her old friend's advice was sound. The sooner she forgot Lebno, the quicker she'd find tranquility. Her thoughts had been skipping over themselves, imagining moments she shouldn't.

The sun dipped beneath the horizon before she reached home. Never had her cave seemed so empty.

∞ O ∞

The next few days, she toiled in the west end of Voolhry Bay. Each berg she courted held a pink tint. The wrongness of it, the suddenness and relentlessness of this unknown scourge set her nerves jangling. The elements' discomfort permeated the very air itself.

Knowing that Haryon wouldn't take them, she released the pieces from her bonds and worriedly studied them as they floated out to the open sea.

At the end of the third day, on the long, empty walk home, she passed Lebno. Though the road held many travelers, he walked alone, carrying a heavy pack on his back.

She calmed herself and forced her gaze toward the ground.

"Faya?"

Pretending not to hear, she shifted the harness on her shoulder and raked her empty sled over a patch of rock. The screech echoed against the high walls of the cliffs beyond.

"I say, Faya!"

She turned to face him, her eyes still low, and said, "Aye?"

"Good day to you."

Afraid that a blush would color her cheeks, she continued looking down. After all, little had happened between them. He was simply a man. Yet a thousand thoughts and feelings driven by her intense loneliness had shaped him into so much more in her imagination.

He said, "Isn't it late to be beginning your day's courtship?"

"I've sent them all adrift to find other keepers. Seems they've acquired an unknown scourge."

"A what?"

"A tinge of pink, suggesting a blood infection. Yet I've not found evidence of fouled animals."

Lebno set his load onto her sled. "Do you mind?"

"Not at all."

"I've been gathering roots to make powders for the apothecary." His mouth turned down, as though an earth courter tugged at his face, and he added, "To fortify Daslak's arsenal."

Arsenal? Faya wondered what dangerous tasks Lebno performed each day. "Do your courtships cause you pain?"

"Often." He paused. "Though fire can also warm and comfort."

She crossed her arms, imagining a fire in the corner of her bedchamber, and Lebno sitting on one of the empty chairs.

"The pink tint is likely my doing," he said. "I shouldn't linger."

"Wait." She watched his muscles ripple with the weight of the pack as he bent to retrieve it. Faya sensed the uneasiness of frozen water both far and near. This man frightened the ice. She shivered, but could not allow their fear into her heart.

"Well?" He stood before her, his face blank again. Or had a worried smile flitted across it for a moment?

She opened her mouth to speak, but shut it. After a shrug she looked at her feet and said, "Good luck to you."

"And to you, Faya."

Heat radiated from him as he passed. She raised a hand to her cheek and felt not only him, but the fire of her own desire. Dragging her sled across the largest stretch of exposed rock in sight, she noisily made her way, as rude as she could force herself to be, hoping her actions would erase his attention.

∞ O ∞

All evening, she sulked in her cave. Twice now, she'd stood in his presence and each time she had felt aflutter. The elements screamed their warnings and yet she waved them away like she would a mosquito in summer. Logic had abandoned her, for she barely knew the man. Attraction, as well as an instinctual wariness of him, had taken hold.

She tried to hate him, to push him out of her thoughts and convince herself that he wasn't worth the effort, that his smile and kindnesses were false.

Her heart felt otherwise.

Instead she imagined a thousand ways to hold him, a multitude of schemes that would allow her to press her flesh against his without regret. She had been alone for so long.

His smile flashed through her mind, warming her. She closed her eyes and remembered every crease of his face.

∞ O ∞

In her dreams that night, she swam in pink water. With each stroke, the color sank into her flesh, turning her pink then red, thickening her skin, until she became a red seal.

She barked at the ice to forgive her. It calved and pounded forth an avalanche of huge masses, each as red as a bog swallow's breast.

The surface was lost within the chaos. Desperate for a breath, she pounded her snout into the cracks, searching, needing. When a beam of sunlight pierced the darkness, she surfaced and inhaled sweet air.

Eyes open, she scanned the shoreline. Lebno sat by a fire, embracing it. Though he held a flaming log, his clothes did not catch and his flesh did not burn. He turned to her, angered by the intrusion. The fire erupted, spewing flames high and wide. Faya tried to dive below the surface, but too late. Flames seared her eyes and flesh.

She awoke, screaming, panting, sweating. Her heart worked hard, as though she'd hauled a full sled uphill. The elements' contempt lingered in Daslak, saturating her ice, condemning her desires and soon her people. A seal in a dream usually foretold its dreamer's death, a final warning from the elements to heed them or suffer the consequences.

She must forget Lebno. Purge him. She pulled at her hair and screamed for him to get out of her head.

∞ O ∞

The next evening, the double moons aligned to announce the nearness of spring blossoms. Faya lay in her sleeping chamber under her furs but sleep wouldn't come. Instead she dwelled on the day's events— her empty sled, the bay filled with floating, pink bergs. In the glow from the embers, she stared at the cracks in her ceiling; the one shaped like a jagged tree met up with the one shaped like a dog's tail. She followed them back and forth, having stared at them a thousand times, finding comfort in the certainty of her home; the rock, never changing, never faltering.

At the sound of feet scraping on stone, she sat up and turned towards the entrance of her cave. A dark figure stood beyond the fire's light.

"I came to say goodbye," he said, his voice barely a whisper.

"You're returning to Cape Trebnay?"

Lebno ducked under the overhang between the main chamber and her sleeping chamber, running his hands through the soft fur of her outer clothes as he passed them. When he approached her fire he waved his hand and the flames surged higher, roaring back to life. He threw a log on the blaze and stepped right up to the chair she always used. With careful precision, he set it next to her and sat.

Despite his closeness, she shivered.

"You must know how wrong we are together." He reached down and placed his hand on her chest, feeling her heart pulsing. "Somewhere in here."

She sat with her hands immobile, wondering what to do. Thoughts of the ice, pink, tainted, screamed their warning to shun him. All the while an ache started in her chest, and was joined by physical urgency. She stared at the ground.

He nudged her chin, making her look at him. "But I can't stop thinking about you, Faya."

She leaned close to him. Her arms opened of their own accord, and he knelt down, pressing into her embrace. Tears streaked both their faces. "Lebno, if only...."

She couldn't finish. Fear of the elements' wrath should have made her wish him well on his journey, showing her respect for his great gift. But when he gazed at her, his face filled with grief and longing, she pressed forward, touching her lips to his.

They sat motionless, a fraction of their skin in contact, afraid and unsure. He moved away, and brought his fingers up to her lips, tracing them. She kissed each fingertip, tasting salt from his tears. Then she drew them into her mouth.

He gasped. Her breathing quickened and she pulled him closer.

His lips felt buried beneath the hairs of his beard, as though they feared hers. She pressed on, her tongue probing into him, searching for his gift, hoping that it would allow her safe passage to his soul.

Her hands wandered his cheeks, his neck, his hair. Sweat soaked his shirt. The moisture tickled at her thoughts, a reminder of her dance with its solid form.

His hands found her body and pressed hard against it, sending waves of anticipation through her.

She moaned.

Her hands traveled to him, in return. When his body responded, she smiled and whispered his name. The sound of it, bouncing against the walls of her cave, reminded her of the wrongness of their actions.

She pulled back, hesitated.

He allowed the distance to linger, then said, "What?"

"We *can't*."

He trembled from his own desires, gripping her with surprising strength, as he maintained the slight distance between them.

"We *shouldn't*," he said. His hands felt ablaze, as though he'd been digging through hot coals, and still, he held on. "I'll say goodbye, then."

"Wait." She said.

With a burst of fury she kissed him, hard, pressing her body close to his.

They traded their passions, her heart pounding in rhythm with his. For the first time in her life she felt whole; woman, lover, courter, all poured into a single body. After their lovemaking, they lingered under a single layer of furs, sweaty and drunk with rapturous content.

"Faya," he whispered. "My ice courter."

"My fire," she said.

The truth stung them both, ending their connection like the last bolt of lightning before a storm moves on.

He stood, retrieved his clothes, and dressed in silence.

Pulling a second and third fur over her still-naked body, Faya could not replace the warmth he had provided. Part of her wanted to insist he return to her embrace, but the dream's warning had returned to her mind.

As he stood before the overhang, ready to take the last step from her sleeping chamber into the main one, he paused. Silent.

Many words lingered on Faya's tongue, but she could not find any that matched her jumbled thoughts. She wondered whether he did the same, for he remained as silent and unmoving as the rock surrounding them.

Then he took one step away, sapping all of the fire's strength.

She willed him to look back, gaze at her one last time. Speak words she would sew to her heart.

Instead he took two steps, then three more, shuffling silently; his shoulders slumped as low as the sun in winter.

He did not look back.

∞ O ∞

Pink taints appeared in greater numbers. Haryon, desperate to appease the wharf's needs, begged Faya to bring whatever she courted. The market outcry, of disgust mixed with relief, carried over the rocks and fields.

Two days after Misha gave birth to a son, Haryon accompanied Faya on one of her courtships, to thank the elements for his new joy. They headed for Voolhry Bay. Each attempt to court there had resulted in only pink wastes.

Haryon pointed to the far side of the bay. "There. The ice looks clear."

She linked with a berg, whispered in the language of crystal forms. Words were sculpted for the living; ice demanded immediacy too primal for common speech.

"Come," she said aloud, more for Haryon's benefit than effect. With a creaking moan, the sheet of ice calved, and a man-sized berg drifted toward them.

"Amazing," he said.

A smile settled on her face, more innocent than she'd mustered since her night with Lebno. As the ice drifted closer, the unmistakable tint of pink dusting came into focus.

"Is this why my cavern floor is turning red?" he asked.

"Aye. I've placed Daslak's livelihood in peril."

"Lebno's gone."

"But not forgotten."

He shook his head. "I thought you a smarter woman than this."

"It's easy for you, isn't it? To condemn me for having hope? You, with your beautiful Misha and wondrous new son. It's hard to be alone. And Lebno was as exceptional as a fissure in the center of a berg— the sort that will split ice so profoundly that I complete a week's work with only one courting."

Haryon shook his head. "I'm your friend, Faya. You have to move on. These feelings are poison. The elements are showing you the truth of it. Why won't you see?"

"I can't help it."

"You *must*, or I will call the question to the council myself."

His words lingered in her ears as he left her alone with the ice.

∞ O ∞

Haryon did call the question, leaving the council no choice but to sentence Faya to a cleansing. The ritual, meant to appease the elements and return their favor to Daslak, rarely ended well for the courter.

She sat on the cold ground, shivering, her wrists tied behind her back. She sensed the snow around her and courted a small patch, singing to it, feeling its sadness. It felt its approaching transformation, to trickle below the earth and meet with its kin, or evaporate into the sky above. It sent a greeting, to the two of them.

Two?

Quickly, Faya counted the days since her last cycle. Surely the snow was wrong. Had it been too long?

She stared in disbelief at the snow, now tinged pink. Too many days. She would bear not only a bastard, but an abomination as well. She had forsaken the elements, bearing a child with dark powers, a doer of unspeakable ills.

Tears spilled down her cheeks while she longed to touch her belly.

The sound of boots on snow, pounding towards her, shook her free of the courting. She pulled herself tight and small, hiding her shame from the world.

In the darkness, a figure emerged. They'd sent her friend to carry out the sentence.

"Are you ready?"

She nodded.

Haryon grabbed her, then fussed with the bindings until they loosened. Fearing that others might be watching, she remained silent, not acknowledging his kindness.

Tears rolled down her cheeks. She willed them to freeze, so she might court them for comfort. "What have we done?" she said aloud.

"I tried to warn you, to make you forget him."

"I'm pregnant."

He turned to face her. "What?"

"Moments ago, before you arrived, I courted the snow and it saw me as two, not one. I'm carrying Lebno's child."

Without another word, Haryon dragged her along, step after step, over terrain that tripped her. Blood trickled from both her knees. Fear overwhelmed her, more for the baby she carried than for her fate. She refused to cry out or engage her friend in conversation, afraid that he might break.

Finally, they stopped at Voolhry Bay. She said, "Where are the elders?"

"On that ridge, see?"

She stood part-way above the bay atop a cliff face marred by a toppled tree. The winds had been strong here, and the young tree had lost its battle with the rock.

Haryon had chosen the site for her judgment with deliberate care. The cliff sheared well below the water's surface and the pool would be deep enough to survive the cleansing's plunge. With any luck, the fallen tree might even slow her fall.

The ice on the water below begged her to court.

"I cannot untie you," he said.

"I know."

She longed to place a hand on her belly, to connect to whatever creature grew there.

Come, the ice whispered.

She drew in a deep breath, sensing the moisture in the air inside her lungs, and held it as Haryon pushed her over.

She blocked out the pain of the tree branches bashing her flesh on the way down. But when she broke through the ice, its presence tore through her senses as she splashed into the frigid water beneath.

She embraced the adored all around her, and opened her mouth to allow liquid to fill her lungs.

I'm home.

The water sensed the second life. It should have condemned the fire courter's presence, but the power of an old courter lingered within the salty pool's depths. Faya sank further, giving in to death, wondering what kind of mother she would have been.

Fight for your child. The presence filled her mind. Knowing. Loving.

Fight, my daughter.

Faya closed her eyes, trying to shut out the demand. She wanted to die here, among her kin. Then the realization of the source snapped her free of her despair.

Mother?

I lost you to my lover, the sea. Don't make the same mistake.

I miss you.

Go. Breathe.

She opened her eyes and the salt stung them closed. *I will fight for my child. For love.* She remembered the red seal from her dream and finally understood its purpose. Drawing on her connection with the ice and the power of her mother's presence, she willed the seal to form, and imagined it biting at her bindings, freeing her hands. As in her dream, she drew the tint into her body, a steady stream in ribbons of pink. Mimicking the seal's powerful strokes, she swam for the surface, pounding her feet and hands against the hard sheet until she broke through the ice. Her lungs emptied of water and she drew in aching, welcome, gasps of air.

The taint had served two masters. The first master had brought the taint to life as a warning for Faya to shun Lebno. The second master, overseer of the cleansing, had been satiated the moment that the young ice courter had broken through the surface alive. Now, with both duties fulfilled, the taint surged through her body, filling each crevice with a bounty of forgiveness. The elements present within, accepted the child of two opposing courters, and gifted it with the characteristics necessary for survival. As the powers tickled at the child, its tiny essence reacted with a brief but perceptible response.

The two masters, single in purpose, formed their message in Faya's mind: *You have appeased us, and so your child will thrive.*

With a burst of relief and joy, Faya propelled herself for the shore. There, bleeding, shivering, choking, she collapsed.

∞ ◯ ∞

"Faya, drink this." Haryon's voice. She opened her eyes but saw only his hands.

She lifted her head, sipped at a cup of tea, and fell back, eyes closed. The hot liquid suppressed a flutter in her stomach. She put one hand on her belly.

I will love this child. The cleansing should have brought her death, and yet, she lived.

"How long?" she asked, her voice a whisper.

"Six days."

Though she wanted to look at Haryon, to thank him for his leniency, exhaustion gripped her and she lost consciousness once more.

∞ ◯ ∞

The next time she opened her eyes, she was home, in her cave. A small fire burned close by. Haryon sat in his chair beside the blaze, poking at it with a stick. He turned to Faya, and said, "You're awake."

"Yes."

"How are you feeling?"

Her stomach growled in answer. She shrugged. "Hungry, I suppose. And weary." She reached out her right hand.

He took her hand, and squeezed it, saying, "I'm sorry."

"You did what was required. I understand. And I forgive you."

"The council is satisfied with the cleansing." He drew another blanket over her. "The clear ice won them over."

She tried to speak but only managed a cough. When she brought her left hand up to cover her mouth, she couldn't bend her elbow, for it was bound in a brace.

"It's broken," he said. "Your leg as well."

She coughed again, but managed to say, "Clear ice?"

He nodded. "All the stock, in my cavern and at the wharf. Not to mention the hoards you loosed during your cleansing. Every last taint is gone. Seems the elements have also forgiven you."

"Have you?"

He smiled. "Aye."

"Good." Tears trickled down Faya's cheeks. "Without a father, the baby will need an uncle."

"Uncle, I'll be, regardless. But our council sent word ahead to Cape Trebnay. Your fire courter may yet return."

She smiled, relieved, and then struggled to sit, managing the gesture enough to embrace Haryon. The hug felt better than a hearty soup in a cold, empty stomach. "How's Misha?"

He pulled back. "She and Boeh are staying here, helping to watch over you. They went out for some sunshine."

"Thank you," she said.

She imagined the child in her belly nodding in agreement, as though it too was grateful for all that Haryon had done for them. Deep in her heart, Faya wished the baby could already be here, snuggled and warm in her arms, a gift and miracle from the elements.

Outside, sheets of ice tore free, in a dance of joy for their courter.

Hot Furball
on a
Cold Morning

It wasn't the first radioactive furball to hide in my backyard. But it was the first monkey.

I was nuking a mug of last night's coffee when I spotted the little shit. It had climbed the big maple in the backyard then proceeded to hug itself and shiver. I stared out the kitchen window, wondering whether to call animal control or the lab. The creature was obviously *hot*; its fur had fallen off in clumps leaving nasty open sores. It wouldn't live much longer.

I yanked my coffee from the microwave. It slopped on my hand, scalding me. The red sore blistering there reminded me of my own rad count. I wasn't as far gone as the monkey, but most scrubbers my age had about two good years left.

Cold water from the tap took the sting away. That gave me an idea.

In the basement, I dug a bucket out of a pile of long-forgotten gardening tools. Since the corporation built a lab within two klicks, the yard was too contaminated to grow anything. I opened the tap, but nothing came. *Damned pipes froze again.*

Knocking on the faucet a couple of times, I coaxed enough water out to fill the bucket. *Better plug in the truck.*

I carried the sloshing bucket upstairs and set it by the back door.

One check out the window confirmed that the monkey hadn't budged. I threw on my coat and boots, grabbed the heavy-duty extension cord from the front closet, and braved the driveway. Instantly I regretted not wearing gloves, but I was too tired to go back for them.

The truck was buried under a pile of snow. I swiped some onto the driveway with my sleeve. Once I'd found the door handle,

I opened the driver's side, my fingers sticking to the metal, and popped the hood. The cold had turned the block heater rock-stiff. I jammed at the plug, smashing my sore hand and the damned prongs only slid about halfway in. The unmistakable clicking of the heater told me it was good enough.

I hurried inside, blowing on my hands. After digging out my gloves, I tromped out the back door with the bucket. Snow squeaked under my boots all the way to the maple. I looked up, but the monkey was gone.

"Here, fella. Where'd you go, monkey-brain?"

The neighbor's junk-pile wiggled. I took a few steps closer, squeaking through the snow.

"Come on out, shithead."

The little furball jumped into the open. It stared at me with beady eyes, flicking its tail back and forth.

"I got something for ya."

It reared on its hind legs. I moved one step closer and lifted the bucket. Nice and slow. The monkey jerked, but it didn't run. Just stood there, staring at me and my bucket.

I pulled the handle back and grabbed the bottom. The furball dropped to all fours.

I tossed the contents, pummeling the thing with a gush of cold liquid. Bits of its fur fell in soggy globs, marking the snow with gray and red. It bolted, tearing past the junk-pile and beyond, leaving a dripping trail of paw prints and blood.

I caught a glimpse of it clearing Joe's yard, heading west towards the lab. I wasn't sure if I'd hurried his death or prolonged it. Maybe he'd be lucky and go quick.

Critters always ran back to the lab. I sure as hell wouldn't return to a place that put me through that kind of hell.

Except for the fact that it pays my bills.

The bucket continued to sway back and forth by the handle. Monkeys are close to humans with their DNA and shit. He'd been running, hiding, and I fucked him up some more. What did that make me?

Damn. Should've just put it out of its misery.

I threw the bucket at the neighbor's junk pile and a long metal pipe caught my attention. Leaning over the fence I could reach it. With a quick check for Joe or any other nosy neighbor who might enjoy ratting on my ass for stealing, I grabbed the pipe.

It felt good in my hands. Solid. Cold. Merciful.

In the silence of the morning, the sounds of the wind and passing traffic muffled by the snow, I could hear the clicking of the truck's engine block. "Get moving," it ticked at me. "They'll fire your ass if you're late again, and then what'll you do?"

"Fuck 'em," I said. Not loud enough to bring out the neighbors, but enough for a moment's satisfaction.

I followed the bloody tracks, snow clogging my boots, the pipe's cold seeping through my glove and into my aching fingers. The monkey had scaled a chain link fence and fallen into a neatly stacked cord of wood. A few stove lengths had tumbled onto him. He lay there, stunned, panting, trapped by the weight of a couple of hunks of wood. In his glory the little shit could've easily scampered away, but he was too weak to fight.

"Sorry about before."

Its eyes didn't look beady now. Just fucking tired.

"This ought to help." I raised the pipe over its head. I expected it to run or bite me, but it only lay there. Waiting.

With a home-run style whack I smashed its head in. The tail twitched, not once, but three times before it stopped.

I fell to my knees and puked like a sissy, the pipe still in my hand. I stared at the end where clumps of fur and blood and brains stuck like snot on a finger. I sniffed them, and for a moment I almost licked the mess as if it was some freak-show lollipop.

"What's good for the monkey is good for the scrubber."

I yanked my puke-stained gloves off and raised the pipe over my head. One good whack was all I'd get.

JELLY
AND THE D-MACHINE

My name is Austin and I'm a disaster.

Okay, I'm exaggerating; more of a testosterone challenged, ubercerebral tragedy.

This week, fate's bingo parlor dropped me three bad balls in a row. First, I failed my trigonometry mid-term; a fist to the gut in the self-esteem department, with the added bonus of crushing my mother's hopes for my acceptance at Waterloo.

Second, my attempt to secure a prom date failed. Susan said no. Her quick response was, "I'm busy." Then she bit her lip and stared at me like I might not believe her, and said, "I don't really like you." To be honest, I'm glad she admitted the truth. Because that warm feeling I get when I look at Drake Ferris isn't going away. I could listen to his Irish brogue all day long.

Which brings me to the third and final ball. Jelly caught me staring at Drake in math class. By tomorrow, the entire school will know I'm a fag, which is really annoying when I haven't quite decided if homo rather than hetero tastes better on my eggs. In terms of my overall popularity, though, my catapult from the closet won't matter. Because Jelly will knock my lights out and then, hey, problem solved.

Carl *Jelly* Fraser is a self-righteous bully. You're thinking, with a name like Jelly, he's more a victim of scorn, but that's not the way karma descends on the town of Schmuckville.

He chose the nickname for himself because grape jelly makes a mess of you. If you spill it, it gets on your fingers, your clothes, hell, all over your kitchen, and if your shirt is white, you'll never get out the stain. I would give anything to kick that bastard into the next county. So would every guy like me; even Drake.

My encounter with Jelly will last longer than the traditional tussle. Jelly will have me like a dog has a pig's ear: to chew on and suck on and drag into the yard where he'll forget about me until it's time to pick me up and work me over some more.

So I'm lying in bed, listening to the ceiling fan click while it spins, hot as a frying pan for a June night, and I'm doing what I do best: worrying. If Jelly brings a knife, what will I do? Should I pretend to fall unconscious or fight back? And even if I deny being gay, will he believe me? Will I believe myself?

I've watched the moon's light slowly paint my room, from the door a couple hours ago, to my computer, and now it's moved out the window to the tree house.

There's an idea. If I disappear, how long will Mom take to look in the tree house?

Days? Weeks?

I wonder how long I'll have to live off the grid, waiting for the world to change enough so I can safely re-emerge. I'm a pretty patient guy.

Time, man, that's it. I need more of it, tons of it, a googolplex of its beautiful bounty. Better yet, Dad's ultimate nerd weapon: the time machine. I can leap into the future to a time when no one will care about my personal preferences. To a place where Jelly is a bitter night manager and his minions have spawned newer and more sophisticated fish to fry.

Dad used to ramble about how time machines are only products of quantum mechanics and the fourth dimension. His deepest and clearest desire had been to build one, become uber-famous, and live a life of fame and fortune. Or better yet, be in a *Science* textbook. And he had been so damned close when...

I decide it's time for me to step up and finish what he started.

I figure that if I climb high enough and plummet through a small enough hole, I can separate the quantum likelihood of my existence into two versions of myself. Just like the light experiments with the tiny hole in the piece of paper and the big, bright bulb. At the critical moment, I will rupture a membrane along the edge of the fourth dimension and drop out on the other side. I could hang in other-land, make a few friends, maybe lay low, especially if no one recognizes me. Or better, if I *also* exist there, I can watch my other self, maybe, if I don't freak myself out too much, have a long chat over coffee and a couple of donuts and figure out who we really are. It's cheaper than therapy; that's a given.

When I and other-me are ready, I'll reverse my steps, take another plunge, and slip back into my life. Mom'll cry, and I'll be in the news, "Lost Boy Found after Unexplained Absence." Possibly rake in a little side cash, enough for a car, spinning a few white lies about alien abduction; hot probes and such, get myself a tidy story-bonus for the tabloid spread.

Definitely.

∞ O ∞

After assuring myself of Mom's continued slumber, I find Dad's stash, including the rubber-chicken-toss target-board from the school Fun Fair, marked with "This must be it!!" in Dad's red-Sharpie-handwriting on the back. Finally, my Mom's endless volunteering comes in handy. The "double prize" hole has been triple-circled in red. Chuckling to myself, I haul it upstairs and outside, then go out to the garage to snag our supply of bungee cords. I want to be sure, so I use several packs, so many that any spider will be envious of my design. From a spy satellite circling overhead, my machine can pass as a trampoline— no late calls to homeland security required, move along, pal.

Remembering Dad's insistence that light plays a crucial role; I hook up our two painting lights and point them so they converge right below the hole.

A final check through Dad's journal to be sure I've set up the equipment correctly, then I sneak into the study and grab my father's laptop. Dust has piled pretty thick on top. Mom will kill me if she walks in, so I'm extra, super quiet. Dad was working on fourth dimensional formulae the night before the dump truck smashed him out of our lives. He had told me so. Late that Thursday after too many beers.

"Son," he slurred, "you're gonna be so proud of me. Oh, people will laugh, especially your mother. Don't tell her I said so, because she's mad enough about the money I'm *wasting*. But I'm certain these calculations are right this time. She's finally going to be proud of me. God, I love her."

And she had loved him right back, as much as I did, maybe more. After the squish, she set up a corner of the study as his shrine. Minus the candles and incense of course; she isn't a *zealot*.

Laptop under my arm, I sneak out and awkwardly climb the ladder to the tree house. I boot the computer, set dad's iterative calculations to auto, and stand in the open doorway.

The target looks damned small from up here. For at least a minute, I wonder if the Jelly-beating can theoretically be a more pleasant option than the unqualified pain if I miss my mark. But self-inflicted-stupidity always wins the teen debate against bully-plus-humiliation, so I lean forward.

As I find the air, I have at least one second to think, *This one's for you, Dad.* Then I find the hole.

Skin scrapes free of my arms as they rub against the rough edges of the wood. The brightness of the painting lights blinds me, numbing the pain like somehow not seeing the wounds makes them hurt less. Sound adds its personal spin, splinters and rushing air, a scream that's more like a whimper when my lungs are compressed.

Then the thud. It's a crackless thud, giving me hope that I haven't snapped a bone. Down here, in the shadow of the tree, the soft light nudges my courage in the open-your-eyes direction.

So I do.

There's Dad's car. And not Mom's.

Whoa. Not squished.

I brush off the splinters and remember my torn skin too late. The scream is enough to wake the dead.

"Austin? What the hell are you doing out there? It's five am, for crying out loud."

∞ ○ ∞

This is the part where I tell you he's alive, and I'm so glad because I've missed him, and dump trucks are stupid, and karma may finally have been *fair* for a change.

But then he's downstairs and out the door and hovering over me, probably wondering how I so massively hurt myself by falling from the tree house through a hole. Except there is no tree house, and there is no hole. I throw my arms around him and, for the first time in years, I hug him like I'm five and he's brought home the biggest bag of candy to ever grace this wonderful planet.

I can feel his awkwardness underneath, like he can't fathom what's come over me. But another, more important thought finds its way to my frontal lobe; Mom should be here, too, just as angry and confused.

"Where's Mom?"

He drops his arms to his sides. "Very funny."

I refuse to release him. "Seriously."

His voice, muffled by my constriction of his chest, comes out in gasps, "Did Jelly put you up to this? Because I thought you were staying over at his place tonight?"

"*Jelly's* place?" I release my grip and give him the biggest dose of sarcasm-plus-confusion my pained body can muster. "*Overnight?*"

That's when he starts to pick at my hair, checking for a brain injury. "The video game slam-down, not ringing a bell? Or did you damage your hearing, too?"

Without hesitation, I flip from I'm-so-glad-you're-alive to contemptible teenager. "It's a throw-down, not a slam-down, Dad. Don't you *ever* watch TV?"

"I'm waiting for an answer."

I launch into a blur of explanation-laced-with-B.S., enough to distract and confuse while I find my bearings. The contraption worked, although I'm pretty sure that the year and my age are bang-on identical, so I guess I didn't build a *time* machine, more a *dimension*-machine. Dimension-machine sounds lame, though. D-Machine: there's an epic name that will look good on any supermarket shelf. I coined the term without hesitation. "I'm exhausted, and to be honest, my arms really hurt," I say.

He takes a long, intense look at me, then at his own hands, which are stained with my blood. "Yeah, maybe we should get you cleaned up. Think it's hospital-worthy?"

I shake my head. "Peroxide."

"That'll sting like you-know-what."

No worse than having my dad come back from the dead and my mom be controvertibly absent. "Better pain, than an infection," I say.

"Agreed."

He leads me into the house and up to the bathroom where there isn't one stick of feminine stuff to be seen. No makeup, no night cream, no hair straightener; not even the box of *products* she leaves in plain sight so embarrassingly that I cover them with a towel whenever a friend comes over.

I had found my way back to my father and had forgotten to show Mom the way.

"I miss her," I say.

He chooses that moment to dab on the peroxide.

∞ ◯ ∞

Austin the disaster strikes again.

Allow me to clarify.

If you're considering fabricating a D-Machine to visit another version of your reality, make sure to pick a destination where you will at least be able to find the parts you'll need to build the return-portal. Because when your mom dies, your dad is likely to be so distraught that the last item on his massive to-do list will be going out for the PTA. And without his finger in that volunteer pie, I doubt you'll have a rubber-chicken-toss target-board still stored in your basement. And he may never get around to hiring that dude to build you a tree house so you won't feel like you'll miss out on a part of your childhood from only having one parent available.

Oh, and remember to slip out the back door and find a great hiding spot as soon as you can, because the other version of you is due home any minute, and you don't want to get that egg on your face in the first twenty-four hours.

But I am in too much of a stupor, a combination of the peroxide pain and the loss of my rubber-chicken-toss target-board, to remember to hide. Sure enough, along I come, the other-me, home from a night of frolicking and fanciful play at Casa Jelly. Adding another nail to the Austin-coffin, Drake and Jelly arrive in tow.

I hear their footsteps on the stairs only moments before the inevitable big entrance, so I dive under the bed.

Oh, here's another tip: Used socks smell incredibly bad. *Truly.* Don't kick them under the bed; it's not worth the agony.

One at a time, each boy crashes on the bed. I can tell which dent belongs to the Jelly-man, because face it, with a name like that, you must've guessed he carries a few extra pounds. The three of them are still high from the all-night video frenzy.

The conversation is the usual, "So then my guy kicked your guy," game chatter, but when Dad wakes up and makes a point of stumbling downstairs, the topic sways in another direction. Drake gets all quiet, and he's mumbling something to Jelly that sounds a little too friendly, and then other-me says, "Come on, you two. Bad enough I have to cover for you at school. If my dad walks in—"

"He won't," says Jelly. "I can hear the cereal crunching from here."

Then the room goes quiet and I hear a soft sucking sound. Like a kiss.

"Stop," other-me says.

But I don't sound disgusted. I mean, other-me, he doesn't sound like he's revolted by their kiss. No, he sounds *hurt*. Turns out, no matter which dimension I find myself, or a *version* of myself, in, I have my eye on Drake. Both eyes in fact.

Add to that a dash of the Jelly roadblock.

I want to jump out and confront them. All of them. Right then and there. Granted, the stinky sock factor is a contributing persuader in the equation. The possibility of permanently messing up my multi-dimensional karma stops me. So I plug my nostrils and breathe out of my mouth as quietly as possible.

Jelly keeps on making his moves on Drake, until sanity returns to the worlds-at-large and the other-me says, "I need fuel, or I'm gonna crash."

"Eggs," says Drake.

"I'm in," other-me says.

"Perfect," says Jelly.

Then they're gone, and I'm alone once more in my other-room. I decide to get out of D-Dodge, find my way back, and take my chances with evil-Jelly. I will need a new D-Machine, and an immeasurable number of minutes to properly say goodbye to my Dad. And not in that order.

∞ O ∞

Other-me doesn't have any D-machine-worthy parts in his room, so I sneak down to the basement. Tough gig, because the basement stairs are in a big sight-line from the kitchen, where the four of them are laughing and planning their Saturday. A couple of times I'm sure Dad has spotted me in his peripheral vision, but he doesn't react, so I assume I'm clear.

The basement has been hit by a nuclear explosion, or some other weapon of mass destruction. I'm leaning into an oversized plastic bin chock full of circuit-board-and-wire-spaghetti when someone's hand is on my back.

I fall on my ass, shrieking like a girl.

"They're gone," he says.

That silences me. I open my mouth to tell him the truth, okay, to exaggerate a *little*, but then I close it again because he looks delighted; as though he may have finally invented something good.

"I shouldn't have given up," he says. "Tell me how I did it?"

"Did what?"

"Finished the dimensional disruption device. And why didn't I take the first trip?"

"How did—"

"Your hair can't grow four inches in an evening," he says.

I touch my hand to my head. Yeah, I admit it, I'm a guy *and* I take good care of my hair: sue me. "Busted," I say.

"Tell me. *Every* detail."

I start with his laptop and the dimensional formulae, but when I get to the rubber-chicken-toss target-board, his face gets scrunchy and he looks like he's going to cry.

"Back in your world, your mother, she's… *alive?*"

"Yeah," I say.

He crosses his arms on his chest and bites his lip. I can tell he wants to cry, but he's trying not to. "No dump truck?" he whispers.

My turn to hold back the tears. Only I'm not as good at it as he is. "Oh, there was still a dump truck."

He leans down and puts his hands on my shoulders. Both of us have tears leaking out now, but we're still holding a fraction of our dignity together. "Is she paralyzed? Or mentally incapable? That would—"

"She's fine," I say. Then I hit him in the chest like somehow it's his fault, and I add, "You're dead. Not her. *You!*" I hit him again, and suddenly I'm pummeling his chest, except he's blocking me, and the punches are more like shoves, and then I'm crying so hard that he's holding my hands, and I'm letting him.

"The worst of it," I say, "is that I can't stay here. I can't. Not with Jelly, and Drake, and—" My throat closes, and I'm choking, but I need to say it. "It's not fair!"

He's holding me, and running his hand down my back like he used to when I was little. "Shush," he says, "I understand."

"Why can't I have you both? At the *same time!*"

He doesn't speak for a while.

I begin to feel too old for this, too mature to be crying in my father's arms. Too much of a man to be afraid, but I don't have the will to push away.

"You know, I didn't believe in God," he says.

I look up and nod at him.

"Well, when she died, I prayed. I spoke to God over and over, demanding to know *why*. But he didn't answer me. Maybe because he only answers if you truly believe. Maybe because he thinks I can't take the answer. Maybe because he has a twisted sense of humor. In any case, she's gone." He gestures around the basement, and says, "From here."

Then he points to his heart and says, "Not from here. She will always live here." Then he points to my heart, and adds, "And here."

"Come back with me," I say. "We'll be together again. She misses you so much. She doesn't talk about it, but she's always so busy with her committees, and her events, and I know it's because she doesn't want to think about how empty our lives are without you."

He holds me again. And I can feel him shaking, like he's crying, but the quiet kind of cry, where you want to hold some of it back because if you let it go, you'll finally feel better and you can't feel that good; you don't *deserve* to be that happy.

"Please come back with me," I say.

"I can't leave you behind."

I open my mouth to object, and he says, "The other you. He misses your mother so much, he doesn't have the strength to stand up to Jelly. I need to be here for him. For *you*. Because one day, he'll realize that Drake isn't worth it. And he's going to need all the help I can give him to admit it to himself."

"Back in *my* life," I say, "I like Drake." I pause, take a deep breath, and come clean. "Back there, I'm gay."

"Here, too," he says. "Have been since sixth grade."

I shudder. "I came out to you and Mom in sixth grade?"

He laughs. "You— *he* still hasn't admitted it, *out loud*. He will when he's ready."

"But you know?" I say.

He nods. "Your mother figured it out ages ago. I took longer to convince, but she kept pointing out the signs."

"When did she die?" I say.

"Three years ago."

"And four months, and twelve days?" I ask.

He nods, and looks at his watch. "Seven hours, and... *nine* minutes."

I look down at my watch. Yep, the karma clocks are perfectly synchronized.

We stare at each other, knowing. Then his hand is on my shoulder again. "I'm glad you told me. About being gay. How does it feel?"

"Lighter," I say.

"Yep."

"If you're going to help me get back, we need a big board with a hole in it," I say.

"I have just the item."

∞ O ∞

Recreating the D-machine with my dad is fun. We don't speak of our impending separation, or of Mom. We're simply two guys exploring their geek side.

I'm holding a piece of plywood and Dad's using a jigsaw, which I can't believe he can do without severing a finger, and he says, "Jelly's an idiot."

"Yep. Back where I come from, though, he's worse. A complete bully. He's the reason I left."

"How so?"

I explain about the prom and Drake, and Jelly likely bashing me into next week after he tells the world I'm gay.

"Most of your friends probably know already."

"I don't have any friends."

"What about Drake?"

I rethink the Drake situation. Sure, I find him handsome, but we have also been lab partners, and we've eaten lunch together on a fairly regular basis. Come to think of it, whenever he misses class he always asks me for my notes.

"You're right."

"Drake is gay, here. And his relationship with Jelly is more one-sided than you, I mean the other you wants to admit. Do you want my advice?"

"Sure."

"Tell Drake how you feel. And if Jelly says a word about your sexual orientation, tell everyone it's because he's gay and can recognize it in you. In fact, he's secretly in love with you."

"Yeah," I laugh. "Like *anyone* will believe that."

"You'd be surprised. The truth has a way of outing itself."

He finishes with the saw, and I let go of the plywood. I'm staring at him, processing what he's said, and I wonder if maybe he's right. Maybe all that teasing was actually *flirting*.

"You're right," I say.

"It's astonishing, I know. But it happens with surprising regularity here."

We both laugh then it multiplies until we're both cracking up so hard that we're crying. I can't believe how good it feels to let loose with him. My *dad*. I had resigned myself to never experiencing a moment like this ever again.

"We should be recording this," I say.

"I hear you."

He hugs me and I don't want it to ever end.

∞ ◯ ∞

Dad rigs up a quick pulley system to recreate the D-machine that night. Without the tree house, I have to climb the tree. With a ladder, of course, because let's face it, I'm a geek and we're not known for our jock-ular prowess. We use bungees and lights, like before.

The hardest part for Dad has been recreating the dimensional formulae. In my reality, he left them on his computer. Here, in a fit of frustration, he deleted them all. But he'd kept the journal, which was buried pretty deep in the basement. We find it and re-enter them. I trust his judgment that they are identical to the ones I've set in motion in my old life.

Other-me has spent the day at the mall. When he arrives home, Dad distracts him with a pizza and then heads back outside. I stay out of sight, hiding high in the foliage of the tree. Luckily, other-me doesn't show interest in Dad's latest experiment. Apparently, these still occur with enough frequency to qualify as lame.

When all of the components are in place, Dad looks up, and says, "Any time you're ready."

"I'll climb down and say goodbye," I say.

He shakes his head. "It's better this way." He pauses. "Easier."

"But." I bite my lip because he's right. "Easier," I agree.

"Tell her I will love her forever," he says.

"So will she," I say. "Love you, I mean. Because I know she does. I do, too."

He smiles. "Now jump."

"Right."

I lean forward, staring down at the hole, and it's just as tiny and pain-inducingly-scary as it was before. I've had the foresight to borrow a long sleeved shirt so as not to open up the scabs all along my arms.

My father is watching me with enough love to make me cry, and I don't want to cry again. So I aim for the hole, close my eyes, and push off from the tree.

While I'm falling, I have enough time to say, "Dad, I love," but the, "you," doesn't make it out because I'm hitting the hole and scraping open my wounds, and my head feels as though it may split open and release watermelon guts over a hundred meter radius, and then I'm on the ground.

It's brighter than before, and I look up to see the rubber-chicken-toss target-board above me, and the painting lights. I stand slowly, and painfully. The tree house is where it should be. Mom's car is in the driveway. Not Dad's.

Above me, a window opens. "Austin?"

Mom is wearing the ratty sweatshirt she uses as her pajama top. It used to be Dad's. Here, he will never wear it again. But she will.

"I'm fine, Mom."

"What are you doing with... oh my God, look at your arms!"

She disappears from the window. I can almost hear her running down the stairs to come to the aid of her wounded son. When she bursts into the yard, she hugs me like I'm a baby.

And I let her.

∞ O ∞

Jelly is waiting on the front steps of the school to beat the crap out of me. Everyone who passes hears Jelly's proclamations of my sexual preference. Some glare at me, others laugh. I meet all of it with a smile.

I can hear my Dad telling me how he knew all along, and how most people would've figured it out already. Not only was he right, but somehow his acceptance makes me proud of who and what I am, acting like a shield against what I feared would be the Jelly-wrath, but turns out to be more like Jelly-failure.

When I get close enough that he can deck me, I stand still, toe to toe, and wait for it. He hesitates, as though he can't decide what part of me to hit first.

I take a deep breath, and say the words I've been refining all night. "Took you long enough to notice, Jelly. But too late, because I only have eyes for Drake. Sorry to break your heart."

"I'm not gay," he sputters, "you fag."

"That's what you tell yourself."

I keep walking.

This is the part where I figure he will jump me from behind. I brace myself for the impact.

Laughter.

Not from Jelly, either. But from everyone who's had the good fortune to overhear our confrontation. Like they've all been waiting for confirmation, and it makes total sense. Better, Drake is at my side and he's taking my hand.

You'd be surprised, my father had said. *The truth has a way of outing itself.*

The truth, like me, is out. And it tastes as sweet as grape jelly.

Everyone Needs a Couch

(The Couch Teleportation Universe)

"Crap. Double crap."

I stood there, mouth hanging open, door ajar, jacket in hand, staring at what was left of my couch. The left half looked normal — stained, ratty — but normal. The other side was gone. I thought back to an image I'd seen of the sinking of the Titanic; after the hull had cracked in two. Its insides exposed for the world to see along a jagged tear. My couch, like the Titanic, foundered.

I never should have given Lorna a key.

I dropped my jacket on the floor and walked over to what remained of my couch. I touched the only intact cushion, testing it out for strength. After a pause, I gingerly sat down. It held. Thank you God, I still had a place to sit down.

I glanced over at the vid. The message envelope flashed crimson in the corner. Probably a "kiss-my-ass" letter from Lorna. I debated whether to open it, but my desire to humiliate myself further won out. I trudged over to the counter and pressed the icon.

Dear Mr. Lazier:

Thanks for your recent submission to Impact Quarterly. *It does not suit our current needs.*

"Just what I need, more rejection."

The envelope icon was still flashing, so I pressed it again. *Five credits have been withdrawn by* Impact Quarterly *for message delivery charges. Your account is now below zero. Unless a deposit is made in two days, your status will change to off-world.*

"You forgot to mention that my rent's due tomorrow, dickheads." I looked around for items to pawn. The couch was out. I had the vid, but public access machines always cost more in the long run. My clothes weren't worth one damned credit. From the looks of the apartment, Lorna had taken everything of value that wasn't nailed down. I opened the cooler for a drink, but I knew what to expect. All she'd left were a few half-eaten food packs long past the edible stage and a can of orthan flippers.

I slammed the unit shut and climbed on the counter to reach the back of the vid. It was screwed to the wall, and I didn't have a screwdriver. Probably why Lorna hadn't taken it. I leaned over the unit and threw my weight against the front. The screws popped out and I fell forward off the counter, with the vid about to break my fall. My reflexes were quick — thank you Lorna for taking all my booze — and I leaned back, holding on for dear life. I spun and the vid landed on me, *saved*. My back was another matter. Naike could sell me something to make the pain go away.

∞ O ∞

Gidder's was still open, and the Drip behind the counter gave me two-fifty for the vid. I told him to put it in my account right away. When he tried to lay the "waiting time" rule on me, I told him how far I could stuff my fist up his ten orifices. He backed down after turning red and wiggling like a worm. All Drips are pansies. Thank God Earth had stronger gravity than Forbi, giving even losers like me the ability to pull off the tough-guy routine.

I hurried across the street to my favorite bar, *Luna's Wake*. Naike, an Earthling, was working as usual. I headed straight to the rear.

"Thought I'd see you in here tonight, Tanker," he said to me as I slid onto my stool.

"Oh yeah, Naike, why's that?"

"Cause that stiff you've been boinking was here earlier—cursing your name."

"She left me a surprise, too."

"Oh yeah? Stingers in the can?"

I shook my head. "*Worse*. She pulled a Titanic on my couch."

"A what?"

"She cut it in half. With an axe from the looks of it. Took the right side with her." I grabbed the drink he'd put in front of me and downed it in one swig. The blast of a thousand cannons exploded in my throat on their way to destroy my gut, but it blurred the edges.

"That's tough."

"Yeah, no kidding." Raising my glass, I said, "Give me another, would ya, Naike?"

"That's another six credits Tank. You good for it?"

"I know you checked. I've got about 240 or so in there, don't I?"

"Tomorrow's the first, and I know your rent's 235. We have the same scum-lord, remember?"

"Right." I tilted back my empty glass and sucked the residue from the last drink. "Boy do I need to sell another story."

"Why don't you get a real job, Tank? I could use a guy for the morning shift. Earthlings draw in business."

"I'm a writer. I swore I'd go home before I gave up."

"If you're statused to *off-world* for bad credit, you'll be packing your bags anyway."

"You always know how to cheer up a guy, Naike. That's what I like about you."

He smiled. "Take the job. You can write at night."

"If I take it, will you give me another drink?"

"When you've earned it."

"What? No freebies for the staff?"

"I'll think about it."

I waited, expecting smoke to puff out his ears from all that *thinking*. Desperate for a drink, I said, "Half-pricers maybe?"

"Done."

We shook on it. A couple of Drips came in and while Naike took their orders I headed for the door. He was my boss now, not my friend. No point making small talk.

As I left the bar, someone nudged me from behind. I turned to see a creature I didn't recognize.

"Excuse me?" It spoke with accented English, through a translator that was probably hiding under its oversized clothes. The alien looked like a cross between an octopus and a camel. At least it had the decency to cover itself, unlike Drips who let their ten slimy tentacles flail all over the place. But who was I to judge alien etiquette?

"What?" I said. Diplomacy wasn't my forte.

"I could hear you in there. You are a writer." It said it flat out, like a statement not a question.

"I'm a writer, yeah. Why?"

"We need what you call a *story* about teleportation."

"Yeah? D'ya need it for credits?"

"Yes. We will pay one thousand credits for a story about teleportation. But it has to be scientifically possible."

"Well, if it was *possible*, wouldn't we have teleportation already?"

"Perhaps it could be believable?"

"For a thousand credits, Bud, I can be *very* believable. What's the market?"

"The market?"

"You know, the name of the publisher, the magazine? What's the length?" Despite how much booze I had consumed, my fear of starving made the offer sound like my big chance.

"We are new to Forbi. Market is not understood, but it would be sent to our homeworld, Cravdop. We are in need of stories about teleportation. The length does not matter, as long as it is believable."

"Okay. When's the deadline? Where can I send it?"

"Tomorrow. We will meet you here tomorrow at the same time."

"Tomorrow?" I paused. My first reaction was to tell it to get lost. Besides, it kept saying "we" and as far as I could tell, it was an "it" not a "we". Could I write a story by then, especially if I had to be working for Naike all day? A thousand credits would buy me plenty of booze, plus a new vid, hell, a new couch. Before the sane part of me could stop me from making a stupid decision, I said, "Deal. I'll meet you here tomorrow with the story."

"Good. Thank you."

It hobbled away and turned the corner with amazing speed. Apparently Cravvers were fast. I was home before I realized I didn't even have its name. *Crap.*

The apartment looked emptier than it had before. I sat down on my half-couch, with my scribbler, and started to write. The first character to be teleported to hell would be named Lorna. That was a given. But how would it work? It had to be believable. No smoke-and-mirror bogosities. I leaned back hard and the couch collapsed. *Double crap.* I guess it held me up as long as it could. Then it hit me— not unlike how the floor just had. The couch was my ticket. It was my teleporter to fame and fortune.

∞ O ∞

I stumbled into *Luna's Wake* bright and early for my shift. I'd had no trouble waking up, since I hadn't slept. The story was finished; the fastest I'd ever churned one out. In it, a teleportation couch malfunctioned, accidently crossing itself with a power-hungry

Strunjox. The resultant sentient teleporter sucked its victims into another world, a hell-world, where all its passengers were tortured and mutilated, then processed into new couches that took over the planet Forbi. It was my best work, or so I thought, in my half-conscious euphoria.

Naike put me to work and promised me four morning shifts a week, twenty credits per. That would more than pay for rent. Plus, he would supply up to three half-price drinks a day, but only at the *end* of the shift. Fine with me. I wouldn't be in a hurry to go home. After Naike got me set up, he left to go sleep, on the promise to cover me with Drip ooze if I screwed up. I knew he would too, so I toed the line. He kept a jar of the stuff under the counter for emergencies. Drips constantly secrete a variety of liquids from their ten orifices. Most are benign, but if you mixed them together and fermented them awhile, they turned into a noxious acid.

Time dragged and by the end of my shift I could hardly wait until Naike came back. And I almost forgot about my rendez-vous with the Cravver. But it showed up, on time, looking even creepier than the day before.

"Is it believable?" it asked.

"Yes. I enjoyed imagining one particular teleportation over and over last night."

"Good. You will get your credits after our colleagues analyze the details."

"And when will that be?"

"Tomorrow. We will come here at the same time."

"It's always tomorrow for you Cravvers, huh?"

"We what?"

"Never mind. What's your name, anyway?"

"Slevron."

"Is that a male or female name?"

"Slevron."

"Right. Do you have a signa, or a message address?"

"No. We are new to Forbi."

"So, you'll meet me here tomorrow then, with the credits?"

"If it analyzes well."

"Right, if it analyzes well." I wanted to shake the thing's hand, but God help me if I could even imagine which part of it was a hand. I nodded, and it attempted a similar maneuver with something that could've been a head. Then it left.

Naike kicked me out after my half-price drinks. I staggered home, exhausted. The sight of my broken couch barely fazed me as I collapsed on it.

∞ O ∞

The next morning, in a flash of brilliance, I decided to submit my teleportation story to *Impact*. Slevron hadn't said I couldn't sell the story elsewhere. I figured it was worth any shot to get credits for the piece. I used a public access machine to submit it before my shift at *Luna's Wake*.

My second day was easier. Sleep can change a man. Slevron showed up, on time, and I escorted it to the best table in the joint.

"Your story brought success Mr. Tank Lazier. We will pay you a thousand credits."

"Yes!" I shouted and the patrons all stared at me in disdain. I had never hauled in that many credits for a story. I was big time now, baby. Tanker on a roll. "When do I get the transfer?"

"Tomorrow. We will submit it to the appropriate financial account."

"It's always tomorrow with you, isn't it?"

"What?"

"Never mind." I passed it my banking details and it got up to leave, then changed its mind.

"Our analyzers would like to thank you, with the gift of a couch. You Earthlings hold them in high esteem. Where is your home?"

"That's not necessary."

"We insist."

"Whatever." I gave it my address and it left. I just wanted the credits, but if they were going to throw in a free couch, who was I to argue? A part of me would hate to see the old one gone though— especially since it had been my inspiration.

∞ O ∞

The next day, the credits showed up in my account, as promised. I bought my vid back from Gidder's. I still didn't have a screwdriver to anchor it, so I propped it up in its old location on the counter with pieces of the old couch.

I had messages waiting. One from Mom, begging me to come back to Earth, and one from *Impact*, acknowledging receipt of my couch story. *Crap*. I forgot about that little side angle. They couldn't publish it now that Slevron had paid me. I sent them a reply, asking them to throw it out, since it sucked and I didn't mean to waste their time.

I made the mistake of opening the last message. It was a vid of Lorna, looking out a transport cruiser's porthole and smiling as she waved at an object. I cranked the zoom to see what made her so smug, and there was her side of the couch, floating in space. Figures. At least I knew where the other half was.

I was late to work, but Naike wasn't around, so I hoped he wouldn't find out. The place was dead in the mornings anyway. I turned on the vid over the counter and watched the news. The lead story was about a man named Robert Black who'd vanished from his complex. His wife had left the room for a minute, then poof, he disappeared. He was some big honcho from Transcore. They were the biggest Earth-based company on Forbi, controlling shipping and immigration. He was "resting on his new couch" when she left him. What was it with couches lately?

When Naike arrived, he said I was good for business, but if I was ever late again, he'd ooze me in a heartbeat. Figures, he'd find out. Probably had a stoolie coming for the first drink every day.

When my shift was over, I belted back two half-pricers then trudged home. To my surprise, Slevron was waiting outside my door.

"We have come to measure your quarters for your new couch, Mr. Tank Lazier."

"Oh, yeah. I forgot."

"It was brilliant of you to use a common couch for the teleportation device. Everyone needs a couch, especially Earthlings, yes?"

"Sure. Come in."

I opened the door and it stopped before entering. "Is there a problem?" I asked.

"What is wrong with your couch?"

"Lorna is wrong with my couch."

"Did she damage it when you tested your story?"

"What?"

"You will need a new couch very soon. Our colleagues will bring it by—"

"Let me guess. Tomorrow?"

"Yes, tomorrow."

It measured the space and slumped out the door. I still couldn't figure out how those Cravvers moved.

I'd brought some food packs home for dinner. Now that I had some cash, I could afford to treat myself like a human being. I was a regular guy with a job and an author, to boot. If only I could figure out how to get a copy of the publication from Slevron.

I turned on the vid as I heated the food, and the top story made my blood turn colder than Forbi ice-rain. Twenty more citizens, all Earthlings, had disappeared from their quarters. In every case, they were sitting on their new couches right before they vanished. The slidges were tracking down where these "super cheap" couches were coming from.

"Crap. Double crap."

∞ O ∞

Drevik thumped on my door. "Open up, Earth scum."

Through the closed door, I said, "Beat it, Drevik. I've got plenty of credits in my account."

"Lying Earth scum. Your account is frozen. I want my money, or I'll take a piece of you for lunch."

Crap. Slevron must have messed with my account. Why did I ever trust it? "I'll get it from Naike. I've got a job now."

"You've got three hours."

I could hear Drevik storm down the hallway. He was a Braklez, a carnivore native to Forbi. They owned the planet. The only reason they didn't eat us on a regular basis was because they thought we tasted bad. Kinda like squirrels on Earth— not worth the bother. Unless they had a *reason* to bother.

I looked at my watch. I had time for a rinse before work. Where would I get enough credits in three hours? Naike was probably good for it, but I hadn't exactly earned a month's pay. When I was ready, I opened my door and two Earthlings in suits stood in my way.

"Mr. Tank Lazier?"

"Who's askin'?"

"Mr. Lazier, may we come in?"

"I'm late for work."

"You won't be going in today, Mr. Lazier."

I stood there, blocking their entrance while they blocked my exit. It was a standoff. Then the suit on the left pulled out a Taser. "Come in," I said jovially.

They took one look at my half-couch then murmured to each other. "You are under suspicion for the kidnapping of several Earth-Forbi. You'll have to come with us."

One of them grabbed my arm and I tried to yank it away. "I don't know what you're talking about."

"You gave the design to the Cravdoppers for the couches. One named Slevron is already in custody. He coughed up your name. The details were confirmed by a magazine called…" He pulled out his scribbler to look it up. "*Impact Quarterly*. You sent them the story then told them to, quote, 'throw it out, since it sucked' end quote. Quite the choice of words Mr. Lazier, wouldn't you say? The couches do suck, don't they? Suck people directly to Cravdop."

"It's a story, you idiots. *Fiction*. You know, pretend? I made it up."

"What happened to your couch, then?"

"Lorna ripped it in half, but not how you guys think. She chopped it up and took her half with her. She left me— stormed off in a womanly rage. She's probably back on Earth by now. All of it happened *before* I wrote the story. Just ask Naike at *Luna's Wake*. He talked to her the day she dumped me."

"Naike Sanchez, of *Luna's Wake*, is also missing."

"Missing? How can he be *missing*? How can they all be missing, when they're all on Cravdop? Can't you just go get them?"

"We *suspect* they're on Cravdop. Besides, Mr. Lazier, these people were taken against their will. That constitutes kidnapping."

Crap. I guess the suit figured he'd told me enough, because he chose that moment to wrestle my hands behind my back and link them together. Forbi had laws against lawyers, so I couldn't weasel my way out of this one. I'd have to plead my case to a slidge— a kind of police officer and jailer. These goons were only hired muscle. They led me out into the hall.

Drevik was coming. "Hey, that's my lunch."

"Not any more. He's due at the jail for slidge interrogation."

Drevik bared his rows of sharp teeth as we passed. I glanced at the slaughter knife in his hand, glad the muscle-goons were on my side.

∞ O ∞

When we got to the jail, a Forbi slidge was assigned to my case. A very agitated Slevron was in another room with his own interrogator.

"Hey," I said nodding towards Slevron. "That's your bad guy. It's the one responsible, not me. I just wrote a story. It's fiction." I was hoping the honest approach would spring me faster.

My slidge said, "The Cravdopper, Slevron, refuses to explain itself. It said it needed to speak with you, to apologize. We do not allow collaboration between suspects."

"Slevron's the brains of this fiasco. I'm willing to allow this apology, or whatever, so long as Slevron owns up to its guilt. You can be my witness, if that's what you slidges need to preserve your shove-a-microscope-up-my-ass procedure."

"Our what?"

"Never mind. Just give Slevron a chance, would ya?"

"One moment." The slidge left the room and staggered across the hall to speak to his counterpart. All Forbi talk with their hands, not literally, but a lot of gestures were flying in the other room. Finally, the two slidges brought Slevron.

The Cravver was jumpy. "We are so glad to see you, Mr. Tank Lazier. We have been waiting to apologize to you."

"I could use some help here, Slev. These guys seem pretty pissed. What'd you do with all those people?"

"We are sorry to cause you pain. You have helped us to esteem our Cravclass. We are grateful."

Slevron's slidge addressed mine. "That's enough collaboration. The apology has been stated, now back to the sentencing room. Don't continue your interrogation until I've completed mine."

Slevron accompanied its slidge back to the room across the hall. They were in there awhile. The slidge gestured, Slevron wiggled. I stared at the ceiling, bored, scared, and in desperate need of a drink. The suits paced back and forth. I kept asking them who they worked for, but the slidge kept telling them to keep quiet. No collaborations. At least they had the decency to unlink my arms so I could bite my nails.

Finally, Slevron left the sentencing room. Its slidge motioned mine across the hall. More gestures, more pacing, more nail biting. Then my slidge came back.

"You are sentenced *clear*. Another infraction and we will change your status to *off-world*. For now, you can go about your business."

"So that's it? No explanation?"

"The sentence is concluded."

"What about the goons?" I pointed to the suits.

One of them answered, "We'll be in touch."

I left the jail wondering what had happened. Was this for real? Did the Cravvers build my teleporter? I was afraid to go home — Drevik was probably still hungry — so I found an Earthling bar across town. I sat in a dark corner and watched the news on the vid.

To my surprise, the two goons were being interviewed for their heroic efforts. They worked for Transcore, and helped one Mr. Robert Black to secure a lucrative trade and transportation deal with a planet new to Forbi. Cravdop. Plus, all the planets in our jurisdiction could now use — for a price — the new teleportation device. "Travel in style with ease. From the comfort of your own couch." Somehow I got the feeling Transcore was getting more than a thousand credits out of the deal.

My account was working again, so I drank half my body weight before I stumbled home. Drevik had tacked a receipt to my door. He'd have to chase someone else for dinner.

When I opened the door, I almost passed out, and not from the liquor. My half-couch was gone, replaced by a new, shiny one. Curious, I sat down. The room blurred, spun, and faded to black. I wondered if it was the couch or the drinks, but when it all came back, I was in a room as bright as the sun and three Cravvers were standing around me.

I puked on the closest one's feet— if you could call them feet. Diplomacy definitely wasn't my forte.

"Hello, Mr. Tank Lazier. We are so glad you are here."

"Thanks— uh, Slevron?"

The Cravver on my left wiggled closer. We are Slevron, this is Ferdrack, of our Cravclass."

"Pleased, Ferdrack. Sorry about the mess."

"We are so excited to have you on Cravdop. Your teleporter disguise worked perfectly. And our Cravclass collected more 'Earthlings' — a very unique species — than ever recorded for a studies bonding exercise."

"You lost me there, Ferdrack. What's it talking about, Slevron?"

Slevron slumped up to explain. "When a Cravdopper begins our advanced studies, our Cravclass performs a bonding exercise. We are to collect a series of items, all of varied and unusual nature, in a short amount of time. The Cravclass with the most items, particularly those most unique, wins a prize."

"Let me get this straight," I said. "You were playing some kind of frosh-initiation-scavenger-hunt game?"

Slevron paused. I figured its translator was on overload trying to decode what I'd said.

"Yes. We are proud to say that we won. Our disguise for the device will count towards our first engineering credit."

"We won, yes, we won," added Ferdrack.

"So, what did you win?" I asked.

"A type of liquid consumed for intoxication."

Booze. *Perfect.* "Where are the people you collected?"

"They returned to Forbi."

"How did they get back?"

"The couch is able to teleport in both directions. We modified that from your story, Mr. Tank Lazier. Your one way model was not as useful."

It was useful enough for Lorna. Too bad she wasn't *actually* trapped on a hell-world.

Slevron continued. "We wanted to collect Earthlings since they control transportation on Forbi. We gave the head of Transcore, Mr. Robert Black, a free sample, hoping he could help us draft a deal for legal access to teleportation. Once Mr. Robert Black was able to confirm the details of our agreement, we opened up the couches for return trips. We did not realize the delay would cause trouble. Mr. Robert Black did not show concern."

"I'm sure he didn't," I said. *The snake wanted the best contract for himself. All I got was a thousand lousy credits.* "So what happens now?"

"We can show you how to go back, but we hoped you would stay, Mr. Tank Lazier. Perhaps you could write us a story about elimination devices? As long as they are scientifically possible."

"Would you settle for believable?"

WASTE MANAGEMENT

(THE COUCH TELEPORTATION UNIVERSE)

I stormed into *Luna's Wake*. The customers lurking at the back tables ignored me. They knew better than to mess with a woman on a rampage. I stepped in some Drip ooze and my shoes squeaked with every stride as I approached the bartender.

"I need a drink, Naike." I slammed my credit chip on the counter.

"What'll it be, Lorna?"

Why do bartenders always wipe the glassware with those white towels? "Whatever Tanker hates!"

"Trouble in paradise?" Naike looked down as he spoke, feigning interest when we both knew that he didn't give a crap about my problems. *Too bad, I'm gonna tell him anyway.*

"Tanker's broke! What did I ever see in him? *Artists!* They're a bunch of losers."

Naike nodded.

"Heard of any work off-world?" *God, I need to get off this rock.* I tapped my credit chip on the counter— a mass of sticky glass-rings. Naike gave me a stop-that-it's-annoying look. I kept right on tapping.

"Nothing lately," he said. He put a purple foaming drink on the counter. It sloshed, adding another stain to the mess. "Ten credits."

I handed him my chip. "Take an extra for yourself."

"You're too generous."

Blow it out your ass. "No problem."

I took my drink to a table near the window, noticed the rain had started, and watched sheets of water pummel pedestrians.

God, I hate rain. I needed to get my ass off Forbi, the sooner, the better. Tanker brought me here, saying it was a great place for creative people. In reality, it was a piece of space garbage inhabited by scum-lords and losers who couldn't afford to go anywhere interesting in the universe.

The sign on the shop across the street blinked on. Gidder's. Buy, Trade, Sell. *Want to buy my loser boyfriend?*

I sipped at the purple drink. I couldn't stand another night with Tanker in that tiny unit. I gave up my own place the night he gave me a key to his. No point wasting credits. But now that I'd hit the wall with him, I had two options: find another micro-scopic dive-of-a-unit run by a scum-lord like Drevik, or take the next transport cruiser off-world.

I downed the rest of the purple drink and slammed my glass down. A Drip two tables over rippled in shock at the noise. All Drips were scared of their own shadows, although they barely cast shadows through their translucence. The jelly-like wigglers have no backbone, literally. I mumbled, "Sorry," then left the bar; no point making an enemy. Didn't matter if everyone else thought Drips weren't worth two shits.

I walked through the downpour, feeling the burn and itch of the acidic rain through my shirt. I passed the job board but didn't see any off-world work for engineers. By the time I reached the apartment complex I was soaked.

Drevik, our scum-lord, stood outside our unit, pounding on the door. "What do you want?" I said.

"Tanker's account's pretty damned low."

"I'm aware of that."

"If he doesn't make rent—"

"I know. You'll eat him."

Drevik clenched his hand and his forearm muscles bulged. "Until I choke on his scrawny flesh."

"Well don't eat me. I'm getting out of here."

"You need another unit? I've got one in the next building. Rent's four hundred. Nicer than this hole."

"That's a bit steep for me."

Drevik sniffed. Carnivores have a tendency to sniff at you, deciding whether or not you're worth eating, I guess. Drevik was a Braklez, a native carnivore of Forbi. Most of the time they leave humans alone. They have some kind of don't-eat-sentient-creatures code, or so they whine to the interstellar cops. But they are permitted to eat you if you don't make rent.

Drevik sniffed at me again, inside my personal space. I took a step back.

"How much do you make?" he asked.

"Four twenty a month. Why?"

"You're an engineer, right?" He stepped closer.

I stepped back. "Yeah, why?"

"My cousin, Alapud, is branching out. He's starting up a lodging satellite. First of its kind to orbit Forbi. Needs an engineer. A *female*. I heard he's paying over six hundred a month."

"How much over six hundred?"

"Depends on the engineer. But he needs someone right away."

"Would today be soon enough?"

Drevik showed his mouth full of pointy teeth. "You'll find his office in the transport station. Tell him I sent you."

"Why are you doing this, Drevik?"

He put his hand on his slaughter knife. "Because if you leave, I get to eat Tanker." He smiled.

I smiled. "Where in the transport station?"

"Fourth floor."

∞ O ∞

I found Alapud's office. The Drip at the desk reached a tentacle under the counter, so I quickly mentioned Drevik's name. She pointed at her boss's door and I let myself in.

Alapud was taller and brawnier than Drevik. When he stood up from behind his desk he stooped below the ceiling. His forearm was broader than my thigh. He reached out his clawed hand to shake mine. His grip practically crushed my bones. I tried not to sigh too loudly when he finally let go.

"Drevik tells me you're an engineer."

"Yep. Mechanical."

"Excellent." He clapped his hands together. "We're having problems passing code. The sooner we open the lodging satellite the sooner I'll start making money." Alapud sat down.

"Code for what?" I sat down in the visitor's chair. It had a hole in the back big enough for a Braklez tail to slip through.

"Waste management."

Toilets? For a second, I almost high-tailed it out of there, but I *really* needed to leave this shit hole. "When can I start?"

"I've got a crew leaving on the last cruiser of the day. I'll buy your ticket and give you a week's pay in advance, to tie up any loose ends on Forbi."

"Thanks. I'll be on the transport." *Just enough time to get my stuff.* "What's my weight allowance?"

"Fifty dregs."

"That's tight."

"Fuel isn't free."

"Good point." I bit my lip, doing some calculations in my head. "Will the weight be a problem?"

"Nope. Anything to get off-planet."

"I hope you can solve our code problems, Miss, uh…?"

"Lorna Watkowski."

"Make the transport, Miss Watkowski." He reached out a clawed hand. I shook it, counting the seconds until he let go.

∞ O ∞

I emptied the apartment of everything that I had paid for, which was basically everything. I borrowed Drevik's dolly to haul the stuff. I closed the door for the last time, eyeing the two things I'd left behind: the vid and the couch. The vid was attached to the wall and I didn't have a screwdriver. I'd paid for half the couch. Tanker called it our "marriage license". Everyone needs a couch, so paying for it together symbolized our commitment to each other. *Half of that is mine.*

I called Drevik and asked him to bring up an axe. He was so excited about my idea, that he must have run the whole way. By the time we'd separated my half from Tanker's, his smile was naughtier than a slidge party. We shook hands. I tried not to whimper.

∞ O ∞

The Drip in Gidder's gave me four hundred credits for all of my stuff. He kept looking outside, eyeing my half-couch with suspicion. I slammed my hand on the counter. Globs of ooze dripped out of his ten orifices as he wiggled red with fear. "Let's focus on the transaction, shall we?" I lifted up my hand and pointed at the credit chip. "Put it all on this."

"There's a four day waiting period before we shelve your property for sale," he said. "In case you change your mind and come back for your items. If you do, we apply a twenty-five percent service charge."

"That's fine."

I left the shop with my life stored in one backpack, plus the half-couch. I couldn't fit the couch on the bus, so I hailed a truck-cab; to hell with the expense. *It'll be worth every credit.*

During the trip to the transport station, the truck-cab driver kept putting his claw on my elbow. I had seen his species around, but I couldn't remember what he was called. They all looked like melons-on-sticks (this one more like a watermelon than a canta-loupe). I don't know what kind of turn-on elbows were for his species, but I let him have his fun. I had no intention of setting foot on Forbi again.

When we got to the station, the driver backed into one of the loading docks. I tipped him two credits, and he groped my elbow one more time before he drove off. The loading gorillas were humans, thank God. I'd had enough weirdness for one day. They carried my couch from the dock to the weigh scales. With my backpack I had less than three dregs to spare on my weight allowance. I decided to pick up some alcohol in the duty-free. But before I left, I gave special instructions for the couch.

I picked up three bottles of tequila, imported from Deslot— a planet with little water and many criminals. The Drip behind the counter seemed pleased with my choice. She turned a translucent green and shimmered with delight. Maybe it was the two-credit tip.

I waited in the check-in lounge for over an hour. By the time I boarded the cruiser, my patience was exhausted and I had come dangerously close to opening one of the sealed-by-duty-free-interstellar-cops bottles of my tequila. Best not get busted on my first day.

I spoke to the flight attendant about my cargo. She had access to a portable vid-recorder. I thanked her, and told her to let me know when we were far enough out to eject our trash.

When she nudged my elbow to wake me, I thought I was back in the truck-cab with that weird elbow-fondling driver. She escorted me through the passenger compartment to a porthole beyond the garbage hatch. I had the honor of pushing the "jettison" button. She worked the vid-recorder, capturing shots of me waving to the couch and a good one of it floating in space. I gave her Tanker's message address and asked her to send the images with my best wishes. She promised to send them as soon as she finished her shift. I tipped her more credits than I should have, then hurried back to sleep in my uncomfortable chair.

∞ O ∞

We docked and unloaded in the middle of the night, which turned out to be noon by the lodging satellite clock. A human, Dansk

Flenkel, greeted me. He called himself my new "partner in waste". As I shifted my backpack, he offered to take me to the loading area to pick up the rest of my gear. When I told him I had it all, he asked, "Did Alapud cheap out on your weight allowance?"

"No. It's a long story."

"I'd like to hear it over a drink sometime." He smiled in that I-think-you're-sexy way.

I responded with my in-your-dreams stare.

"I get off at eleven," he said, stepping a little closer. "I'll be in the plexi-lounge after my shift. Care to join me?"

I'll join you to a venting shaft. "Not tonight." I stepped back. "Space-lag."

"Maybe tomorrow?"

"We'll see." Desperate to change the subject, I said "Feels like about point five gee here."

"Point six-five," he said. "Enough for the toilet pumps to work and not crush Drips and Rejdars."

"Speaking of toilets, can you point me in their direction?"

"I could show you to your sleep unit first."

"Thanks, but I'd rather check out the facilities."

"Whatever." He hurried through a fancy-looking lobby.

Crews of Braklez stood on scaffolding, welding metal ceiling tiles and wiring lights. The lodging satellite still looked pretty rough around the edges, but I could already tell that the lobby was going to look uber-expensive by the time they finished. Most of the crew looked like teenagers or *runts*. On Forbi, almost all Braklez owned real estate. The children worked construction, prepping them to maintain their future investments. *Runts* inherited squat so they worked the trades for life.

I nodded to one of the gawkers. He clamped down his jaw while he pulled back his lips, exposing all his teeth. *Everyone's a dreamer.*

Beyond the lobby, there were a series of waste rooms. The first two were marked "bipeds". The next two were marked "multi-peds" for Drips and Rejdars.

I stopped outside the last one, marked "miscellaneous." "What's in there?"

"I'll show you." Dansk nudged me inside. In the center of the room was a stainless steel rectangular enclosure with half-meter walls. Inside, it had a metal grating lined with pebbles. Above, huge shower-heads hung from the ceiling, swaying slowly back and forth.

"High pressure water and air sprays down when you card out," said Dansk, pointing up to the showers.

"Card out?"

"With your facility card." He pointed to a card panel near the entrance. "It activates lights, airlocks, and the waste rooms. It also unlocks the dining areas and sleep units."

"Ah."

"The cleaning process is automatic."

"Is it working yet?" I asked.

"Only if you card in and out. Because Sheepics have infra-red vision, they don't bother with lights. No lights, no automatic cleaning. And the next guy gets a smelly welcome."

"It could get pretty ripe in here," I said.

"That's one of the reasons we haven't made code yet." Tapping his chest, he added, "And why Alapud pays us the *big* credits."

He laughed at his clever wit. I shook my head. This guy had a one-track mind. "Show me the multiped facility."

He led the way into a room more spa than toilet. Three huge hot-tubs bubbled. As I approached one, I caught a whiff of the steam, which smelled like a mix of fermented Drip ooze and chloramoxide. "What do you put in there?"

"The recipe's from Hycoof, the Drip home planet."

"I'm familiar with it." I knew squat about Hycoof, but I didn't want this guy to think he was smarter than me.

"It's some kind of chemical bath that keeps their skin moist, is buoyant enough to hold them in position while they defecate, and prevents the place from stinking."

I stepped a little closer and peered over the edge of one of the tubs. "Can Rejdars use it?"

"In theory. We haven't had a live one to test it."

I pointed at the exit. "Show me the biped units."

We walked down the hall. Dansk ducked into the male biped unit, so I followed. A Braklez was pissing in a urinal. He turned and saw me, then hissed at Dansk. I turned away, but not before I got a glimpse of his privates. *Thank God they only eat us.* He zipped up and hurried out, hissing again.

Dansk looked a little scared.

Moron. "So you've set up standard urinals?"

"Yes." He pointed towards a pair of cubicles. "And toilets for the harder stuff."

"Can I see the female unit?"

"I'll wait in the hallway."

"Seriously?"

He nodded. "Alapud doesn't pay me *that* much."

Wuss. The female facility had standard cubicles, but the toilets looked huge. I'd never seen a female Braklez, but I'd heard they were enormous, especially when they were about to lay eggs. A human woman would have trouble sitting on the seat without falling in.

I met Dansk in the hallway. "We're going to need some sort of potty-type seats to lower down over the toilets, for humans."

"They're on backorder." His I-think-you're-sexy smile returned.

I adjusted the backpack, feeling it dig into my shoulder blades. "I think I'm ready to get settled in now."

"I can show you to your unit."

"I'm fine," I said. "*Really.*"

∞ O ∞

The next morning space-lag smacked me in the head. I trudged down the sparse hallways of the space station to the staff meeting. I was the last one to arrive, and I ended up sitting beside Dansk. He leaned in close. I leaned over until I was practically in Alamek's lap. He was another Braklez, head of construction and Alapud's brother. He was also in charge of the meeting and he drawled on endlessly about construction details. Blah, blah, wire shortages, blah, blah, tile die lots. Dansk kept leaning closer and I kept edging towards Alamek.

Alawas gave me an evil stare. She was Alamek's mate, and head of "decorum", whatever that meant. She was monstrous. *That's why the toilets are so big.*

While I waited for them to reach my section of the agenda, I doodled on my scribbler and watched the Drip in the corner record the minutes of the meeting.

Finally, a clawed creature, same species as the truck-cab driver (this one more like an egg than a melon), introduced himself as Too-oo and explained the code issues with the sewage pumps. A Sheepic named Baaque added his own comments, complaining about the pumps in the waste reclamation converter. The fluff-ball was wearing a glare-shield that made his eyes look like giant fishbowls, and I had trouble listening to the details while I fought back the urge to make fish-faces at him.

"What species is Too-oo?" I whispered to Dansk.

"He's a Schtem."

Too-oo glared at me. *Mental note: Schtems have good hearing.*

Dansk stared at my breasts as though they might have the answers to Too-oo's pumping problems.

Baaque continued. "We still can't convert the solid waste into useful particulates."

"Useful?" I asked.

"Food," said Dansk. "To save money, the Baaque chefs got the brilliant idea of turning shit into food. I don't touch the stuff myself."

The Braklez all nodded in agreement.

"What's the trouble with the conversion?"I asked. Fishbowl-eyes swiveled his head in my direction.

"Well," said Baaque, "the biped and miscellaneous facilities produce workable waste. But the multiped pellets sink to the bottom of the tubs, and we have to send maintenance in there to extract them manually."

I drew a mental image and it wasn't pretty. "How big are these pellets?"

"The size of my fist," said Dansk.

Too-oo said, "And the pumps jam on them. They're like rocks. How can jelly-blobs poop rocks?"

Everyone laughed. Except me. I had always had a soft spot for Drips, though I wasn't sure why.

Too-oo said, "We also have the major issue of Vissies in the pipes."

"Vissies?" I asked.

"Little parasites," said Too-oo. "They can jump up your urine stream into your circulatory system, sucking the life right out of you."

"Not to mention biting your ass if you sit on the toilet too long," said Dansk.

"I say we run an electrical line through the pipes," said Too-oo. "Zap them all."

"But they're sentient!" said Alawas. "The interstellar guidelines clearly state that all lodging satellites must respect *every* sentient species while it resides in their facility."

"Sentient, my ass," said Dansk.

"All our asses," said Too-oo.

Dansk snickered, and said, "We can't meet code or pass inspection until we eliminate them."

∞ O ∞

Back in my unit, I had to piss a river. I sat down on the toilet, a biped unit way too big for me, and held the sides so I wouldn't fall in. I remembered the Vissies and didn't linger.

After a nap, my head felt ready to split open. I gave up on shaking the space-lag and headed down to the main pumping station to talk to Too-oo and Baaque. They gave me the full tour. Three huge storage containers held the intake, liquid, and solid wastes respectively. From the liquid one, a huge green pipe sent the mixture to a standard set of filters, the final output potable water. From the solid one, a series of pumps, screens, and centrifuges separated the components. A Drip was wiggling down one of the centrifuge screens, scraping away the Drip shit that clogged the unit.

I'm glad it's him and not me.

Too-oo pointed up. "See. They clog the screens, the pipes, everything!"

"What do they do on Hycoof?"

Too-oo shrugged. "Their treaties are extensive. We can only implement the designs included in the *official* blueprints."

"Couldn't we ask one of them?"

"A Drip? Are you *serious*?"

I moved closer to the Drip on the scaffolding. "Hey!" He looked down. "Come here a minute."

He slid down and plopped onto the floor beside me. I said, "We're having trouble with the Drip pellets. How do you deal with the problem on Hycoof?"

"Vissies." He stared at the floor, looking a little on the purple-side and wiggling.

"Not the Vissies," I said. "The solid pellets."

"Vissies," he said, still looking down, turning absolutely terror-scarlet.

"Ask a Drip," Too-oo said.

The Drip hurried away before I could object.

Baaque pointed at a large oven-like machine beyond the waste separators. "That's the main converter," he said. "It produces quality proteins, but they need some color adjustment."

He walked me through the process, but all the time I kept thinking about the Drip and his Vissies.

∞ O ∞

After the tour I headed for the plexi-lounge. Dansk sat at a small black table, sipping an orange drink. I ducked for the opposite side of the room, hoping he wouldn't notice me.

"Lorna!" he shouted.

Damn. I sat down with my back to him and pretended not to hear.

"Lorna!"

Leave me alone.

He appeared at my table, orange drink in hand. "I was calling your name."

"Sorry." I pointed to my ears. "Bad hearing."

"Oh," he said. Then he proceeded to talk louder. "How was your day down in the bowels of the ship?"

"Do me a favor? Don't say bowel."

He laughed. I pointed at the dark vid in the corner. "Can we get any news on that?"

"Not yet. The Forbi wireless feed is insanely expensive up here. Alapud won't authorize the hook up until *paying* customers arrive."

I started to stand up.

"Where're ya going? You just got here."

"I need a drink."

"I'll buy you one." He motioned for the bartender to bring another orange drink before I could stop him.

When she brought it over, I sipped at it. My eyes watered. Dansk snickered, but I took another sip. "Listen," I said. "Any word on the toilet-seat backorder?"

"Another week, at least." He gulped down the rest of his drink.

"Maybe we should contact Hycoof. Find out how they process the Drip pellets?"

"No way."

"Why not?"

He gave me a you're-a-pain-in-the-ass look. "For one thing, it's a bureaucratic nightmare. Besides, I've seen the facilities on Forbi. The tub-design is standard."

"But they don't have problems with Vissies on Forbi, do they?"

"Where are you going with this?" he said.

"Just a hunch. A Drip mentioned Vissies."

"Ask a Drip."

"Yeah, whatever. They're not all morons, you know."

He smiled and stared at my breasts.

I gulped down the rest of my orange drink, trying not to flinch as it set my throat on fire. "I'm tired. G'night."

∞ O ∞

When I got back to my unit I flushed the toilet to watch the water swirl down. How many Vissies had jumped the gap the last time? How many were inside me, getting drunk on that orange crap?

That gave me an idea. I left my unit and strode down the hallway. I took a corner near the docking area too quickly and almost knocked over a newly arrived Drip. "Sorry," I said.

She started to hurry away without answering.

"Don't rush off. I need to ask you a question."

She waited, looking down, turning purple.

"You're from Hycoof, right?"

"No. I separated on Forbi," she said, still looking down.

"Right." I sat down so that her eyestalks were at my height and she could look at me. "I meant your species, the Drips. You're from Hycoof?"

"Yes."

I wiped away a blob of ooze that was about to drip from one of her orifices. A ripple of relief streaked through her and she turned yellow. I'd never seen one turn that color before. "Do you know about Vissies?"

"Small sentients," she said. The yellow flashed back to bright red.

"Yes." *God, these Drips are scared of everyone.* "Do you know their planet of origin?"

"Hycoof." Her wiggle-pace cranked up a few notches.

"Are you afraid of them?"

She wiggled redder, if that was possible, answering my question. "Why?" I said.

"They take us over. They live inside us. They turn us to slaves."

"But not on Forbi?"

Desperate to put her at ease, I wiped the ooze from several of her orifices, one gentle effort at a time. Her red slowly faded to pink. Not quite the yellow from before, but light enough to hope that she might trust me.

"What's special about Forbi?" I said.

"The Rejdars have... *sanitary stations*. Against the..." She turned back to bright red, and continued, "Violating interstellar laws. They kill the Vissies, freeing us."

That's the connection. I nodded, wiping another glob of ooze from an orifice. She faded to a dark pink. "I appreciate your help. I won't tell anyone that we spoke, okay?"

"Go now?" she asked.

"Yes."

She hurried away, leaving a slurping trail of ooze behind her.

I headed for the company offices where I found a download terminal. While I was waiting for my scribbler to connect, I read a news article on the web. "Couch-teleporters soon to be in widespread use." I almost closed the window, but then I noticed the image at the bottom. A weird creature, "Slevron from Cravdop" according to the caption, waved an appendage at the camera. He was credited as one of the inventors of the teleporters. Beside him stood Tanker. I couldn't believe it. *Tanker*. What was he doing hugging a scientist?

I closed the news window and instigated a search of Vissies and Hycoof, all the while wondering why Drevik hadn't eaten Tanker for lunch. From what I could determine, the Vissies invaded the Drips, breaking down their waste into manageable putty instead of hard rocks. The whole thing sounded harmlessly symbiotic to me.

Digging further, I found a few posts on a conspiracy site that alluded to rumors that as payment for their waste-eating-assistance, the Vissies wrapped around the Drips' thought centers, so that they could hitch a ride on the Drips, using the wigglers for mobility, and countless other acts. No wonder Drips on Forbi were so meek. They didn't want anyone to discover their freedom at the expense of sentient-species-extermination.

I didn't want to be responsible for enslaving the Drips with Vissies, so I couldn't use the sentient parasites directly. But if I could find a way to coax Vissies out of the liquid system and into the solid waste system, maybe they could break down the Drip pellets. We wouldn't need to kill the Vissies. All we needed to do was extract any new Vissies from the liquid system, and then trap them all in the solid system. A little *karmic payback* for their consistent enslavement of the Drips.

I called Baaque on the vid. He sounded sleepy, but when he heard my ideas, he woke up. "I'll meet you in the pumping station," he said.

Before I left, I sent a brief report to the construction department heads.

I arrived at the pumping station shortly after Too-oo, Alamek, Dansk, and Alawas. "News travels fast," I said.

"That it does," said Alamek. He was holding his slaughter knife, making me feel pretty uncomfortable. "Explain your idea, human."

I didn't want to give him a reason to eat me, so I dumped the whole Vissies-are-evil scenario. "If we shoot the liquid waste through the vat of solid waste, maybe we can inject the Vissies into the Drip pellets to soften them."

"But the whole point," Baaque said, "is to separate the liquids from the solids."

"I know," I said. "But we need the Vissies to process the waste."

"I read your report, Miss Watkowski," said Alawas. "You're treading on dangerous ground. The Vissies will object to the entrapment."

"True," I said. "But we can't in good conscience give them direct access to the Drips. We'd be sanctioning slavery." They all looked a little confused, so I said, "The way I see it, we have three major stumbling blocks to pass code. We need to turn the waste into useful particulates, soften the Drip pellets into a more manageable effluent, and get the Vissies out of the liquid lines, right?"

Everyone nodded.

"Well, the Vissies are the solution. They feed on Drip waste. We need to get them into the solid flow. If they're happily chewing away, so to speak, that should distract them from the liquid effluent. Maybe we could set up a stop valve to prevent them from washing back into the water lines. And Baaque, the by-product of their snacking will make an excellent protein for your reclaimer."

They all stared at me. I couldn't tell if they were happy or stunned.

"What about any worker Drips who are already contaminated?" said Alawas.

"We will clear the Vissies from the fresh water pipes, so the Drips won't be re-exposed. For all the Drips that show symptoms of enslavement, we force them to take a few vacation days and encourage them to spend the time on Forbi."

"But then they would—"

Alamek said, "What they do on Forbi is *their own business*. I like the idea."

"Thanks," I said. As he ordered the others to make my ideas a reality, I turned to walk away.

"Where are you going?" he asked.

"I'm exhausted. I'm going to bed. I'll report back in the morning." I ducked into a lift.

∞ ◯ ∞

I arrived late to the morning staff meeting, where I found Dansk and Alamek.

I wasn't sure if I should sit beside the carnivore or the weasel. I picked the carnivore.

"Miss Watkowski," said Alamek.

"Yes, Sir?"

"Too-oo and Baaque had crews up all night refitting the pipes. This morning, we lured the Vissies into the solid waste. Looks like your idea works."

"So we'll pass code?"

"I've scheduled the waste facilities inspection." Alamek stood up and walked over to me. His hand paused on his slaughter knife, but then continued to his side. He slapped me on the back, his sharp claws biting into my flesh. "Good job."

"Thanks."

"Of course you'll get a bonus," Alamek continued.

"How much?" Dansk and I asked together.

"Two thousand credits."

I tried to contain my glee, but failed.

"At this point," said Alamek, "we don't need you here any longer."

I didn't want to go back to Forbi, but two thousand credits wouldn't last forever. It wasn't enough to secure transport back to Earth, or any decent planets. "Can I stay here?"

"As a guest, for a few days," said Alamek. "For a small fee, of course."

"You can share my unit," said Dansk, giving me that I-think-you're-sexy stare again.

I shuddered. "Any transports due in today?"

"Forget transports," said Alamek. "I've ordered some of those new couch-teleporters. They should be installed tomorrow. The usage rates are low enough, you could travel anywhere on two thousand credits."

"Great," I said. "I wonder how much to Deslot?"

"Deslot?" said Dansk. "Who'd want to go there?"

"Me. They make damned fine tequila."

FUZZY GREEN MONSTER
NUMBER TWO

(THE COUCH TELEPORTATION UNIVERSE)

Greenie waddled toward the alley on his hind legs. A female human stared at him from the curb. He raised a paw, unsure as to the proper reaction to her scrutiny.

"What's with the costume?" she said.

He looked down at his fur. "This is my natural appearance."

"Huh."

He scratched his shoulder with his front paw. "Did they bring out the trash yet?"

"How would I know? I don't eat garbage."

"I would prefer not to as well, but my circumstances warrant the action."

Every Wednesday night, the restaurant threw out linguini. Greenie loved pasta, but he couldn't cook it himself since his paws lacked opposable digits.

The back door opened and Greenie dropped down to all four paws. The busboy said, "I'm tired of your messes. Put back what you don't eat. Got it?"

"Yes." Greenie rummaged through the first bag and ate the linguini. The second bag held other foods, none to his liking. He preened himself, licking his paws and rubbing them over his snout. Then he ran his claws along his teeth and between them, scraping away any lingering bits of food as he exited the alley on his hind legs.

"So you're an alien?" The girl's long brown hair shimmered in the light from the street lamp, adding luster to her forlorn appearance. She was a youngling, no more than fifteen Earth years, and her clothes required preening.

"I'm Greenie." He bowed slightly.

"That's original."

"Not true. I'm actually Fuzzy Green Monster Number *Two*. The immigration officials at the Couch Teleportation Authority couldn't pronounce my true name, and I was the second green Strunjox to pass through their station, so—"

"Enough with the life history. I get it. You're green."

"May I join you, Miss?"

"Whatever." She slid closer to the street light. "The name's Dree, not 'Miss.'"

He settled himself beside her, hunching his shoulders to appear smaller. "Pleased to meet you, Dree. I'm from Deslot."

"Why'd you come to Earth?"

"My home planet is saturated with corrupt and depraved individuals who sell illegal chemicals for profit. My cave-nest elders are addicted to the substances and they show little respect for me or their fellow Strunjox." He ran his claws through his leg fur. "I came to Earth to avoid falling into misconduct myself."

"Of all the cities, why'd you pick L.A.?"

"My planet's environment is littered with deserts. Los Angeles has a similar climate. Why do you live here?"

She dug her shoe into some sludge in the gutter. "I ran away to be a star."

"You can't possibly become a celestial body."

"No, fuzz-brain." She punched him in the arm. "An *actor*, you know?"

He pressed his ears back.

"You have no clue, do you?"

"No."

She laughed. "I can't believe someone hasn't eaten you alive by now."

"But your laws prohibit sentient consumption, do they not?"

"For a big hairy monster you're pretty tame."

Greenie fidgeted with his claws, clicking them back and forth against one another.

"Cut it out," she snapped

"I don't understand."

She pointed a finger at him. The nail was short, past the quick, and looked most uncomfortable. "You're driving me crazy clicking your claws like that."

"Oh."

"You got any money?"

Greenie wiggled his ears forward and backward. "I wish I did, for then I could consume adequate nutrients. A Strunjox cannot live on linguini alone. We are omnivores."

"I could go for some hot pizza. The food at the shelter's barely edible."

"You have shelter?"

"I stay at a home for teens."

"I've lived for approximately one hundred and twenty-seven thousand of your Earth hours. Perhaps I could live there too?"

"I'm not packing a calculator. Translate that to English."

"Approximately fourteen point five Earth years."

"You're a teenager then, but I'm not sure about the fuzz-factor. We don't see a lot of giant green ETs downtown."

He stood up on his rear legs and hung his head down.

"The shelter's that way. They lock the doors after one. Are you coming?"

"Are you inviting me?" He clicked his claws again.

"Only if you stop that."

He dropped to all fours. How exciting to be invited to dine by a *human*. He wasn't certain of the reason for her friendliness, but he longed for companionship. He hadn't seen another Strunjox since arriving on Earth, and the humans shrank away, from fear, loathing, or perhaps something worse.

They walked past some zealots chanting their ritual monologues of "sparesomechange, sparesomechange." Greenie hurried by, hoping that they would not recruit him to pray with them.

A Braklez — a tall, scale-encrusted carnivore native to Forbi — stood amongst a group of male humans huddled around a vid-booth. The humans smelled of gunpowder and metal. Braklez adolescents were drawn to violent humans. Their cultures followed similar codes of conduct, particularly those involving slaughter. The carnivores ruled illegal substance alliances on Deslot. Greenie stared at the sidewalk so as not to make eye contact with the other alien.

"When will we arrive?" he asked Dree.

She pointed at a brick low-rise a few blocks ahead.

They walked the remainder of the distance in silence. Outside the shelter entrance, youths stood in clusters, engaged in various activities that Greenie found unpleasant. Of all human habits, inhaling carcinogenic fumes in particular assailed his sensitive nostrils. And ejecting saliva was not only rude, but an unforgivable waste of fluids on Deslot.

The humans shied away from Greenie. He dropped to all four paws to appear smaller. A tall human, wearing garments with multiple tears and dangling threads approached him. He wore a gray cloth tied around his forehead and bore skin ornaments with several frightening scenes. "Get off my block, freak," he said.

"Lay off, Stratt." Dree leaned close to Greenie and added, "He's a creep. Just ignore him."

Greenie shifted his weight, from his front to rear paws and back again.

Stratt flicked glowing ashes from his smoke-stick at Greenie. "I said beat it. This ain't no alien shelter. Go find another planet to invade."

Dree stood between Greenie and Stratt. "Give it up. The alien's with me."

"Who asked you?" He shoved her aside. She fell into a puddle of stagnant fluids.

Greenie raised himself on his hind paws and glared down at the ragged human. "Your quarrel is with me. She has invited me to accompany her and I will do so. Now if—"

Stratt lunged at Greenie, grabbing fistfuls of fur, punching and kicking. Greenie dropped down to all fours and shook the human off his coat like a spray of water. Stratt rolled towards the street. The other humans stood frozen, their mouths open in shock. They remained motionless for what seemed like forever, staring at Greenie, awe and fear filling their eyes. He leaned back on his rear paws and walked behind Dree on two legs into the shelter.

"That was awesome," she said.

"I despise confrontation, but allowing him to punish you for accompanying me would have been thoughtless."

"Stratt's a moron, but surrounded by Gray Boyz he's scary. I'd watch your back from now on."

"Must I?" He twisted his neck so that he could peer at his backside. "This position is most uncomfortable."

She shook her head. "It means be careful. Watch out for trouble."

"Oh."

She led Greenie through a large room with several worn couches and a television. Hoping against hope, he bounded over to a couch and sat down. Maybe, if he was really lucky, the lottery rumors were true. He waited, wiggling his rear haunches. The couch did not activate.

"C'mon," said Dree. "The sign-in sheet is upstairs."

"The unit is well used." Greenie pointed to the seat with his claws. "I have heard rumors of free teleporters hidden in the city that randomly activate, based on a lottery system."

She laughed. "A crappy, run-down shelter is no place for a teleportation couch."

"My apologies." He stood and followed her out of the room and up a stairwell. They stopped next to a bulletin board bearing a piece of paper with names and activities scribbled on it. A crudely sharpened pencil hung down from a chain, each end affixed with copious quantities of tape.

"You'll have to sign up for a duty."

Greenie hung his head down and hid his thumbless paws behind his back.

"I know the perfect job for you," she said.

∞ O ∞

"I won't," said Greenie. "I don't wish to hurt others."

Dree crossed her arms against her chest. "Being a bouncer isn't about hurting people, it's about *acting* tough. You're a big guy. You've got the claws and the sharp teeth for effect. C'mon. I know you've got it in you. You scared the crap out of Stratt. Show me your claws."

He held them up.

"That's it. Now your teeth."

He did as she asked.

"Perfect." She stepped back and studied him top to bottom. "Now growl. Can you growl?"

"Grrrrrr."

She jumped back. "Man, that was good. Do it again."

"Grrrr-aaaa-rrrrr"

She shuddered. "I wouldn't mess with you."

"But I do not desire a fight."

"No one's gonna attack a clawed monster."

"But Stratt and his boys—"

"They're regrouping. You'll be safe tonight." She yawned. "I'm going to catch some sleep. Are you good?"

"I try to be."

"No, I meant are you ready? You know, good to go?"

"I suppose." He sat and scratched behind his ear with his rear paw. "When will I see you again?"

"In the morning."

He pointed his claws and growled at her.

She smiled, and said, "That's my fuzz-ball!"

"Thank you for all that you have done for me."

"No problemo." She raised her fingers as though they were claws and growled at him and then left.

Greenie guarded the entrance to the teen shelter. As Dree predicted, the other humans stayed clear of him. Stratt did not return.

∞ O ∞

An hour after dawn, Dree put her hand on his shoulder. "Hey, fuzz-ball. How'd it go?"

"Very well." He settled on his hind paws.

She stroked his fur. "Did someone assign you a bunk? You must be wiped."

"A Strunjox requires little sleep."

"I'm getting breakfast. Wanna come?"

He followed her to the cafeteria. She set down two bowls full of brown crisps on a tray. Greenie sniffed at the offering closest to him, then stirred the bits with a claw.

"It's cereal." Dree opened a carton of bovine extract. "Tastes better with milk." She poured the white substance over her crisps and they crackled.

He avoided the bovine liquid, and he ignored the spoon, which looked far too small to grasp between his enormous paws. He dove into the bowl, snout-first.

"Why did you run away from home, Dree?" he asked between mouthfuls.

She shrugged and stirred her crisps. "My parents. They're both jerks. My Dad drinks too much."

"Aha! A water hoarder. I know all too well what it feels like to be thirsty."

"He drinks too much *alcohol*. It's an addictive substance that makes you stupid."

"Oh. My cave-elders were addicted to *canoxile* and *phlabat*." He pressed his ears back. "It is difficult when your elders cannot properly care for your needs."

She nodded. "It sucks. My mom stares at the TV all day. She's given up on the world."

"Do they care for you?"

"Maybe. I don't know. Sometimes I wonder if they've even noticed I'm gone."

"Family bonds are important to your species. They most certainly would have noticed your absence. Perhaps you should try to mend your grievances?" Greenie rubbed the outside of his paw along her arm.

"Don't." She yanked her hands away and buried them in her lap. "I don't need your sympathy. I can handle myself. I'm glad to be on my own."

Greenie sucked the remainder of his cereal from the bowl. "Do you ever desire returning home? If only to mend your conflicts?"

"Are *you* going back?" she said.

"Perhaps." This youngling's plight was all too similar, too intimate. "I must earn money first. The Couch Teleportation Authority charges many, many dollars."

"What's it like, traveling by couch?"

"It's quite pleasant. You close your eyes and within moments you're sitting on a similar couch on a new planet." He licked a paw and wiped it over his snout several times.

She ran a finger along the rim of the empty bowl. "Sometimes I dream about seeing the cosmos, having an *adventure*." She used her spoon to dig the last few drops of bovine liquid from the bowl. "Then again, this one didn't exactly work out the way I planned."

"We have a saying on Deslot. *To catch a grain of sand, you must open your eyes*."

"That sounds painful."

"It is a riddle of sorts. If I were to try to catch a grain of sand from the wind, using my paws, or a vessel of some description, I would capture plentiful quantities, but miss the beauty of acquiring a single grain. An eye can not only capture a solitary granule without effort, but it endures great discomfort in the process. Such is the nature of the life of a Strunjox. If I had remained with my cave-members, I would have been easily trapped by their routine, and I would now be selling *canoxile* and *phlabat* or worse, be addicted to them myself. On my own, I am honorable, as glorious as a simple particle of sand. But I have also become a discomfort, like a speck of sand trapped in an eye. My elders will shun me for abandoning my cave. And here on Earth, I don't belong. Without thumbs I would likely face similar discrimination on another planet."

"We have a saying here on Earth. *Hard work cures a pained heart.* Maybe we both need a job."

"All the employment opportunities are designed for humans. Deslot was the same. Full of Braklez and Schtems. The whole universe is ruled by creatures with thumbs."

"Stop feeling sorry for yourself! Plenty of animals manage without thumbs. I'll make you a bet."

"A what?"

"We'll both get a job and whoever gets paid first has to take the other one out for dinner."

Greenie pressed his ears back in thought. "What sort of job?"

"You pulled off the bouncer gig last night."

He pressed his ears forward, then backward again. "But I am not paid for that service."

"Lots of places pay for it." She stood up and grabbed the breakfast tray. "If we're going job-hunting, I need to get cleaned up. I'll meet you in the lounge in about an hour, okay?"

"I will be waiting for you there."

She placed the tray in a rack and hurried upstairs.

Greenie lumbered outside and sat on a cement bench to preen. A hand shoved him from behind.

Stratt stood behind the bench along with three younglings on his left and four on his right. All of them wore identical strips of gray cloth around their foreheads. They smelled of gunpowder and metal.

"Get up," said Stratt. "We're going for a walk."

"I do not wish to accompany you."

"I *insist*." Stratt leaned closer to Greenie. "I have a gun, and so do my Boyz. Get up."

Greenie walked on all fours around the bench. The Gray Boyz surrounded him, leading him through a park and across an open field. Finally, they climbed a cement slope under a highway overpass. The walls had been decorated with complex patterns that seemed to make words, but Greenie could not decipher the messages.

"Dree expects me to be waiting in the lounge for her. I do not wish to be rude. Will our business resolve quickly?"

Stratt pulled a gun from his pocket. Greenie had been warned about guns when he first arrived in Los Angeles, but this was the first time he had faced the rounded end. The smell of gunpowder assaulted his nose.

"Should be real quick," said Stratt. "Hold him."

Several of the Boyz stepped up to Greenie, pinning his front and back legs. Stratt took a step closer so that the gun touched Greenie's fur.

"I do not wish to harm you," said Greenie.

Stratt fired. The intense bang of the weapon shocked Greenie as much as the pain in his chest. He could feel his blood pounding beneath his fur. His body could self-heal, but not an injury of this magnitude. He fell back on his rear haunches, freeing his legs from Stratt's assistants and roaring in rage and fear. The injury awakened an instinct honed over generations of Strunjox. His hindbrain took over and for the first time in his life Greenie embraced his ancestry.

He shook off the humans holding his arms as though they were made of paper. Then he pounced on Stratt, biting at the hand that held the gun. The taste of metal in his mouth shocked him back to the moment, back to a more civilized state where the pain in his chest reminded him that he needed to escape. He spat out the gun and then flung it aside with his left front paw.

One of the Boyz swore then fired *his* gun. The bullet grazed Greenie's left haunch.

Echoes bounced against the cement. Greenie lunged past the shooter, knocking the human to the ground. Then he dashed away, using every advantage four limbs could provide. He did not hear any further gunshots nor did he look back. Before he could reach the teen shelter and his one true friend, he collapsed in exhaustion and pain on a crowded sidewalk, panting and whimpering. Humans hurried past him, some looked away, others stared in shock. The last thing Greenie heard was the wailing of a siren.

∞ O ∞

He woke in a cage. Other animals, all smaller than Greenie, had been locked in similar pens.

"Hello?" said Greenie.

An adult human male wearing a white coat appeared. "You're awake. You gave us quite the scare. I'm Dr. Lennox. I've been studying Strunjox physiology, and I believe you'll be better in a few days."

Greenie pressed his ears back. "Am I a prisoner? Must I be punished for the wounds I inflicted on the youngling?"

Dr. Lennox rolled a stool over and sat down in front of Greenie's cage. "I'm to release you to the police when you're well enough. You'll likely be deported to your originating planet."

Greenie scraped his claw along the metal bars. "May I say goodbye to someone? I made a friend, a female youngling."

"Dree?" said the man.

"Was she injured?"

"She came by for a visit. Even if she had been ill, I'm a veterinarian, not a human doctor."

"Oh." Greenie tried to sit up, but his left haunch ached and he flopped back down. "Will she visit again?"

"I'm certain of it. You should rest. I'll wait a day before I call the police. Hopefully, she'll stop by before then."

"Thank you." Greenie closed his eyes and slept.

∞ O ∞

"Hi fuzz-ball. How're you feeling?"

"Dree!" Greenie sat up in his cage. Although he still ached, he wanted to appear healthy and strong in front of her. "I am so pleased to see you."

"I heard about the shooting. The Gray Boyz claimed you started it and they shot you in self defense. But the cops aren't buying it. Every one of them has a sheet."

"Of what?"

"A record. Of all the bad crap they've done. Make sure you tell the cops the truth."

Greenie pressed his ears back. "The police will deport me back to Deslot." He stuck his nose between the bars.

"I'll miss you." She rubbed his snout. "I got a job."

He pulled back. "Wonderful. Do you owe me a meal now?"

"Any time."

"What type of task are you performing?"

"I'm a sales clerk at a grocer. It's only part time, but it's nice to earn some money. Maybe I can save up and visit you."

"Deslot is too dangerous. But if you wish to travel to my quadrant, you should visit Forbi. My cave-cousin traveled there. It has many species, including humans."

"Forbi it is. I promise, if I ever make enough money I'll take a couch. Here." She shoved a piece of paper between the bars. "That's how to reach me. Vid-mail, the address of the shelter, my work, even my parents' place. Don't forget about me."

"I will never forget you, Dree. You are my friend. On Deslot, you would be my cave-match. That is what we call another Strunjox who is not a direct litter-relative, but is trusted enough to dwell within our cave."

Dr. Lennox entered the room. "Time's up. The Strunjox needs his rest."

"Bye, Greenie."

"Goodbye, Dree." He squished his paw through the bars of his cage. It wasn't a proper hand shake, but it made Greenie feel human.

∞ ◯ ∞

The police arrived the next morning. They released Greenie from his cage, only to place him in a vehicle with bars. The electric engine whined in a most annoying manner. Greenie stared out the window. The sidewalks in this part of the city were crowded with eccentric humans and a variety of aliens. One man wore a cardboard box over his head that looked like a vid. Two Braklez wore full battle armor and metallic helmets. Some humans had groomed their hair in strange colors and shapes. One had tinted his locks the same color as Greenie. They studied each other for a moment, comparing shades through the barred window. Towering fences topped with sharp wire surrounded many of the buildings. Most had security vid-recorders at the entrances.

Greenie groomed himself nervously. The vehicle stopped and the police officers stepped out, their weapons at the ready. He followed them through a series of stark, windowless corridors until he arrived outside another cage, this one tall enough for Greenie to stand in. He walked through the door and waited.

"What's your name?"

He pressed his ears back. "Greenie."

"What kind of a name is that?"

"My full name is Fuzzy Green Monster Number Two."

"You've gotta be kidding," said the man.

"My birth name is Ktraploxjabtuvcta."

"Spell it."

Greenie did so.

"We retrieved your blood from the veterinary clinic, so we have your genetic code on record. An investigator will record your statement about the mauling."

Greenie nodded and sat back on his haunches. "When will I return to Deslot?"

"That's not for me to decide." The officer walked away.

Hour upon hour passed while Greenie sat on the floor of the prison. An officer brought a metallic tray of food. To Greenie's delight they had brought him linguini with meat sauce. The meal reminded him of his first encounter with Dree. After he groomed himself, he curled up in the corner of the cell and whimpered.

The investigator arrived and asked Greenie a long list of questions. He detailed his experience, recalling each incident—the Gray Boyz, the gun, his attack on Stratt, being shot, running away, Dr. Lennox, Dree. He explained every action whether he deemed it relevant or not, until the officer closed her notebook.

"That meshes with Ms. Water's story," she said.

"Who?"

"The teenager from the shelter."

Greenie pressed his ears forward. "Dree?"

The officer checked her notebook. "Yes, that's the girl I interviewed."

What a wonderful last name. The one quality prized most on Deslot. "When will I be deported?"

"The investigation is still pending. You'll serve your sentence on Earth until your case is resolved. The injured youth, Mr. Stratt, will never regain the use of his hand and that will likely affect the ruling. You're going to be in jail for a while."

"And then?"

"You'll be deported." She closed her notebook again.

"Will I get linguini every day?"

"Maybe once a week." She thumb-scanned the room's door lock and left.

During the months that followed Greenie endured more investigation and scrutiny, but in the end the authorities deemed his actions excusable.

The meal service provided linguini every seventeen Earth days. It was not as frequent as the restaurant, but it had more flavor and he did not have to search through the trash. Other aliens inhabited his cell block, including two Braklez who were appealing their sentences. In Greenie's home quadrant, Braklez were permitted to slaughter other sentients under certain conditions— broken rental agreements, failed contracts, and familial interferences. They spent many days meeting with human legal agents.

On Greenie's deportation day, two police officers transferred him to the Couch Teleportation Authority and escorted him to the Economy couch area.

A uniformed Authority man said, "Name?"

"Fuzzy Green Monster Number Two."

"Destination?"

"Deslot," said both the officers together.

"Wait!" came a cry from the long line of travelers waiting for their turn on a couch. Greenie turned around. "Dree!"

He bounded up to her and pounced. They tumbled head over rump, Greenie protecting Dree from harm. "I am so very pleased to see you!"

"Whatever." She wiped a stray droplet of water from the corner of her eye.

"Did I pounce too harshly?"

"I'm fine." She sniffled. "Just glad I got here in time." She reached in her purse and handed him a piece of paper.

The policemen hurried over. One shoved Greenie onto the couch and the other grabbed Dree by the wrist.

"Don't interfere, Miss."

"I'll make it to Forbi," she called.

"I cannot wait," he replied.

The room faded and Greenie closed his eyes. Within moments he was sitting on a sand-brown couch on Deslot. Two Schtems stood waiting.

"Ktraploxjabtuvcta?" said the closest one.

He pressed his ears back. "That is my name."

"This way."

Before Greenie followed, he read Dree's note.

I've been thinking. If they don't like your name, Ktrawhatever, how about suggesting they call you Scary Green Monster Number One?

He pressed his ears forward with delight. She *was* his friend. Feeling a surge of confidence, he stood on his rear legs and walked with his snout held high and proud, ready to face his cave-elders.

DESTINY LIVES
IN THE
TATTOO'S NEEDLE

I dropped from the airship like a rock, praying for my chute to open.

It did.

Below me the airship crashed into the ground. On impact, the fuel tanks erupted, turning night into day. The midsection bounced once and then landed sixty meters east. The navigation cone remained intact, from what I could see at this distance. With any luck, the primary officers had all followed my lead and jumped the moment the aftsection broke away.

My landing jolted me from ankle to jaw, but I remembered my training and hit the ground without snapping any bones.

Although the transport had been dangerously close to the front, I had calculated the flight path myself. The course provided the optimal route to the staging area for our upcoming offensive.

The enemy was out there, filling me with the dread that follows a man in war. Especially a Thinker, like me, for whom torture might be worth the effort.

The Pacificers would arrive soon, honing in on the location of the wreckage, searching for anyone who might have survived.

I inhaled as I scanned around. Tall grasses brushed at my thighs. I accessed my data on the sage grass that grew in this part of Pacifica, a grass so vile that even goats would not eat it. The smell was heady, like moldy bark. An urgent desire to expand my understanding of the parameters of vile and the need to eat, to keep shock at arm's length, pushed me to tear off a piece and sip at the end.

Bile rising, the bitterness spoke volumes on the intellectual brilliance of goats.

To my left, the remnants of a wooden fence lay crumbled along the base of a rolling hill. On the other side, the wild grass looked a little different, more like an intentional crop, though it was overrun with weeds and bushes. I headed for the densest patch, hoping to find some dandelion leaves.

On closer inspection, the fence wasn't rotten so much as carefully broken to appear worn. I climbed over and dropped to all fours. By moonlight, I clawed at a clump of dandelions, brushing the dirt away before I munched on the leaves. The roots were edible, similar to carrots, so I took a bite. Though bitter, they didn't engage my gag reflex like the sage grass had, so I ate two and saved a bunch for later.

I crawled up the hill and, from the crest, a vista opened up before me. The amber hue of the downed airship caught my attention. Remembering the last course I'd plotted before the ship lost containment, and using the stars, I determined the crash site was north of me. The remains burned bright enough to build a partial day-bubble in the darkness. It called men with weapons like moths to a porch light.

I could see them, some on foot and some on troop transports, gathering around the edges of the wreckage. Worse, the unmistakable hands-in-the-air gestures of prisoners added their dejected silhouettes to the crowd.

Damn.

They'd be searching for me. I carried a plethora of secrets, though not on paper. Every airship had a Thinker. We were worth more in a war than ammunition, more than a handful of officers or a battalion of grunts for that matter.

Back to crawling, with my rear a little closer to the ground, I headed down the hill, putting some land in the line of sight between the ship and my position. The fence followed a crooked line all the way to the next ridge and beyond. My instincts told me to ditch the field and go my own way, because where there were fences, there were people loyal to the Pacificers. But the wooden construct's clever design spoke to me. Dandelions, sage grass, and grain in beautiful randomness; no simple farmer would build such a marvel.

Past the second ridge, the fence took a sharp turn to the south and ended at a pile of rocks arranged to conceal an opening.

My nerves turned the corner from worried to hyper-alert while my Thinker curiosity drove me forward. I felt more exposed than

I had on the high ridge. I might as well have shouted, "I'm an Atlanticer. Come and take me. Free torture material, no waiting!" Yet I kept on crawling.

I paused to slow my breathing. I counted ten inhales before movement near the rocks caught my eye. The guy had a bow pointed at me, making me wonder if I had hopped dimensions to a land where guns and grenades didn't win all the playground fights. On my knees, I raised both hands, hoping I wouldn't learn what it felt like to have a shaft of wood sticking out of me.

"I'm unarmed," I said.

He didn't speak. But I could hear the squeak of the bow bending. "I'm not what you think."

Then the twang of release sounded, followed closely by the thump of wood sinking into the dirt less than a meter away.

I waved my arms in the sky. "Okay, maybe I am, but could we calm it down?" I threw the dandelion roots to the ground, to prove my good intentions. "I didn't mean to steal. I was hungry, is all. And I thought them only weeds."

Escape scenarios flowed through my mind like water over falls. Still kneeling, I put both hands behind my head, and said, "Those soldiers by the wreck would give you five, maybe six hundred standards for a find like me, delivered *alive*."

I could hear the man pulling back the bow again. I waited for the twang but it didn't come. Finally, he left the security of the rocks, bow drawn in front of him, and moved out of the shadows into the moonlight. He wore a cape, the hood covering his face with a grim-reaper-meets-black-hole pit of nothing.

"Don't move," he said, though the voice wasn't low or masculine. Either he was a kid, or the woodsman-reaper was a woman. "The next one's aimed at your heart."

Yep, *he* was definitely a *she*. "I believe you." I kept to my knees, my hands still on my head. I wasn't sure if she could see my face, as the moon was behind me, so I turned a bit to the left, revealing the tattoo on my right cheek.

She released the tension on the bow string, but kept the arrow nocked.

I thought about shouting, "I'm a Thinker!" but she had started the cloak-and-bow dance, so I followed her lead.

"Get up," she said. "Keep your hands behind your head."

With the awkwardness of a guy who'd fallen from the sky, crawled around a while, then kneeled for too long, I stood.

"Move towards the door." She indicated with her bow towards the rock-obscured opening.

My need to see her face grew. I scanned my data archives, but couldn't find a reference to this stranger-who-felt-familiar. The cadence of her voice was unique; I was certain I had never heard it before, yet some deep and irretrievable archive within me knew it, knew her, knew my whole life had been building to this moment. Immersed in my data-space, my hands fell to my sides.

"Hands up!"

I jolted back to the moment and returned my now-shaking hands to the please-don't-kill-me position. Close now, her frame was discernible under the cape. She was my height, my build, and she smelled as though baths were rarer than straight fences in this part of the world.

After clearing my throat a couple of times, I found my voice. "If you don't mind me sayin', your fence sings of a Thinker's handiwork. Your husband?"

"Don't have one."

"Oh." More words would've filled the awkward gap, but I'm much better with calculations than I am with women. She moved aside so that I could pass her on my way to the opening. The moonlight found its way onto the tip of her nose. Her skin was as pale as the moon.

Still aiming at me, she said, "Keep moving."

A question lingered at the back of my throat but I didn't allow it to escape. "It's pretty damned dark in there. I don't suppose you brought an emitter?"

I took her silence as a "no."

Shuffling between the rocks, I lost my balance and both hands rushed out of my neutral position to save my head from smacking into the rough-cut walls.

"Forgive me," I said, straightening a little with my hands in the air again. "I was falling." With any luck, my apology would keep her arrow out of my back.

"I'm watching you," she said. Her bow string squeaked in protest as she drew it back once more. For a moment, my mind reached out and plucked it like a violin. My archives chose a low G as the note that should vibrate along its desperate length. Before I continued into the total blackness in front of me, I took a final direction bearing.

I didn't like not being able to read her movements, but her breathing sounded easy, not the quick panting of fear. For now.

The tunnel led to the left, heading northwest. It was dug from the earth and braced with more wood of the same vintage as the fence. The floor sloped at a steep twenty degrees and the top was low, so I had to stoop as I scuffed along. With each step, dust stirred, filling my nose with earthen smells and my mouth with grit.

"How far?" I asked.

The bow string answered in taught silence.

The passage curved to the right, then left again, and I lost one percent of my directional certainty. A part of me needed to know my precise location, as though it could spell my fate. The more westerly a route, the deeper I moved into enemy territory.

We reached a branch and I stopped. She nudged my right shoulder, so I took the right fork, relieved to be heading more east. Thirty steps ahead, the tunnel opened into a room.

The overhead emitter glowed dim green. Wires snaked down the ceiling and met more wires on the far wall. A sideboard held a few dishes. On top sat a thermalater and below was a storage cupboard, for water I guessed. *All the comforts of home*.

"It's nice," I said.

"Kneel down."

I dropped back into position, my hands behind my head again. She released the bow and set it down in the dirt, well behind my reach. Next, she pulled first my left, then my right hand behind my back and tied them together. Neither of us spoke. With her knee, she knocked me face first into the dirt.

My jaw hit hard, hurting like hell. "What was that for?"

"Your choices," she said.

Choices? As far as I could figure, every move since the airship had lost cohesion hadn't been chosen, more like thrust in my face like a sharp poker.

"You could've killed me back there. If you do me here, you'll be stuck dragging my body topside for burial."

"Who said I'd bury you?"

I looked down at the dirt. The greenish light made contrast tricky, but I could make out darker patches in the floor, blood stains maybe, bigger than what would leak out of a rabbit or a chicken.

She moved over to the sideboard. Her hood remained firmly down, hiding her face from mine. I wondered if she was ugly— scarred or savaged by some past indiscretion. Tapping the top of the thermalater, she said, "Can you fix this?"

"Got any tools?"

She opened the sideboard. A water purifier with a full tank took up most of the space. Tools had been tucked in around it, and some hung from the inside of the door.

"I'll need to walk over there."

Her head moved down, slightly, the smallest excuse for a nod I'd ever seen.

Standing was tricky without the use of my hands, but I managed it with a fraction of my dignity intact. "Take the cover off," I said.

Close enough to touch her, my curiosity peaked. The hood was so damned low and the cloth so thick that I'd never get a good look. As she popped the metal top off to reveal the machine's workings, a good stream of green light found its way into the dark-hood zone. For a second, I glimpsed her eyes reflecting the light back. Their intensity could've cut through me more efficiently than one of her arrows.

She motioned with her head for me to focus on the thermalater. I leaned in closer, angling hard to each side to try and see past my own shadow into the gloomy innards. I opened a maintenance file in my mind and called up the schematic for a unit of similar size and power. A quick comparison to what I saw before me revealed the problem.

"There," I pointed with my nose.

She didn't move any closer.

"You see the striped wire leading down to that triangular component with five posts?"

"Step back," she said.

I gave her room to move in and check the workings.

"Yes."

"The wire's corroded. Probably not bringing enough current to the aggravator. Without enough juice, it can't get atoms busy enough to warm anything. You need to replace the wire."

"I've misplaced my spool of spare wire," she said. I could've done without the sarcasm, but she was the one with the upper hand, and mine weren't exactly in offensive positions.

"Take a length from up there." I pointed with my head at the ceiling. "The emitter could move a meter and still throw enough light around the room. And that'd give you two lengths of wire. One for the repair and one as backup."

She nodded.

"You'll need to strip them."

She pulled a knife from beneath her cape. A big butcher's kind of knife that would be awkward to use for close work.

"Got anything smaller?"

She shook her head. In my mind, I imagined the smile on her face, telling me she probably did have a smaller one, but she wanted to play.

"It'll do," I said. Sitting back, I butt-shuffled my way to the far side of the room while she worked. The bigger the distance between me and the knife, the better. The bow wasn't far from her grasp. She worked the wire as though she'd been born an electrician. When she finished, she said, "You found it faster than I predicted."

I shrugged, too afraid to thank her for the compliment in case it wasn't one. Then the scenario unfolded for me. The thermalater had been a test. I'd been so busy trying to think my way out, I'd forgotten to pay attention to the moment.

With the unit fixed, she warmed a cup of water, sipped at it, and then turned her hooded face towards me.

"I miss coffee," she said.

"Don't we all?"

"You're an Atlanticer." Not a question.

If the uniform hadn't given me away, the symbols in my tattoo should've spelled it out for her: my family crest at the center, an old Boston name. My Thinker level swirled around it, and my battalion logo and rank had been burned onto the fringe. At the far right, two outstretched lines tapered to points— the only part of the design that my mother had chosen for me. On my first birthday, when my parents had sent me to be tested, I had scored off the standard charts. Enticed by the reward, they had decided right there in the facility to enlist me. Thinkers were rare, and one of high caliber would eliminate their debt and buy my sergeant father a promotion.

"The men in town would kill me for keeping your kind and collect the reward themselves. Convince me not to eat you."

"Well, ma'am, I helped you fix the thermalater."

"We both know I could've done that alone."

"I have a spare emitter in my pocket. A yellow one. It'd make your room twice as bright."

"Keep going."

I wasn't sure how much more I could reveal that she hadn't already figured out. Whatever game she was playing with me, I wasn't privy to the rules. Eating me wasn't a threat she'd carry through, only another attempt to unsettle me, keep my thoughts jumbled to slow my data access, maybe prevent me from calculating my escape. Whatever her ultimate goal, I had a feeling that I wouldn't be happy with the outcome.

I swallowed, tasting more grit than saliva, and shuddered. Hours ago, I had been happy to hit the ground intact. Now I wondered if maybe I should've prayed for a hole in my chute.

Alternatives flipped by, each one ending with my death. The only variable seemed to be the amount of pain before the release. With nothing to lose, I threw my cards, hell, the whole damned deck, in front of me. "I'm a *high* Thinker. Designed for strategic plotting, navigation, and deployment. I carry more secrets than a four star general. With my reward you could upgrade your equipment and have enough standards left over for a half a side of cured pork."

She smirked. "With a high reward comes increased risk. A better chance I'd be murdered, not paid."

I saw my chance, then, like the flash of data that sparks a chain reaction. "I could help you plan the handover, to ensure you get what's coming to you."

"I don't like the sound of that."

"Neither do I. But I'd just as soon not be eaten, if it's all the same to you."

"There're worse things than being eaten." Her voice turned the corner from hardened to bitter. Her life here — the cave, the well-planned fence, the sage grass — held twists of its own. Whatever the Pacificers had done to her, she wasn't loyal to them.

Another logic spark flashed. My capture was *personal*. I should've slit my own throat instead of following her down this hole.

"What do you want?" I said.

"When the time is right."

∞ O ∞

She left me alone, my hands tied behind my back, wondering when she would return. In the dim green light my sense of time had distorted. I certainly felt exhausted enough for it to be day, but the combination of hunger, tension, and over-thinking had messed with my internal clock.

Though I'd been trained to compartmentalize, storing the most sensitive data below layers of operation manuals and navigational charts, I couldn't help but dwell on the accumulation of secrets I carried. The next strategic offensive, code name *Snowfall*, wasn't due to begin for another six days. With almost a week's notice, the Pacificers could meticulously search for our camp and ambush our battalions. We'd take huge losses, probably half the airship fleet. A dozen of my colleagues and I had spent three months on the strategy; choosing which waves to send on the primary mission, waiting for the weather to be on our side.

She'd heated a bowl of stew in the thermalater and never retrieved it. The aroma of cooked roots and onions, mixed with a lamb-ish meat smell, filled the cave. My stomach growled loud enough it should have knocked dust from the roof.

Saliva poured into my mouth. I hadn't eaten since the dandelions. By now, the stew would be tepid, but I could run the thermalater for another cycle.

Checking behind me, I stood and made my way to the unit. With my hands tied behind my back, I opened the door and stuck a finger in. Not too cold.

Nothing would have made me happier than to lick my finger, but that wasn't going to happen. She'd taken the knife, so I didn't have a way to cut my hands free. Instead, I grabbed the bowl, and then, with shaking legs, slowly kneeled down to set it on the dirt floor behind me.

In my haste to turn around, I stirred up a good-sized cloud of dust, most of which would end up in the stew. But with the kind of hunger spawning in my gut, anything would've tasted damned spectacular.

Leaning forward with my hands behind my back threw off my center of gravity. I knew before it happened that I was going to face-plant into the stew, but it would taste great, so long as I didn't drown. When it splashed up my nose and into my eyes, I was glad that the contents had cooled.

"Want a spoon?" she said.

I should've turned around and looked at her, but I had committed to the food, and at that moment I was a rabid dog who'd chew off any hand that got between me and my meal.

"Greg!"

I spat out a precious mouthful of stew in shock. Gobs of vegetables and sauce stuck to my nose, my chin, and my cheeks. With the slow precision of a well-crafted plan, I turned to face her.

She still wore the cape and her face still hid in the shadow of the hood.

"How'd you know my name?"

She stepped closer, within reach. Pulling a rag from her pocket, she wiped away the mess on my tattooed cheek and pointed at the family crest, then my rank.

All along, I'd assumed the cave was her home. I shook my head, irritated that hunger and her endless games had clouded my thoughts. Her facility must be beneath the hill I'd traversed only *yesterday*. Ten seconds of network access would be all the time she would have needed to search on my tattoo.

She stepped back and crossed her arms on her chest. "How are your wrists?"

"Sore."

From beneath her cape, she pulled the knife free of a leather holder. "Can I trust you, Greg?"

"Seems kind of unfair that you know my name and I don't know yours."

"As a high Thinker, you shouldn't ever contemplate fairness. Only precision, elegance, or logic."

"That's not how it works," I said.

Leaving my hands still tied, she tucked the knife back into its holder. "Lying isn't the way to get what you need."

With that, she grabbed the near-empty bowl of stew and left me alone once more.

I maneuvered myself closer to the wall and leaned against it. I closed my eyes and drew my thoughts deep inside my mind, distancing myself from the pain in my wrists and the congealed stew up my nose.

Embracing data, I floated through my favorites— a list of the first one hundred prime numbers, the coordinates of every evac hospital in Atlantica, the height of every building in Boston. Each idea blanketed me, adding a buffer of comfort between the futility of my situation and the hope of rescue.

A trade was still a theoretical possibility. But she wouldn't dare bring anyone down to her cave. Nor would she reveal her cleverly hidden farm.

The trip for any such exchange would provide my only chance for escape. Whether the kind where I ran and hoped to find shelter, or the kind where I slit my own throat, had yet to be decided. But now I had the spores of a plan.

Decision brought comfort. For the first time since my sudden exit from the airship, I found sleep.

∞ O ∞

I woke with a full bladder. The room was quiet. If the woman was near, she was awfully still.

"Hello?"

She didn't answer.

In the dim green light of the emitter, I recognized her shape. She lay in the dirt, about as far from me as she could get in the room, and appeared to be sleeping.

Every muscle in my back, shoulders, wrists, legs, hell; *all* of me, ached. I needed to stand, walk around, and take a leak, maybe not in that order.

More than anything else, I wanted to pull back that hood of hers and have a look at her face. I couldn't shake the haunting feeling that I knew her.

My mind flashed a thousand warnings. She would never sleep in my presence, especially when she had another place to go, to hide, to do whatever it was she did when she wasn't with me. But despite the glaring risk, I struggled to my feet. My actions would destroy any trust I had built with her. Since she was baiting my response, I needed to learn *why*. I awkwardly made my way across the room. And as the danger volume made my head pound, I knelt on one knee beside her.

The cloak had been cinched tightly around her body, the hood drawn nearly closed, leaving a small opening for fresh air. Her chest lifted and fell with the long, slow breaths of sleep. If she still carried the knife, I might be able to fumble for it, but could I do so without waking her?

Instead, I turned so that my hands were positioned over the hood and craned my neck around to see my way to undoing the string holding it closed at her neck.

"Greg?"

Her voice made me jump. With my mouth as dry as sand, I said, "Yeah?"

"Have you ever had a dog?"

The question threw me. I had expected her to pull out the knife and cut me, or to scold me for touching her. Deceit hadn't worked for me yet, so I followed along. "A shaggy one," I said. "Named *Sol*."

"A male?"

My hands still waited, right above the string. "Sol was a bitch. The kind that never stops yipping, eats through everything that means something to you, and pisses in your bed."

She could've moved by now, sat up, grunted even. Instead, she lay in her prone position. Part of me believed she wanted me to undo the hood. She said, "How long did you keep her?"

"A few months, until the army deemed her gratuitous."

"Do you miss her?"

"I barely remember her." My determination wouldn't last much longer. I bit my lip, grabbed a string, and pulled.

Her hands unfolded from beneath the cloak, the knife in her right. It moved in a slow, deliberate arc, and I braced myself for the pain of a thick hunk of metal sliding through skin, deep into my flesh.

Instead, she cut the bindings holding my wrists.

My arms flopped to my sides with an excruciating round of pain. I couldn't will them to move. Control wouldn't happen for a while yet. But I turned to face her and smiled.

"Thanks," I said.

She set down the knife like a line in the dirt between us. I stared at it then back at her. Without another word, she loosened the hood's string and pulled it down, revealing her face.

Nothing could have prepared me for the shock of her tattoo pattern. Nearly identical to mine.

"Yes," she said. "It's real." After a pause, she added, "Think, Greg. Deeper than you've ever delved before."

My thoughts tumbled, a flurry of questions, repercussions, and analyses until the room wouldn't stop spinning. I swallowed down the bile rising up my throat. After years of war, endless offensives, and then the fall from the sky, I should've simply accepted the reality. But Thinkers analyze. They make sense of the senseless. And what this woman had revealed to me was so incongruous, so unlikely, that my mind and body would not allow the truth of it to sink in.

"*You* shot down the airship," I said.

"I've been waiting a long time for the opportunity. The cost was worth the benefit."

"People died," I said. "The survivors were probably tortured. If they confessed our plans, you might've changed the course of the war."

"I didn't. There's no word of it on the network. This was about you, Greg. Nothing more."

"Thinkers never make a decision based on one parameter. But I don't need to explain that to you, do I?" My fingers graced her left cheek. Her tattoo, the family crest in the center, identical to mine. A cousin perhaps? Her Thinker level swirled around it, with two more loops than I carried. I had never met a thinker ranked that high. The bare skin where her military designations should've been were so pristine, I had to touch them, again and again. How could she have hidden from recruiters her entire life?

She closed her eyes and I could almost hear the data connecting and re-forming. At the far left, two outstretched lines, identical to mine save for the tapers, reached out into the world. Her tapers ended in v-shaped forks. If I could pull my tattoo from my face and place it next to hers, my tips would fit precisely into her forks.

"I thought the marks were like snowflakes," I said. "Never this similar."

"Destiny lives in the tattoo's needle. No other pattern could ever find its way onto me."

"What do we do now?"

She rubbed at my wrists, bringing pain, but also the relief of blood circulation. "Keep digging Greg. *Think.* "

"You didn't answer my question."

"We run. North. I've spent years scouting safe stops and surveying trails. In five days, we can cross into the Northlands. Old Kanada. Neither side will look for us there."

She stood and picked up her bow which had been leaning against the wall near the tunnel. I saw her life as an operatic opus of choices: proximity to the border, high ground, along a logical flight path, the cave setup, the broken thermalater. All strategically placed like chess pieces, while she waited for the first white pawn to move.

"By tomorrow, they'll have finished with the airship," she said. "We can scavenge what we need from the wreckage. Can you walk?"

I shook my legs, one at a time, testing their workability and regretted the gesture. My now over-full bladder felt about ready to burst. With a glance at her for permission, I staggered over to the corner and pissed. After, I dug a glass from the sideboard and slowly downed some water.

Another glassful.

After gasping with relief, I said, "Got any stew left?"

"In the kitchen. And clean clothes. The trip should loosen your muscles."

She reached out a hand and I took it. My thoughts felt fractured, disconnected. I'd gone from fugitive to prisoner to conspirator. "How long have I been down here?"

"Forty-one and a half hours, give or take six minutes."

I nodded. We moved into the tunnel. She pulled a portable blue emitter from her cloak and lit the way. I'd always hated the feel of blue light, as though it shouldn't count as light at all, more like an eerie glow that doesn't belong in the world.

She must've sensed my discomfort because she said, "They draw less power. Makes the batteries last."

I considered explaining to her that I understood the reason, and the feeling wasn't rational. But she knew.

"The facility had blue lights," she said. "Where they tested us. I despise the color, too. It makes me feel vulnerable."

And with her revelation, a compartment door blew outward in my mind. Its contents seeped across every aspect of the knowledge that built Greg. I'd buried every moment with her, from the warm, wet womb of our mother to the final grip of our chubby hands as they yanked her away from me.

"Alyssa?"

She nodded.

I closed my eyes and prayed for the strength to follow her north, to a place where we might find peace. My tattoo tingled at the tips. I opened my eyes to see her cheek lightly pressed against mine. I longed for a mirror, yet I knew the tapers had finally found each other.

∞ O ∞

After I ate, washed, and re-charged with a quick nap, we readied ourselves and ventured outside. Alyssa grabbed fistfuls of sage grass and ordered me to eat them before we approached the navigation cone. To avoid gagging, I chased every swallow of grass with two of milk to coat my throat and gut.

She explained how the chemical composition of the grass blocked my frontal synapses. Otherwise, my proximity to the wreckage and all of these dead soldiers would trigger embedded beacons and call the good guys to extract my still-alive ass before the Pacificers found it.

Just as she'd said, the crash site appeared deserted. Most of the wreckage had been picked over. Alyssa's pack nestled on her back like an old friend. Mine simply made my shoulders ache.

A prisoner of the military machine my entire life — save for that first year — the instinct to regroup, to debrief, clung to me. Loyalty to the cause had never been negotiable, but the thought of a war-free zone with a cabin in the woods brought a level of peace I'd never experienced before.

My *twin*.

I had blocked her existence for so long that acceptance fought against every neuron firing in my head.

"Hurry," she said. "We need to put some distance between us and the site. The grass isn't fail-safe."

I nodded. The gesture was easy, small, neutral. Hardly worth the attention of a mind overflowing with more important thoughts and decisions. But gestures can mean so much more, and this one, unbeknownst to me, would have initiated my homing beacon, if not for the protection of her crop of vile weeds.

To distract me from puking another mouthful of the stuff, Alyssa shared her history. At the age of three, she had outsmarted facility security protocols, an act many tried but few accomplished. Alone, she fled Boston, making her way from culverts to abandoned sheds, hiding from the world while building her own place in it. Living off the grid meant no formal education, no military training, no family, no friends. She had constructed a hole in the world and waited for me to join her.

I spoke of my own life, my service, but it all seemed selfish and heinous compared to the purity of her choices. When I described my former platoon, giving life to the memories of the other Thinkers who trained with me, she said, "They'll come for you."

"But the grass—"

"It only blocks deliberate communication. They might have planted a deep initiative, just in case. To protect their investment."

"Is that all I am?"

"Not after I'm through."

Three hours and seventeen minutes later, a squad of Atlanticers caught up to us. We hid at first, but they outnumbered us twenty to one. We had discussed this inevitability, and dreaded our only course of action.

Alyssa buried herself and slowed her breathing to a near comatose state. I moved as far away from her as possible, and then snapped a twig so they'd find me.

As they cuffed my hands, I embraced a flow of data. It did little to block out my fear and guilt, but its solace was all that I had. I held the data stream close to my heart, a buffer of hope while I braced myself for the long ride back to the life I was now determined to escape.

∞ O ∞

As the airship neared the Pacifica border, we followed my route north to avoid the enemy.

I hadn't seen or heard from Alyssa in two years. I had buried her so deeply within my mind that I often wondered if I had simply dreamed her existence to escape the ugly turn this relentless war had taken.

The enemy shell took us by surprise, so far from the current engagement. As the men and women around me prepared for the crash, I donned a parachute and stepped out an emergency door. My second sudden departure from an airship was infused with an uneasy calm brought on by my constant diligence to check and recheck my exit strategy.

I dropped from the airship like a rock, praying Alyssa would be waiting for me.

Synch Me, Kiss Me, Drop

When my nose stopped aching, I smiled at Rain. She had snorted a song ten minutes before me, and I couldn't quite figure why she waited here in the dark confines of the sample booth.

"Rain?" I said. "You okay?"

"Do you hear it, Alex?" she said, not really looking at me. More like staring off in two directions at once, as though her eyes had decided to break off their working relationship and wander aimlessly on their own missions. "It's so amaaazing."

She held that "a" a long time. I should've remembered how gripping every sample was for her, as though her neurons were built like radio antennae, attuned to whatever channel carried the best track ever recorded. I needed to distract her, get her ass on the dance floor before I ended up with another Jessica-situation. I still had eight months left on my parole.

"Do you hear it?" Rain nudged me, hard on the shoulder. "Alex!" Her eyes had made up and decided to work together, locking on me like I was the only male in a sea of estrogen.

"Yeah, it's awesome," I lied. For the third time this week, I'd snorted a dud sample. My brain hadn't connected with a single, damned note.

Beyond the booth, the thump, thump of dance beats pulsed in my chest. Not much of a melody, but since they'd insisted I check my headset with my coat, I couldn't exactly self-audio-tain.

I grabbed her arm, feeling the soft flesh and liking it. Loving it. Maybe the sample *was* working on some visceral level beyond my ear-brain-mix. "Let's hit the dance floor."

"In a minute. Pleeease."

Over-vowels were definitely part of her gig tonight.

"Wait for the *drop*," she said, stomping her foot.

"Right." I watched her sway back and forth, in perfect rhythm with the dance music coming from the main floor. The better clubs brought all the vibes together, so that every song you sampled was in perfect synch with the club mix on the speakers. When the drop hit, everyone jumped and screamed in coordinated rapture.

I would miss the group-joy here in this tiny booth, with this date who was more into her own head than she would ever be into me. If I could get Rain out on the floor, I could at least feel the bliss, whiff all the pheromones, feel all those sweaty bodies pressed against mine, soft tissues rubbing together.

"Yeaaaah!" She shouted and grabbed my hand, squeezing it. Harder. She leaned her head way back; her eyes pressed shut, her mouth wide open.

The drum beats surged, and then, for a fraction of a second they paused. Everyone in the club inhaled, as though this might be the last lungful of air left in the world and then...

Drop.

But *drop* doesn't say it all. Not even close. Because when it happens, it's like the most epic orgasm of all time and pinching the world's biggest crap-log in the same moment.

Rain opened her eyes and pressed her hand against the side of my cheek. Lunging with remarkable speed for a woman who over-voweled, she kissed me. Her tongue pressed against my lips.

I tasted her. Wanted her. An image of Jessica popped into my head: the look of terror on her face when I accidentally yanked her under.

The euphoria gone, I closed my mouth and turned away from Rain.

"Whaaat?" she said.

For a second, I thought about explaining what I had done to Jessica. Spewed on about how the drop isn't always built of joy. Instead, I went with the short, obscure answer. "Probation."

Rain looked at me funny, like she couldn't quite figure out how the judicial dudes could mess with our kiss-to-drop ratio. Finally, she smiled, and said, "Riiight."

Desperate to avoid another over-vowel, I shouted, "Let's dance!" This time, when I grabbed her arm, she followed along like a puppy.

Scents smacked at us as we pushed our way through the seething mass on the floor. This week's freebie at the door was *Octavia*, some new perfume marketed at the twenty-something set. It was heavy on Nasonov pheromones, some bee-juice used to draw worker-buzzers to the hive. When the drug companies cloned it, the result was as addictive as crack and as satisfying as hitting a home run on a club hook-up.

My nostrils still ached from snorting a wallop of nanites, but scent doesn't only swim in the nose. The rest is all neurons, baby, and I had plenty to spare. Apparently so did Rain, because she was waving her nose in the air like a dog catching the whiff of a bitch in heat. The sight of her made me want to take her and do her right there on the floor.

But *Conduct* was a high-end club. The bouncers would toss us both if they caught us in the act anywhere on the premises, so I kept it in my pants. I still had another two hundred in my pocket. Enough for three more samples. Maybe I'd pick up a track from an indie-band this time. High rotation popular drivel never seized my brainstem.

Unlike Rain.

The beats were building again. This time, with a third-beat thump, like Reggae on heroin. I could feel the intensity from my fingertips to my teeth to my dick. Even if I couldn't hear more than the background beats, I anticipated the drop. Rain opened her mouth again, raised both her hands in the air with everyone else, like a crowd of locusts all swarming together.

Pause.

Drop.

My date kept her eyes closed, her hands on her own breasts as she milked the release for all it was worth. Any decent guy should've watched her, should've wanted to, but I caught sight of a luscious creature, near the high-end sample booth, in the far right corner of the club. The chick was about to slip between the curtains, but she caught me staring.

Her eyes glowed the purple of iStim addiction, reminding me of Jessica. My thoughts drifted to memories.

Jessica had grown up in the suburbs, her allowance measured in thousands not single dollars. The pack of girls she hung with had all bought iSynchs when they first hit the market. The music sounded better when they could all hear the same song at the same time. For the first time in more than a hundred years, getting high was not only legal, but ten times more amazing than it had ever been before. We all lived in our collective heads, the perfect synch of sound and sex.

I should've turned away from the sight of the purple-chick, should've reached out to Rain and kissed her again. Close tonight's deal. Instead, I approached Rain's swaying body, and next to her ear shouted, "Back in five."

She nodded.

Fueled by fascination, and the two hundred burning a hole in my pocket, I headed for the high-end booth.

One of the bald bouncers with tribal tattoos worked the curtains. Yellow earplugs stuck out of both ears, so conversation, or in my case, pleading, wasn't an option. Feeling in my pocket for the two hundred, I scrunched the bills a bit, trying to make the wad appear larger than its meager value, then pulled out the stack in a flash. I had never dealt with this particular bouncer. *Conduct* was more Rain's club than mine, so I hoped the bills would get me past. The guy didn't even acknowledge me, as though he could smell my poverty, or maybe my parole. His eyes stared straight ahead.

My head scarcely came up to his bare chest, so I was uncomfortably close to his nipple-rings, but I held my ground, and pointed at the curtains.

He remained statue-like. More boulder-like. Then a woman's cream-colored hand with purple nails ran from the guy's waist to his pecs and he turned to the side, like a vault door.

Purple-chick stood in the gap between the curtains. Her black dress was built of barely enough fabric to meet the dress code. Her hair stood on end like a teenager's beard, barely there and oddly sexy. She must have dyed it every night, because the stubble matched her eyes and nails. A waking wet dream.

"Come in," she pointed beyond the curtains.

"In what?" I mumbled to myself.

"Very funny."

"You're not laughing."

My body neared hers as I moved past into the sample booth. I carried my hands a little higher than would have passed as natural, hoping to cop a feel of all that exposed flesh on my way by. But she read me like a pheromone and stepped back.

A leather bench-seat lined the far wall of the booth. Three tables were set with products in stacks like poker chips. The first was a sea of purple, tiny lower-case "i's" stamped on every top-forty sample like a catalog from a so-called genius begging on a street corner for spare music. The second was a mish-mash of undergrounds like *Skarface*, *Audexi*, and *Brachto*.

The third table drew me like fire. Only one sample. The dose was pressed into a waffle-pattern, which was weird enough to make my desire itch. But the strangest part was its flat black surface that sucked light away and spewed dread like mourners at a funeral.

Purple-chick watched me stare at it, waiting for me to speak. My mouth kept opening and closing, but I couldn't find words.

Expensive. Dangerous. Parole. All perfectly legit words that I couldn't voice.

I had forgotten my two hundred. My palms must have been really sweating, because what had once been a quasi-impressive stack, now stunk of poor-dude-shame.

With practiced smoothness, she liberated my cash and said, "The *Audexi* works on *everyone*."

Distracted from the waffle, I said, "How'd you know I couldn't hear the last track?"

"Your throat," she said. "You're not pulsing to the beat."

My fingers felt my pulse beating like a river of vamp-candy. Her observations were bang-on. I wanted to illustrate my coolness, or, at the very least, my lack of lame-ness, but all I could manage was, "Oh."

She laughed.

My eyes wandered back to the waffle. I licked my lips.

Grabbing my chin, she forced me to look at tables one and two. "Your price range."

"What's the waffle?"

"New."

"Funny."

She didn't laugh. "Far from it."

"Addictive?" I asked, staring at the purple on the first table. How this woman could work the booth without jonesing for her own product made me rethink her motives.

"The absolute best never are," she said.

"No black eyes allowed in the boardroom, huh?"

She nodded. "Precisely."

I remembered Rain. By now, she'd have noticed my absence.

Purple-chick still held my two hundred. Her eyes locked on mine. "Try the *Audexi*. You won't be disappointed."

Like a Vegas dealer, she shoved all of my money through a hole in the wall, selected an *Audexi* sample from table two, and held it in front of my nose.

I probably should've reported her. All of the clubs had to be careful not to push products hard; end up drawing the cops. But my money was long gone and Rain wouldn't wait much longer.

I exhaled; the moisture turned the poker-chip-shaped disk into a teeming pile of powder-mimicking nanites, and I snorted. For several blinding seconds, I felt as though a nuclear bomb had blown inside my nose. I could feel Purple-chick's hand on my arm, making sure I didn't wipe out and sue the club. Then the song erupted in my mind.

Sevenths and thirds. Emo-goth-despair. Snares and the ever-present bass, bass, bass. Music flowed like a tsunami through a village, grabbing ecstasy like cars and plowing through every other thought except for the tweaks of synths and the pulse-grab of the click-track. The song was building, and all I could think about was finding Rain before the drop.

∞ O ∞

Rain and I danced in nanite-induced harmony until the early dawn. Exhausted and covered in sweat and pheromones, we grabbed our coats and carried rather than wore them outside.

The insides of my sore nose stuck together in the frigid air, a wake-up call for the two of us to don our coats or end up with frostbite. I didn't want to, I was so damned hot and pumped, but I figured I should set a good example for Rain. And the way our night was progressing, I wouldn't have much time to scan my barcode at the parole terminal before curfew.

Jessica's fucking choice of words would be killing my buzz for eight more months.

That fourth of October had been hot as hell. After clubbing, we both stripped and headed into the lake for a skinny dip. Except she wasn't skinny and I wasn't much of a dipper. She'd called me over to the drop and I thought she meant for the lingering song, not the drop-off hidden in the water. When the drop blissed me, I lost my footing and plunged over my head.

"Shit, it's cooold," said Rain.

I snapped back to reality. "Still with the vowels?"

"Screw you." She pushed me away and called a cab with the same arm-wave.

"Don't be that way, baby."

"Now I'm your fucking baby? After ditching me for a dozen drops while you plucked that purple fuzz-head."

"You saw?"

"Who didn't?"

"Sorry. But you gotta admit, you and me, we really synched *after*." I nudged her, maybe a little too hard. "The last sample I snorted was worth it. Right?"

A cab squealed a U-turn and stopped in front of Rain. She started to climb in and then looked up at me.

I shook my head. Shrugged. "Tapped out."

"Fine." She slammed the door in my face and the cab took off up the street.

I stood there, watching my breath condense in the air, its big cloud distorting her and the cab. The cold clawed its way into me, sucking away my grip on reality. The shivering reminded me to at least wear my coat.

As I stuffed my arms into the sleeves, I sniffled, feeling wetness and figuring the cold was making my nose run. But then I noticed the red drops on the ground and the front of my coat. I wiped with one finger and it came back a dark and bloody mass. Dead nanites, blood, snot, all mixed together. Two shakes didn't get it off my finger, so I rubbed the mess in a snow bank and only managed to make it worse.

The nearest subway was blocks away. I should've kept my mouth shut, shared the cab with Rain and then stiffed her for half the fare. But I'd hurt her enough for one night. Hurt enough women for one lifetime.

Jessica had been the closest thing to a life preserver, so I grabbed on. Tripping on the samples, her brain couldn't remember how to hold her breath, or at least that's how my lawyer argued it at the trial.

As I trudged for the subway, I concentrated on not slipping and falling on my ass. I found the entrance, and headed down the stairs, gripping the cold metal handrail, even though my skin kept sticking to it. The *Audexi* sample still pulsed through my system and I couldn't walk down in anything but perfect synch. The song was building to another drop, and I had to make the bottom of the platform before that moment, or I'd become another victim of audio-tainment.

The platform was nearly empty, save for a few other clubbers too tapped out to cab their way home. The Nasonov-pheromone-scent of *Octavia* hung in the air, calling us all home like buzzers to the hive. Much as I loathed their company, I couldn't resist the urge to huddle with the others in the same section while we waited for the train.

Off to our right I caught sight of Purple-chick. She wore a long, black faux-fur coat. The image of her here, slumming it with the poor, was as wrong as a palm tree in a snow bank. She belonged in some limo, holding a glass of champagne.

I tried to break the pull of the scent-pack, but couldn't step far enough away from my fellow losers to get within talking distance of Purple-chick. When the train arrived, I watched her step inside, then waited until the last second before I climbed aboard to make sure we were both on the same train.

The train was so empty I could see her, way ahead.

Standing near the doors, she held a pole while she swayed back and forth. I couldn't figure out why she didn't sit down, especially after a long night at the club. The rest of us were sprawled on benches, crashing more than sitting.

I considered the long trek up to her part of the train, but I didn't trust my balance. Instead, I watched her. Waited until she stepped in front of the doors; announcing her intention to exit.

Once again, I waited until the last second to leave the train, in case she decided to duck back on without me. I could tell that she knew I was watching. Following.

Okay, *stalking*.

She hurried up the stairs. Either she was training for a marathon, or her samples had all worn off, because I couldn't keep up. When she reached the top, she turned around and said, "What?"

Instead of rushing off, she stood there, at the top of the stairs. Waiting.

Her eyes were blue.

Not purple.

I hurried until I stood in front of her, nose to nose. "You took the waffle?"

She nodded.

"Tell me."

She shook her head. "Can't."

"Figures." I turned away.

"But I can show you."

"Yeah?"

"Kiss me," she said.

I sure as hell didn't wait for her to change her mind. We shared it all: tongues, saliva, even our teeth scraped against each other, making an awful sound that knocked my sample completely out of my head.

What filled the void wasn't the pounding of my heartbeat. Or hers. Or any song that I had ever heard. Instead, I could hear her thoughts, as visible as a black blanket on a white sand beach.

"Wow," I said.

Isn't it? Her words, not spoken but thought to me. They reverberated around my skull like noise bouncing in an empty club.

I lost my footing and fell. Down. In. Far away. Suddenly I was six years old and my father leaned over and hauled me back up onto my skate clad feet. We skated together, him holding me, his back stooped over in that awkward way that would make him curse all evening.

"Find your balance, Alex. Bend your knees. Skate!"

I had forgotten how much I loved him. Forgotten what it felt like to be young and innocent, to enjoy the thrill of exercise for its own sake, and feel a connection that didn't cost the price of a sample.

"I love you." But when I looked up at him, he had morphed back into Purple-chick, now Purple-and-blue-chick. She held me, preventing my crash down the stairs.

"Cool, huh?" she said.

"A total mind fuck."

"That's why it's so expensive."

"How much? I mean, you're on the subway, so if I save —"

"In my experience, those who ask the price can't afford it."

"Why me?" I said.

She smiled. "Marketing."

I needed a better answer, so I listened for her thoughts. All I sensed was the wind from another subway, blowing up the stairs behind me.

She turned and hurried for an exit.

"Wait!" My head buzzed, confused by the difference between waffle and real, trapped by the synch-into-memory-lane-trip that lingered on my tongue like bad breath.

Her boots stopped clapping against the lobby of the subway station, but she didn't look back. I was glad of it, because my memories were still swimming in my head. I wanted her to be Dad.

Not Dad. *Rain*. My former date's cute outfit lingered in my synapses, replacing nostalgia with guilt. I wondered if Rain had made it home okay in the cab.

Then naked Jessica filled my head, and it was October again.

"I didn't mean it," I said aloud, my voice echoing against the tile walls. "The high confused it all. I'll do another year of parole. I'll spend my sample money on flowers for your grave. Please, forgive me?"

Still with her back to me, and in a voice that sounded eerily like Jessica's, she said, "What about Rain?"

I shook my head, even though she couldn't possibly see me. "She'll understand."

Far ahead, Purple-and-blue-chick turned to face me. I saw her as *them*, she had somehow merged with Jessica, the two of them existing in perfect synch, like a sample and the club music stitching together; twins in a corrupted womb. They both saw me for what I was, a lame guy who would always be about eight hundred shy of a right and proper sample. Whose love would always be shallow, too broke to buy modern intimacy.

"You've got less than ten minutes to clock in your parole." She started walking again, and I watched her leave; one synched step at a time until she exited the station and disappeared along the ever-brightening-street.

Drop.

Only this drop — waffle-back-to-real — felt like nails screeching on a blackboard. I wasn't in my usual subway station, and I had no idea where to find the nearest parole scanner. The station booth was empty, too early for a human worker to be on duty. The only person in sight was an older woman with the classic European-widow black-scarf-plus-coat-plus-dress that seemed to broadcast; *Leave me alone, young scum*.

So I did.

I hurried onto the street, and looked towards the sun. It was well above the horizon now, but hidden behind a couple of apartment buildings.

"Fuck," I told the concealed ball of reddish-yellow light. "How'd it get so late?"

The judiciary alarm buzzed inside my head.

For a moment, I could feel a drop, the biggest, most intense and amazing drop I would ever experience. The sort of nirvana that people pursue ineffectually for a lifetime. Or two.

I had less than ten minutes until the final warning.

Rushing for the nearest, busiest street, I tried to wave down car after car, hoping someone would point me to the nearest scanner or let me use their phone. I should've brought my portable scanner, but I'd been fixated on getting into Rain's pants when I left.

People ignored me.

Shunned me.

I smelled of trouble. Which, technically, I was. But I didn't mean to be. It wasn't my fault.

It was never my fault.

One cab slowed, but didn't stop. The driver made eye contact, and then rushed away.

"Hey!"

I'm not sure why the cabbie stiffed me. Maybe he read my desperation. Maybe he was Rain's cabbie and he knew I was broke. In any case, he probably broadcasted a warning to his buddies, because the next cab that got remotely close made a fast U-turn and booked.

Choosing a direction, I took off down one street, then hung a right at the next, jogging, skidding, almost falling on my ass. Every direction felt wrong.

I didn't see a single person. No one. Not even a pigeon for fuck's sake. All I needed was a *phone*.

Stopping at a traffic light, one hand on the pole, I leaned over trying to catch my breath. To think.

My heart was pounding now, no synch in sight. The song was long gone, the link to Purple-chick disconnected. No one had my back.

I turned in a circle, then another, scanning far and near for anything of value: an ATM, a coffee shop, a diner, any place where I could access the judicial database. Plead my case.

The final warning buzzed.

"Fuck!" My spit froze when it hit the ground.

I reached full blown panic. My heart tripped like the back-bass before the drop. Only this time, the other side was built of misery not ecstasy.

If only I had paid my cell bill. If only my father was still alive to catch my sorry ass. If only I had lied to Rain, shared her cab. If only Jessica hadn't called it a drop.

I figured I was cooked. So I closed my eyes. But when the pain didn't come, I sat down on the cold curb, and felt the chill seep through my clothes.

I bit my lip. Tasted blood.

The first jolt ripped through my body. I wanted to writhe in pain on the sidewalk, but my body was stuck in shock-rigor. An immobile gift for the cops.

I imagined Rain beside me.

"You're an asshole," she said.

"Sorry."

She morphed into Jessica, her purple eyes wide with fear. "I'm lost," she said.

"Take my hand." I wanted to reach out, but I couldn't move. My fingers looked nearly white in the cold. Her fingers seemed to shiver around mine, as though they were made of joy, not flesh. Then she touched my hand and I knew in that moment that life existed outside of stimulation, in a place where reality wasn't lame or boring. Life danced to an irregular rhythm that couldn't synch to any sample.

She let go.

The judiciary pulse jolted again. I flopped to the pavement, distantly aware that my skull would remind me for a long time after about its current state of squishage.

The parole-board must have lived for irony, because the jolt lasted for so long that I *welcomed* the release. A pants-wetting, please-make-it-stop, urgent need for the end.

Drop.

TATTOO INK

"I've always wondered how tattoos season the meat."

A whimper escaped, marking her first abandonment of hope. Tattoos of snakes and dragons blanketed her naked body. She squirmed against the chains.

"What do you want from me?" Her lips quivered, but her eyes didn't relinquish moisture.

I stroked her calf, deciding on the primary bite point. "I bet you didn't cry when they inked you." Her skin, seasoned with salt and musk, burned against my fingertips.

"I can pay," she said. "If you release—"

I licked the two-headed dragon on her thigh, tasting curry and ginger with a splash of latex.

My incisors sliced through the first layer. The ink tasted of lime, metal, and licorice.

Fascinating.

GRAY LOVE

The day I saw the gray lady, I froze. Stopped running along Muskoka Road 15, dead in my tracks. She was walking along the gravel shoulder, carrying a road kill carcass. She held it out in front of her, like an offering, or a lunch tray in a cafeteria. At first it creeped me out; turned my blood to cherry freezies, the ones I would suck on back when I ate chips for breakfast and ran for fun instead of exercise.

The whole time she smiled with a big, wide grin. I figured she was distracting me from her color. The instant I eyed her, I had to look twice. Three times even. She looked like cement; as gray as old bacon.

Her smile held me, made me wait near the sign that says, "Road ends in 0.5km" deciding between heading back to the cabin or sprinting towards town. A cloud moved away from the sun and the yellow reflections from the sign painted her skin, melting the freezies. In the golden light she looked pretty, a whispered kind of beauty that fails if you look too carefully. We walked closer to each other and she set down the carcass. With every step she made me all hot and creepy-desperate. I wanted her. Right then. Right there. And I had no idea *why*.

When I take a woman, I'm usually slow, careful, the town chicks like me that way. But urgency took over and I grabbed my usual slowness and squashed it like a mosquito. A messy swat too, the kind that leaves a big splat of blood because the damned bitch already tasted me.

I needed to seize the gray lady and kiss her and tell her my life story. Maybe in that order. She wanted me too. The grin said it all. "Now, baby. Undress me *now*."

I stumbled in the high grass as my ankle twisted over a rock, ruining my slick come-on. She wouldn't want me clumsy and wounded. She wanted me fresh and snappy, hip like a twenty-something, but with the added bonus of my thirtyish *experience*. Since she kept on smiling I kept on limping.

When I was close enough to touch her, I saw that she was older than I'd first thought. Forty maybe. She turned away, well more to the side. Gave me the profile. I saw the mark on her neck— a big purple bruise with yellow and green swirls. It looked like someone had stepped on her neck and held her down. But then I wondered if it was a hickey because it was in the right spot. I could suck neck with style back in high school.

The bruise called to me. It wanted me to touch it, taste it, smell it. So I leaned in close, put my nose right up, and snorted back a big whiff.

The smell was unforgettable: creamed corn, fresh beer, and granny-soap. I didn't think bruises had a smell, but hers did. Something about being gray, like it gives you permission to rewrite the rules.

I stepped back and looked her up and down. She was thin, but not skinny. The kind of woman who had come into her stride, and who passed up dessert but still ate French fries. I put my hand on her waist, above that oh-so-curvy-hip spot that jeans turn into a dream on a woman. She faced me and turned down the wattage on her smile. Only a quarter turn on the dial, but I felt the mood shift. I wondered if she didn't like me up close, or maybe she'd changed her mind.

She opened her mouth, like she was gonna speak, but she didn't. I waited, in case she was drawing out the moment.

Nope. So I said, "I'm Ray."

"Hi, Ray."

"I want you."

"I can tell."

"Can I kiss you?"

"Please."

I leaned in and our lips touched. I wanted to close my eyes, even though I'm not a closed-eye-kisser, but my body was block-ing the yellow glare from the sign and she looked even grayer this close up. But something about the smell of creamed corn and beer made me keep staring, eyeballing her every pore.

Her lips were dryer than dead flies. I thought they'd be cold or slimy, but they were scratchy. Rough. I pressed in, trying to share my spit, to wet her up.

She opened wider and her tongue touched mine. I shook, like a jack pine in a winter wind. I thrust my own tongue into her, reaching, probing, and marking my territory between her teeth. My hands found her hair and I leaned in, harder. I took turns pulling back for air and then diving back in, finding different ways to suction-lock our mouths. I switched nose sides, I turned sideways, then upright, then the other way.

She tasted like candy. The kind that you wear around your neck, biting one piece after another, until all that's left is a sticky elastic. I bit her lip, only a little, but enough for her to pull back.

"Ray?"

"I'm sorry."

"Never say you're sorry."

I ran my hands down her neck, along her shoulders and forward. Her knockers were big enough to enjoy, but not huge. Not like a stripper or a bingo junkie. I squeezed and she moaned.

That started the snow blower. I didn't want to make a mess so I cradled her in my arms as I lowered her to the dirt.

She kissed me all the way down. I took that as a *yes*. An alarm bell in the back woods of my brain yelled something about latex, but I plunged ahead.

Her belt loop, her zipper, and then her jeans slid into the grass. I hauled her shirt up and over her head to get the full view. Grayness, everywhere. Like elephant skin, but not as hairy or wrinkled. I caressed the gray, up and down; touching her any-place I could, mostly in the places that made her moan because that kept my mind off the weirdness of it.

I kept inhaling her, pressing my nose against her, and every spot brought another surprise. Wet wool mittens, day-old donuts, copy-machines, new cars, cut grass, and rubber bands. She was a buffet line of scents and I wanted to try everything.

My nose was getting overloaded so I licked her. That started another round of moaning, and most of it wasn't coming from her.

I yanked my sweaty shirt and running shorts off, and tossed them into the woods. The grass brushed against my skin, rough but so alive. I was glad for the height of it when I took off my boxers. I didn't want a neighbor driving by and catching a glimpse of my ass. The bugs were at me, but I didn't care. I could scratch the itches later.

We cupped and found each other. My dick danced like a pro, but the DJ played a short song because it was over quick.

Gray lady nudged me off. I flopped onto my back and she snuggled close, resting her head on my chest, playing with the hairs, twisting them, grooming them. The after was better than the big moment. We lay there for a long time, touching, remembering.

"What's your name?" I asked.

She moved her head off my chest and pressed it against the grass, once, twice, three times. Each thud a bit louder than the one before.

"Never mind," I said.

Her head settled back on my chest. I inhaled. Her hair smelled like moth balls and dusty books. I buried my nose, going deeper. Hair spray and bug repellent. I sniffed around for a better scent, that didn't remind me of dark basements, but the good smells had all faded.

Gray lady smiled. I couldn't see it, but I could hear it somehow. She hummed like an old TV. But her gray color was darker. Not black, but on the road to it.

"I'm glad," I said.

"Me too, Ray."

"Tomorrow?"

She shook her head.

I was bummed, but the particulars of her deal became clear in my mind. Gray lady was a onetime girl. No repeat customers. No refunds. No exchanges. The grass rustled in the wind. Bugs buzzed, flew past, and bit me. I kissed her shoulder. Then her neck, on the other side, the unbruised one. I found a spot that tasted like leftover boiled potatoes. God, I love potatoes. Then it was gone and I could smell axle grease.

"I..."

I couldn't say it. I wanted to, but she didn't say a word. And a one-way L-word is worse than silence. So I closed my eyes.

"You're sweet, Ray."

I drifted off. I dreamt in gray. And when I woke up she was gone. The grass was squished down beside me; most of her smells forgotten. My skin was cold so I reached for my shirt, but my arm wouldn't work. My eyes did, so I looked down at my naked body.

Every inch of me was cutlery gray. The bugs were on me too, but not the kind that bite. Nope, these were the kinds that eat rotten meat. Maggots and beetles and shit.

The crows flew down too, they wanted my eyes. It was then that I realized I wasn't seeing the whole picture in the usual way. I had an overhead, top-down view. A postcard shot of the ditch and me.

I had my chance and I blew it. I even started to say it, but didn't finish. Got as far as the "I" but the "Love" part didn't make it out of my mouth. I should have offered the sentiment to her, like she had offered me the road kill carcass. Maybe that would've saved me.

She left me there as a reminder to say what you feel.

I never looked good in gray.

THE TEAR CLOSET

My father was a thief who stole my mother's soul.

The larceny began one night behind the soda shop. Mom thought herself ugly, so when he sweet-talked her, she shut her mind and allowed her heart to sop up the whimsy, her future pilfered by the foreign delights of lust.

They were married in a private ceremony. Grandpa Randall might as well have signed the papers himself. His faith forbade an unwed daughter becoming a mother.

My entrance into the world nearly killed her. I fussed in the nursery while Mom recovered. She begged to hold me, but the nurses pronounced her too weak. My father worked, but not in the sales office like he told Mom. No, he worked his baby maker inside one warm hole after another on the bed with the iron-bar headboard in our basement apartment. His mother washed the sheets for him before Mom and I arrived home.

Within a year, my father abandoned the secrecy of his sinful wanderings. Mom cursed his name and he beat her for it. I screamed continuously. Some people don't remember being babies, but I cannot forget how the salty smell of tears filled my nose like the putrid stink of brackish pools on a derelict beach.

∞ O ∞

On my first day of kindergarten, my father accompanied me to school. I remember he handed me a paper bag with a bread-and-butter sandwich and an overripe banana inside. He tilted his head and smiled.

"Mabel," he said.

"Yes?"

"You're going to meet plenty of boys in school. But I want you to remember that I'm your man."

The bell rang and the parents hugged their children. My father got down on one knee and kissed my ear. It made a loud slapping sound, and the suction from his mouth tugged on my eardrum with a painful pop. I heard his breathing, fast like he had been running. As the teacher called us in, he whispered, "Forever."

The smell of his breath, coffee and sugar, lingered in my nose. I tried to erase him from my mind, but he seemed to hover behind me.

I threw up that first day; right after Miss Gage brought us to the carpet for story time. The pungent odor of vomit chased my father's stink away. The custodian cleaned the mess and Miss Gage sent me to the office. The secretary called home. Mom picked me up.

"Does your stomach hurt?" she asked.

I shook my head.

"Were you scared of the teacher?"

"Miss Gage is nice."

"Oh."

I thought she would say more, perhaps ask about my fear, but she tugged my hand and led me home. She cooked pancakes from a mix, using water instead of milk because the milk truck skipped our apartment when we couldn't pay. We didn't have syrup, only butter. Grandpa Randall brought us butter on Sundays on his way home from church where he prayed for us.

Before my father returned home that evening, Mom cradled me close and wrapped a soft blanket around us— a pink one with ribbon sewn on two sides. "I want to show you a secret," she said.

She took me inside the broom closet beside the fridge. "Here," she pointed at the far wall. With a hard nudge of her shoulder she pushed and the wall opened inward.

I stood with my mouth open.

"Sit," she said.

I crawled into the small space and settled on the floor with my blanket around my shoulders. It smelled of her. She snuck in beside me and closed the door.

In the menacing darkness, she said, "Watch."

Slowly, hundreds of pinpricks of amber light glowed and brightened. When they burned vibrant enough for me to see

Mom's face, they began to fall, inching to the floor where they trickled into a pile around us.

She reached out and cupped a tiny handful of amber brilliance. The light reflected on her cheeks and in her eyes. She was crying. I rarely saw her cry.

"These are my tears," she said. "I keep them safe here, in my tear closet, so that your father won't find them. Would you like to share them?"

I nodded.

"Take a few in your hand."

I grabbed for the pile and the lights scattered.

"Slowly, Mabel. Be gentle."

She guided my hand to the floor. I breathed slowly and tried not to wiggle. A few lights nudged at my fingertips and then moved away.

"Easy," she said.

The lights snuck close once more and moved into my palm. I felt sadness, as though my world had filled with sorrow and I had to cough it out of me. Tears filled my eyes and I encouraged them, crying and sobbing. My entire body shook.

Mom hugged me, still holding the blanket over my shoulders. She cried too, not vehemently, but more than I had ever seen.

I don't know how long we wept, but when the two of us stopped, my body drooped with relief. All around me, amber lights sparkled, pulsing bright, then dim, then bright again. So many tears. The closet warmed from their brilliance.

"Mom?"

"Yes?"

"Do you come here a lot?"

"Not much."

"It's beautiful."

She nodded. I held her and closed my eyes. When I finally opened them, the lights had all faded away.

"We'd best get back," she said.

∞ O ∞

Mom walked me to school for the next two months. But when the pancakes thinned, and my lunch turned into a slice of bread, she took a job with the phone company. She reported at half past seven, so my father had morning duty. He would hug me and rub his unshaven face against mine to awaken me. The whiskers burned, scratching my skin like hundreds of dirty needles. The first time he did it, I told him it hurt.

"Love hurts," he said.

"Why?"

"Because men are strong and women are weak."

"Mom's strong."

He glared at me while he chose a skirt and blouse from my closet, sniffing them before he tossed them on the bed. "Get dressed."

I changed while he made my lunch. Then he brushed my hair, yanking out the tangles and swearing while I bit my lip. After he finished my second pigtail, he sniffed my hair.

I hated his nose most of all.

∞ O ∞

I remember how much I loved Sunday mornings because I would wake with Mom snuggled next to me. We would take our time rising and talk about what I had learned in school during the past week. I considered telling her about my father's sniffing, but I didn't want to waste our time together with sad thoughts.

Most Sundays, my father slept late and spent the afternoon bossing Mom around. She would bring him his coffee and aspirins, and make as nice a Sunday dinner as she could afford.

One Sunday in June, we woke early and Mom showed me how to make pancakes. My father wasn't home yet, so we giggled and played. Mom put red food color in the batter so we would have pink pancakes for our girl-time.

We sat down to eat them, heaping extra butter on.

Then he arrived.

"My head is splitting," he said. "Where's my coffee?"

"I'll put it on," said Mom. "The pancakes are ready."

"I'm sick of pancakes." He slapped her hard across the cheek. She fell from her chair at the kitchen table, her elbow catching a glass on the way past. It smashed on the floor.

"Clean your mess," he said.

When she stood, the broken glass cut her feet. She didn't cry out. Her feet left bloodstains on the floor.

"Now you're making it worse." He slapped her again. When she fell backward, the glass cut her hands.

He pointed a finger at her. "Don't cry. I can't stand your crying. You're so *weak*."

She shook her head and reached for a cloth to clean up the shards.

I hurried to the broom closet and brought Mom the dustpan.

She took it from me. "Go to your room. Stay there. I don't want you cut."

Stepping carefully in my slippers around the glass, I did as she said. I left my bedroom door open a crack and watched her sweep the glass and dump it in the garbage. When the floor was clean, she rinsed her hands and feet in a basin, vigilantly checking for shards. My father paced in the living room, complaining that she was taking too long with his coffee.

She needed to cry. I could feel it filling my head as though a piece of me was still in the closet where the tears waited. I added my own fear to their power and willed her to sneak inside.

The coffee percolator hissed and gurgled as Mom poured the steaming liquid into a mug. She hurried it to my father.

"Finally," he said. After taking a sip, he looked up from the couch and caught me watching.

"Shut your door."

I did. I wanted to slide the bolt lock, but feared his anger. Tears tingled under my fingers. I pressed my ear against the door and listened. Between his slurps, I heard the gentle clunk of the tear closet's secret door.

"Where's the cream?" He slammed the cup down. "Woman?" His footsteps moved towards the closet. "What are you doing in there?"

A slam.

Millions of tear pricks jabbed all over my body. Mom begged him for mercy. I didn't dare open the door. Instead, I sat in the far corner of my room, hugged my knees to my chest, and sucked on my pink blanket while I rocked back and forth. He yelled and he hit, but he never once mentioned the tears. Their pain kept worsening all over me until, exhausted, I collapsed and slept.

Mom left for work before I woke the next morning. While I dressed, my father sniffed my discarded clothes, including my underpants. I couldn't understand why anyone would want to smell something that had touched my bum.

I looked up at him and he smiled. But it wasn't a happy smile. I wanted to cry, but the tears wouldn't come.

As he yanked a comb through my hair, I asked, "How long will Mom work for the phone company?"

"Until the day she dies."

∞ O ∞

In November of the same year, Sean Pensky arrived in our grade-two class. He was about an inch taller than me, skinny, and he had a bad mouth. It always said stuff he didn't mean, or so he told Miss Howard.

One day at recess, he ran up to me on the playground. I was skipping by myself, and he yanked the pink rope out of my hand and said, "You stink."

"Do not."

He threw the rope over the fence onto the baseball diamond where the big kids played. "Do too."

"Get it back."

"No way."

One of the big kids grabbed my rope, then another joined in, until they were playing tug-of-war. The game ended when it broke.

"Thief!" I shouted at Sean.

"I didn't steal anything. Your stupid rope's right there."

I shoved him. When he shoved me back hard, I fell down and scraped my knee. A teacher took me to the nurse's office to slap on green goo that smelled like the dark hallway at the hospital where Mom would get stitches. The office called home.

My father picked me up. He stared at my knee. "Looks sore."

I nodded.

"I'll kiss it better."

"It doesn't hurt that bad."

He signed me out and smiled at the secretary. She smiled back. He covered the wedding ring on his finger.

As the school doors clanked closed behind us, he said, "I'll kiss it better at home."

He kissed more than my knee. He touched my private places and smelled them too. His whiskers scratched and scraped me. His tongue dirtied me. I wanted to cry, but I couldn't. He had stolen my tears, just like Sean had stolen the skip rope.

The next day at school, I hunted for Sean at recess. Before he spoke, I punched him. He collapsed like an old shoe. I kicked him. He screamed and cried, begging me to stop.

"I'll steal your tears," I shouted at him.

The principal dragged me into the office and made me tell my story. He said that stealing my skip rope was wrong, but hurting Sean was worse.

"Is there anything wrong at home?" he asked.

"My father loves me."

"Your Mother's on her way from work."

"Mom?"

He nodded.

I waited in the office. When she arrived, she stared at her shoes and apologized to the principal. They called Sean down from class. I apologized to him in front of everyone. Mom signed me out and handed me a rectangular, yellow ticket.

"We're going for a ride," she said.

We walked from the school in the opposite direction of home. Mom took me to a stop where a red bus picked us up and took us downtown. From there, we walked to the phone company.

"You can stay here for the rest of the day."

"Really?"

She nodded.

I sat on a stool beside Mom. She wore a headset and answered all sorts of questions. Her voice sounded full of hope. Not sad or hurt like at home. When she had a break, we walked to the ladies' room holding hands.

I recall that afternoon so clearly, even now. Pure elation, as though a weight had been lifted from us both. On the bus ride home, a tear slipped down her cheek.

"You found your tears?" I said.

She nodded. "Your father didn't steal them. They're safe."

She cried and hugged me and I cried too. We wept so much that a lady sitting a few rows up came over and asked if she could help.

"We're more happy than sad," said Mom. "Glad to be together."

The lady gave us a funny look, but left us alone. Mom and I stayed on past our stop. After a while, the driver parked the bus. He opened the front and back doors, and then approached us.

"End of the line. You have to get off or pay again."

"Oh," said Mom.

I thought she would pay our fares, but she didn't. Instead, we exited by the back doors and started walking, but not towards home.

"Where are we going?" I asked.

"Away."

"For how long?"

"Forever."

I asked her if that was the same as how my father had said *he* was my man. Forever. She stopped walking and sank to the ground. Her skirt slipped up, showing her panties. I leaned forward to smell them.

"What are you doing?" she asked.

"He sniffs my underpants, to make sure they're right."

Her face turned white, like the chalk they painted on the grass · at school for the baseball diamond. Her hand shook as she stood and pulled me beside her.

"Come on," she said. "Hurry."

I wanted to ask her where we were going, but I don't think she knew.

The sun dropped low in the sky. We continued walking. Mom limped and said her shoes hurt her feet. I told her to take them off, but she wouldn't.

The streetlights came on, illuminating the bridge over the valley. Brown water, the color of Mom's high-heeled shoes, flowed far below. Miss Howard had taught us the name of the river at school, but I couldn't remember it. Mom walked us right to the center of the long bridge. We were up so high, I felt like a bird. The wind roared in my ears. Cars sped past on the road beside us. She stopped, gripped the railing, and looked down.

"Isn't it beautiful, Mabel?"

I nodded.

"It's a long way down," she said.

"I'm scared."

She sat down with her back against the railing and said, "Me too."

The cold made me shiver, so she wrapped her arms around me. "I wish I had my pink blanket," I said.

"Sorry, sweetie. There wasn't time to get it." We sat in the middle of the bridge, shaking and silent.

"I'm done," she said. "I can't go back."

"Home?"

She nodded. She had her tears and I had mine. She didn't want anyone to take them.

I started crying. "Why does love have to hurt?"

She wiped the tears from my cheeks with her fingers and dried them on her skirt. Her hand felt as cold as the basement cement floor.

"Love only hurts when you don't deserve it." She stood and leaned over the railing. "I'm too ugly to deserve love."

"*I* love you, Mom."

"You deserve better. We've come here to hide our tears. Climb up here and I'll show you where we'll keep them."

I stood. The wind hit me hard, and I almost fell into the traffic.

She put one leg over the railing. "Come on, Mabel. The tear box is right here." She pointed past the railing, where I couldn't see.

I stood on my tiptoes and leaned over. Hovering below the railing, a swarm of her tears drifted together, their amber light glowing.

She swung her other leg over the railing. "Come on."

I grabbed her hand, but I couldn't will myself to climb. I shook my head.

"It's okay," she said.

"No, Mom. *Please.*"

She pulled on my hand. I dug my feet in and held on. She swayed in the wind, twisting my arm until I thought it would pull off. My hands were sweating, and her grip slid.

The cloud of tears enveloped her. Poised for a heartbeat, our eyes locked. Then she and the amber lights disappeared over the side. She didn't scream on the way down. I knew she had found the bottom when I heard a faint thud on the wind.

I sat. On something. I pulled it out from under me. She had lost one of her brown shoes. The thin heel reminded me of Sean and his skinny legs. It smelled of the stockings Mom hung in the bathroom on Sunday afternoons.

For a long while I shivered and waited. For what, I didn't know. My father had stolen her from me sure as he had stolen her soul. He had taken all that we had.

Three times, I stood and leaned over the railing.

I thought about throwing her shoe over. She needed both shoes. It was too dark to see to the bottom of the ravine, but I thought I could see a dim orange patch of light below. Her wide eyes kept flashing in my mind, afraid, determined, alone. My teeth chattered in my mouth. Maybe the tears had helped her fly away? I tried to lift my leg to climb over, but I lost my balance and fell backwards. Strong hands grabbed me.

A man.

"What are you doing out here alone?"

I stared up at his broad shoulders and smooth face. "Nothing."

"Where do you live?"

I should have lied, should have run and never looked back. Instead, I recited my address as I had learned to do at school. The man walked me home. My father was there, with liquor on his breath and anger in his eyes.

"Ran away, did you?" he said. "The principal phoned."

The man said, "I'll leave you to it, then." He left us, taking hope with him.

∞ O ∞

The night after the funeral, where we said goodbye to Mom, I had a terrible nightmare. I was falling and falling for what seemed like forever. When I woke, I could barely catch my breath.

My father's snores drifted into my room. Mom used to make me a snack whenever I woke from a nightmare, so I tiptoed across the cold basement floor into the kitchen. When I opened the fridge, I feared the light would wake him.

It didn't.

Inside was a cake the neighbor had given us to help with our sad time. Mom had baked a cake for my birthday once. She had stuck candles in the middle and told me to make a wish and then blow them out. The first wish that had popped into my head was for a puppy. But I never got a puppy.

I set the cake on the counter and took out a knife. With all of my heart, I closed my eyes and wished for tears. The knife slid easily through the rich chocolate frosting. It was brown, the color of the river and my Mom's shoe. As I glided the knife free of the cake, I stared at the goo clinging to the blade. Inhaling deeply, the chocolate smelled as rich as cream and as pungent as the dirt surrounding my mother's grave.

I lifted the slice of cake onto a plate, found a fork, and approached the broom closet. I had wanted to sneak into the secret part since mom had left us, but my father had always been watching, touching, sniffing. The back wall squeaked as I shoved it inward. I stopped and listened.

My father snored on.

I crawled into the closet, sat, and tasted the heavy frosting while the cake melted on my tongue. As I raised a second forkful, amber lights began to arrive. The chocolate tasted salty; I found tears on my face.

I licked my fingertips, one at a time, tasting salt and chocolate together. As I pulled each finger free of my mouth, the lights scurried out of the way.

"No," I said to them. "Don't leave me."

They did the opposite. They doubled and doubled again, adding more light to the small space. I remembered how my mother had held me here, how her love had comforted me. I missed her so much.

"Mom?" I said to the tears.

Some hung silent in the air around me, others pooled in my lap and on the floor nearby. Though they warmed the small space, I still felt cold.

"I miss you."

On and on the tears arrived, and with each new volley I wept. I cried as quietly as I could so my father wouldn't hear. "Please come back to me, Mom. I need you."

I could almost hear her voice, the way she would say, "I love you, my sweet Mabel," right before she tucked my sheets tightly around me for sleeping. I think the tears missed her, too.

For a long time I lingered in the tear closet, sobbing alone until I thought I would dry up like a shrunken apple. "Why does forever have to be so long?" I asked the lights.

They gathered around, hovering closer, until they seemed to fade inside of me. I lost sight of them. My sadness lingered, but my crying lessened, turning to whimpers and then shuddery sighs.

Exhausted and with my empty plate in hand, I crawled out of the closet. The clang of the dish in the sink seemed louder than a glass breaking. The knife, still covered with cake and frosting, lay on the counter where I had left it. The shape of it appealed to me so I picked it up.

Holding it made me feel brave.

Determined and armed with the dirty knife, I walked into my father's room. He was still asleep, sprawled half in and half out of his blankets. His head lay on an angle against the iron bars of the headboard. Without thinking, I held the blade above his nose. Would it slide as easily through him as it had through the cake?

He awoke and looked from me, to the knife, to me. His eyes opened so wide I thought they might get stuck like the glass eyes on a doll. For the first time in my life, I saw fear there, as though my father was actually afraid of *me*.

"What're you doing, Mabel?"

I couldn't answer, couldn't move. As the seconds ticked past, fear left his face. The contempt he had always shown for Mom took its place. With a sneer, he slapped at my hand. The knife flew across the room. It sprayed bits of icing and cake as it tumbled into a pile of his clothes on the floor. In that moment, I understood my mom's years of terror.

Afraid, I stood there, staring at him. He sat up and drew his hand back, readying a violent, backhanded slap.

The tears began to drift out of me, swarming, and then advancing towards my father. In huge clumps, they landed on him, making the faintest of plunking sounds as they hit.

He swatted at them, swiped them, scratched them. They eluded his every effort. I watched his hands with fascination, stunned. Despite his strength and size, he couldn't hurt these tiny lights.

When I looked back at his face, he was crying. Huge tears streaked his face. His nose, that horrible, awful nose, dripped snot in two matching ribbons over his lip.

I knew how much he hated crying. I couldn't help but stare at him as he did.

"Get 'em off. Get 'em off me." He kept repeating it, over and over, while he cried and swatted at the tears; his eyes as wide as Mom's had been when she learned to fly.

I found my voice. "Love hurts. But not because men are stronger than women."

I took a step back and then another. When I was far enough away that he couldn't touch me, the tears around him began to fade. My father continued to scrape and swat at them, even when I couldn't see them any longer. A small army of tears stayed around me, on my arms, my legs, my hair, ready to defend me if he got too close.

I turned my back on him and started for my room, but stopped to face him once more. "Love hurts because you don't deserve it."

∞ O ∞

The next day, when he walked me to school, my father kept his distance. The few times that he ventured too near, or tried to sniff me or touch me, he would start to cry. Though I couldn't see any tears on him, my father continued to brush and swipe at his arms and legs and scratch his skin raw. I wore the tears like a blanket, my amber blanket, bigger and brighter than the pink one my mother had shared with me.

When Miss Howard saw us, she came over.

"I'm so sorry for your loss," she said to him.

He nodded and wiped another tear with his sleeve. Without answering, he started for home.

The bell rang, but when I tried to hurry for the line, Miss Howard said, "Wait, Mabel."

She knelt down in front of me. "If you need time alone, or to call home, just ask."

"Okay."

She nodded. "Your father is so sad. He must have really loved your mother."

"I don't think so," I said.

"Why would you say such a thing?"

I shrugged. "Because they aren't his tears."

"Whose tears are they?"

"They used to be Mom's, but now they're mine."

HELL'S DEADLINE

Every day in hell sucks. I wake on the hard cold floor of the empty bedroom, blinding sunshine streaming through my curtainless window, and proceed to roll over into a patch of my own vomit. Never fails.

The countdown on the wall advances. Today's marked as day thirty of thirty.

The shower doesn't work, so I rinse myself and my vomit-stained clothes with the water from the toilet.

I squirm back into my soggy clothes and head for the kitchen. The bread smells of mold but it isn't blue. I shove two slices in the toaster and crank the indicator up. They pop up light and soggy. Doesn't matter how many times I toast the bread, it won't get any darker.

Hell's all about the details.

The S-man's left a note. I'm careful opening it, but I slice my finger on the envelope anyway. The boss has a sense of humor that keeps on giving.

Dear Debbie:

Good luck. I'm rooting for you.

I head for the door and grab the key from the hook on the wall. I've scribbled "Jamie" above it in black marker, but it's not my brother's key.

Maybe it's the trigger. The S-man blocks me from remembering much between attempts. One day, I *will* figure out the puzzle; decipher whatever it is that will flip the deciding switch and earn myself a ticket north.

Outside my cabin, the gravel of the path crunches under my feet. The air's humid and still, like the worst day of summer.

Reeks of exhaust too, though I don't hear or see any cars zipping past on the road beyond the swamp.

The gravel trail leads to the same place no matter which direction I follow. The S-man does enjoy a good mind-fuck. Today, I head right.

The smells around me thicken; sap laced with rotting leaves. The birch and poplar trees close in until the light vanishes and I can't see past my hand, stumbling through the brush, hearing the growls and padding paws of the creatures who track me. My nerves ignite.

I stumble on until the woods brighten. I've reached the pine stands. Towering poles grow straight toward the reddish sky, planted in endless rows.

I follow the fourth corridor to my left. Between the giants, the lower branches are broken or dead, protruding like sharpened talons. They scratch my face and arms, dig into my legs, tear my pants.

I duck past mammoth trunks, picking one aisle then another, searching for safe passage. No matter how many times I change direction, I always reach the shed as the sun's setting.

Mom's screaming.

I don't want to use the key, but I do. Gotta fix things so I can get the fuck north.

Inside smells like smoke, sweat, and raw meat. Jamie's cowering under the table in his usual hiding place, his hands pressed over his ears, tears smudging his cheeks.

Dad's gripping Mom by the hair with one hand and pounding her with the other. He's right handed, but he's using his left jab today.

"Get your hands off her," I say.

"Mind your own fucking business," he says.

I step closer.

He drops her and faces me. Nose to nose. I can smell his breath. He's rotting from the inside out. I imagine killing him, cooking him, the taste of his flesh vile, like poison. Like victory.

"I never liked you," I say.

He grabs my breast. "You like this, though, don't you."

The knife appears in my hand. I don't know how, but it's always ready when his fingers pinch my nipple.

He closes his eyes.

"Debs?" Jamie's out from under the table.

"Get back and hide," I say.

Dad's hands are lower, in my pants.

"I don't want you to see this," I say.

Jamie shoves Dad from behind.

I don't know if this part's new. The S-man always blocks what happens from when the knife appears until the deed's done. This performance is how I earned a ticket south. Stabbed my father with the kitchen knife over and over until he stopped twitching. The *why* doesn't change the verdict. Despite motive, I rode the down escalator.

Jamie grabs my wrist. "Don't." He yanks at the knife handle.

I hold tight. "Hide!"

"Not this time."

We fight over the weapon. The old man stands frozen, uninvited to the party until we siblings agree.

Jamie shrieks, "It's my turn."

I look down. He's got the glint, the one I've seen burrowing in my own eyes. The one that says, "Fuck the consequences, I've waited my whole life for justice." Maybe that's why I wrote his name over the key.

I release the knife.

He holds it close to his chest, triumphant. Then he turns on the beast. For a split second, I want him to do it, to take the rap. He's young; maybe they won't ship him south.

No.

I obstruct his arms mid-lunge. He fights, but I seize the knife. Dad un-freezes. I kill him.

Blood splatters us.

Mom sobs, mumbling about how Dad didn't mean it.

Then I'm walking through the woods with the knife. The carnivores race towards the blood. A few wolves to my left, a bear beyond. An immense cat screams.

"Come and get me." I drop the knife, blade down. It sinks into the loam.

The wolves advance, baring their teeth. I welcome them.

"Nice work."

The S-man's beside me. He waves the carnivores away.

"You had your ticket north."

I shrug. "Jamie wouldn't survive here."

The S-man buttons his blazer. "Kids are resilient." He's smiling like he knows a secret.

"I'm never leaving here, am I?"
"Contracts are tricky," he says.
"I did the world a favor."
"You broke the rules."
I nod. "What now?"
He shakes his head. "No point spoiling the fun."

∞ ○ ∞

I wake in a bed. A bug-infested, half-rotten, bare-mattress in the middle of the bedroom, but a bed none the less.

The shower works. Clean clothes hang over a chair. The toaster's still broken. The countdown on the wall says day one of thirty.

I bite into my soggy toast and use the butter knife to open the S-man's note. No paper cuts— I'm learning.

Dear Debs:
Luck is for losers. Surprise me.

MOD ME DOWN

I hurried from the elevator to our dingy apartment, holding the mail that would change our lives.

Mary stared at the letters. She still wore her waitress uniform. Her brown hair appeared redder than usual, tinged by the light reflected off the adjacent brick building.

I handed over her notice and tore mine open. After skimming the contents, all I could do was laugh.

"What'd you get, Lucas?"

I shoved the paper in my back pocket. "*Gray Squirrel.*" Close enough. I didn't have the balls to tell her that I was due for a shot of rat. Squirrels were rats with good P.R., so it wasn't exactly a lie. "How about you?"

She held the letter at arm's length. "I'm afraid to look."

Sitting beside her on the couch, I rubbed her back. "When you're ready. It can't be worse than mine."

She slowly separated the flap from the envelope and tugged the letter free. "No, I won't—"

"What?"

She passed me the notice. Her DNA assignment: *American Cockroach.*

"At least you'll still be *American,*" I said.

"That's not funny. I want squirrel. We'll insist."

"Only married people can dispute." I shrugged.

"We could get married."

"The lineups—"

"Don't you love me?"

I pulled her into my arms. "I do." She resisted at first, then after a sniffle or two she hugged me back, crying. I ran my fingers through her hair.

"It's all about status, about *money*," she said. "My boss got *Arctic Fox* and we get vermin?"

"Tons of roaches live in New York City. Maybe *we'll* be the lucky ones."

"I squish bugs." She shuddered. "They're disgusting."

"Fine. We'll marry."

"Right now?"

"Yes."

She blew her nose. Nodded. "I'll get my coat," she said.

∞ O ∞

Crowds rushed past us. No matter how many people were modified, New York was too busy. Too colonized.

We grabbed applications from a bin outside Mary's church, and then filled them out in silence while we sat in a pew waiting our turn. Mary held my hand, wringing it hard enough to numb my fingers. I drowned in her olive scent. God, she was beautiful.

I thought back to the olive groves in Tuscany near my grandparents' villa. In Italy I had felt connected, as though I belonged. I was eight that summer and already counting the years until my father would welcome me into the study, where men drank *Frangelico* from highballs and smoked *Toscano* cigars.

Now, after only two years as an adult, rathood fell into my lap. The irony flicked me in the head, like my brother Tony used to.

"Hmm," I said aloud.

"What?" Mary whispered.

I leaned against her shoulder, absorbing her warmth. No matter what the modifications did to me, or my Mary, her love made the whole mess bearable.

When Father DiTosto called our names, we handed him our applications and our DNA assignments.

"We both want to be squirrels," said Mary.

He glared at me. I flashed him the don't-tell-her-I-lied signal. Mary beamed her waitress smile.

The Father handed back our papers. "Too late, I'm afraid. New rules. You have to be married at least a week *before* you receive your assignments."

Mary stood, silent, as the words sank in. I opened my mouth to object when the Father said, "Do you still wish to marry?"

I shrugged. Mary shook her head.

We shuffled out of the church and took the subway home. As the train rattled through a dark tunnel, its lights blinked off. When they flickered on, a few people scurried for cover near the exits. Bug DNA in action.

The well-dressed passengers looked away, comforted by their own elite-status DNA assignments.

I touched Mary's hand. Soon she'd be scurrying too.

∞ O ∞

The line-up outside the clinic snaked several blocks along Delancey Street and ended near the subway entrance. Our breath hung in the chill morning air. Bad enough they forced the mods on us, let alone making us stew for hours in the cold first.

"We should have come earlier," said Mary.

"We needed the sleep. Besides, we'll have more time to ... uh ... *prepare*."

A family of six joined the line behind us. The dad wore paint-splotched pants and a pencil behind his ear. The mom looked like she drove a minivan and devoted her life to her four sons. Three of the boys were school-aged, and the youngest had a snotty nose and chubby little hands. The one in the middle looked about eight, my age on my summer visit to the old country. He would never wander olive groves or make love to his wife. I stomped my feet, left then right, more out of anger than from the cold, mourning the kid's loss.

The sun holed up behind thick rain clouds. My hands were damn cold.

"I should've brought gloves," said Mary.

"Me too."

After an hour, the sun poked free. It energized the crowd, as though God had finally turned the music on at the prom. A man wearing a blue flannel shirt jumped the ropes and ran for the subway. Two guards in fatigues and flak jackets raced after him.

Flannel-guy had a good head start.

"Stop! Last warning!" They readied their weapons, the serious kind with the big clip full of ammo.

He didn't stop.

They took care of him.

The people in line watched. Whispered. The blue flannel turned purple, like blue and red paints mixed together. A thick bank of clouds swallowed the sun, turning the grim display dark.

Prom's over, go home, I thought.

A woman, who had to be at least seventy, politely excused herself from line. She ripped her notice to shreds and threw the pieces down a sewer. I thought the guards would threaten her, but a tech hurried over and urged her inside. When she refused, more techs appeared and they dragged her through a side entrance.

Mary shivered.

"You're freezing," I said. "Maybe you could get us a couple of coffees?"

"Didn't you *see* what just happened, Lucas?"

"We could explain it to the guards first," I flashed my *love-you* face.

She stood, silent, for a few minutes, then sighed and waved a guard over. She handed him her wallet, less her debit card, and offered to buy him a coffee so he wouldn't shoot. Her smile won his trust.

"That shop." He pointed to the place across the street. "Make it fast."

"Yes, sir."

While she was gone, I watched yellow taxis rushing in swarms along Delancey. Tall buildings stood like sentinels, parting the street for their passage. The city teemed with life. Would rathood be easier, or harder?

Mary returned with a tray of coffee, enough for us and two guards. "I'm scared, Lucas."

I took my coffee from her and sipped. The shot of espresso shook the fuzz from my brain. My hands warmed, holding the cup. "Try and relax."

"A woman in the coffee shop said the government is turning us into *food*."

"She lied." I sipped again, wincing as the coffee scorched my tongue.

"Roaches and squirrels like us will be prey for the predators. The higher ups, like politicians, get to stay human. They'll eat us all."

I shook my head. "I don't believe it. She's paranoid."

Mary glared at me. Lowered her voice. "The woman said the scientists are lying about reversing the mods. Once we change, we *can't* be human again."

"They *promised*. We'll be re-humanized as soon as the ice backs off."

"That could take centuries, Lucas."

"Thirty years, tops." I looked around. The couple ahead of us in line leaned in, listening, as did the family behind. The eight-year-old boy stared at Mary as though she'd sentenced him to death. In a way she had.

"Think, sweetie. We either get the shot or we *get* shot. I want to live. I'll count the days until we change back. I'll find you. I love you." I kissed her.

"I love you, too." A faint smile flitted across her face. We both said little after that.

Time dragged. We trudged ahead, one numb step at a time. The kids behind us got restless, shoving and poking. They drove their parents nuts, but their behavior didn't bother me. Tony and I had been the same, back when our days were limitless.

During the *Kestrook Implementation*, the world had watched the news, hoping for a reversal of global warming. Every night we listened to reports of the micro-scrubbers dropped into the atmosphere. Scientists crunched numbers.

Then they released their findings.

We'd overcompensated. The scrubbers had mutated, surpassing their objectives to the extreme. The planet had less than ten years before plunging into an ice age.

The Health and Human Services Department passed the *DNA Act*, ordering *Mandatory Modifications*.

Riots erupted nightly in my neighborhood. I threw rocks with my buddies and ran from the cops. The president ordered nation-wide Martial Law. Tony was mowed down by a tank ten feet away from me.

I dropped my rocks and complied.

A gaunt tech in an oversized lab coat said, "Next. Show identification."

I passed him my driver's license.

He swiped it through a reader. "Index finger in the scanner."

I watched the machine track my fingerprint.

The tech said, "Gray line." Pause. "Next."

Mary was assigned the maroon line. We hugged and she disappeared around a corridor to my left. Alone, I followed the maze of lines painted on the tile floor, finding my gray in the mix.

The building smelled of disinfectant and sweat. Loud fans moved bad air through filthy vents. I passed a T-intersection where a yellow line branched off to the left. Dozens of men huddled along the side corridor. One guy was picking at the yellow paint on the floor, trying to scratch the line away.

An orange line ended near a steel door with an inset window, the glass blocked with black paper. One guy waited outside, muttering, "I can't, I can't," over and over.

My line stopped outside a white door. I waited for about ten minutes, hoping to chat with other soon-to-be-rat men. No one showed.

I knocked, waited. The espresso shot lingered on my tongue, like my passion for Mary. As I thought of how *she* tasted, I lost myself in the scent of olives.

The door swung open.

"Lucas Marcusi?" A tech with a stern face and a buzz cut glared over his metal clipboard.

"Yes?"

"Inside."

I sidled past him.

He closed the door, and said, "Sit," nodding toward a black dentist-type chair.

I eased into the seat. "How long will it take for my tail to sprout?"

He lifted a needle and tapped the plastic syringe with his nail. "It varies. Before it touches the ground, you'll be living in the sewers with your kind."

I gripped the arms of the chair, turning my fingers white.

He swabbed my shoulder with a cotton ball. "Relax, Marcusi. It'll hurt less."

"No offence, needle boy, but you're not the one about to be verminized."

He squeezed my flesh and jabbed the needle in.

A burning sensation started in my shoulder and raced to my heart. I screamed, and then gasped for air. A weight pressed down on my chest. My hands twisted, pushing my thumbs back so hard I thought they'd snap off. My back arched as though the vertebrae were being welded together. When the pain subsided, I felt an odd sense of urgency to find a girlie magazine and a private room. Then the espresso demanded a way out and I vomited over the chair, coughing and gagging as wave after wave turned my insides out. The room started spinning and I plunged all the way to nowhereville.

∞ O ∞

After moaning in recovery for a while, I finally grabbed hold of reality. The nurse on duty walked from bed to bed. He wore purple scrubs, far too bright and cheery for such a dour job. Fifty men or more rested in various stages of consciousness on gurneys with the metal sides pulled up. The unmistakable stench of vomit permeated the space. An industrial-sized mop sat ready in its murk-filled bucket.

The nurse handed me a sheet of paper bearing my reassignment. Colony AT347, at the corner of Moore and Water Street.

"When?" I asked him.

"As soon as you can make the arrangements. No more than ten days from today."

He purple-shuffled down the row of beds. Ten days, two hundred and forty hours, a bunch of minutes — I couldn't do the math — left of my old life. And I had to waste the first few minutes with fifty strangers in a room full of fear.

∞ O ∞

Two hours later, strong enough to be discharged, I followed the signs to the waiting room.

The place was jammed with women and children. Mary sat in the third cluster of orange plastic chairs. She held a paperback in her lap, her slender fingers nestling it like a prize. Her eyes were closed and gentle snores escaped her mouth. No antennae had sprouted through her mane of thick brown hair. *Yet.*

"Mary?"

She blinked. "Lucas?"

I flashed my sexy smile. "Who else would it be?" I kneeled and drank in her scent. "Did the bug stuff take?"

"You should've told me."

"Told you what?"

She stuffed the book in her purse. We stood up slowly, our eyes locked. When she turned to get her coat, her perfect ass took my mind off all things bug and rat and ice. It filled out her jeans like water in a balloon. I wanted to kiss her more than ever.

A bump tented the shirt on her back, maybe a wing. I reached out to touch it but she whirled around, facing me.

"We can't be together," she said.

"Why?"

"They posted updates on the men in recovery. You're a *rat*."

I reached behind myself, to see if my tail had started to sprout. "I'm still *me*."

She slung her purse over her shoulder. "Rats *eat* bugs."

"I would never hurt you. I *love* you."

I waited for her to say it back. She didn't. "Why'd you wait, then?" I said.

"To say goodbye."

"So say it."

"Goodbye." She started away.

I stood frozen beside the ugly plastic chair, feeling more like a rat with every breath. "Wait," I said, hurrying to catch her.

She walked faster.

"C'mon, Mary, wait up."

Outside the clinic she stopped. Panting, I drew her into my arms, rubbed my nose up and down her neck, and inhaled her luscious olive scent. I licked a small patch of skin then nipped at her.

She slapped me. "See!"

"What?"

She shoved hard, knocking me down. Before I could stand, she scurried away.

I scrambled up and rearranged my clothes, pretending I hadn't just been humiliated. From somewhere ahead, a waft of fresh-baked-bread-aroma rolled over me. I sought the source, my stomach urging me to hurry. The front window of a bakery was full of knishes. Steam condensed on the glass as they cooled. I caught a glimpse of my reflection. The guy in the window was me, or maybe ninety percent me. Were my teeth longer?

Inside, I asked, "What's fresh?"

"The spinach." The haggard baker moved knishes from a baking sheet to the display shelves.

I paid for four. While I waited for my change, drool dribbled out of the side of my mouth. The counter beckoned me. I leaned forward and sniffed the wood. It smelt of grease and onions. I nibbled, enjoyed the way the grain felt against my teeth. I bit down harder.

The woman scowled. "Get your rodent teeth out of my counter."

Releasing the wood, I said, "Give me my knishes."

She threw the bag at me. The warm steam emanating from the contents had already softened the paper.

"Now, *get!*" Keeping my change, she raised a broom, bristles up like a deadly weapon.

I wouldn't need money in the sewers anyway.

Outside, I ripped soft chunks of onion-and-spinach-flavored potato from a knish and shoved them in my mouth. The taste spoke of heaven and earth united.

∞ ◯ ∞

My tail grew an inch a day. Bending it above the waistline became too painful, so I ripped a hole at the back of my jeans for it to hang through.

On my last day above ground I left our apartment door wide open. Mary had cleaned out her stuff as soon as she got home from the clinic. I didn't know why she wanted it all. I slung my old high-school backpack over my shoulder. I'd stuffed it with small items that held the most memories: my senior yearbook, some family photos, plus Tony's football. It was big and awkward, but my brother had *loved* that ball.

I rode a cab to Battery Park. Liberty held her torch high. The Staten Island Ferry chugged towards the pier full of human passengers with human destinations. I stared at the most famous statue in America and considered the irony, given my current lack of freedom.

My sense of smell had increased dramatically. I caught whiffs of perspiration from the bench beside me, cotton candy on the ground, and car exhaust.

Leaning over the railing, Upper New York Bay spread before my eyes; a vista of filthy water. Mods broke the blue-brown surface, shooting air through their blowholes like dolphins. Lucky bastards. I would have paid good money to score that mod— the sound of water rushing through my ears, the feeling that I could swim forever and never get tired.

"They're beautiful, aren't they?" A woman stood beside me, her pink tail poking out from under a short skirt. Her lips were thin, shrunken-looking. I wondered if they'd always been that way or if her face had started to change.

Her body, so close, awoke my desires. "Nothing should swim in that water," I said. "It stinks." I grimaced. Not the smoothest pickup line.

"I'm Natalie." She leaned in closer. "Today I'm reporting to Colony AT347."

"Me too. The colony, I mean. I'm Lucas."

She reached out to shake my hand and I grabbed her, bringing her close, sucking in the smell of her shampoo. Her hair rubbed painfully against my newly sensitive whiskers.

She stepped back, out of the embrace. Smiled. "Wanna go together?"

"Sure." I glanced once more at Liberty's green body. *I still had the moves.* Hand in hand, we descended to our new home.

∞ O ∞

The smell below ground was worse than disgusting. Every moment I wanted to run for air. The entrance to our colony was nothing but a hole dug in a wall and a tunnel about six feet long.

All of the other rat-mods assigned to our colony were women, making me Alpha. The reassignment guys had left four shovels so I started digging. Natalie helped some, but she didn't have the stamina for much.

After three days I abandoned my pants, frustrated by my tail and enthralled by my ever-enlarging gonads.

More women joined us. Some dug with me, others shored up the walls with our designated supplies. The government depot provided enough construction materials to build a minimal sanctuary. After that, we had to scrounge.

Some of the women were shy at first, hiding in the corners of our tunnels with their tails wrapped tightly, trying to hide their *changes*. All of us covered our noses with cloth. I thought we would have been used to the stink by now, but it kept getting riper. Body odor, our own waste, and gases unleashed from the mud all added to the stench.

I sent Natalie to the depot for advice. She returned with ventilation equipment. It was all manual gear — no point getting hooked on electricity when it wouldn't last — so I drew up a crank-duty schedule.

Natalie kept me company at night. When we'd press together in the mud, I'd try to love her, but my thoughts drifted back to Mary. If only they'd made her a rat.

One evening, a brown, shaggy young male entered my territory. He said he was assigned to our colony but I sensed the lie. He was too small to challenge me as Alpha. I didn't want him sniffing my females.

"Get out," I said in English, not rat. The words were sticky, as though my mouth had forgotten them. "*My* colony."

He came at me, teeth and claws aiming for the hurt zones. I bit back, got him in the eye. He squealed, tore away. Years of fighting Tony paid off in rat-to-rat combat.

The rat-mod returned a few days later, half of his tail bitten off, the wound weeping puss. Natalie took pity on him and nursed his wounds. I allowed it. Compassion would buy me points with the ladies. Besides, the little turd was submissive now. I could use a minion.

Grant became our colony's first Beta male.

More rat-mods came down to us, bringing news from above and filling our colony beyond capacity. Their voices hurt my ears. Too low, not rat-like yet. They told us the President and First Lady had flown to a shelter near the equator. The wealthy had paid their way out of the cold zones. Everyone else topside was either DNA-modified, or would be, soon.

∞ O ∞

The colony tunneled and bred, bred and tunneled.

"Am I smaller," I said to Lorna, the second-gen rat-mod warming my back.

"Nope. Ceiling's higher."

"That joke never gets old," I laughed. It came out shrill. Squeaky. Her face had lost the human features she'd inherited from her first-gen mother. Her chin was longer and her nose pointed out to meet it. She wiggled her whiskers at me.

"Was that a laugh?" she asked.

I flicked my tail. "Go back to sleep."

Lorna had taken Natalie's place as my Primary female. She birthed two daughters— my tenth and eleventh offspring, third-gens. They were born with full whiskers, thick fur, and rat-shaped snouts. Human features faded as each generation bred into the rat kingdom. Childhood didn't last long down here. Second-gens had larger-sized litters— twins, triplets, and sometimes quads.

Several colonies had established a *waste zone*. We all used it, and re-routed our ventilation to avoid out-gasses. I'd grown accustomed to the stink. But with all the bodies, moisture was one of our biggest frustrations. I assigned several of the former scientist first-gens to create a more efficient way to recycle the liquid into potable water.

Five years later, the full grown third-gens grew to sizes even smaller than their mothers, reaching forty inches from nose to tail at most.

In quiet times I held story-nights. I'd gather all of the children, and even the second-gens who asked to join, and told stories of *before*. I sketched pictures in the dirt of power lines and taxis and skyscrapers. I'd put on plays, imitating a traffic jam with a few of the first-gens. When I told them about the sky, the sun, and the stars, they'd wiggle their whiskers and gaze up at me, spellbound. Some would beg me to take them topside, to see for themselves. I'd make promises that we all knew I wouldn't keep.

One night, Grant entered through gate fifteen, his harness full of foodstuffs. "Good haul, huh sir?" He nudged me with submission.

"What took you so long?" I said.

"Food's harder to find. There are more rat-mods now. And other mods too."

"Recruit more foragers," I said.

He bobbed his head then flicked his tail near my nose. It was drenched with the unmistakable odor of roaches. Like a snack-beacon.

I thought of the woman from my past and her beautiful olive skin. I wanted to rut with her, but I couldn't remember her name. "I can't eat her. It's wrong," I mumbled.

"What?" said Grant.

I snorted at him and inhaled more roach-scent. A word drifted into focus.

Mary.

∞ ◯ ∞

The temperature plunged. We huddled together, rutting and sharing warmth. A rocket sled to the bottom of *Maslow's Hierarchy*.

Two of my lesser females lost their newborn litters. The babies were too small to warm themselves. We needed fire.

I sent Grant and twelve females for wood. They gnawed what they could from frigid buildings. Inside the colony, we burrowed for fuel. Cave-ins brought odors from the *waste zone*. All of my keepsakes, including Tony's football, were buried in a sudden collapse. The loss hit me hard, as though he'd died twice.

Fires filled the tunnels with acrid smoke. Our ventilation couldn't circulate enough fresh air. Extra tubes brought in cold drafts, defeating the purpose of the fires.

Body warmth saved us from freezing. *Barely.*

Others came, rat-mods in search of their kind. We shared our fires. They shared their ventilation contraptions. The air quality improved, and with the extra bodies so did the temperatures. But our increased numbers caused in-fighting.

I took a third-gen mate, Patty. Lorna didn't like sharing our nest. She'd whip her tail against the wall, night after night, whenever I rutted with Patty.

During one of Lorna's tantrums, she curled up in pain and started to shiver. Patty and I licked at her fur but she didn't respond. Lorna's wails brought other females, and Tandori, the midwife.

"She's in labor," said Tandori.

"It's too soon," said Patty.

Lorna started bleeding, but no babies emerged. Tandori rubbed Lorna's back and uttered soothing whimpers.

When Lorna quieted, Tandori stroked the blood-smeared fur. I crept closer to say goodbye.

"Eat her!" said Patty.

"No." I smacked my tail down. Hard. "We don't eat our kind."

"I'm starving," said Patty.

"Me too," said Amy, a third-gen. The other females pleaded for nibbles.

"No cannibalism. Not while I'm Alpha."

The smell of blood filled the small space. It turned my stomach, reminding me of how long it had been since my last satisfying meal. My females, the mothers of my children, stood all around me, pressed forward by hunger. I shoved them back, nipping their hides.

Once I'd ushered them out of my nest, I started digging. It took me hours, but I buried Lorna.

∞ O ∞

When topside became uninhabitable, our colonies prepared for battle against the predator-mods. Foragers became warriors. The colony had stores of food, but none of us knew how long it would need to last. Whenever possible, we ate found foods— carcasses the predators had abandoned, molds and fungi growing near our light sources, bugs. But not bug-mods. As Prime-Alpha, I ruled them off-limits.

Sticks were sharpened into spears, but few of us could hold them in our paws or charge with one in our mouths.

The bigger predators stayed in the upper tunnels, unable to force their huge bodies through. A pack of seven wolf-mods dug down to our levels to feed. The first wave of the attack landed on some fifth-gens who were nesting in the north cavern. The lupines broke through the roof from seven different spots simultaneously. They ravaged through dozens of our younglings who had no defense against forty pounds of tooth and muscle.

"Grab a spear," yelled Grant.

"Stick together," I shouted, joining the fight.

Three wolf-mods had advanced deep into our tunnels. They picked up females by the scruff and shook them, one after another, until they flopped, lifeless.

Too terrified to fight, the forth-gens and some of the thirds scattered. The urge to flee screamed at my nerves, but I held my ground.

The largest wolf-mod closed on me. His coat glowed amber in the dim light of the fire. Fear grabbed at my balls and squeezed.

As Alpha, I had to attack, risk my life to protect my kin.

But he'd *eat* me.

The wolf advanced, teeth bared.

Terror exploded inside my rat-mind. I fled, abandoning years of our collective efforts.

Most of my colony stuck with me. The rest, too brave or too scared to flee, were lost.

I headed down, beneath our storage compartments, to levels I'd never visited. Hundreds of us, a huge pack of rat-mods, squeezed through tunnels dug by creatures much smaller than us. Two levels below, the smell hit me. The floors reeked of cockroach. We'd reached the bug-mod levels, the domain I'd declared off-limits. Terror drove us on, from the hunger in our bellies and the predators at our backs.

I nudged at a narrow opening, widening the hole until I could see the level below. A massive pack of roach-mods carpeted the floor, squirming, crawling over one another, flicking their antennae, and buzzing their wings.

They varied in size, but they were all smaller than our fourth-gens. Some were the size of bugs, not mods. Pure roaches could have integrated with their non-human cousins, or the roach-mod bodies might have shrunken more profoundly than ours. Either way, the room erupted with the unmistakable smell of *American Cockroach*.

Her name wouldn't come, lost in the panic, but I remembered a woman. One of *them*.

A dim iridescent glow filled the space, but I couldn't see the source. I looked for her, searching for an olive-colored body in a sea of red-brown.

My stomach ached, reminding me why I'd led my colony here. But I wouldn't. I shouldn't.

A bunch of roach-mods charged past my line of sight. They all had yellow patches behind their heads, except for one. Its patch was greenish.

I jumped through the hole. My pack followed.

"Now?" said Claire, an old first-gen like me.

"Wait."

Rat-mods continued to pour through the hole and drop to the roach-carpeted floor. Some of the bigger roach-mods investigated us, rubbing their feelers along our fur, but the rest scuttled to a safe distance.

The greenish one crept closer, five of its kin on either side. It opened and closed its wings, blowing its scent my way. I recognized her, despite the overwhelming whiff of roach-dinner.

Her carapace glowed maroon in the eerie dimness, not olive like before. The smooth curves of her hips, the ones I used to caress with my long-gone human fingers, had been replaced with an oval body and six spindly legs.

Her antennae wiggled in a frantic patter, up, down, all around, pounding on each other then frisking the air in front of me. Her feelers were sexy in an odd way. I nudged them with my snout.

She shrank away then returned, examining me with her antennae-for-sight.

I squeaked at her and she clicked in response. Pressing my tongue against my rodent incisors, I managed the word, "Love," in English, I hoped.

She sat back, her under-side exposed. Her antennae slowed, moving back and forth in a steady rhythm. Did she understand?

Other roach-mods took up the rhythm, waving feelers. My rat-mods advanced, frustrated at the slowness of the confrontation. The roach-mod female reached a leg tip out to me and I held it in my forepaw.

Our eyes met. She had more than two now, all showing caution, hunger, restlessness. I sniffed at her and bit my tongue. My empty stomach boiled at the taste of my own blood. My former lover, my last connection to humanity stood in front of me, so close. So *wrong*.

"I love you." My words slipped out, in rat. My females gasped.

The roach-mod's antennae wiggled in a fit of complexity. The other roaches stopped their rhythmic motions and picked up the flurried feeler-dance. I nodded in false comprehension. Leaning closer, I pressed myself against her, where I used to fit.

She rubbed her legs along my back.

I squirmed.

The roaches retreated.

I mounted her, needing to mate. Make babies. *Her* babies.

She smelled of prey-fear.

I nibbled her abdomen.

She kicked at me, but her legs were ineffective. She beat me with her antennae, screaming in a high-pitched bug-wail.

The bugs shrieked in unison; a foreign shrillness that immobilized me. Betrayal blazed in each of her multiple eyes.

Climbing above the din of insanity, I acted on my one, clear thought: *Eat!*

A frenzy of ripping and tearing began.

I forgot the wolf-mods, our lost fifth-gens, our homelessness. Survival had the keys to my brain and it was racing, blindly, for the edge of the cliff.

I inhaled a deep lungful of roach. What was left of the female's ravaged body drooped in my forepaws oozing foreign liquids.

My colony joined in the banquet. Some of the roach-mods fought back, but most dashed to safety through tiny crevices.

When the turmoil ended, I huddled with several female rat-mods. Their bodies warmed me, soothing my aches.

"I'm finally full," said Claire.

"Not me."

"Eat more, then." She nudged at my gonads. "You need to recover."

Lust took over. I rutted with her, screaming, "More babies!"

After, I fell to the ground, unsatisfied. Neither the rutting nor the carnage had filled my empty core. We'd eaten mods. Once they had been... *human*, the word faded from misuse.

Another word circled the outskirts of my thoughts. *Murderer.* I ignored it.

Exhausted, I slept.

In my dreams I tasted olive skin and remembered her name for the last time.

Mary.

THE NEEDLE'S EYE

Lise held the needle up to the light. A single drop of vaccine nestled between the twin points, glistening amber. She hesitated, hating the cure for the slow ravages of Retiniapox. But she'd seen the horrible devastation the scourge could bring. Entire villages wiped out. Bodies doused with bleach and left to petrify in the sun, as no one would risk the dangers of burial or cremation.

Her patient, a young girl, wailed on the cot, held down by her mother. The cot's canvas, once green and now a drab shade of gray dotted with splotches of blood and fluids, groaned under the pressure of two bodies pressing down. The stench of it wafted up, adding to the reek of sweat and fear that permeated the medical station.

The girl's mother wore a bandage over her left eye from her own inoculation. Red and yellow blotches stained the white gauze; the eye would never function again, but her chances of contracting the virus had dropped by sixty-eight percent. Lise had vaccinated the mother only moments before, yet it felt like hours. *So many eyes ruined.* When she'd signed up for overseas medicine, she had prepared herself for the horrors of makeshift facilities and understaffed clinics, but nothing could have prepared her for Retiniapox. Or for making the brutal decision to relinquish sight in one eye to care for the defenseless. Back in university, medicine had called to her, with its noble pursuits and its promise to help, to cure. Now she felt like a crusader, storming through a new dark age with a bifurcated needle instead of a sword.

"*Où est ton Papa?*" Lise asked about the father's whereabouts in the hopes of distracting the girl while the Alcaine numbed her eye.

The mother shook her head.

I shouldn't have asked. They come from the northeast, where the last outbreaks were reported. Choosing silence over further reassurances, Lise leaned forward and held down the child's head. Taking a moment to steady her hand and re-check the needle's position, she began the scratching. Two strokes left and right, pressing the serum with both points just below the surface of the cornea. The girl squirmed and shrieked, more from fear than pain. She shouldn't be able to feel the needle. Two strokes up and down and the amber liquid disappeared into the layers of her eye. Lise pressed gauze over a closed lid and taped the dressing down.

Next.

A young man, about the same age as Lise's beloved Rideau, lay down on the cot. She tied his arms in the restraints, sanitized her needle, and gathered another drop of serum.

∞ ◯ ∞

Working in the sweltering biohazard tent, sweat poured down Rideau's back. The Hazmat suit made the dry heat unbearable. He leaned over his next patient simultaneously cursing and thanking the layers of PVC separating him from the virus. With sight in only one eye, depth perception was all the trickier through the wrinkled plastic face plate.

The woman's body wept from countless pustules, most concentrated on her face, neck, and chest. Her eyes had liquefied the previous day; always the first casualties. A biological weapon of war, the virus had been designed to blind its victims, rendering an opposing army helpless. Nature, in its random cruelty, had mutated the pathogen to a deadly cousin of Smallpox since its introduction in the battle of Baqa el Gharbiyya.

The woman moaned, unable to scream, throat clogged with erupting sores.

"*Bientôt,*" he said. *Soon, it'll end.* One in a thousand would survive the illness. About three in ten would succumb despite vaccination; a high price to pay after trading sight in one eye for hope.

He readied a dose of morphine to add to her IV. A seizure gripped the patient in the next cot. Arms and legs flailed, knocking Rideau off balance. He fell onto the woman. His arm brushed across her neck and chest, ripping open a swath of pox. In his haste to push himself back up, he twisted the morphine syringe in his hand.

Pop. Rideau started, stunned, terrified, at the unmistakable sound of a suit breach.

He hurried for the rinsing station, searching for the suit's weakness. The needle had poked through a smear of pus. Contamination. *No, I must think positive.* Other doctors had endured a suit breach without infection.

He showered the suit with bleach until the buzzer sounded. Next he stripped, set the bleach to half-dose, and cleansed himself. Caustic welts erupted on his skin and he dared not open his eyes, though they stung mercilessly. At the buzzer, he lunged blindly for the eye wash and rinsed the bleach from his face.

In two hours he would learn the true effectiveness of his vaccination; whether the trade of sight in one eye for his safety had been fair. He headed for the quarantine tent and scribbled a note on the chalkboard outside, "Rideau, needle through suit, Wednesday, 1027 hours."

Inside, he clung to thoughts of Lise; fleeing this room of despair for better times. He remembered the previous Saturday, bringing the thought to the front of his mind, reliving its exquisite beauty.

He rested on their cot, watching her run a sponge along her arm. She turned to face him and said, "Like what you see?"

He smiled. "Always."

The air in their tent was dry but cloying; like laundry at the bottom of a hamper. His skin was slick with sweat. He sat up and the sheet fell from his chest, pooling around his waist. Part of him wanted to grab her in his arms, make love to her again. Watching her bathe electrified him; his muscles twitched with desire and bliss.

The lights dimmed then returned to their yellow murk. "The generator needs to be filled," she said.

"I'll get to it. Are you finished with the water?"

"Not quite."

"Hurry and come back to bed."

She lifted another sponge full of water along her thigh and the excess dripped slowly back into the basin she had placed below. "I think we've wasted enough time today."

"Wasted?" He crossed his arms. "Is that what you think of our time together?"

She glanced out the mesh window. "The queues have started already."

He clicked his tongue against his teeth. "I shouldn't have to take a number to be with my own wife."

She shook her head. "Pardon. I've so much on my mind."

He tugged at the sheet, wrapped it around his waist, and approached her naked body. As she dabbed the sponge along her neck, he followed her movement, kissing her hand and then her neck.

"Rideau...."

He turned her around to face him.

She trembled in his arms. "What is it?" he said.

"I'm late."

He traced the line from her chin to the base of her neck. "The clinic can wait."

"No. I'm pregnant."

He dropped the sheet and pressed his hands against her belly. "Vraiment?"

She nodded.

He pulled her close. Her trembling intensified and he pressed her chest against his, feeling her heart beating in synch with his own.

"The clinic's no place for a baby," she said.

"Kiss me." He found her tongue with his, absorbing her passion like cracked earth soaked by rain.

When their rhythms eased and her breathing slowed, he said, "We'll put in requests for a transfer. They'll grant yours on medical grounds and I'll meet you in Montreal as soon as I'm able."

"I won't leave without you," she said. "We're in this together."

He kissed the back of her neck. "We should dress."

∞ O ∞

"Rideau!" Lise peered through the quarantine tent's plastic window. "What happened?"

"A needle through the suit."

She pushed at the tent flap, and poked her head inside.

"Stay out!" he snapped.

"I won't come any—"

"Close the flap, Lise. I couldn't live, knowing I'd contaminated you."

She backed outside, glanced at the chalkboard, and then her watch. "We'll know in another twenty minutes."

"Oui."

"I'll wait."

"No," he said. "Get back to the clinic. The time will move quickly if you're busy."

She touched the tent fabric with her right hand, willing it to turn into his skin so that she might comfort him. With her left, she pressed at her belly, at the tiny life growing there. *Not now. I need him more than ever. Please, God, protect him.*

"Go on, Lise."

"*Je t'adore*," she said.

"*Moi, aussi*," he responded.

Biting back her grief, she hurried to her work.

For the longest thirty minutes of her life, she vaccinated patient after patient. Every other woman was with child. Her mother had once said to Lise, "When you're pregnant, it seems that everyone around you is, too. That's the way of the world; people making babies, loving along the way in their own manner. Enjoy every minute of this special time. I never felt as much a woman as when I carried you inside me."

A pregnant woman with near-black skin lay on the cot. With her arms at her sides, she waited for Lise to tie her down. Her eyes full of fear, she closed the left one, indicating that was the eye she wanted vaccinated. As Lise moved closer, the vaccine held between the needle's twin points, the woman's belly shuddered. The unmistakable shape of a foot protruded against the skin. Lise laughed, nearly choking on the sound of it. A smile passed briefly along the patient's face and then terror filled it once more.

With careful and deliberate strokes, Lise scratched the vaccine into the soon-to-be mother's eye.

Glancing at her watch, she returned with a kit and a Hazmat suit to the isolation tent. She stripped to her underwear and tugged at the thick plastic, yanking it over her sweating body. Sebastian had offered to examine Rideau. Though tempted to dodge the duty, she stuck by her resolve to do it herself.

With her suit sealed, she lifted the tent flap and entered the dark space. She touched Rideau's cheek with her gloved hand and stared at the red blotches blossoming in the white of his good eye. Soon it would weep the toxins building in his body. His empty, vaccinated eye stared out, still clear and unmarred.

She choked back a sob.

"I know," he said.

"I brought serum. If I scratch your good eye it will reduce the severity of the symptoms."

"I'll spend the rest of my life blind and scarred by the pox. How could you love such a man?"

Tears erupted, lining her cheeks. In the suit, she couldn't wipe at them. "I would love you blind and deaf with no legs. I will keep on loving you. Don't make me raise this baby alone."

He was silent for a long time. Lise listened to her breath in the suit, the loud echo of life, reminding her that she was healthy. For now.

While she waited, she longed to kiss him, to press her lips against his and insist that life was worth living. "*S'il te plaît.*"

"Don't beg, Lise. I can't bear it. You're right. I want to be a father."

He sat up awkwardly, and kissed the plastic of her face plate. "Do it."

She kissed him back and then gently pressed him down onto the cot. Two restraints hung from her belt. She pulled the first one free, her hands shaking beneath the thick layers of plastic.

"Tie them tightly," he said. "I don't want to accidentally infect you."

She strapped him down, doubling over the fabric then clipping the clasps together. Welts criss-crossed his body— burns from the bleach wash. She ran a gloved hand along his skin, hating the way it stuck to his body, agonizing over the barrier between them.

"Don't hesitate. You've done this hundreds of times. I'm only one more patient." With that, he stared at the ceiling, his eye full of resolve and bravery.

Holding her breath for a long time, she let it out and dropped Alcaine into his right eye. While she waited for it to numb, she slowly and carefully opened the vial of serum and dipped in the bifurcated needle. Her skin stuck to the inside of the suit. The smell of her breath, overpowering in the small space, reminded her of the coffee she'd shared with Rideau only hours before. The memory lifted the dam on another flood of tears.

"I'll never forget your beautiful smile." His voice cracked, as though he hadn't spoken in a lifetime. "*Je t'adore.*"

"*Moi, aussi.*"

Her vision, distorted by her anguish, turned his face into a streaky blur. She tried to find him through the waterfall, blinking frantically. With time, his blue eye came back into focus and she leaned in close with the needle.

Her every instinct told her to pull away, flee from this madness. Finding her inner resolve, thinking of the needs of their unborn child, she focused all of her energy into steadying her wavering hand. She whispered, "Forgive me."

∞ ◯ ∞

Months later, Rideau waited impatiently while he picked at the wax in his ears. The long hours, by Jeep, then train, then plane, had exhausted him and clogged his remaining senses. He'd never realized how loud transportation could be. Now he stood in the customs line, the last hurdle between him and his family, and listened to the conversations all around. A couple discussed in whispers how much to claim on the duty form. A child complained about the cold. How many of them stared at him, saying nothing? Victims of the pox were rare in Canada, and survivors rarer still. How many times had he brushed his fingers along his pocked cheeks and wondered how hideous he had become?

On that fateful day, after she'd vaccinated his good eye, they'd agreed that, for the safety of their child, she should return to Montreal as soon as possible. So when his fever had broken, they had said their good-byes. In her absence, he had truly understood the meaning of despair.

The long months in the hospital had passed with sickening slowness. His illness had relapsed four times before he was finally well enough to leave the biohazard tent. Weak from so much time on his back, he was forced to take even more time to build up his strength for the journey home.

A lifetime had passed, Théophile's lifetime.

When his turn came, his aide led him ahead to the customs officer. Documents were produced and with a loud stamp, he was sent towards his future.

The aide asked, "Is someone meeting you?"

"My wife. Lise."

"Wonderful."

"And our new son, Théophile."

"Will this be the first time you've seen him?" The woman's voice faltered. So many idioms were based on sight.

"Yes," he answered, before she apologized for the comment.

Their shoes clicked on the hard floor, echoing along a narrow corridor. Then the whoosh of automatic doors and the noise of a crowd. All around him, cries of *"Bienvenue,"* and, "We missed you," erupted from unseen faces.

And then the touch of fingers he remembered and the whisper of her breath against his neck.

"I've never been so happy to see you, my love," she said. "Would you like to hold your son?"

She handed him the baby. Rideau steadied himself for the boy's cry at the sight of this horribly disfigured stranger. But the boy cooed instead.

"Bonjour, mon petit Théophile." Rideau flashed a smile of relief.

"He's been wondering when his father would come home to spoil him."

"I brought presents," he said, as he felt the soft nose and chubby cheeks. "For both of you."

She squeezed his hand, then nudged him to take her arm.

"What does he look like?" he asked.

"Healthy and handsome," she said. "Just like his father."

THE
FLOWER GATHERING

My son, Eli, hurried ahead of me. "Look, Mommy. The crane!"

"Madam Prime Minister," said Aurisandra, the forewoman for the north wing construction project. "Please calm your *son*. Children usually aren't permitted—"

"I appreciate your accommodation. Eli's fascinated with large machinery."

Aurisandra glared at me. "*He* should *listen*."

Leaning down to his level, I whispered, "Pay attention to the forewoman. Safety first."

He nodded, but delight made him squirm beyond compliance. Under the transparent dome, his mood had burst forth; his exuberance almost as large as Saturn itself. On the day that the crane had arrived from Earth, he had begun his relentless pestering to visit the construction site.

The crane engine started. "It's working, Mommy!" he said.

"Yes." To see him bathed in the constant glow from the rings was to watch an angel fluttering in heaven's light. I patted him on the head, and turned to my assistant, Shurrana. "Rather loud, isn't it?"

"Indeed," she said.

Aurisandra pointed up at the crane. "It is buried in the center of the new apartment complex."

As we all watched, a large, black-and-yellow-striped disk about ten meters in diameter, shaped like a giant serving tray, retracted away from the dome. The telescoping poles making up the arm of the crane stacked into one another, drawing the tray closer to the control box. At the other end of the pole, counterweights ratcheted upwards, swinging as they rose.

The control box looked unoccupied.

I shouted, "Where's the operator?"

"Automated," shouted Aurisandra. She came closer, so she wouldn't have to shout, and pointed at the disk. "The outside of the disk is slightly convex, matching the curvature of our dome. It heats and shapes each piece of glass to fit into existing sections of the structure."

I asked, "How are the pieces added without jeopardizing the seal?"

"It's simple, Madam Prime Minister. The pieces of the dome overlap, creating a failsafe barrier in case of breakage." Aurisandra linked her fingers together into a bowl shape. "We add extra panels beneath the existing framework, making the layer three to four panes thick in places."

She pointed at some pieces of equipment that looked like mutant toilet plungers: three-meter-long metal rods with meter-wide black suction cups attached at their ends. "Then the crane uses clumps of pressure cups, six at a time, to push out the dome."

The crane's base began to pivot in a counter-clockwise direction. The main pole rotated on a ball-and-socket joint, bringing the disk down, ever so slowly, until it settled onto the next piece of glass.

Eli watched, mesmerized. I thought he would have grown bored of the activity, as the manipulation of the glass proceeded so slowly that at one point, I wondered if it had halted for our tour.

Finally, the disk lifted away from the pile, the glass firmly attached, and the pole began to swing back up towards the dome.

At the same time, the crane's base rotated, bringing the disk in a broad arc towards where we stood.

Aurisandra said, "The dome will always be intact; its thickness varies as it expands to fit the new structure."

Eli hopped on the spot, pointing. "The disk is coming."

He said more, but I couldn't hear him over the screech of glass against metal.

I felt Shurrana's hand on my arm. At my ear, she shouted, "We should step back."

"Mommy!"

I turned to Eli, marveling at how his face had lit, so full of wonder.

"Yes," I shouted. "Soon it—"

Screams erupted from our group, and a fraction of a second later I heard a sound that clung to me like a second skin: a hard object slamming against flesh. Someone grabbed me and yanked me back so fiercely, I was not able to reach Eli. I watched him in slow motion, his hand outstretched towards mine. The glass panel reached him, smashing into his tiny body with the force of an explosion.

"Eli?"

Shurrana held my wrist with a fierce grip.

The glass had carried his body twenty or more meters beyond where I could see. And when the two hit the ground, the glass shattered into countless splinters, mixed with clumps of bloody flesh, pieces of Eli's sweater. Worse, one of his arms, flung towards where I stood.

I stared, transfixed by the mess of it, the *remains* of what had been my son. I couldn't cry, or look away. Instead, I continued to gawk at the chaos. Mute.

"Madame Prime Minister?" Shurrana's shout in my ear.

With a near-audible snap, I became acutely aware of the moment. The members of our tour group, all staring at me. My assistant, releasing my wrist, leaving a hand-shaped red mark. The forewoman shouting into her comset. And the crane's pole, slowly pushing the disk back to the dome, seemingly unaware that it no longer held the requisite piece of glass.

I remembered to breathe, scanning for his body. "Where's Eli?" I asked Aurisandra, my voice lost in the din of the crane.

The forewoman didn't answer, didn't move closer to hear me, didn't ask me to repeat the question.

"He needs me." I shouted to Shurrana. "Get a medical team."

My assistant looked afraid, though of what I couldn't be sure. She held my shoulders, her lips nearly touching my ear to compensate for the noise, "You shouldn't look..."

"He's my child!"

A medical team entered through the far hatch, pushing a stretcher, then pausing to survey the disarray.

Why aren't they running? I began to bark orders, "He'll need pressure bandages. The sooner he's to the hospital—"

The sting of a slap across my face. My teeth rattled against one another.

Aurisandra's hand still hovered next to my cheek. At that moment, the crane's engine halted. The silence fell on us like a leaden blanket.

"The *Fourth* is *gone*, Madame Prime Minister." Her voice quiet. Calm. Unfeeling.

Reporters appeared through the hatch, most headed towards the pieces of... A pair slunk towards me, their cameras at their sides, catching the scent of my despair.

"Madam Prime Minister," my assistant again. "You're shaking. Perhaps you should sit."

I wrenched free of Shurrana's hold and walked towards the arm. Unsteady at first, then, as my legs stopped wobbling, I took longer strides. My heart raced. I had to reach his body. Had to find him and connect his pieces back together.

The medical team stood motionless.

A tall woman, with the facial tattoo of a medtech looked up at me, and said, "Madam Prime Minister." Her voice barely a murmur, she added, "I'm sorry."

"No." My voice cracked, no longer the Prime Minister, merely a mother, I said, "Please?"

People were speaking, to me or one another, I couldn't be sure. I pushed the medtechs back. "Give me a moment."

They moved away, leaving the gurney close to what was *left* of... I knelt where I stood. Tears filled my eyes, blurring my vision.

"You finally saw the crane. I hope...."

Words clogged my throat. Trying to take a deep breath, I failed, lost all poise, and sobbed.

I collapsed and wrapped my arms around my own body, as though I held him close, could prevent him from departing my world. I lingered, despite the nudges of the women around me, whether reporters or medtechs or my people, I didn't care.

Shurrana beside me. "Tecmessa?" she asked. Intimate. Urgent.

"What!"

"I'm so sorry about your son."

"Eli. His name is Eli."

"Of course it w... is. You're our leader. Let's go somewhere more private."

I should have agreed. Should have dug deep within myself for the official face, the one that the colony would expect me to wear when surrounded by a frenzy of cameras and microphones.

More sobs. My body a quivering mass of anguish.

Shurrana offered her arm. "When you're ready," she said.

∞ O ∞

With a calm resolve, Shurrana guided me to the housing wing. In the privacy of my room, she gathered my three daughters and filled them in.

I listened. Hands wringing.

Within an hour of Eli's death, Shurrana helped Norinda, my eldest, to prepare and deliver a statement on my behalf, outlining our sorrow at the loss of our Fourth.

Broadcasts of Norinda's message and footage of the accident endlessly looped on every console in the *Pyleian* settlement.

Except for mine. My console had had an unfortunate accident of its own.

∞ ◯ ∞

Hours later, dark circles under her eyes and shoulders drooping, Norinda entered my chamber. "The reporters are spreading rumors," she said. "That the incident might not have been an accident. That the Fourth-Abolitionists are to blame."

"They claim responsibility whenever a Fourth makes the news," I said.

Norinda leaned over and would have looked down on me had she been a bit taller. Her short-cropped black hair looked perfect, as always. Though Eli's death had turned me haggard, she seemed oddly serene. "But Eli wasn't just *any* Fourth, Mother."

I tried to speak, found my throat wouldn't work. I cleared it, twice, and managed, "No."

The door chimed. "Who is it?" said Norinda.

"Kjillu."

My eldest crossed her arms as though to protect herself from my Second Minister, then said, "Enter."

Norinda and Kjillu shared a greeting. The two could have been sisters with their matching hair and slim bodies, but separated by a decade or more. My daughter nodded at me then left through the adjoining door for the girls' chamber.

I lay down on the bed and rubbed the tender spot at the back of my skull.

My Minister shut the door behind her and walked over to me, her usual boldness subdued. She sat beside me and said, "Tecmessa, we're all pained by the death of your *Fourth*. But the settlement must continue to function."

"See to it," I said.

"For how long?"

"Until I'm whole."

"You're my friend, Tecmessa. Please, I beg of you, weigh each word, every action. All of *Pyleia* witnessed your behavior at the construction site. Tears shed for a male will not soon be forgotten."

"He was my *child*."

"He was a *boy*. The newscasts are using the incident to fuel debate over the Fourths' Law."

"He was kind. Creative. Loving. I will *not* subscribe to the propaganda of reporters *or* radicals."

Kjillu grabbed my shoulders. "Everyone is watching."

I shoved her away. She wavered but did not step back. "Handle it," I said.

"Fine." On her way to the door she added, "Get some rest," and then left.

I buried my head under the pillow and cried. Eli's scent lingered in the bedding, from the night, two past, when a frightful dream brought him to my bed for comfort. I inhaled his smell deeply, savoring hints of his soap, his sweat, his individuality.

The door to the girls' adjoining chamber chimed. "Mother?"

I lifted the pillow and considered what to tell my second-eldest, Tumeda. No words came to mind.

"May I come in?" she said.

I sat up and lost Eli's scent. "Leave me alone."

I expected her to protest, but she waited in silence. At eleven Earth-years, Tumeda acted more mature than her older sister, now fourteen. Though Norinda had been groomed for politics, Tumeda possessed a natural ability for insight and empathy unmatched in her generation.

"Please?" she tried.

"Go away."

"Mother?"

"Go. *Away*."

I held back my grief for a count of ten while I waited for her to leave.

No more knocks. No more protests.

Relieved to be alone, I collapsed on my bed. The walls and ceiling seemed to press in, choking the air from my lungs. Our lengthy confinement in these harsh buildings wore down my soul. I longed for the sky and open spaces.

On Titan, our settlement, named after the Greek Amazon *Telepyleia*, had been populated only with women. To escape the war-ravaged turmoil of Earth, our foremothers organized the evacuation, built the transport ships, and gathered supplies, all with minimal male assistance. Radical lesbians, the original colonists believed men were a threat to a sustainable civilization. They sought a place to build a new culture.

Though the premise was still foreign to some, we had allowed males to be birthed into our ranks. The Law of the Fourths, written by my mother, Prothoe Ikanolijos, our Chief Justice, allowed male fetuses to be inseminated only if three sisters preceded them. Our stocks of sperm would not last indefinitely; some samples had already shown hints of degradation in cold storage. To perpetuate our colony, our supply required an upgrade. But men would never be allowed to outnumber women, nor would they occupy positions of authority. Male off-colony transport personnel were not even permitted to enter beyond the outer delivery depot. We had severed our allegiance to Earth and the endless aggression that testosterone delivered to an ecosystem.

I called up my mother's image in my mind, following the deep creases on her face to her green eyes. She would have known what to do, how to cope with this kind of grief. I heard her voice, sharp yet kind, calling me to the table for our weekly gathering of three: my grandmother, my mother, and I. The slight fragrance of pollen lingered in the air, from the fresh bloom residing in the mug at the center of our table.

I had forgotten Grandmother Dela's love of fresh flowers, a luxury enjoyed solely by the Chief of the harvest wing. At her remembrance gathering, my mother and I had placed a fresh bloom beside her photo. My blossom had been cut from a tomato plant, bright and yellow, but small, with a slight fragrance that reminded me of the green stains that would seep into my skin when my grandmother took me pruning. She would tell me stories of flowers grown purely for their beauty — roses, daisies, tulips, lilies — an indulgence we couldn't afford in the necessity-driven coldness of space. She showed me images she kept in her private journal, to help remember the precious blossoms we had left behind.

Such a trinket might comfort my broken soul. After sending Shurrana a request to track down a flower, I drifted to sleep.

∞ O ∞

Veranisey, my eight-year-old, chimed at our door. "Mother? Please unlock the door. I need help with my homework."

"Ask Norinda."

"She already left."

"Later."

Veranisey stomped loudly across the next room.

"She'll be fine," I said to no one.

The room wasn't convinced.

I shuffled to the wash basin and splashed cold water on my face. I felt nothing, not even the shock of the coldness against my skin.

Switching to the hot, I scrubbed my face raw.

My hands blistered, and still I felt nothing.

"Eli?" I called, hoping to attract his essence closer to mine.

Silence.

Moving to my bed, I sat, staring at the main door, willing Eli to return.

Emptiness.

I lost track of time.

∞ O ∞

Moments after the tech repaired my broken console and left, Kjillu entered without knocking, carrying a mug filled with water. An okra bloom swayed back and forth with her steps.

She set the flower on the table beside my bed. "How're you feeling?"

With concentrated effort, I forced a bland smile. "I'm alive."

She pointed at the mug. "Why a flower?"

"Family tradition. It represents the essence of life— its beauty and vitality."

"The harvest forewoman objected. Harshly. Don't expect another."

I smirked. "Okra-coffee. How dare the Prime Minister interfere with the lifeblood of *Pyleia*."

"You've found your sense of humor."

Looking up at her, she wore the obligations of the office, *my* office, like a second skin. Allowing the silence to stretch between us, I studied her composure, which never varied, not even once.

Kjillu grasped her hands in front of her, gently, but with assurance— a gesture tailored for press conferences. "Ready to resume your duties?"

Another pause, though this one not nearly as lengthy. "Not particularly."

Leaning over the mug, I inhaled a whiff of the okra. No aroma emanated from the blossom. Lifeless. Like my soul.

"All right," I said, standing. "Might as well be now."

Typing up a quick note on my newly repaired console, I forwarded a promise to the girls. I had been ignoring them for so long, their requirements were my next priority.

Kjillu stood in my doorway. "Shall we?"

With a shudder, I followed her beyond the safety of my room.

We traversed corridors of metal and concrete, stark materials designed for durability not aesthetics. Few women passed by; the shift had changed more than thirty minutes before. Rounding the last corner, the clicks of console keyboards and the chattering of my senior staff filled my ears.

Shurrana sat in her cubicle. As soon as she saw me, she stood and said, "Welcome back, Madam Prime Minister."

The other staff stood and quieted. I nodded at them and said, "Thank you."

"The construction of the north wing has been delayed due to the investigation," said Ghastadi, Chief of the Development Committee.

"They're taking the Abolitionists' claim seriously?" I asked.

"Certainly, Madame Prime Minister."

I sensed uneasiness among my staff. The women glanced at me, then Kjillu, and then back at me again, unsure of who was in charge. Focusing on the first order of business, the north wing, I retrieved the latest report.

Kjillu, reading over my shoulder, said "Shall I set up a meeting with the forewoman. Aurisandra?"

I shook my head. "I'd rather visit the site alone. In person." I paused, remembering the forewoman's attitude towards Eli. "The woman owes me an explanation."

∞ O ∞

Three times, I paged Aurisandra to meet me at the entrance to the north wing. Receiving no response, I ground my teeth as I charged my way through corridor after corridor on my way to the site.

Kjillu had reluctantly remained at the office. Shurrana had demanded to tag along, but I hadn't allowed it.

"I need to think," I had told them. *Find answers.*

A worker wearing a red construction helmet stood at the gate. When she noticed me approaching, she stood straighter. Funny, how my position either turned people into statues or buffoons.

I looked beyond, and said, "Where's your boss?"

She shrugged then blanched, "I'm sorry, Madam Prime Minister, I didn't mean to act so casual, I mean—"

I cleared my throat to interrupt her meandering. Speaking as slowly and clearly as possible, I said, "Where's Aurisandra?"

"Ma'am, I'm sorry, but no one's seen her today."

I pointed at the crane, idle, silent. "Have they finished the investigation?"

"Yes, Ma'am, I mean no, they aren't *finished*, but they've left for the day."

"Who *can* I speak with to get an update on the delays to the north wing?"

"The forewoman left notes in her office." The woman turned toward the office to the left of the gate's entrance.

I strode through the gate, headed for the crane.

Red-hat shouted, "Madam Prime Minister!"

I stopped. "Yes?"

She hurried to my side, taking off her hat, handing it to me. "You can't enter the site without a hard hat."

I didn't need one before. None of us had.

"Fine." I donned the bright red hat and proceeded.

The site felt ominous now, as though all of its promise and possibility had been shattered along with Eli. Workers went about their business, though from the looks of their numbers, many of them had been sent home. What few remained seemed to concentrate their efforts near a cement mixer that turned and turned while they shoveled in gravel.

As my feet neared the crane, my heart beat faster. The disk had been removed so that only cables dangled from the pole where it had once been attached; the cables pooled on the ground like pasta.

Turning away, I headed for the cement mixer.

Before I was close enough to speak to any of the workers, they noticed me and stepped away from the machine.

"Hello, Madame Prime Minister," said a tall blonde, wearing a yellow hard hat.

"Hello. What're you working on?"

A redhead arrived beside the blonde. Wearing a white hat, she walked and acted like a manager. "We're testing the cement. The gravel from the automated mines doesn't have the proper consistency. The geologists are searching for a new vein. In the meantime, we're making do with what we have, laying some minor foundations that don't require the—"

"Fine," I said.

My comset rang. Kjillu needed me back at the office.

"Carry on, ladies." Before any of them could respond, I turned my back on them and hurried away.

∞ O ∞

Back in my chamber, the okra had drooped. I stared at the withered white petals then pulled one back to examine the purple-red center. It saddened me that its beauty, a living example of evolution and adaptation, had worn out so soon.

A knock.

I opened the door and found my assistant.

"Come in," I gestured for her to join me.

"Thank you, Ma'am."

Shurrana stood a few steps inside my room, surveying. Her attention fixed on my table, the dead blossom still sitting in the mug.

"Okra?" she said.

"Yes."

"People used to adorn death rooms with flowers," she said. "To cover up the stench of the decomposing body."

I stared at her, more shocked than insulted, trying to imagine the proper response to such a thing.

"We need to discuss Eli's... uh."

"His what?"

"Remains"

"Oh."

She stared at the droopy okra blossom, then back at me. "You need to decide whether we're to ship the ... *arm* ... to recycling."

The question hung between us, like moisture clinging to a cold glass in a hot and humid room.

"As a child of the Prime Minister," I said, "he deserves an honorable disposal— a ceremonial burial beneath the sea."

Could I send him into the cold depths where he would sink alone, forever?

Though tears formed, I willed them inert.

"I suspected such," said Shurrana, staring at her shoes.

Finally, she looked up. "The more of these... *demands* you make, the more you degrade your credibility."

I crossed my arms over my chest. "I don't *care!*"

I heard the panic in my voice, too late to stop it.

She stared, but with a kindness around her eyes. "I'll pass along your wishes, Ma'am."

Taking another look around the room, she pointed at the okra blossom. "I make artificial blossoms," she said. "Carnations."

"What?"

"Ornamental flowers. I'll send one over."

I heard her words, watched her leave, wondering how a woman who had worked at my side for so many years could still surprise me. With a glance at the wilted okra, I said, "Thanks," to the empty room.

∞ O ∞

That evening, when I didn't join the girls for supper, Veranisey brought me a tray. My eight-year-old had prepared a dessert in the kitchens. I lifted the lid to reveal a yellow sweet-cake.

"My teacher gave me the recipe in class."

I broke off a piece and before I put it in my mouth, I asked, "What's it called?"

"Honey-cake."

I swallowed before the word could sink in. Honey. One of Eli's favorite foods. The look of pride of Veranisey's face spoke of my need to not only *eat* the cake, but to *love* it. Though my stomach clenched, I forced my mouth into a smile that didn't reach my eyes and said, "Wonderful."

"I wanted to help you feel better." She stepped closer, setting her hand on my leg, like I often did to comfort her. "He loved honey." As she spoke the words, tears welled in her eyes.

"Come here." I pulled her close to me and hugged her, my own tears falling freely. The sorrow lingered between us, like rising smoke in a room on fire. I wondered if Eli had felt any pain. Or sadness. Or fear.

Veranisey pulled away from the hug.

I wiped her tears with my fingers, and she did the same for me. In a voice that I hoped would sound calm to her ears, I said, "I'm not sure I can finish the cake."

"Is it the honey?" she asked.

I gazed at her innocent face, wondering if she truly understood the magnitude of her statement.

"Yes," was all I could think to say.

She gave me another hug, a quick, empty one this time, and departed.

∞ O ∞

My girls needed their mother, especially Tumeda. Whose rage snuck free of her at odd times, when she reached for her toothbrush or cleared the dishes; an embodiment of her unacknowledged grief. I shielded her from the prying eyes of reporters.

Even Norinda, who often accompanied me to the office, had begun to question the radicals who picketed the atrium. In an interview the reporters had dug from the archives, the still-absent Aurisandra had discussed my "sympathies for the Fourths." Worse, Kjillu was quoted out of context concerning her fear that my ability to lead had been compromised by my "unnecessary grief." Norinda had stomped to the console. For a moment, I thought she might break it. Like mother, like daughter. Instead, she simply turned off the interview mid-sentence.

During the previous two nights, I had waited for the girls to settle, and then had left my chamber for the shuttles. Each time, reporters had lurked in every corner on the way to the Clyemne Wing, ready to catch me acting irrational, so they might garner more proof that their leader's judgment faltered.

On the third try, I left nothing to fate. I assigned Kjillu to a press conference announcing the latest shipment of gravel that facilitated the resumption of the north wing project. After listening to her statement, the reporters bombarded her with questions about my leadership. I used the distraction to sneak through the dimly lit corridors of the housing wing to the shuttle station where I took a train to the recycling facility.

∞ O ∞

The lowest floor of the building was marginally heated, providing only enough warmth for the custodians to function. I grabbed an insulated work suit from the hooks near the bulkhead door. I stood at the hatch, afraid to proceed, fearful of witnessing the deterioration of what remained of my son on the other side.

I glanced at the clock, aware that the press conference would likely be over by now, and entered the room.

Eli's shriveled, naked arm lay in a clear plastic bag on a steel shelf. Above it, fragments of what appeared to be a desk had been collected into a waste bin. Below, discarded syringes sealed in a recyclable hamper bore the biohazard symbol and incineration instructions. I edged closer to his arm. Someone had scribbled his disposal instructions on the inside, between his elbow and wrist. *Shred and reclaim.* I gasped. My baby's body had been torn apart enough.

The custodian appeared. "There's no unauthorized personnel allowed here." She paused. "Excuse me, Madam Prime Minister. I didn't realize—"

"When is he... *it* scheduled?"

The woman checked her portable console. "The large chopper is malfunctioning, Ma'am. Should be a couple more days before we're able to reclaim this room."

"I don't want it shredded."

"We need to reuse everything."

"I'm the Prime Minister, am I not?"

"Yes, Ma'am."

"What's your name?"

"Hannah Roth."

"I order you, Hannah, to freeze my son's arm until further notice."

"Yes Ma'am."

"You won't speak a word of this to anyone. Clear?"

She nodded, appearing scared enough to heed my warning. "Move on."

"Yes, Ma'am."

I waited until I was sure she couldn't hear me then stood over what remained of Eli. "You won't be treated like garbage. You're the Prime Minister's child."

I suspended my hand a centimeter above his fingertips. This tiny portion of his body wasn't Eli. He had been a furnace of enthusiasm. What lay before me was a memory, like a nightmare not quite remembered in the morning. He had slipped beyond me without asking, without taking my hand and begging me to show him the way.

I took a quivering breath, then another, forcing back the grief. "I will always love you, Eli."

The next movement I recall was of my feet plodding up the stairwell. I had returned the work suit, though I didn't remember doing so. Reaching the shuttle stop, I glanced back at the recycling station sign. From compost to salvage, from death to dishes, every scrap of reusable material was diverted to a new use. Hannah processed endless discards daily. She and her team deserved a special ration for such disheartening work. I would have Shurrana scrounge through the stores for an appropriate bonus next allotment cycle.

By the time I reached my chamber, I had less than two hours before breakfast. My bed stood empty, too cold to provide comfort. On the table, in the mug that had held the shriveled okra blossom, all the water long evaporated, sat a trio of artificial flowers. The blooms contained endless rows of tufts; all crimped together into a base so packed that I could hardly believe it strong enough to hold the blossom upright. All were white with faded red-and-blue patterned "P's"; official maintenance uniform fabric.

A short message waited on my console from Shurrana. "As promised, the carnations. Enjoy, Madame Prime Minister."

A genuine, heartfelt smile crept across my lips. I could hardly remember when I had last felt un-forced joy.

The girls had left their chamber unlocked, so I crept in and cuddled next to Veranisey. She wiggled a little then settled. Though I could barely hear her breathing over the circulation fans, I felt her chest rise and fall— a steady reminder of her vitality.

When she woke, she turned to me and said, "How long have you been there, Mommy?"

"A couple of hours."

"I'm glad."

I hugged her tightly.

"We all miss Eli," she said. "But life goes on."

I shook my head. "You're growing up so quickly."

My stomach growled loudly.

Veranisey stood and stretched, giggling a little. "We'd better eat," she said.

I sat up at the edge of the bed, steadying my legs before standing. "I'll grab something on my way to the office. Have a great day at lessons, girls."

Norinda chose that moment to surprise me. She walked over, grabbed her two sisters by the wrists, and pulled them close. Together, we shared a group hug. The rightness of it seeped through my clothes and skin. For the few seconds that we all embraced, I almost forgot that Eli wasn't among us.

∞ O ∞

Kjillu radiated the gritty temperament of a sleepless night. As she dropped her portable console on my desk, she scrutinized me, staring at everything from my boots to my hair. I looked a mess, having worn my clothes for more than twenty-four hours straight, but I kept my face blank.

"The large recycling chopper is on the fritz," she said. "But you knew that already."

So much for Hannah's extra ration.

"The press will feast on the story for a week, Tecmessa. What were you thinking? Visiting his remains was a bad idea. But ordering it frozen, well that's just plain crazy. He's *gone*. The sooner his body is put to good use, the sooner you'll be able to move on."

"He deserves a proper burial."

"He's a *Fourth*. Listen to yourself. You'll be committing political suicide, not to mention the disgrace you'll bring to your daughters."

"They loved him as much as I did."

"In private, perhaps. If you can't do this for yourself, do it for Norinda. She has a promising political future. Don't ruin her chances before she can even begin."

I stood with my mouth open, trying to think of a way to disagree. But Kjillu was right. Without waiting for my retort, she said, "Think about what I've said," then left my office.

My staff shuffled at their desks, pretending not to have overheard our exchange. Kjillu's dominance lay thick in the office long after her departure. I delved into my work but I could not shake my Second Minister's warning. She had always been more conservative; a good balance to my liberalism. Together, we appealed to a great majority of the population and garnered well-earned victories.

Though I had embraced the Law of the Fourths, my Second Minister lived by the stringent rules enacted by the original colonists. My grandmother, Dela, though a lesbian herself, had raised my mother to choose her own path. Most of the first generation born in the colony had taken female companions, even if their desires had been forced down in favor of conformity. My mother had loved another woman, yet I don't believe that either of them would have chosen such a lifestyle had they been born on Earth.

To illustrate my liberal tendencies in a favorable manner, I founded a celebation group — a combination of celibate and celebration — for women born in the second generation, other like-minded individualists and broad-thinkers who chose solitude over falseness. My position gave the group respect, though Kjillu reviled our purpose. Her mate, Lauriana, a cook at *The Wild Harp*, "put forth the proper image for a Minister in charge of the future of our civilization," or so she reminded me whenever I attended a formal function unaccompanied.

On my console, I blocked off half an hour of time and said, "Shurrana?"

My assistant looked up. "Ma'am?"

"I'm headed for an okra-coffee break. Would you join me?"

She nodded.

On our way out of the office, we found Kjillu in the archives, searching citations on a large console. "Keep me updated as to the status of the shredder," I said. She nodded and continued with her work.

On the stairs to the cafe, Shurrana said, "Tecmessa, please tell me that you didn't visit the recycling center last night."

"What if I did?"

She hurried ahead of me and blocked our path down the steps. "You're only adding fuel to the media frenzy. Let him go."

"He will have a proper ceremony." The words echoed up and down the staircase. I wondered who else used the thoroughfare; would she recognize my voice?

Leaning closer, using barely a whisper, I said, "Doesn't it ever bother you? The discrimination. We're hypocrites, no better than the sexist men back on Earth. As Prime Minister, I owe it to our future to question all of our choices."

"Be *careful*." She stepped aside and we continued down the hall. "We're raising boys into men," she said. "Doesn't it worry you, wondering what will happen when they reach adulthood?"

"They'll be whipped and curtailed into the most useless of beings," I said. "*Men should cower, not contribute.* Isn't that our mantra? The one kindness about Eli's early death is that he hadn't been taught to hate himself, yet."

"I spoke more of the girls' needs, Tecmessa. Your daughters might pursue encounters with the Fourths. The biological drive to reproduce is strong."

"I manage without a partner. Though my hormonal urges spring forth, I set them aside."

"Some of us struggle to quench them."

"What are you saying?"

"The archives satisfy my needs. I have my favorite images, as do many of the women in the celebation group you founded."

I stared at her in surprise.

She shrugged, her cheeks red.

∞ O ∞

From the table in Cafe Eurybe, Titan's orange-colored sky shone through the thick glass of the dome above us. Though liquid methane "rain" was exceptionally rare, the thick atmosphere made the sky appear stormy. Combined with the extreme cold, the outside conditions forced us to remain trapped inside our artificial habitat.

"I appreciate the imitation flowers you left in my chamber. Not roses, but..."

"Carnations." She sipped at her okra-coffee.

"Right," Enjoying the warmth of the mug in my hands, I said, "I could make one." *For Eli.*

"I could show you how," said Shurrana.

"I'd like that."

We finished our okra-coffees in silence while I cut and shaped delicate fabrics together in my mind.

∞ O ∞

Each evening, after finally leaving the office, I locked myself in my chamber and made flowers. My daughters thought I was meditating, that I'd discovered solace and inner strength through self-reflection. On the contrary, after a few patient instructional sessions from Shurrana, I managed to create artificial carnations, one painstaking bloom at a time. The first attempts had been hideous, misshapen monstrosities. After carefully disassembling them, I repositioned and adjusted the petals until I created my first recognizable flower.

By the end of the second week, I'd become proficient enough to make two flowers in the half-hour I set aside, bringing the total bouquet to seventeen. I hid the finished products on the top shelf of my closet, beneath the sweater my grandmother left me when she died— an old wool cardigan her mother had knitted by hand. As my collection grew, the sweater did little to hide the stash.

On the four-week anniversary of Eli's death, Aurisandra turned up in an emergency room. She had "lacerations of undisclosed origin" that required a total of twenty-eight stitches. The incident gave me pause. On one level, I was almost *pleased* at the idea that my supporters might have taken the law into their own hands to retaliate against Aurisandra and the anti-Fourth radicals. But as the leader of a civilization based on peace and understanding, I had to condemn the violence.

Publically.

Shurrana set up a press conference outside the hospital wing. I began with a brief statement:

"The missing forewoman for the north wing construction project is recovering well, with no anticipated long-term complications. She remains silent, refusing to answer to the accusations of her involvement in the anti-Fourth movement, or her alleged tampering with the crane on the day of my son's death."

I paused for effect, readying myself for the barrage of questions from the press.

"Madam Prime Minister, if the allegations are true, how will Aurisandra be prosecuted?"

"To the fullest extent of the law."

"Madam Prime Minister, do you have a formal statement concerning this, our settlement's first murder charge?"

"I trust in the judicial system. Next question."

"Madam Prime Minister, is it true that you've ordered the remains of Eli, in particular his arm, frozen for a ceremonial burial in the future?"

I glanced at Shurrana, looking for guidance as to how to answer. She shrugged.

"Yes."

Gasps rippled through the women before me. For a few seconds, the crowd hushed, as though everyone present had forgotten how to breathe. Then the shouts began; a mish-mash of noise my mind couldn't decipher into anything short of bedlam.

I raised my hands, in the classic demand-for-silence gesture, but to no avail. Finally, Shurrana stepped up to the microphone and repeatedly demanded quiet.

Once the crowd complied, I said, "Thank you for your patience. As soon as I have more information on the ceremony, I will distribute the details. Now I must return to more pressing matters of the colony."

I gripped my assistant's hand and we hurried to a train, the reporters hounding us until my security detail blocked them from entering our car and the doors closed behind us.

∞ ◯ ∞

My grief clouded my daily routine. When the recycling report crossed my console, my thoughts dwelt on Eli's waiting arm. I'd avoided the decision to either bury it in the sea or allow it to be reclaimed. That same morning, I was called to attend the dedication ceremony for the newly completed northwest atrium.

I listened attentively to the speeches and studied the new facility. As soon as the architect used her pointer to sever the holographic ribbon, I hurried to a shuttle. The extra time bought me a chance to scrounge for more fabric.

The Asteria complex housed the manufacturing facilities. The automated weaver droned loudly from the east building, drawing me towards the promise of scraps. A long mural depicted the history of fabrics from hand-looms to textile mills. Women owned the culture of cloth. From seamstresses to sweat shop laborers, our sisters had clothed humanity for thousands of years. Stopping in front of one image, I scrutinized the scene. Shown from the back, her ear protectors protruding, the tension in her shoulders and pain of her hunched back spoke of her countless days enslaved by the dance of machine and thread. I touched her hair and felt cold cement, not the warmth of her hard existence.

"We honor you," I said aloud.

I followed the corridor to a junction with two branches, spinning to the left and weaving to the right. Multiple doors interrupted the mural on the right-hand wall. I checked the first one.

Stacks of spooled threads filled the compartment.

I shut the door and checked the next one. Bare, save for shelving, the scuffs in the floor indicated a heavy load had been removed recently.

Further down the corridor, the rhythmic smack and clang of the weaving machines drowned out the ever-present whirling of the air scrubbers. I opened the next compartment.

"Get out!" said a familiar voice.

I threw the light switch. Norinda sat atop a metal crate. Beside her, his face hidden inside his shirt, sat a boy.

"Show yourself," I said.

He pulled the shirt down to reveal his features. He was of African origin, with straight hair. He looked remarkably like Eli might have as a teen. I'd seen this Fourth in the corridors. His mother was Tumeda's teacher.

Norinda stood. "What are you doing here, Mother?"

"That's my question," I said.

"Nathan and I were talking."

"Yes, Madam Prime Minister," he said. "Talking."

"I didn't address you." I grabbed Norinda's arm, yanked her down from the crate, and dragged her close to me. "Come with me."

"Not without Nathan," she said.

"You shouldn't be alone with a Fourth."

"I like him." She snorted, sounding more like Eli than I thought possible. "I knew you wouldn't understand."

"Oh, I understand *perfectly.*"

Without waiting for a response, I hauled Norinda out to the corridor.

"We were only—"

"Not another word!" Glaring into her eyes, I added, "Not one, *single* word."

Breathing deeply, I searched for calm. "You're never to see him *alone* again."

"Why don't you order him killed? I'm sure that'd boost your popularity."

The slap echoed against the walls. My hand stung. A red image of my fingers welled up on her cheek.

"It's your *duty* to respect our laws." My words sounded hollow, even to my own ears.

"I'm not a lesbian," she said.

"Neither am I."

"You and your celebation group sit around and talk about how you don't need anyone because loneliness is nobler than homosexuality. *A woman doesn't require the love of a man.* Isn't that the edict of your group— to live a full life without love?"

I shook my head. "Love and intimacy aren't interchangeable. I can live without sharing my bed. Mothers have a stronger bond with their children than they will ever feel for a *man.*"

"*Eli* was a man. And you *loved* him. You're such a hypocrite. The whole damned colony is the ultimate propaganda-filled hypocrisy," she said. "I've memorized the mission statement in school: *Women built* Pyleia *as a utopia free of the subjugation of men.* But we're all fooling ourselves. We can't survive as a species without them."

"That's why we have the storage banks."

"Why the Fourth Law, then?"

"To replenish our supplies," I said.

"So Eli existed solely for his sperm? He was completely disposable once he banked deposits?"

"Of course not."

"What then, Mother? A job scrubbing floors? Who would he love? In your warped little promised land, he wouldn't even know his children."

I opened my mouth to answer, but couldn't think of what to say. What would Eli have done with his life? Who would he have loved?

"Nathan's a year younger than me, but he's smart," she said. "So smart that the teachers thought he should be taught math. They allowed him to join my class two months ago. He fidgets in his seat and pushes back his hair all the time, just like Eli did. Our teacher does her best to shush him. But he keeps right on speaking, as though his opinion matters."

In that moment, I saw Eli in her— his stubbornness and his black and white view of ethics. I also saw Tumeda and her never-ending ability to reason us all to death with logic. "His *opinion* isn't the problem," I said.

In an attempt to lessen the tension, I lowered my voice and spoke very slowly. "As leader, my family must set an example. If my eldest daughter flouts the rules—"

"You're so convinced that loneliness is noble. My generation isn't."

An image flashed through my mind, of Norinda engaged in a sexual act with Nathan. I raised my hand, ready to strike her again. *Violence as a means of expression. Typical male behavior.*

She stared at my hand in silence.

I lowered it to my side. In that moment, all of my thoughts focused into a singularity of empathy. Eli's death, Norinda's choice, the sperm banks; all of it jelled into a pattern I had been trying so hard not to see. For the first time since becoming Prime Minister, I was ashamed of the settlement.

I wasn't aware of how much time had passed while I came to this realization, but Norinda looked impatient and worried at the same time.

"Come on," I said. "I want to show you something."

"What about Nathan?"

"Bring him."

We hurried through the corridors, Norinda walking to my right and Nathan behind us.

I led them into my chamber and locked both doors. "Please, sit."

Norinda sat on the bed and Nathan on the floor. Inside my closet, I pulled out the pile of carnations hidden beneath my grandmother's sweater.

I set them on the bed, handed one to my daughter, and one to the boy.

"What are they?" she asked.

"Carnations. I made them."

The boy studied his. "What are they for?" he asked.

"For Eli. To commemorate his life."

"Why, Mother?"

I picked up a carnation and brought it close to my nose, pretending to smell its non-existent fragrance. "Because we need this. All of us. We need pieces of our past. The foundation of our new civilization is flawed. You're not the only woman born in our third generation to gaze at a boy with longing. Love is more powerful than politics or philosophy. My love for Eli never faltered. Not once did I love him less than I would a daughter. Yet seeing you with Nathan made me angry. Why? Because I've been *taught* to fear males, mistrust them, loathe them. Just like Aurisandra. And look what fruit her hatred bore."

Norinda raised a hand. "Mother—"

"Let me finish." I paused. "You've both reminded me of what's truly important. You've clarified my view. I'm in a position to curb this hypocrisy before it ruins what we've worked so hard to build."

∞ ◯ ∞

My carnations had evolved into exquisite replicas of natural magnificence. When I found a discarded sheet made of pale blue cotton, it reminded me of the images in the archives of Earth's sky. I salvaged the pieces not ripped or stained and produced my favorite flowers to date. The hue captured Eli, not only his abundant joy, but also his maleness, bound to the stereotypical gender-based color.

I brought the last blue carnation down to the storage chamber. I donned a life suit, tucking the blossom inside the protective layers, and then ventured through the airlock to see what had become of him.

His arm had been stuffed in a corner, once upright but now sagging in an unnatural curve. I touched it. Even through the layers of the life suit, the flesh felt tough and rotten, like a piece of meat that has been overcooked then stored for too long. His arm no longer bore any signs of life or movement. The word "corpse" came to mind, but I stopped it there, refusing to admit its existence or speak it into reality.

Crying inside a life suit is a futile exercise, for the fans and reclamation devices are most uncomfortable, but knowing did not stop my tears. I wrenched my head left and right, avoiding the tube that slithered out to suck my fluids and recycle them into drinking water. "No," I shouted at the suit. "You won't take this moment from me." But the mechanisms were neither sentient nor courteous. If anyone had been observing me while I struggled against the life suit, I would have appeared mad, batting my arms at a non-existent opponent, flinging my head and torso away from unseen tormentors, and all the while maintaining eye contact with the decrepit remains of my son's arm.

I lost my balance and collided with the shelf. I watched in helpless terror as his limb fell to the floor with a dull thud.

My scream activated the intercom.

"Madam Prime Minister," came a voice in my headset. "Is that you? Are you injured?"

"Yes," I said. "My heart's no longer whole."

I turned the sound off before suffering her frantic questions. Without looking back, I moved away from the arm and hurried through the airlock. My life suit fell to the floor as a medtech appeared with a kit in hand.

"I'm better," I said.

"Let me check you out, Ma'am."

"That won't be necessary." I stored the suit in the rack. "I would like my son's remains placed in a sealed container. I'll send word once I secure its final destination."

"Yes, Ma'am."

I hurried for the shuttle before she objected.

News of my encounter beat me to the office. Kjillu stood by my desk, arms crossed. She said, "Tecmessa, his arm should have been reclaimed over three months ago."

"I'm in the process of arranging his funeral."

My Minister moved closer and murmured, "It's about time." The other staff stopped working and tuned their attentions to our conversation.

"Everyone," I said. "To the boardroom."

While the women arranged themselves around the table, I searched through my office for a picture that my mother had given me on my seventh birthday. When I entered the boardroom, Kjillu stood at the head of the table. Norinda appeared, as though she had sensed a pivotal moment not to be missed. I leaned over her and said, "I might regret this one day. But for now, I want you to know that I respect your convictions."

I activated the light beneath the table's display glass, removed the picture from its frame, and placed it in the center of the table. A large image of Earth glowed bright for all to see. The bleakness of it, once the blue planet now turned gray and brittle, added a layer of dread to the atmosphere in the room.

"We left our home to build a new civilization. My hope for the future began the day my mother, Prothoe Ikanolijos, first gave me this photo and described the devastation we left behind. Twice since then I've felt true despair. First, on the night that Prothoe suffered an aneurism and left me alone. Second, the day my son Eli died. I haven't enough fervor left to lead you. I've decided to resign."

An unheard sigh of relief drifted through those present.

I had captured my staff's full attention. Every nervous face pointed at me. "Kjillu will assume my role until a proper election is held."

Kjillu's relief was now mixed with fear, or perhaps exhilaration, I could not be sure which. She said, "I accept your resignation, Madam Prime Minister."

"But first," I said. "Every Prime Minister is allowed a legacy."

The women leaned forward, ready to support me in my last official act.

"Males, *men*, deserve dignity. Intolerance breeds anger and resentment. We must nurture them — respect them — to create a sustainable society."

Accusations broke out, like bees scurrying from flower to flower. My daughter remained silent, waiting.

"I will step into a new role. *Teacher*. The boys in this colony will be my priority. Under my guidance, they will learn to succeed, to achieve, and most of all, to love."

I called up an image of Eli on the console. "My son was most likely murdered. I cannot tell you how many nights I have stared at the ceiling from my bed, imagining all of the violence I could inflict on Aurisandra. The witch deserves to suffer for her part, even if she didn't control that crane herself, or lead the Fourth-Abolitionists in their actions."

I paused, swallowing back my anger, bringing my voice back from the quivering brink. With practiced political poise, I released my fists, returning my hands to open palms at my sides. "But I will not harbor revenge or resentment. His spirit lingers in me. His love of life, of discovery, of kindness will never be forgotten. As a member of the Prime Minister's family, he will be accorded a proper funeral. The ceremony will occur tomorrow. I expect all in attendance to show him the highest respect."

Though our colony's hierarchy mimicked that of Earth's Western politics, we did not follow the procedures of men. Rather than shaking hands, I hugged my staff one by one. Norinda cried openly. I had never been so proud of my daughter.

∞ O ∞

We held the flower gathering in the banquet hall on the plaza. Many of my Ministers and staff showed their respect. Every male in the *Pyleian* settlement attended, eager to hear their new teacher's words.

I had enlisted the help of Veranisey, her classmates, and friends to assist with the overwhelming task of preparing enough blooms for the anticipated guests. We had worked well into the night before the gathering, crafting hundreds of replicas of the Earthly blossoms.

I had commissioned the harvest forewoman to diffuse a floral scent in the room. She extracted oils from pods and stems, roots and leaves discarded for compost. The three remaining live members of the original generation who had the courage to attend the gathering confirmed that the concoction did not remotely resemble the slight fragrance of a true carnation. The jibe didn't diminish my determination. So long as it smelled of something other than body odor or last night's soup, I voiced my appreciation of the botanist's efforts with enthusiasm. She did not attend the gathering herself, for her allegiance rested with the more conservative women in the settlement.

The media called for a fifteen minute work stoppage; in protest. Even some of the life support mechanics joined in, shutting down fans, turning the colony eerily quiet. Ironically, the research facility was the only area to maintain vigilance. So our sperm, the most precious of male contributions, were able to show their support on Eli's special day.

After considering Norinda's avowal to seek a male partner, I embraced her choice. I would attach the love once born of my son's existence to this new man in our lives. My future son-in-law perhaps, if the judicial system would allow such a radical change in settlement philosophy.

Inside the tiny casket-like-container, the flesh of my son's arm no longer belonged to Eli. Like my beliefs in our society, the arm had been stripped of its value. My baby had moved on to another realm, one where he would never be forced to hang his head in shame for what he was. As an atheist, I mocked my illogical faith, yet a part of me held firm to the notion that his spirit lived on. This belief emanated from all of me, every nerve and muscle, especially my heart.

On arrival, I handed each person a carnation. Once they found their seats, I stepped up to the podium.

"Ladies and, most notably, *gentlemen*, we share a common desire for hope. Not only the hope that the colony will be sturdy and bountiful, but also the hope that our foremothers' values will uphold and sustain our society. My son, Eli, taught me otherwise. Love has no bias. Every soul deserves respect, regardless of the number of X or Y chromosomes housed in their DNA."

I stepped down from the podium and walked up to the container holding my son's remains. No flag adorned the case, for we had eradicated the concept of a "nation" from our judicial vocabulary. His coffin rested on a cart to allow me to wheel him away. On top of his final vessel sat four blue carnations, the finest I had constructed of all of my artificial flowers. I lifted one and inhaled its fragrance of worn cotton. With a shrug, I placed it back on the coffin. Clearing my throat, I hummed the wordless lullaby my mother, Prothoe, sang for me every night of my childhood.

Singing calmed me. With authority, I said, "My mother wrote that song. She named it 'Molpadia', literally 'Death Song' after the Greek Amazon. History says Queen Antiope was wounded in a battle of the Attic War against King Theseus. As the king approached his prey, Antiope could not defend herself and so Molpadia killed her, with an arrow or spear — no one is certain which — to protect her queen from violation at Theseus's hand."

I ran my fingertips along the smooth surface of Eli's coffin.

"Though murder is abhorrent to me, and my own son was killed for what he was, I might have been tempted to end his life, years from now, as a form of mercy, to protect him from the continual persecution inherent in our culture. For that reason, I've stepped down as Prime Minister. I stand before you as a simple teacher and mother," I glanced over at all three of my daughters, "and a human being. If babies will be conceived naturally, not with insemination, then we have fulfilled a biological obligation as *Homo sapiens*. To not acknowledge the importance of all male members of our settlement is irresponsible and hypocritical. I'm as guilty as anyone seated here of such crimes. On my dead son's honor, I beg him for forgiveness."

Lowering my voice, I touched Eli's coffin and whispered, "You taught me so much. I can never live up to your innocence, but I will spend each of my remaining days instilling tolerance and peace into our *Pyleia*. I hope that when I breathe my last lungful of processed air, you will grant me the same."

Addressing the crowd once more, I said, "I loved my Fourth. My *son*. And as each and every one of the mothers in the audience must understand, all mothers grieve hardest when they outlive a child."

I could sense the rising tension. "As our society continues to integrate these young males into our culture, we must make adjustments to our predecessors' radical views. In the long run, our objective remains the same: to nurture peaceful democracy. If Eli's death contributes to a greater understanding and clarification of the place of *males* in our society, then his loss will not have been in vain."

Picking up the carnation once more, I pointed to the audience with it. "We must all continue to value love over hatred, respect over ridicule, and peace over violence."

In a slow and grand sweep, I brought the carnation close to my heart.

My grief ascended, threatening to dissolve my courageousness. Norinda rose, stood beside me, and handed me a handkerchief.

"Thank you," I whispered to her.

"I'm proud to be your daughter."

We hugged. My girl, now a woman, fueled my resolve to complete the ceremony with decorum.

I held her a few seconds past when her grip loosened. I stepped away and nodded. Norinda remained beside the coffin. She placed her carnation, a white one with a faint pattern of pink rosebuds, beside the blue ones.

"It's time," I said to the crowd, "for all of you to approach with your flowers in hand."

Women and boys stepped towards Eli's container. "You're welcome to keep your carnation, or place it on the casket. I've read in the archives that at traditional grave-side ceremonies, only family members threw their flowers down, but I consider every person in this colony a part of our extended family."

Row by row, people spoke to me or Norinda. Some gave me their flower, some left the token for Eli, and others cherished the hand-made gift. I maintained a noble stance for as long as mourners lingered.

When the last guest left the hall, leaving me alone with my daughters and our security detail, I smiled. "Norinda, Tumeda, and Veranisey. My three girls, though I think Norinda's crept into womanhood while we weren't looking."

"*Mother*," she said.

"Eli would have agreed. He often said that you and I were alike."

Norinda nodded. "He was perceptive."

"And cute," said Veranisey.

"And kind," said Tumeda. "I miss him."

"We all do," I said. "But this is our chance to say a proper goodbye."

After gathering the flowers on top of the case, I walked around to its short end and pushed the cart towards the door. "I'm going to take him on a shuttle to the sea's edge and then bury him in the depths. Head home, if you like."

"I'll come," said Tumeda.

"We all will," said Norinda.

The four of us wheeled Eli out of the banquet hall and across the courtyard to the shuttle station. On the train, we sat in silence until the last stop. There, we disembarked and pushed the cart slowly to the airlock at the edge of the colony.

"What about the flowers?" said Veranisey.

Returning the pile of carnations to the top of the case, I said, "They'll go out with him. So that a piece of him is always close to a piece of us."

I opened the inner door and we all gently maneuvered the case into the airlock. Bringing a few flowers to my lips, I kissed them one by one. Then I exited the vestibule and closed the inner door.

Metal clanked, steel against steel. Through vision distorted by tears, I worked the levers and entered the code that opened the outer door and pushed the contents onto the ramp. For a moment, I was relieved that the inner door had no window. I could not watch his remains splash into the methane sea.

"The Fourth-Abolitionists will fight you," said Norinda.

"I know."

"I think you're right, Mommy," said Veranisey.

I knelt down to her height. "Why?"

"I loved Eli as much as I loved Norinda or Tumeda. I don't see the big deal about boys anyway. They aren't *that* bad."

"No," said Norinda. "Some of them are actually quite handsome."

"Yes," I said. This time, the thought of seeing Norinda in the arms of a boy didn't rouse my anger. For an instant, I imagined myself nestled in a man's arms. Though foreign, the thought appealed to me, despite my utter lack of live specimens mature enough to bring to life such a fancy.

I grasped Norinda's hand, and then Veranisey's. They each, in turn, took one of Tumeda's. We stood in our circle of blood, swaying back and forth. I hummed the first few lines of "Molpadia" once more.

"No sad songs, Mom," said Tumeda.

"What shall we sing?"

"Something happy," said Veranisey.

"Something boyish," said Norinda.

"Why don't we make up a song?" said Tumeda. "On the shuttle ride home. We could call it 'Eli.'"

"Among the Flowers," I added.

The four of us made up a tonal disaster of a song with awkward lyrics. Over the years we embellished it, until we'd refined it into a piece worthy of public performance. And on Norinda's wedding day, I sang it aloud to celebrate the first official male-female marriage in the *Pyleian* settlement.

I had become the embodiment of my newly developed ideals. Eli would've cried, but my eyes remained dry, despite my pride and happiness. Since that fateful day, I had spilled more than enough tears for both of us.

MUFFY
AND THE BELFRY

I bite my lip as I tiptoe into my mother's room. She gets real mad when I wake her at night, but I need her. With Muffy under my arm, I poke her. "Mom?"

"Huh?"

"I need to go to the bathroom."

She squints at the big red numbers on her clock. "Don't wake me, Penny, just *go*."

"Sorry."

The nightlight from my room paints the floor pale yellow so I can find my way to the bathroom. The wood squeaks under my toes. After turning on the light, I blink the brightness away and set Muffy on guard in the doorway.

Don't look up. I sit down, but I can't stop myself from peeking. Way above me is the dusty and dark opening that Mom calls the "skylight." It has four crinkly glass panes shaped like triangles. A big crack zigzags along the one closest to me. The black wood posts holding it together meet at a point and an old piece of rope with a knot at the end hangs down from the center. A bunch of spider webs cling to the knot, and on windy nights, like tonight, it sways back and forth. I look up because I have to make sure the spider that built the web isn't about to land on me and suck my blood.

My friend Becky has a skylight in her kitchen. The hole above me doesn't look even remotely like a skylight. It looks more like the haunted belfry in a Halloween picture book my teacher read to us. In the story, a monster lived in the belfry, and I'm scared that one lives in mine.

I wash my hands, pick up Muffy, and turn out the light. I wait in the hallway until my eyes adjust to the dark. The wind whistles through the belfry. The rope will be swaying up there, knocking the spider down. I listen for its feet but the wind covers all the quiet sounds. I keep Muffy close. He smells like the lemon soap my mom uses to wash him. When I can see better, Muffy and I hurry for the bed and dive under the covers. The air gets hot and stale, but I can't pop out. Not yet. The monster from the belfry may still be awake.

"Easy, Muffy. We have to listen a while longer. To be sure."

The wind shakes my window. After a long time, I pull back the covers and inhale fresh air. The monster must be asleep. I squeeze Muffy and close my eyes.

∞ O ∞

Every day I walk the same route home from school: seven streets down Merner, then right onto Lackner. Russell lives on Lackner too, right across the street from me in a big green house with shutters and a long wooden porch. He always gets home from school before me 'cause his mom drives him.

I stare down at the sidewalk and hope today he will leave me alone.

"Look at *Nickelhead*. She's five pennies crazy. Going to cry today, crazy brains?"

He blocks my path.

Still looking down, I whisper, "Let me by, Russell."

"Oh, I'm shakin' in my boots now, *Nickelhead*. Look me in the eye, and maybe I'll be *really* scared."

He shoves me on the shoulder. I stare at my shoes. "I used up my milk card today. I don't have another one. Please, let me by."

"If you say pretty please."

"Pretty please, Russell."

"I didn't hear you." He shoves me harder.

Louder this time, "Pretty please, let me by."

"On one condition."

I wait.

"Halloween is next week. Bring me three chocolate bars a day, starting tomorrow." He leans in and I can smell his stinky breath: rotten candy mixed with dirt. I turn my head away.

"My mom bought raisins not chocolate bars," I say.

"I don't care. Three a day. Got it?"

He shoves me aside, and I fall onto the street. Russell's favorite way to say goodbye. One day a car may come and *splat*. Lucky for me, Lackner isn't busy with cars. I wait until he crosses the street, then step up to the curb.

Mom and I live above a store, the only apartment on the block. Old Mr. Quiggly owns the building. He's always been nice to us. When Mom was young, she worked in his store after school, selling candy to her friends. When Dad died, Mr. Quiggly rented us the apartment above the store for cheap. Mom needs to get things for cheap. Otherwise there won't be milk in the fridge.

I walk inside the store. Mr. Quiggly looks up from a newspaper and smiles.

"Hello, Penny."

"Hi, Mr. Quiggly."

"How are you today?"

"I'm okay." I point at a bag of chocolate bars. "How much for those?"

He tells me the price. I drop my hand to my side.

"Are you sure you're all right?"

Still a little scared from being pushed onto the street, I force out my best smile. "I'm sure."

"Well, see you later then."

"Bye."

I walk around back, up the stairs, and unlock the apartment door. Inside, I turn the bolt as quick as I can. Russell never comes to the door, but I don't want to take any chances.

I remove my coat, bring my knapsack to the living room, and turn on the TV. I always keep the volume on low and sit close so I can hear. Mom says not to make too much noise during store hours. Mr. Quiggly needs quiet. I take out my homework. I have to finish before five o'clock. If I don't put dinner in the oven by five it won't be ready when Mom gets home. Work always tires her out, but dinner makes her smile. She hardly ever smiles since Dad went to heaven.

After I finish my homework, I count my piggy bank money. I have enough to buy the chocolate bars. Muffy stares at me as if to say, "Don't do it. That money's for your future."

"It's okay, Muffy," I say. "I'll find a way to put it back. I need to get past Russell." Muffy understands. We talk a lot about Russell.

I hurry downstairs, remembering to lock the door behind me. Mom gets mad if I forget, even if I'm only going out for a minute. I walk around front and into the store. I grab one of the bags of candy by the cash register and look around for Mr. Quiggly, but I don't see him anywhere.

"Mr. Quiggly?"

Nothing.

"It's Penny."

I put the candy on the counter. When I still don't see him, I walk around and see a foot. Dropping my money, I run over to where Mr. Quiggly is lying on the floor. I shake him and shake him, calling out his name, but he won't move. I run to the back of the store and find the phone with the big sign above it that says, *not for customer use*. But this is an emergency.

∞ O ∞

The police car lights are flashing outside the window when Mom gets home from work.

"I'm sorry dinner isn't ready. I put it in the oven at five-thirty. It'll—"

"Penny!" She runs over to me and hugs me while we stand in the hot kitchen. "I don't care about dinner. I talked to the police. They said Mr. Quiggly died and *you* found him."

"I was in the store, because… I wanted to say hi, and I saw him."

"Oh, sweetie " She hugs me again, the way she does when she cries about Dad.

"I'm okay."

"Are you sure?"

"I've seen dead people before."

"I know." She looks as if she might cry, but then she gets down on one knee and holds my shoulders. She always does that when she has something *important* to say. "Do you want to talk about what happened? It hasn't been long since Dad—"

"I'm okay." I don't want her to talk about him. I don't want to think about dead people anymore.

"Well, okay, if you say so." She stands up. I guess the important part's over. "This is bad for us. With Mr. Quiggly dead, we might not be able to stay here."

I check the oven timer. "Dinner's almost ready. You can set the table if you want."

∞ O ∞

I sneak into Mom's room and nudge her. "I need to go to the bathroom."

"How many times do I have to tell you? Just *go*."

"Sorry." I clutch Muffy. After seeing Mr. Quiggly all dead, I have the spooks really bad. I inch from Mom's room to the bathroom as carefully as I can, looking all around me with every step. Muffy's scared, too. I can tell. He doesn't smell lemony any more, he smells old.

I turn on the bathroom light. The bulb shines extra bright then blinks out.

Squeezing Muffy, I stand still and suck on a bit of his fur. The fluff sticks to my tongue making me gag. I flip the switch up and down a few times, but the light stays off. Mom keeps the extra bulbs in the top cupboard of the kitchen where I can't reach. I wonder what to do then I notice the hallway is dark. My nightlight is off too.

Maybe the power will work in a minute.

I switch the light to the on position and wait. Muffy and I rock back and forth hoping the lights will come back on.

They don't.

Finally, I can't hold it anymore. I take tiny steps into the bathroom, one hand ahead of me, gripping Muffy with the other. I don't look up this time. After, I close the lid slowly, trying not to make a sound, and skip the flush. The sink is right next to me, so I lean over, and turn on a trickle of water, enough to rinse. With my empty hand out in front again, Muffy and I inch back toward my room.

That's when I hear it. A squeak. Or maybe it's a creak. It sounds like one of the boards in the belfry. Maybe the one that holds the cracked glass. It sounds as if it will give way under the weight of the monster.

I take bigger steps toward my room and stub my toe.

"Ouch," I say, louder than I meant to.

Mom won't wake up, but the thing in the belfry may have heard. More steps in the dark. My feet make too much noise. I can feel it now, something alive, something creeping toward Muffy and me, waiting to grab us and eat us. When my knee bumps the edge of my bed, I yank my blanket off and, with Muffy under my arm, I crawl under the bed.

Another squeak.

My body shakes all over. If I call Mom, she may come and hug me. But I shouldn't wake her. So I press my back against the wall. It's dusty under the bed and I feel a tickle in my nose. I stick my finger under it like Becky taught me. It's the only way to hold back a sneeze.

Another squeak.

This one doesn't come from the belfry. It comes from the room. Someone is standing by my light switch. Maybe Mom is going to turn on the light and tell me not to be scared.

Another squeak.

From the bed this time. It can't be Mom because she would have turned on the light. Except that the power isn't working. She would have spoken to me by now. If I stay still maybe the monster won't find us.

"Penny?"

"Muffy, not now." I squeeze him and whisper in his ear, "We have to stay quiet until the monster goes away."

"Penny."

I look at Muffy and whisper, "Did you just talk out loud?"

"Yes."

"Oh. Okay." I try to think, but it's hard when I'm scared. If my bear can talk, then maybe he'll scare away whatever is up there. I push him to the edge of the bed.

"Is it gone, Muffy? Can you see if it's gone?"

"It's not gone, it's inside me."

"What?"

"It's inside me," he says, a little louder. But not loud enough to wake Mom.

"No, I meant what's *inside you*?"

"A friend."

"Becky?"

"No."

"I don't have any other friends." If Muffy is carrying a monster inside him, I definitely don't want both of them in my bed.

"Muffy?"

"Yes?"

"Can you move?"

"I don't think so."

"Try."

We both wait while he tries. I study him as best as I can in the dark room, but he doesn't seem to move. I wiggle out from under the bed and peek over the edge. No monster.

The lights come back on. Mom will get mad if I leave the bathroom light on all night. Money doesn't grow on trees. But I can't go back in there. I hurry over to the closet and lay Muffy on the floor by my dolls. "I love you Muffy, but this is for your own good. Goodnight." I run back to my bed and sleep under it for the night.

In the morning, Mom doesn't yell about the light. I guess she's still worried about me seeing Mr. Quiggly dead. I open my closet to grab my day clothes. Muffy rests in the same spot. He doesn't say a word. I close the door.

After breakfast, Mom says, "It's going to be cold today. Go get a sweater."

"Would you get it for me? Please?"

She gives me the stop-this-right-now-or-I'm-going-to-get-mad look, so I walk back to my room.

When I open the closet door, Muffy says, "Take me to school today."

"Why?"

"Because."

"Mom says 'because' isn't a reason."

"Please, Penny. For me?"

Mom always says not to bring toys to school. Kids lose toys at school. I don't want to touch Muffy now that he can talk, but he looks up at me with his happy eyes. He doesn't look mean, or scary. So I get my knapsack from the kitchen, and walk back to my room. I put him in, hoping Mom won't check my bag.

∞ O ∞

At lunch recess, I grab Muffy from my knapsack and run to the far corner of the schoolyard by the baseball diamonds. He stares at me with his Muffy smile.

I figure he isn't going to talk, but then he says, "Penny?"

"Yes?"

"I have a plan for Russell."

"What is it?" I sit down in the grass.

"He wets the bed almost every night."

"How do you know?"

"His mom buys him big-kid diapers in my store."

I shake my head. "You don't have a store."

"Mr. Quiggly's."

I pick up Muffy and stare into his yellow eyes. "Is that you Mr. Quiggly? In Muffy?"

"Yes."

"How can you make Muffy talk?"

"Because I died."

"How come my dad doesn't make him talk?"

"It only works for a little while. Your dad's been gone for too long."

I swallow hard. "Can you ask him questions?"

"Maybe."

"Well, can you ask him why he left us? Mom's always sad, and we need him to come back."

"He can't come back."

"But *you* did."

"I'm here to help you with Russell, and then I have to go."

"Why?"

"That's the rules. I'm sorry."

I want to be strong because I hate it when girls cry, but I can't stop myself. I squeeze Muffy and rock back and forth, trying not to get tears or snot on him. When the bell rings, I sit there. A teacher comes over and tells me to go back to class or say what's making me cry. When I won't, she brings me to the principal's office. I sit on the waiting bench until the principal comes out and tells me that it's okay to cry when people die. Then she says she'll call my mom.

I stop crying. "Please don't. She doesn't like to miss work. I'm okay."

I sniffle. She passes me a tissue. I blow my nose and sniffle again.

She passes me another tissue. "Go to your class. But if you're feeling sad then come back, okay?"

I nod.

The rest of the day I try to forget that my dad's never coming back like Mr. Quiggly.

On my way home from school, I stop and gasp. Russell is waiting on Lackner and I haven't got the chocolate bars.

Maybe I can run around the block to avoid him. But he can see me coming from that direction, too. If I try to outrun him, he'll probably catch me. He's fat, but not *that* fat, and he's older than me. Even fat boys can run faster than little girls.

I guess he's tired of waiting 'cause he starts after me. I hear Muffy's voice inside my knapsack. "You have to stand up to him, or he'll never leave you alone."

"But he'll hit me."

"Trust me."

Russell runs into me and knocks me onto the road. A car motor roars. I jump back onto the sidewalk before the driver zooms by, honking. We both wait until the car turns a corner.

Russell glares at me. "Where are my chocolate bars?"

"I couldn't buy them. Mr. Quiggly was dead."

"I heard about that, *Nickelhead*. Now you're *really* crazy brains 'cause you touched a dead guy." He slaps my head.

I look down at the sidewalk.

"I bet you have candy. Gimme your bag."

I don't want him to find Muffy. I stand there, cross my arms, and say, "No. Leave me alone."

"What did you say?" He grabs my knapsack by the top handle and yanks, lifting me off the ground.

"Stop it. That hurts."

"Gimme!" He shakes the knapsack off my back and jerks it open. His fat hand digs in and pulls out Muffy.

"*Wookit da widdwe teddy beaw. Baby Penny's got her widdwe beaw wif her.*" He grabs Muffy's body in one hand, and his head in the other, as if he's going to rip my bear's head off.

"Give him back, *right now*, or else."

"Or else what?"

"I'll tell the whole school that you wet the bed like a big, fat *baby*!"

"Do not."

"Do too. Mr. Quiggly told me. I mean it. I'll tell the *whole school*."

My heart pounds. Russell makes a fist, but before he can hit me I ram head first into his stomach, knocking him onto the road.

He falls down hard, still holding Muffy. Russell doesn't look mean anymore. He looks scared. So I shout, "Russell wets the be-ed! Russell wets the be-ed!"

"Shut up!"

"Gimme my bear."

He throws Muffy at me. I shove him in my knapsack and yell, "Russell wets the be-ed!" one more time. Then I run as fast as I can for home. I take the steps two at a time. My hand shakes so badly I can hardly get the key into the lock. He's going to catch me and hurt me. Finally, the door unlocks and I hurry inside and slam it shut.

For the first time in my life, *Russell* was scared of *me*. I run to my bedroom window and search the street. He must have gone home because I can't see him. Still holding my knapsack, I pull Muffy out and set him on the bed. I give his paws two high-fives.

"I did it, Muffy. I stood up to Russell."

"I know."

"Do you think he's going to hurt me tomorrow?"

"No. I think he'll leave you alone now."

I grab him and hug him so tightly that I squish his body out of shape. All sorts of smells leak out of him: lemon soap, dust, and candy, like the loose sweets Mr. Quiggly used to sell in paper bags.

"I hope you're right," I say.

"Penny?" His voice sounds muffled.

I stop squeezing him. "Yes?"

"Don't be afraid of the belfry. Your dad told me that he looks out for you from up there. He knows you're afraid of the dark."

"Dad hides in the belfry?"

"Not exactly. He watches over you when you're scared."

I hold Muffy's head up high so that his eyes are close to mine. "Really?"

"Yes."

I stare at my cute bear. "Muffy?"

"Yes?"

"Thanks for helping me."

He doesn't answer. I watch him until five o'clock when I have to put dinner in the oven. I sit him on the kitchen table with his back leaning against the wall so I'll hear him if he speaks. But he doesn't.

When Mom comes home I have dinner on the table. She says we shouldn't worry about the apartment 'cause somebody at work has a place we can rent. She even lets Muffy sit on the table for the whole meal.

At bedtime, I climb under the covers with Muffy. I ask him a thousand questions while the air gets hot and stale, but he doesn't answer. Not a word.

The next night I wake up and start into Mom's room. I get as far as her door and change my mind. When I reach the bathroom, I don't turn on the light. Instead, I sit on the floor and gaze up at the belfry. The rope sways from the wind and the spider webs float back and forth. Moonlight shines through the glass, poking through the crack. The dark wood looks creepy, but solid.

I hold Muffy in the crook of my arm and listen for my dad.

SOUL-HUNGRY

I should've adjusted to being dead by now.

The time-slips are the worst part. Blending into my after-reality would be easier if I could join a posse. Then I'd have others to slip with. Funny how being an introvert turns out to be just as crippling in my afterlife as it was in my alive-life.

Back when my soul hadn't caught a ride on the cursed train, my therapist had reassured me every other Tuesday that *structure would save me*. Turns out she was wrong. My routine made me an easier target for the soul-hungry. On *this* side of dead my attachment to routine has been sabotaged by the random skullduggery of the slippage of death-time. Day becomes night becomes day with each unnecessary blink of my not-real eyes. My morning walk becomes my whenever-walk in search of sustenance.

Since I can't seem to release my attachment to my final apartment, my outdoor adventures begin with a trip past the park on Eighth Street.

If I had ever found a husband, and we had ever decided to make ourselves some babies, we would've taken the little monkeys to this park, despite its lackluster appearance. Kids love climbing-forts, and who doesn't crave the occasional bob back and forth on a giant plastic hippo-on-a-spring? But the best part of the pathetic playground had been the single wooden swing. No kid under five could've sat on it without falling off, but I hadn't cared. I had loved to sit on that ancient piece of comfort, pumping my legs and twisting my fingers around the ropes. If the swing had been one of the more modern styles with safety straps, I would never have been able to indulge. As it was, my ass had fit snugly on the plank.

In my new dead-form, I can sit (sort of) on the swing, but I can't pump it up and down. Without the fun-factor, I choose to forgo my old standby and simply settle against the fence that separates the park from the nearby townhouses. There, I watch. And wait. For someone to drop by the park. And maybe, just maybe, I'll jump them on the upswing, suck the life out of them, and curse their soul.

I'm so damned hungry.

Eating means killing.

And killing is hard.

I saw my fair share of the cursed while I was still fighting to stay alive. Their essence materialized right before they struck, and if I was quick enough, which I used to be, I could run. And I did run. Often.

True believers used talismans. Their unwavering faith in God combined with their sin-cleansed confidence worked most of the time.

But the talisman classes never made any sense to me. Having never learned Latin, the words felt like cockroaches on my tongue, always squirming into the corners and falling out as half-chewed carapaces. Since I couldn't fake my belief in God, the talisman would've barely worked anyway.

Agnostics and atheists like me had to rely on warning systems and purification squads, but our protectors couldn't be everywhere at once. The afterlife is a crowded place and the cursed are always hungry.

Now that I'm dead, I can understand — from the pursuer perspective — why running is effective, even from posses. Because one moment I'm about to pounce on a victim, and the next it's twelve hours later and my potential dinner is long gone.

As a matter of fact, I recently watched a posse of five try to capture a young woman who looked to be about my former age. (Which is sort of my age forever although it doesn't seem to matter here.) She was climbing the steps from the subway, carrying her midget fluff-dog in an ornate purse. This particular posse — they call themselves the SubSet — own that subway exit, the five of them lurking around the top of the stairs whenever the purification squads are elsewhere, feasting on victims like jelly beans in a jar. On that particular day, at the last moment they all materialized to eat her (and probably the dog, too). The chick let out a scream that was shrill enough to wake the living *and* the dead. Then poof— the posse slipped as a joined-at-the-soul collective into another time. The woman was left clutching fluffy to her breast, panting and praising God that she had been allowed to survive another day on the living side of reality.

While she was standing there I probably should've pounced on her myself. But if I had, her cursed soul would've likely lingered near the subway exit. When the time-slipped posse meshed with the woman's new timeline she would've snitched on me, blabbing to the SubSet that I had weaseled into their turf.

The posse could choose to retaliate; unleash their wrath on *me*. Only posses have the amplified, linked-together power to destroy another cursed soul. I really don't want to end up in the after-afterlife, or wherever double-cursed souls go.

Soon after I arrived here, I pleaded for the SubSet to take me on as a member. They laughed in my face, and then... well, I'd rather not remember all the ways they humiliated what's left of me.

I have my sights set on the Bookzies. They're an all-female posse who linger near the entrance to the coffee shop inside one of those big bookstores. I love floating in and around the books. All of the paper makes me feel a little more solid, even though I'll never be able to read another book cover-to-cover. Occasionally, I hover far enough behind a real person to read over their shoulder. Sometimes I can read an entire chapter before the urge to eat becomes too strong. Then, like always, I materialize, they freak out, and poof— reading time's over. And if I time-slip away, not only do I miss what happens next in the book, I'm even hungrier by the time I reorient myself.

Regardless of whether or not God exists, or whether said God would spend any time here in the afterlife, I believe that the time-slips act as mediators. Maybe that dude near the windows who's been reading *Forbes* isn't quite due to check out. On his behalf, karma invokes the slip to prevent the soul-hungry from cursing him into a premature death. Maybe he deserves an easier afterlife.

Another theory is that the slip could be the cosmos's way of equalizing the ratio of cursed-by-the-soul-hungry to dead-by-other-means. If too many souls are cursed, they would all live their afterlives here. Cursing that many people might solve some overpopulation issues in the real world, but *this* afterlife would become severely overcrowded. With a shortage of alive-victims to feast from, we would all be so soul-hungry that my death-life would be an absolute misery-fest.

Right now, I'm hovering near the *Fiction and Literature* section, watching the Bookzies snag an unsuspecting latte drinker. As they succeed in cursing the guy's soul, the latte drops to the ground along with its dead drinker, spraying brown liquid on the two people sitting nearby. The living all flee for their lives. The Bookzies are huddled around their victim, slurping and sucking the soul bits like fat off a chicken wing, and I'm feeling particularly cordial. So I sidle up to their circle, clear my not-quite-a-throat, and say, "Hey, there."

The closest one turns to look at me, makes the L-shape with her fingers over her forehead, and says, "Beat it, loser."

"Look," I say. "That was one smooth kill, and while we're all still in the same time zone I thought I'd inquire as to the possibility of an opening in your posse."

The Bookzie in the red hoodie — we're stuck in the same clothes we died in, and she always sports the same gaudy sweater — says, "We're full up."

I cross my arms over my chest, and say, "I didn't mean this *particular* soul, because, hey, I'm not all that hungry right now." *Even though I'm starving.* "But I've seen your posse around, and I'm as impressed with your kill ratio as I am with your political and philosophical leanings, so I think I'd be a great fit."

"Buzz off," says the one in the black leather jacket.

I watch her lick her lips and wonder how long she's been dead, because no one says *buzz off* any more. Do they?

I say, "If you'll only—"

But I slip ahead, and the bookstore is dark and empty, including the coffee shop which is closed and cleaned for the next morning rush. Where the Bookzies had been snacking on their victim, there isn't even a fragment of alive-soul left to taste.

Figures.

I head for the staircase to the main floor. Standing at the bottom is the latte-drinking victim, now a newly cursed member of this afterlife.

"Do I know you?" he says.

"Maybe." I shrug.

He's looking around, acting more than a little nervous as though he thinks someone's going to throw him in jail for hanging out in the bookstore after hours.

"Relax," I say. "They can't see you."

"You can."

"I'm dead."

He takes a step back. "Oh, right," he says. "And so... I'm..."

"Yeah." I take a step closer to him. "You're dead."

"I'm cold," he says.

"You're hungry."

That gets his attention. He's staring into my eyes, with that question that none of us like to admit we know the answer to. Because while we were all still living, we saw enough of the soul-hungry and we are infinitely and uncomfortably familiar with their culinary choices and the consequences thereof.

"How does it work?" he says, as if cursing people is as easy as ordering a pizza. He tucks his hands into his pockets, looking as casual and sexy as a model on a billboard.

I take a deep breath in and let it out, though the effect is useless here, like screaming with the volume set to zero.

"You hover. In places where you feel comfortable. At least at first. Until you join a posse. Then you're obligated to stick within their territory so they can protect you and slip with you."

He nods and his confidence makes me wonder if he was rich when he was alive. "That group. The ones who... I remember..." He scratches his head. "They called you a loser."

"Yep." I don't know what else to say. The guy's been dead for almost no time at all and he's already cooler than me.

"Why," he presses, "did they call you a loser?"

I feel the desperate urge to sit, even though I don't physically require the rest. "I'm a posse-less loner."

"So join one."

"I've tried."

"So try again. What's involved?"

Feeling more anxious, I say, "I'm no expert, but from what I've seen, you hang around their territory and try to impress them with your soul-snatching brilliance. Be careful. If you're lingering too much they'll see you as a threat. And then..."

"Then?"

"Let's just say, you don't want to piss them off. They'll punish you." I pause, remembering when the SubSet dragged me to the pound and forced me to suck on the rancid souls of abused dogs. "Or worse."

He laughs. "We're dead. How can they make things worse?"

"The posses have enough connected strength to destroy you."

His smile fades. "What happens then?"

"I'm not sure exactly. An after-afterlife, I guess."

"So basically, I should suck up to them?"

"Or charm them. Charisma's crucial. But I seem to have misplaced mine."

"Okay." He turns to stare at the windows, and I'm guessing he feels the need to get the hell out of this pathetic bookstore, AKA ground zero of his demise. "Thanks," he adds, somewhat absently.

"You're welcome."

For the first time in a long while, I'm actually hoping for a slip. I mean, this guy's *hot*, and I wouldn't mind starting my own posse with him as the inaugural member, but he's obviously not into me. And I'm more than a little sick of rejection.

He walks over to the windows, presses his hand against the glass, and learns that he can pass through.

"Thanks for the tip," he says over his shoulder.

"Any time." I want to add "Really", but the sentiment will only make me sound needy.

Once he's outside, I walk over to the glass, wholly intending to follow him. Then I time-slip.

∞ ◯ ∞

Three soul-sucks later, I'm still alone. I haven't bumped into latte-guy, so I figure he's found himself a posse far away from my stomping grounds.

The sun's up, but I know full well it won't last. I walk through the door of my former apartment (the Asian couple living there are such devout Buddhists that I don't have a hope of cursing them) and head for the park on Eighth Street.

A mother is sitting on the swing, watching her young daughter bounce back and forth on the giant plastic hippo-on-a-spring. I haven't eaten in a long time. If I move any closer to either one of them, I will definitely materialize. And in my current desperate need to feed, I will kill one of them if I have the chance.

They don't deserve to be cursed.

But I'm so bloody hungry.

For the second time since I ended up in this afterlife, I consider the idea of starving myself. I've seen the emaciated shells of the cursed, even watched one slip once. She didn't disappear quickly like the rest of us do. She seemed to evaporate, the bits of her fragile cursed soul floating and lingering before finally slipping beyond my sight.

Maybe that's the way out of this place?

But I'm starving, and I really, *desperately* need to eat something. Some*one*.

Mother or daughter?

I'll only have the chance to curse one of them.

If I go for the daughter, fairness karma is likely to slip me out of here. No way is that little cutie-pie's time up yet. I've got better odds on the mother, but then I'll be orphaning the girl. Maybe.

I don't know why I figure that Dad isn't in the picture. Something about the way the mother is half-swaying and half-twirling lazily on the swing makes her look so bone-weary tired that she must be a single mom. Probably got herself pregnant and the guy ran.

Or maybe he was cursed?

Either way, if I kill the mother then I will crush this little girl's spirit. She won't last much longer on the living side of reality, and then she'll end up a different kind of orphan in the afterlife. Because for as long as I've been here, I've never seen a child. Which means if they're cursed, they go elsewhere.

I have my theories as to where.

Heaven's my first guess. But that involves a faith that I've never held.

The second option is a little darker. That maybe kids are cursed differently. Somewhere, on another timeline, there's a place where all of the soul hungry are under the age of twelve. And maybe the only souls they can suck belong to other kids. Or maybe the elderly? I've never seen an *old* cursed soul in this afterlife either.

Turning my attention back to my hunger, I need to make a decision. Mother or daughter?

Kids can run fast.

Mothers are extremely protective.

I'm so goddamned hungry.

I creep closer. One step, then another. The loops on the swing are creaking against the mother's weight. The girl on the plastic hippo-on-a-spring is slowing down her bob-rhythm.

My heart should be beating faster. Should be warning me that I'm a very bad person and the act I'm about to commit is really, truly, horrifically wrong.

One more step and I will have her.

I open my mouth. Reach out with my hands. And materialize.

The girl screams.

She will taste so incredibly fresh. Like the first day of spring.

The mother leaps off the swing.

For an instant, with my young prey squirming in my grasp, I turn to look behind me to gauge the mother's proximity.

With the pop-crack of a time-slip, Latte-guy arrives. He tackles the mother to the ground, slashes her soul open, and says, "I've got her."

The child stops squirming, shocked at the sight of her mother's limp body in Latte-guy's arms. I dig into her.

Behind me, I hear latte-guy sucking and slurping at the mother's soul. At least neither of them will be left alone to mourn the other's loss.

Despite my expectations, the girl's soul is hollow at best. More a snack than a meal. As the last pieces of living soul — the bits that carry the dead soul into the afterlife — brush past, they condemn me. For being a child-killer. For copping out; monopolizing on innocence because of my own self doubt.

"Hey," says latte-guy. "Want some of the mother?"

I wipe my mouth and turn to watch him. Sure enough, plenty of the mother's live soul still hovers around her carcass. If his offer isn't genuine, I can't tell.

Leaving the spent girl, I move over to the opposite side of the mother's body. "Really?" I ask.

"Be my guest." He points with his nose towards her feet.

Still hungry, I dive in.

Between mouthfuls, he asks, "So you're still alone?"

"Yep," I say. "You?"

"Haven't found anyone I like yet." He sits back on his heels, staring at me in a way that makes me wonder the true reason he's invited me to his banquet. "Except for you."

My turn to sit back.

Once again, we're staring into each other's eyes. He's looking even more handsome than the first time I saw him. Apparently he's well over the initial shock of his cursed reality. Maybe more adjusted to this place than I'll ever be.

Still staring into my eyes, he says, softly, "How was the child?"

I shrug. "Hollow."

"Was she your first?" He pauses. "*Child*, I mean."

"Yes."

"I haven't seen any cursed kids." He stares at the swing. It's still moving, though only slightly now. "Either when I was alive or here."

"Me neither."

"Or grandparents," he adds. Now his eyes are back on me, and I can't help but feel a stirring of lust.

I swallow hard. "I think they fill in the time-slips."

"Interesting theory."

I expect him to contribute more, maybe add his own opinion as to the whys and wherefores of our mutually-cursed afterlife. Share his philosophies on the rules for the time-slips. But he simply keeps on staring into my eyes.

"I hate them," I say. "The time-slips. They really mess with my comfort zone."

"Me too," he says. "Although I've always considered myself more of a spontaneous man than a schedule nazi."

"Huh," I say. "So you're my opposite."

"I suppose." He stands, steps around the body of our mutual victim, and places his hand on my shoulder. The instant we touch I feel a buzzing, as though his hand has morphed into an electric razor that's vibrating up a storm.

"Wow," I say.

"Ditto."

"So you haven't... *connected* with anyone here?" I ask.

"Not so far."

"Me either."

"How long have you been... *here*?" he asks.

"Tough question," I say. "With all the slips, it's really hard to keep track of time in this place. A year, at least. The longer I'm here, the less I remember."

"That's started for me," he says. "The forgetting."

I shrug. "Makes some things easier."

"Like the killing," he says. Not a question.

"Especially the killing."

He's still touching my shoulder. I want more of him to touch me. To caress parts that haven't been caressed in a long time, in the afterlife or before.

"My place..." I don't quite know how to explain the Asians living in my apartment without sounding like a bitch.

He stuffs his hands in his pockets. "Mine too."

He gets me, I think.

"Here will do." He walks over and points to the ground near the swing. The little girl's body is far enough away that we won't have to look at her while we settle in.

"I've always loved that swing," I say.

"Was this your neighborhood?"

I nod as I take a few steps toward him.

"Mine too," he says. "Though not recently. I grew up here."

"Oh." I should probably say more, but I move closer to him so that the tips of our shoes touch. All I want at that moment is for him to kiss me.

"I've missed this," I say.

He nods. "Before we kiss," he pauses. "Believe me, I totally *want* to kiss you, but..."

"But what?"

"Tell me your name."

"It's..." My name is just out of my grasp, as though the letters were sucked away, one at a time, with each murder I committed. "I can't..."

"No worries." He brushes his fingers on my cheek and I shudder. "I'm Ben."

I reach forward and touch his left ear. *He* shudders so I bring my other hand up to touch his right. Our faces are so close that we have to shift our gazes left and right, not able to look into both eyes at the same time.

Much as I want to run my fingers through his hair, I'm afraid the not-alive feel of it will be *wrong*. And I don't want any distractions to spoil this moment.

"Do you have a last name?" I ask.

"Does it matter?"

My mouth approaches his. If we could both still breathe I would be able to feel his breath against my lips— smell it and guess what he had last eaten. But my sense of smell is broken here. Even if his last real food was a latte, he's sucked back a few souls since then. I'd rather not taste despair during our first kiss.

"What are you thinking?" he says, his lips still oh-so-close to mine.

"Trivial thoughts," I say.

"Way to stroke my ego."

Plunging ahead, I kiss him. The vibration is different. Wetter, somehow. The kiss is tender, despite my longing for this contact to turn into a more primal act. I feel as though I'm eleven years old and being kissed for the first time. Only better. And maybe worse, too.

Technically, it is a first kiss of sorts. My first afterlife kiss. Although I no longer remember who I am — who I was — I am reborn.

His hands are in my hair, and he's stroking my cheek with his nose so gently, I'm about to explode in pure, unadulterated ecstasy.

I take a chance and touch his hair and it feels real, as though now that we're connected all our not-parts have become real.

"Please," I say.

"Don't beg," he says. "We're equals here."

The swing squeaks one last time, as though our energy has sucked its last momentum from the world. We kneel beneath it, and explore the delicacies of not-flesh become real.

His hands are softer than I expect, like the delicate powder coating a marshmallow that used to melt when it touched my tongue. Although our performance does not last long, we linger after. That time — the quiet solace — fills me up more than any soul I've consumed since being cursed.

I expect a time-slip because I've never felt *good* here. Maybe this is how a posse begins— with an act of intimacy. If Ben and I are able to slip together from now on, we will gain a marriage of sorts. Then whenever we linger in this park, we might dream of the children we could've had.

But I'm afraid to dream, especially of children we will never have. *Or of the one....*

"What are you thinking now?" he asks.

"I'm horrible." I look down, unable to meet his eyes.

He gently nudges me, encouraging me to look up at him. "Because of the girl?" he asks.

"I can feel her," I say. "Inside me, like a slice of innocence pie that I'll never digest."

"We'll avoid them," he says. "The children."

"Eventually we'll forget. That we promised." I pause, and add, "To leave kids alone."

Before he can answer, we time-slip. *Together.*

When we land, the park is empty and dark. Ben is still standing next to me.

"That was a long slip," I say.

"How can you tell?"

I point at the moon. "It was full yesterday, and now it's past the last quarter."

He pulls me close and says, "We won't allow each other to forget the important parts."

"Promise?" I say.

"Cross my heart." He smiles, then adds, "And hope to die."

PUBLISHING CREDITS

"Coolies" Originally appeared in *On Spec*, Volume 20, Number 4, #75.

"The Wind and the Sky" Originally appeared in *Neo-opsis Science Fiction Magazine*, Issue 5, and *The Best of Neo-opsis Science Fiction Magazine*, Bundoran Press.

"Storm Child" Originally appeared in *Cicada* Volume 9, Number 6.

"Hot Furball on a Cold Morning" Originally appeared in *Doorways Magazine*, Issue #6.

"Everyone Needs a Couch (The Couch Teleportation Universe)" Originally appeared in Fall 2003 issue of *Oceans of the Mind*.

"Waste Management (The Couch Teleportation Universe)" Originally appeared in *Challenging Destiny* #21.

"Fuzzy Green Monster Number Two (The Couch Teleportation Universe)" Originally appeared in *Neo-opsis Science Fiction Magazine*, Issue #12.

"Destiny Lives in the Tattoo's Needle" Originally appeared in *Tesseracts Fourteen*, EDGE Science Fiction and Fantasy Publishing.

"Synch Me, Kiss Me, Drop" Originally appeared in *Clarkesworld Magazine*, Issue #68.

"Tattoo Ink" Originally appeared in the *Shadow Box e-Anthology*, Brimstone Press.

"Gray Love" Originally appeared in *Chimeraworld #2*.

"The Tear Closet" Originally in *Tesseracts Thirteen*, EDGE Science Fiction and Fantasy Publishing.

"Hell's Deadline" Originally appeared in *Book of Dead Things*, Twilight Tales.

"The Needle's Eye" Originally appeared in *Chilling Tales: Evil Did I Dwell; Lewd I Did Live*, EDGE Science Fiction and Fantasy Publishing. Winner of the 2012 Aurora Award for Short Story.

Our titles are available at major book stores
and local independent resellers who support
Science Fiction and Fantasy readers like you.

EDGE Science Fiction
and Fantasy Publishing

Our titles are available at major book stores and local independent resellers who support Science Fiction and Fantasy readers like you.

Milkman, The by Michael J. Martineck (tp) - ISBN: 978-0-77053-060-7
Moonfall by Heather Spears (pb) - ISBN: 978-0-88878-306-6

Of Wind and Sand by Sylvie Bérard (translated by Sheryl Curtis) (tp)
- ISBN: 978-1-894063-19-7
On Spec: The First Five Years edited by On Spec (pb)
- ISBN: 978-1-895836-08-0
On Spec: The First Five Years edited by On Spec (hb)
- ISBN: 978-1-895836-12-7
Orbital Burn by K. A. Bedford (tp) - ISBN: 978-1-894063-10-4
Orbital Burn by K. A. Bedford (hb) - ISBN: 978-1-894063-12-8

Pallahaxi Tide by Michael Coney (pb) - ISBN: 978-0-88878-293-9
Paradox Resolution by K. A. Bedford (tp) - ISBN:978-1-894063-88-3
Passion Play by Sean Stewart (pb) - ISBN: 978-0-88878-314-1
Petrified World (Determine Your Destiny #1) by Piotr Brynczka (pb)
- ISBN: 978-1-894063-11-1
Plague Saint, The by Rita Donovan (tp) - ISBN: 978-1-895836-28-8
Plague Saint, The by Rita Donovan (hb) - ISBN: 978-1-895836-29-5
Pock's World by Dave Duncan (tp) - ISBN: 978-1-894063-47-0
Puzzle Box, The by Randy McCharles, Billie Millholland, Eileen Bell, and Ryan
  McFadden (tp) - ISBN: 978-1-77053-040-9

Reluctant Voyagers by Élisabeth Vonarburg (pb) - ISBN: 978-1-895836-09-7
Reluctant Voyagers by Élisabeth Vonarburg (hb) - ISBN: 978-1-895836-15-8
Resisting Adonis by Timothy J. Anderson (tp) - ISBN: 978-1-895836-84-4
Resisting Adonis by Timothy J. Anderson (hb) - ISBN: 978-1-895836-83-7
Rigor Amortis edited by Jaym Gates and Erika Holt (tp)
- ISBN: 978-1-894063-63-0

Silent City, The by Élisabeth Vonarburg (tp) - ISBN: 978-1-894063-07-4
Slow Engines of Time, The by Élisabeth Vonarburg (tp)
- ISBN: 978-1-895836-30-1
Slow Engines of Time, The by Élisabeth Vonarburg (hb)
- ISBN: 978-1-895836-31-8
Stealing Magic by Tanya Huff (tp) - ISBN: 978-1-894063-34-0
Stolen Children (Children of the Panther Part Three)
  by Amber Hayward (tp) - ISBN: 978-1-894063-66-1
Strange Attractors by Tom Henighan (pb) - ISBN: 978-0-88878-312-7

Taming, The by Heather Spears (pb) - ISBN: 978-1-895836-23-3
Taming, The by Heather Spears (hb) - ISBN: 978-1-895836-24-0
Technicolor Ultra Mall by Ryan Oakley (tp) - ISBN: 978-1-894063-54-8
Ten Monkeys, Ten Minutes by Peter Watts (tp) - ISBN: 978-1-895836-74-5
Ten Monkeys, Ten Minutes by Peter Watts (hb) - ISBN: 978-1-895836-76-9
Tesseracts 1 edited by Judith Merril (pb) - ISBN: 978-0-88878-279-3
Tesseracts 2 edited by Phyllis Gotlieb & Douglas Barbour (pb)
- ISBN: 978-0-88878-270-0
Tesseracts 3 edited by Candas Jane Dorsey & Gerry Truscott (pb)
- ISBN: 978-0-88878-290-8
Tesseracts 4 edited by Lorna Toolis & Michael Skeet (pb)
- ISBN: 978-0-88878-322-6
Tesseracts 5 edited by Robert Runté & Yves Maynard (pb)
- ISBN: 978-1-895836-25-7

Warriors by Barbara Galler-Smith and Josh Langston (tp)
    -ISBN: 978-1-77053-030-0
Wildcatter by Dave Duncan (tp) - ISBN: 978-1-894063-90-6